395
104

P9-DLZ-238

Praise for the novels of Sheila Roberts

"Within minutes of cracking open the book,
my mood was lifted...the warm,
glowing feeling it gave me lasted for days."
—*First for Women* on *The Snow Globe*

"Her characters are warm and engaging, and their
interactions are full of humor."
—*RT Book Reviews* on *Bikini Season*

"An uplifting, charming, feel-good story."
—*Booklist* on *Angel Lane*

"Will doubtless warm more than a few hearts."
—*Publishers Weekly* on *Angel Lane*

"Roberts' book of small-town life is as sweet as ginger
cookies and as homey as raisin pie (recipes included).
Readers will laugh and cry with the women lovingly
portrayed in this heartwarming story that explores
the joys of friendship and the power of good deeds."
—*RT Book Reviews* on *Angel Lane*

"A congenial cast of subsidiary characters...meet Hope
at a community garden plot and share their stories
there. Roberts effectively knits these troubled but
kindly characters together in a story line that throws
the reader a few unexpected twists."
—*The Seattle Times* on *Love in Bloom*

"This is an engrossing story
with strong characters and arcs similar to
Debbie Macomber's Cedar Cove titles.
The light romance, delicious descriptions of chocolate
and recipes add to the flavor of Roberts's
promising new series."
—*Booklist* on *Better Than Chocolate*

SHEILA ROBERTS

WHAT SHE WANTS

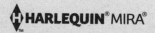

Recycling programs
for this product may
not exist in your area.

ISBN-13: 978-0-7783-1432-5

WHAT SHE WANTS

Copyright © 2013 by Sheila Rabe

Printed in U.S.A.

For Dustin

Dear Reader,

Welcome back to Icicle Falls. I'm so happy you're taking a break from your busy schedule to spend some time with my characters. In this book you won't be hanging out with the girls. It's the guys' turn.

Jonathan Templar is my salute to those quiet, average men with super big hearts who often get overlooked when a better-looking, flashier man enters the room. I think Jonathan is proof that a big heart is better than a big set of pecs any day. His buddy Kyle…well, he finds it very frustrating that he's height-challenged and he gets irritated when women look right past him to the taller men. But maybe Kyle needs to practice what he preaches and look beyond the packaging when searching for Ms. Right. Then there's their friend Adam, who is about as clueless as a man can get. If you've ever had your man take you for granted, I'm sure you'll be cheering when you see Adam's wife giving him a painful but well-deserved refresher course on how to be a good husband.

All the men are on a steep learning curve. But they're about to discover what we women have known all along— there is much wisdom to be found in romance novels.

I had a wonderful time with these three men and their poker pals, Vance and Bernardo. I cried over every setback they encountered and cheered at their every success. These guys stole my heart. I hope they'll steal yours, too!

I love hanging out with readers so I hope you'll check out my page on Facebook (look for Sheila Roberts, author), follow me on Twitter, and visit my website (www.sheilasplace.com), where you're bound to find everything from a new Icicle Falls recipe to a fun contest.

Happy reading!

Sheila

Chapter One

Working in such close quarters with a woman that you could bump knees (thighs, and maybe even other body parts) was probably every man's dream job. Except Dot Morrison's knees were knobby and she was old enough to be Jonathan Templar's grandmother. And she looked like Maxine of greeting card fame. So there was no knee (or anything else) bumping going on today.

"Okay, you're good to go," he said, pushing back from the computer in the office at Breakfast Haus, Dot's restaurant. "But remember what I told you. If you want your computer to run more efficiently, you've got to slick your hard drive once in a while."

"There you go talking dirty to me again," Dot cracked.

A sizzle sneaked onto Jonathan's cheeks, partly because old ladies didn't say things like that (Jonathan's grandma sure didn't), and partly because he'd never talked dirty to a woman in his life. Well, not unless you counted a *Playboy* centerfold. When talking with most real-life women, his tongue had a tendency to tie itself into more knots than a bag of pretzels, especially when a woman was good-looking. This, he told himself, was one reason he was still single at the ripe old age of thirty-three. That and the fact that he wasn't exactly the stuff a woman's dreams were made of. It was a rare woman who dreamed of a skinny, bespectacled guy in a button-down shirt. Those weren't the only reasons, though. Carrying a torch for someone tended to interfere with a guy's love life.

Never certain how to respond to Dot's whacked-out sense of humor, he merely smiled, shook his head and packed up his briefcase.

"Seriously," she said, "I'm glad this didn't turn out to be anything really bad. But if it had, I know I could count on you. You can't ever leave Icicle Falls. What would us old bats do when we have computer problems?"

"You'd manage," Jonathan assured her.

"I doubt it. Computers are instruments of torture to anyone over the age of sixty."

"No worries," he said. "I'm not planning on going anywhere."

"Until you meet Ms. Right. Then you'll be gone like a shot." The look she gave him was virtually a guarantee that something was about to come out of her mouth that would make him squirm. Sure enough. "We'll have to find you a local girl."

Just what he needed—Dot Morrison putting the word out that Jonathan Templar, computer nerd, was in the market for a local girl. He didn't want a local girl. He wanted…

"Tilda's still available."

Tilda Morrison, supercop? She could easily bench-press Jonathan. "Uh, thanks for the offer, but I think she needs someone tougher."

"There's a problem. Nobody's as tough as Tilda. Damn, I raised that girl wrong. At this rate I'm never going to get grandchildren." Dot shrugged and reached for a cigarette. "Just as well, I suppose. I'd have to spend all my free hours baking cookies for the little rodents."

Sometimes it was hard to know whether or not Dot was serious, but this time Jonathan was sure she didn't mean what she'd said. She was only trying to make the best of motherly frustration. Dot wanted grandkids. Anyone who'd seen her interacting with the families who came into the restaurant could tell that. It was a wonder she made any money with all the free hot chocolate she slipped her younger patrons.

She lit up and took a deep drag on her cigarette. Her little office was about to get downright smoggy. Washington State law prohibited smoking in public places, but Dot maintained that her office wasn't a public place. Jonathan suspected one of these days she and the local health inspector were going to get into it over the cigarettes she sneaked in this room.

"I'd better get going," he said, gathering his things and trying not to inhale the secondhand smoke pluming in his direction.

"You gonna bill me as usual?"

"Yep."

"Don't gouge me," she teased.

"Wouldn't dream of it. And put your glasses on to read your bill this time," he teased back as he walked to the door. He always tried to give Dot a senior's discount and she always overpaid him, claiming she'd misread the bill. Yep, Dot was a great customer.

Heck, all his customers were great, he thought as he made his way to Sweet Dreams Chocolate Company, where Elena, the secretary, was having a nervous breakdown thanks to a new computer that she swore was possessed.

The scent of chocolate floating up from the kitchens below greeted him as he entered the office and Elena looked at him as if he were Saint George come to slay a dragon. "Thank God you're here."

People were always happy to see the owner and sole employee of Geek Gods Computer Services. Once Jonathan arrived on the scene, they knew their troubles would be fixed.

He liked that, liked feeling useful. So he wasn't a mountain of muscle like Luke Goodman, the production manager at Sweet Dreams, or a mover and shaker like Blake Preston, manager of Cascade Mutual. Some men were born to have starring roles and big, juicy parts on the stage of life. Others were meant to build scenery, pull the curtains, work in the background to make sure everything on stage ran well. Jonathan was a backstage kind of guy. Nothing wrong with that, he told himself. Background workers made it possible for the show to go on.

But leading ladies never noticed the guy in the

background. Jonathan heaved a sigh. Sometimes he felt like Cyrano de Bergerac. Without the nose.

"This thing is making me loco," Elena said, glaring at the offending piece of technology on her desk.

The company owner, Samantha Sterling—recently married to Blake Preston—had just emerged from her office. "More loco than we make you?"

"More loco than even my mother makes me," Elena replied.

Samantha gave her shoulder a pat. "Jonathan will fix it."

Elena grunted. *"Equipo del infierno."*

"Computer from hell?" Jonathan guessed, remembering some of his high school Spanish.

Elena's frustrated scowl was all the answer he needed.

"Don't worry," Samantha told her. "Jonathan will help you battle the forces of technology evil. When Cecily comes in, tell her I'll be back around one-thirty. Try to keep my favorite assistant from tearing her hair out," she said to Jonathan.

"No worries," he said, then promised Elena, "I'll have this up and running for you in no time."

No time turned out to be about an hour, but since Elena had expected to lose the entire day she was delighted. "You are amazing," she told him just as Samantha's sister Cecily arrived on the scene.

"Has he saved us again?" she asked Elena, smiling at Jonathan.

"Yes, as usual."

Jonathan pushed his glasses back up his nose and

tried to look modest. It was hard when people praised him like this.

But then, as he started to pack up his tools, Cecily said something that left him flat as a stingray. "I heard from Tina Swift that you guys have your fifteen-year reunion coming up."

"Uh, yeah."

"Those are so much fun, seeing old friends, people you used to date," she continued.

This was worse than Dot's cigarette smoke. Chatting with Cecily always made him self-conscious. Chatting with Cecily about his high school reunion would make him a nervous wreck, especially if she began asking about women he used to date. Jonathan hit high speed gathering up his tools and his various discs.

"Are you going to the reunion?" she asked him.

"Maybe," he lied, and hoped she'd leave it at that.

She didn't. "I moved back just in time for my ten-year and I'm glad I went. There were some people I wouldn't have had a chance to see otherwise."

There were some people Jonathan wanted to do more than see. Some people with long, blond hair and... He snapped his briefcase shut and bolted for the door. "So, Elena, I'll bill you."

"Okay," she called.

The door hadn't quite shut behind him when he heard Elena say to Cecily, "He needs confidence, that one."

It was an embarrassing thing to hear about himself, but true. He needed a lot more than confidence, though. How could a guy be confident when he didn't have anything to be confident *about*?

By now it was time for lunch, so he grabbed some bratwurst and sauerkraut at Big Brats and settled in at one of the café tables in the stone courtyard adjacent to the popular sausage stand. This was a perfect day for outside dining. The sun warmed his back and a mountain breeze worked as a counterbalance to keep him from getting too hot. A cloudless sky provided a blue backdrop for the mountains.

During weekends the eating area was so crowded you had to take a number. Today, however, it was relatively quiet with only a few tables occupied.

Ed York, who owned D'Vine Wines, and Pat Wilder, who owned Mountain Escape Books, sauntered across the street to place an order. They stopped by Jonathan's table to say hello but didn't ask him to join them. No surprise. Pat and Ed had a thing going.

According to Jonathan's mom, Ed had been interested in Pat ever since he moved to Icicle Falls and opened his wine shop. But Pat had been mourning a husband and wasn't remotely interested. It looked like that was changing now. Watching Ed's romantic success kept the small flame of hope alive in Jonathan. Maybe, if a guy hung in there long enough, getting the woman of his dreams could become a reality.

Or maybe the guy was just wasting his life dreaming. Jonathan crumpled his napkin. Time to get back to work.

His next client was Gerhardt Geissel, who owned and ran Gerhardt's Gasthaus with his wife, Ingrid.

Gerhardt was a short, husky, fifty-something man with gray hair and a round, florid face. He loved his wife's German cooking, loved his beer and was proud to celebrate his Tyrolean heritage by wearing lederhosen when he played the alpenhorn for his guests first thing every morning.

He played it even when he didn't have guests. Recently he'd gotten carried away celebrating his birthday and had decided to serenade his dinner guests after having one too many beers and had fallen off the ledge of the balcony outside the dining room. He'd fallen about twelve feet but fortunately had broken his arm instead of his back.

"Jonathan, *wie geht's?*" he greeted Jonathan, raising his cast-encased arm as Ingrid showed Jonathan into his office. "I hope you are here to solve all my problems."

"That is an impossible task," said his wife.

Gerhardt made a face. "See how she loves me."

His wife made a face right back at him and left. But she returned a few minutes later with a piece of Black Forest cake for Jonathan. "You're too skinny," she informed him. "You need to eat more."

"You need a wife to cook for you," her husband added.

"My youngest niece, Mary, lives just over in Wenatchee, and she's very pretty," Ingrid said.

"And very stupid." Gerhardt shook his head in disgust. "Jonathan's smart. He needs a smart woman."

"Mary is smart," Ingrid insisted. "She just makes bad choices."

"Well, uh, thanks," Jonathan said. "I appreciate the offer." Sometimes he wondered if everyone in Icicle Falls over the age of fifty wanted to match him up.

Heck, it wasn't only the older people. Even his sister had been known to take a hand, trying to introduce him to the latest someone she'd met and was sure would be perfect for him. Of course, those someones never were.

Gerhardt's computer problem was simple enough. Jonathan reloaded his operating system and he was done.

"You'd better get out of here before my wife comes back with Mary's phone number," Gerhardt advised after he'd written Jonathan a check.

Good idea. Jonathan left by the side door.

After leaving Gerhardt, he fit in two more clients and then headed home.

May's late-afternoon sun beamed its blessing on his three-bedroom log house at the end of Mountain View Road as he drove up. He'd originally planned for two bedrooms, but his folks had talked him into the extra one. "You have to have room for a wife and children," his mother had said. Good old Mom, always hopeful.

Fir and pine trees gave the house its rustic setting, while the pansies and begonias his mother and sister had put in the window boxes and the patch of lawn edged with more flowers added a homey touch. Someone pulling up in front might even think a woman lived there. They'd be wrong. The only female in this house had four legs.

But Jonathan often pictured the house with a wife

and kids in it—the wife (a pretty blonde, naturally) cooking dinner while he and the kids played video games. He could see himself as an old man, sitting on the porch, playing chess with a grandson on the set he'd carved himself. The house would've, naturally, passed on to his own son, keeping the property in the family.

His grandpa had purchased this land as an investment when it was nothing more than a mountain meadow. Gramps could have made a tidy profit selling it, but instead he'd let Jonathan have it for a song when Jonathan turned twenty-five.

He'd started building his house when he was twenty-seven. A cousin who worked in construction in nearby Yakima had come over and helped him and Dad. Dad hadn't lived to see it finished. He'd had a heart attack just before the roof went on, leaving Jonathan on his own to finish both his house and his life.

Jonathan had become the man of the family, in charge of helping his mom, his grandmother and his sister cope. He'd been no help to his widowed grandmother, who had tried to outrun her loss by moving to Arizona. He hadn't been much help to his mom, either, beyond setting her up with a computer program so she could manage her finances. He'd tried to help Julia cope but he'd barely been able to cope himself. He should never have let Dad do all that hard physical work.

"Don't be silly," his mother always said. "Your father could just as easily have died on the golf course. He was doing what he wanted to do, helping you."

Helping his son be manly. The house was probably the one endeavor of Jonathan's that his father took pride in. It wasn't hard to figure out what kind of son Dad had really longed for. He'd never missed an Icicle Falls High football game, whether at home or away. How many times had he sat in the stands and wished his scrawny son was out there on the field or at least on the bench instead of playing in the band? Jonathan was glad that he had no idea.

"I love you, son," Dad had said when they were loading him into the ambulance. Those were the last words Jonathan heard and he was thankful for them. But he often found himself wishing his dad had said he was proud of him.

As he pulled up in his yellow Volkswagen with Geek Gods Computer Services printed on the side, his dog, Chica, abandoned her spot on the front porch and raced down the stairs to greet him, barking a welcome. Chica was an animal-shelter find, part shepherd, part Lab and part…whatever kind of dog had a curly tail. She'd been with Jonathan for five years and she thought he was a god (and didn't care if he *was* a geek).

He got out of the car and the dog started jumping like she had springs on her paws. It was nice to have some female go crazy over him. "Hey, girl," he greeted her. "We'll get some dinner and then play fetch."

He exchanged his slacks for the comfort of his old baggy jeans, and his business shirt for a T-shirt sporting a nerdy pun that cautioned Don't Drink and Derive. Then, after a feast of canned spaghetti for

Jonathan and some Doggy's Delight for Chica, it was time for a quick game of fetch. It had to be quick because tonight was Friday, poker night, and the guys would be coming over at seven. Poker, another manly pursuit. Dad would have been proud.

The first to arrive was his pal Kyle Long. Kyle and Jonathan had been friends since high school. They'd both been members of the chess club and had shared an addiction to old sci-fi movies and video games.

Kyle didn't exactly fit his name. He was short. His hair was a lighter shade than Jonathan's dark brown—nothing spectacular, rather like his face.

His ordinary face didn't bug him nearly as much as his lack of stature. "Women don't look at short guys," he often grumbled. And short guys who (like Jonathan) weren't so confident and quick with the flattery—well, they really didn't get noticed, even by girls their own height. This had been a hard cross to bear in high school when it seemed that every girl Kyle liked chose some giant basketball player over him. These days the competition wore a different type of uniform, the one worn to the office, but his frustration level remained the same.

The grumpy expression on his face tonight said it all before he so much as opened his mouth. "What's with chicks, anyway?" he demanded as he set a six-pack of Hale's Ale on Jonathan's counter.

If Jonathan knew that, he'd be married to the woman of his dreams by now. He shrugged.

"Okay, so Darrow looks like friggin' Ryan Reynolds."

Ted Darrow, Kyle's nemesis. "And drives a Jag," Jonathan supplied. Darrow was also Kyle's boss, which put him higher up the ladder of success, always a sexy attribute.

"But he's the world's biggest ass-wipe," Kyle said with a scowl. "I don't know what Jillian sees in him."

Jonathan knew. Like called to like. Beautiful people naturally gravitated to one another. He had seen Jillian when he'd gone to Kyle's company, Safe Hands Insurance, to install their new computer system. As the receptionist, it had been her job to greet him and he'd seen right away why his friend was smitten. She was hot, with supermodel-long legs. Women like that went for the Ted Darrows of the world.

Or the Rand Burwells.

Jonathan shoved that last thought out of his mind. "Hey, you might as well give up. You're not gonna get her." It was hard to say that to his best friend, but friends didn't let friends drive themselves crazy over women who were out of their league. Kyle would do the same for him—if he knew Jonathan had suffered a relapse last Christmas and had once again picked up the torch for his own perfect dream girl. The road to crazy was a clogged thoroughfare these days.

Kyle heaved a discouraged sigh. "Yeah." He pulled an opener out of a kitchen drawer and popped the top off one of the bottles. "It's just that, well, damn. If she looked my way for longer than two seconds, she'd see I'm twice the man Darrow is."

"I hear you," Jonathan said, and opened a bag of corn chips, setting them alongside the beer.

Next in the door was Bernardo Ruiz, who came bearing some of his wife's homemade salsa. Bernardo was happily married and owned a small orchard outside town, in which he took great pride. He wasn't much taller than Kyle, but he swaggered like he was six feet.

"Who died?" he asked, looking from one friend to the other.

"Nobody," Kyle snapped.

Bernardo eyed him suspiciously. "You mooning around over that bimbo at work again?"

"She's not a bimbo," Kyle said irritably.

Bernardo shook his head in disgust. "Little man, you are a fool to chase after a woman who doesn't want you. That kind of a woman, she'll only make you feel small on the inside."

Any reference to being small, either on the inside or outside, never went over well with Kyle, so it was probably a good thing that Adam Edwards arrived with more beer and chips. A sales rep for a pharmaceutical company, he earned more than Jonathan and Kyle put together and had the toys to prove it—a big house on the river, a classic Corvette, a snowmobile and a beach house on the Washington coast. He also had a pretty little wife, which proved Jonathan's theory of like calling to like, since Adam was tall and broad-shouldered and looked as though he belonged in Hollywood instead of Icicle Falls. Some guys had all the luck.

"Vance'll be late," Adam informed them. "He has to finish up something and says to go ahead and start without him."

Vance Fish, the newest member of their group, was somewhere in his fifties, which made him the senior member. He'd built a big house on River Road about a mile down from Adam's place. The two men had bonded over fishing lures, and Adam had invited him to join their poker group.

Although Vance claimed to be semiretired, he was always working. He owned a bookstore in Seattle called Emerald City Books. He'd recently started selling Sweet Dreams Chocolates there, making himself popular with the Sterling family, who owned the company.

He dressed like he was on his last dime, usually in sweats or jeans and an oversize black T-shirt that hung clumsily over his double-XL belly, but his fancy house was proof that Vance was doing okay.

"That means we won't see him for at least an hour," Kyle predicted.

"What kind of project?" Bernardo wondered. "Is he building something over there in that fine house of his? I never seen no tools or workbench in his garage."

"It has to do with the bookstore," Adam said. "I don't know what."

"Well, all the better for me," Kyle said gleefully. "I'll have you guys fleeced by the time he gets here." He rubbed his hands together. "I'm feeling lucky tonight."

He proved it by raking in their money.

"Bernardo, you should just empty your pockets on the table as soon as you get here," Adam joked. "I've never seen anybody so unlucky at cards."

"That's because I'm lucky in love," Bernardo insisted.

His remark wiped the victory smirk right off Kyle's face. "Chicks," he muttered.

"If you're going where I think you're going, don't," Adam said, frowning at him.

"What?" Kyle protested.

Adam pointed his beer bottle at Kyle. "If I hear one more word about Jillian, I'm gonna club you with this."

"Oh, no," said a deep voice. "I thought you clowns would be done talking about women by now."

Jonathan turned to see Vance strolling into the room, stylish as ever in his favorite black T-shirt, baggy jeans and sandals. In honor of the occasion he hadn't shaved. Aside from the extra pounds (well, and that bald spot on the top of his head), he wasn't too bad-looking. His sandy hair was shot with gray but he had the craggy brow and strong jaw women seemed to like even in a big man. They were wasted on Vance; he wasn't interested. "Been there, done that," he often said.

"We're finished talking about women," Adam assured him.

Vance clapped him on the back. "Glad to hear it, 'cause the last thing I want after a hard day's work is to listen to you losers crab about them."

"I wasn't crabbing," Kyle said, looking sullen.

Vance sat down at the table. "It's that babe where

you work, isn't it? She got your jockeys tight again?" Kyle glared at him, but Vance waved off his anger with a pudgy paw. "You know, women can sense desperation a mile away. It's a turnoff."

"And I guess you'd be an expert on what turns women off," Adam teased.

"There isn't a man on this planet who's an expert on anything about women. And if you meet one who says he is, he's lying. Now, let's play poker." Vance eyed the pile of chips in front of Kyle. "You need to be relieved of some of those, my friend."

"I think not," Kyle said, and the game began in earnest.

After an hour and a half, Vance announced that he had to tap a kidney.

"I need some chips and salsa," Adam said, and everyone took a break.

"Did you get the announcement in the mail?" Kyle asked Jonathan.

No, not this again.

"What announcement?" Adam asked.

"High school reunion," Kyle said. "Fifteen years."

Jonathan had gotten the cutesy little postcard with the picture of a grizzly bear, the Icicle Falls High mascot, lumbering across one corner. And of course, the first thing he'd thought was, maybe Lissa will come. That had taken his spirits on a hot-air balloon ride. Until he'd had another thought. *You'll still be the Invisible Man.* That had brought the balloon back down.

"Yeah, I got it," he said. "I'm not going."

But Rand probably would. Rand and Lissa, together again.

Now his balloon ride was not only over, the balloon was in a swamp infested with alligators. And poker night was a bust.

Just like his love life.

Chapter Two

Poker night hadn't ended well for Kyle. Vance, the old buzzard, had picked him clean. And that set the tone for the weekend.

Saturday was nothing but chores and errands. He filled the evening playing *War on Planet X* with a bunch of online gamers, which left him feeling unsatisfied. He was getting too old for this crap. He needed more in his life. It seemed like everybody was getting paired up but him.

He was even more aware of this fact when he went over to his folks' house for Sunday dinner and learned that his baby sister had gotten engaged. Of course he'd seen it coming for months and he was happy for her. But now it was official—he was the last of the three siblings left unattached. And Kerrie was four years younger, which didn't help. Neither did remarks like, "We have to find somebody for Kyle." He didn't need his baby sister finding someone for him.

He'd found someone. All he had to do was make her realize he was the man for her.

Well, the weekend was over and it was a new day.

TGIM—Thank God It's Monday. He walked through the glass doors of Safe Hands Insurance Company and into the lobby with its modern paintings, the strategically placed metal sculpture of two giant hands stretched out in a gesture of insurance paternalism, and plants that looked like they'd escaped from an African jungle. He kept his eyes front and center, because there, straight ahead, was the receptionist's desk.

Behind it sat a vision. Jillian. She had long, reddish-blond hair that she tossed over her shoulder when she talked, full, glossy lips he dreamed of kissing, a perfect nose and sky-blue eyes. *Blind* sky-blue eyes. One of these days she was going to see him, really see him. Maybe even this morning.

He sure saw everything about her. Today she was wearing a white blouse that plunged in a V pointing to her breasts—as if a man needed any help finding them—and she'd worn a necklace made up of glass baubles to fill the gap between neck and heaven. She'd tucked her hair behind her ears, showing off dangly earrings that matched the necklace. She had a funny little habit of tapping her pencil on the desk as she talked on the phone, which she was doing now. The call only lasted a moment. She pushed a button and sent the caller on, probably to one of the bosses. Such an efficient woman.

Now she smiled as she caught sight of him walking down the hall in his gray slacks and his white Oxford shirt, his hair slicked into the latest style (at least according to the new barber he'd gone to at Sweeney Todd Barbershop—the one highlight of his weekend).

He puffed out his chest and donned his best smile. He did have a good smile; even his sisters said so.

Oh, man, look at the way her eyes lit up at the sight of him. It was the hair, had to be. He forced his chest to swell to its fullest capacity.

Look at that smile. She had a great smile and she used it a lot. When a woman smiled a lot, it meant she was happy and easygoing. That was exactly the kind of woman Kyle wanted.

He was almost at her desk when he realized they weren't making eye contact. She was looking beyond him.

Then he heard a rich tenor voice behind him say, "Jillian, you're especially beautiful this fine morning."

Ted Darrow, the ass-wipe. Kyle's supervisor. Kyle could feel his smile shrinking even as he shrank inside. He mumbled a hello to Jillian and slunk by her desk.

"Hi," she said absently as he passed. Then for Ted it was a sexy, "Hi, Ted."

"Hi, Ted," Kyle mimicked under his breath as he strode to his cubicle. Jillian shouldn't waste her breath saying hello to that fathead. Men like that, they flirted with women, they used women, but they didn't appreciate women. Kyle flung himself into his chair with a growl.

"Starting the day off well, I see," said a soft voice from the cubicle next door.

Unlike *some people,* Mindy Wright always had the decency to acknowledge his existence. It didn't make him feel any better, though. Mindy was no Jillian.

"Hi, Mindy." His hello probably sounded grudging, so he added, "How was your weekend?"

"Well, it was interesting."

Mindy had been trolling the internet for her perfect match. So far she'd hauled in a truck driver who was ten years older than she was and about forty pounds heavier than he'd looked in his picture on the dating site, a man who claimed to be a churchgoer but hadn't gone in two—okay, make it five—years, a shrink who Mindy said was the most screwed-up person she'd ever had dinner with and someone who'd seemed like a great catch until she learned he had no job. "And he wasn't planning on finding one anytime soon, either," Mindy had confessed. "He's writing a book."

"Oh, well, that's good," Kyle had said, trying to put a positive spin on the latest loser.

"About mushrooms."

"Bound to be a bestseller."

That had made her laugh. Kyle made Mindy laugh a lot. If only he could work up his nerve to ask Jillian out. He was sure he could make her laugh, too. But so far, his attempts to get her attention had all been thwarted.

Shakespeare had it right. The course of true love never did run smooth. For Kyle, it seemed to run into nothing but dead ends.

At least Mindy was getting some action. "So, who'd you go out with this weekend?" he asked.

"No one I want to keep, that's for sure. I think I'm done looking."

"Hey, you can't give up. Your perfect man may be right around the next corner."

"The next internet corner?" She peeked around the cubicle wall, a grin on her face.

It was an okay face, fringed with dark hair and decorated with glasses, a turned-up little nose that made him think of Drew Barrymore and a small chin that seemed to sport a zit once a month. (What was with that, anyway?) As for the bod, well, not a ten like Jillian. Still, she was pretty nice. Someone would want her.

"Yeah," he said. "The next internet corner. Or maybe at the Red Barn." If you wanted cold beer and hot music, that was the place to go.

She shook her head. "I haven't gone there in a long time." Then she disappeared back behind the cubicle wall.

"Why's that?" he asked, booting up his computer.

"Too much competition."

"I know what you mean." Funny how the walls of an office cubicle could make you feel like you were in a confessional, willing to say things you wouldn't share face-to-face. Not that he'd been in the confessional for a while.

Maybe he needed to spend some time there. And maybe he should be talking to God more. God saw him, even if Jillian didn't. Maybe God would consider working a miracle and opening Jillian's eyes. At the rate things were going here at Safe Hands, improving her eyesight was going to *take* a miracle.

* * *

It was nine o'clock and time for Jonathan's morning ritual. He grabbed his bowl of cereal with sliced banana and turned on the TV to a station in Oregon. "Barely made it in time," he told Chica, who'd settled on the couch beside him. "We shouldn't have taken such a long walk."

Her only response to that was a big yawn.

"You know, you've got a bad attitude," he said.

She let out a bark.

"And you're jealous," he added, making her whine. He put an arm around her and gave her head a good rub. "But I'll keep you, anyway."

The commercial for laser skin treatment ended and Chica was forgotten as an image of the city of Portland came on the screen, accompanied by perky music. A disembodied voice called out, "Good morning, Oregon!"

Then there she was—trim, blonde and beautiful— seated at a couch in a fake living room next to a gray-haired guy wearing slacks and an expensive shirt.

Scott Lawrence. Jonathan frowned at the sight of him. Media guys, they were just too smooth. *Now who's jealous?*

He was, of course. Talk about stupid. In order to be jealous of other men, you first had to be with the woman. Jonathan was not with Lissa Castle, never had been.

"Well, Lissa, I'm sure your weekend was stellar," Scott said to her.

"Yes, it was." She had such a sweet voice, so full of cheer and kindness. Lissa had always been kind.

"Did you have a hot date?" Scott teased. "What am I saying? Of course you had a hot date."

She neither denied nor confirmed, just sat in her leather chair and smiled like the Mona Lisa in a pink blouse.

Which meant she'd had a hot date, Jonathan deduced miserably.

Her cohost turned to face the camera. "Speaking of dates, some of you out there in our viewing audience might be doing internet dating and finding it frustrating."

"It can be stressful when it comes time to meet that other person off-line," Lissa said. "And that's why I know you're going to appreciate our first guest this morning, who'll be sharing tips with us on how to transition from online to face time."

Sometimes even face time didn't win a girl, Jonathan thought sadly, not when the girl was out of a guy's league.

He'd been in love with Lissa ever since he'd discovered girls. In fact, Lissa had been the first girl he discovered when she moved in next door at the age of nine. They'd become pals, which was great when he was nine. But as they got older and she got even prettier, Jonathan began to look beyond the borders of friendship.

He wasn't the only one. During high school, his friend Rand took a new interest in Lissa once she became a cheerleader. And she was interested right back.

Hardly surprising, since Rand was the cool one. When they were kids, everyone had fought over Rand while picking teams for playground softball games. In high school he'd been captain of the football team. The boys all wanted to be his bud and the girls all looked at him like he was a free trip to Disneyland.

As for Jonathan, he was captain of…the chess team, and hardly any girls looked at him at all. Not that he'd wanted any girl but Lissa.

No matter what he'd done, though, he couldn't win her interest. She always thought of him simply as her good friend.

He'd wanted to be more. When they were juniors, in the hopes of getting her to see him in a new way, he'd sneaked into Icicle Falls High early on Valentine's Day and taped a hundred red paper hearts to her locker.

But she'd thought Rand had done it. Rand happily took the credit and took Lissa to the junior prom. And Jonathan took a swing at Rand. And that was the end of their friendship.

But not the end of Rand and Lissa. They were an item clear through senior year.

As for Jonathan, he wasn't an item with anyone. He'd tried, gone out with a few girls as desperate as he was, but every time he'd closed his eyes and kissed a girl he'd seen Lissa.

After everyone graduated and scattered he still saw her on holidays when she was in town visiting her parents and he was over at his folks' next door. Once in a while they'd talk. He'd say brilliant things like, "How's it going?" and she'd ask him questions like,

"Anyone special in your life yet?" He'd never had the guts to say, "There's been someone special in my life since I was nine."

When his dad died, she'd sent him a card telling him how sorry she was. Mostly, though, she just waved to him while hurrying down her front walk to catch up with girlfriends. He'd tried not to see when she left on the arm of the latest local whose attention she'd captured.

A couple of summers ago, he'd seen her when she came home to surprise her mom for her birthday. He'd been at his mom's, up on a ladder painting the side of the house, when she called a cheery hello from next door.

He'd almost lost his balance at the sound of her voice.

"Jonathan Templar, paint specialist. And I thought you were only a computer genius," she'd teased from the other side of the hedge that ran between their houses.

He'd had a perfect view of her from his perch on the ladder and the view was great. She'd looked like a cover girl for a summer issue of some women's magazine in her pink top and white shorts.

"That, too," he'd said, then asked, "Are you in town for long?"

"Only the weekend."

He knew what that meant. This moment was all he'd have with her.

"We've got Mom's big birthday dinner tonight. Then brunch tomorrow and then I've got to get back to Portland. I don't think I'll even have time to bake you any cookies. How sad is that?" Before he could answer, her cell phone had rung. "I know, I'm on my way," she'd said, and ended the call. "I'm late, as usual," she'd said to Jonathan. "I'd better get going. Good to see you, Jonathan. You look great." Then she'd hurried off down her front walk, her long, blond hair swinging.

That hadn't been the only thing swinging. Watching her hips as she walked away had been hypnotic, addictive. And dumb.

Jonathan had leaned over to keep her in view just a little longer and lost his balance. With a startled cry, he'd grabbed for the ladder but only succeeded in bringing the bucket of paint down on himself as he fell, turning him blue from head to toe. A one-man Blue Man Group act.

He'd bruised his hip in the process, but his ego had taken an even bigger hit when Lissa came running to where he'd fallen. "Jonathan, are you okay?"

He'd been far from okay. He'd been mortified, his face probably red under the blue paint. But he'd said, "Oh, yeah. No problem. I'm fine."

Then his mom had come out and started fussing over him and that had been the final humiliation. He'd tried to wash his clothes and turned his underwear baby blue, and it had taken him days to get the last of the paint off. Bits of it stubbornly lingered under his fingernails to remind him of what a dork he was. Well, that and the blue undies.

Lissa did find time to bake him cookies. She'd dropped them by his place on her way out of town.

He'd tried to play it cool by leaning one hand against the door frame but had missed the mark and nearly lost his balance. Again.

She'd pretended not to notice. "I just stopped by to make sure you didn't break anything."

"Naw, I'm fine." His briefs were another story, but he wisely kept that bit of information to himself.

"That's good," she said, handing over the paper plate of goodies. "But if you *had* broken something, I'd have signed your cast."

Would you have kissed it and made it all better? That had been an unusually clever remark. Too bad he hadn't thought of it until she was long gone. But even if he had, he'd have never gotten up the nerve to say it. Instead, he'd said, "Then I'd have to save the cast 'cause your signature will probably be valuable someday."

That had made her smile and making her smile had made his day.

"See you soon," she'd called as she got in her car.

"Yeah, see you," he'd called back.

And he had ever since, every day on TV. He'd liked her on Facebook, too, not that she'd noticed. It wasn't much, but it was all he had and it was better than nothing. Barely.

"I wonder if she's coming to the reunion," he mused.

Next to him Chica whined.

"Yeah, you're right, what does it matter?" Jonathan

muttered. These days she was way too busy to hang out with nerdy guys she'd hung with as a kid. And if he went to the reunion, history would repeat itself and the high school hunks would squeeze him out.

He listened as the guest expert talked about how to make a first date with an internet match-up successful. If only there was an expert out there who could help a guy have a successful encounter with a woman he'd known all his life.

"I can't keep just seeing her this way," he said to Chica. "And I can't go on doing nothing. She won't stay single forever."

As if, when she finally walked down the aisle, it would be to him! "You're dreaming," he told himself.

Well, so what if he was? A man needed dreams, needed to think big. *Go big or go home.*

Oh, yeah. He was already home. Forget about it, he advised himself.

The morning show ended and Jonathan turned off the TV, leaving Chica in charge of yard patrol and napping, and then got in his car and drove down the long, gravel road toward town. He passed a few large lots with big houses on them, but mostly here, in his neck of the woods, the land remained dense with trees and brush.

He liked it that way. Jonathan Templar, rugged mountain man. Well, mountain man, anyway.

The town itself looked picturesque on this sunny morning. The window boxes and hanging planters that decorated the quaint Bavarian-style buildings over-flowed with red geraniums and pink and white begonias. And with the mountains rising up behind, he could almost believe he was somewhere in the German Alps. A few people were stirring, some running errands, some visiting, others sweeping off the sidewalks in front of their shops.

It sure wasn't New York or Seattle but that was okay with Jonathan. Icicle Falls was perfect the way it was. Who would want to live anywhere else?

Lissa Castle, that was who. Would she ever give up her TV career and move back to Icicle Falls? Probably not. Would he say goodbye to this beautiful place and follow her wherever her career led? In a heartbeat, if only she'd ask him.

Even a man caught in the net of unrequited love had to think about other things once in a while. Jonathan parked his car on Center Street and turned his mind to business.

He had plenty to keep him busy the rest of the morning, so busy in fact that he wound up working clear through lunch. He found himself with twenty minutes to kill before he had to be at Mountain Escape Books to work on Pat Wilder's computer, so he decided to duck into Bavarian Brews for a quick pick-me-up.

The aroma of coffee kissed his taste buds as he walked in. Yes, he was probably going to go a million years without sex, might never connect with the woman of his dreams, but at least he had coffee.

Coffee. Sex. Was there really any comparison? Jonathan frowned at the thought of what he was settling for in life.

Cecily Sterling came in right behind him. "Hi, Jonathan. You need a caffeine fix, too?" she asked as they got in line to place their orders.

"Yeah," he said, showing off his suave to the most beautiful woman in Icicle Falls. Jonathan Templar, lady killer.

He was racking his brain to come up with something clever to say when Todd Black, who had just entered the coffee shop, stepped confidently into the conversation. "By this time of day, who doesn't need a hit?"

Cecily rolled her eyes at him. "You make it sound like you've been up for hours."

Todd owned the Man Cave, a tavern on the edge of town. He kept late hours and so was bound to sleep late.

"I was up early this morning doing the books. Not easy after a hard day's night."

"I'm sure you work very hard watching over your kingdom of Kahlua," she sneered.

"It's not a bad kingdom. By the way, Kahlua and chocolate go well together. Bring me some more of yours and I'll prove it."

"I'll take your word for it."

Jonathan had been standing in line behind Cecily, but somehow Todd managed to cut in front of him. He watched with a mixture of irritation and envy as Todd leaned in close to her and said, "One of these days you're going to watch some sappy movie where the couple is dancing real slow and you're going to remember my offer to give you a tango lesson."

She shook her head and moved away a step. He closed the distance.

Oh, this was a master in action. Jonathan eavesdropped shamelessly.

"Or you're going to get an urge to come check out the action on my pinball machine. You said you were good but so far you haven't proved it."

"I don't have to prove anything to you." She turned to look at him and they almost brushed lips.

"You're invading my space," she said, frowning.

"I bet that's not all I'm invading. How you sleeping these days, Cecily? Do you get hot? Throw off the covers?"

Her cheeks went pink. "I sleep fine, thanks." She took two giant steps away and placed her order, leaving Todd with a confident smirk on his face.

Jenni, the barista, whipped up Cecily's coconut mocha latte and set it on the counter, but Cecily chose that moment to send a text on her cell phone. Todd's drink order came up and she put away her phone and picked up her to-go cup. They stood trading words that, Jonathan suspected, had secret messages attached, then, with her cheeks even pinker, she left the coffee shop. Todd watched her go, smiling like a man who'd just landed a fish and was now contemplating how he'd cook it.

Speaking of cooking, there'd been enough current zipping back and forth between those two to light the giant fir tree in the town square at Christmas and the rest of the town, too. How did guys like Todd manage to stir up a woman's hormones with nothing more than a few well-chosen words? Jonathan wished he knew.

The only way to find out was to ask.

Todd was about to saunter out the door. Jonathan grabbed his drink and hurried after him. "Uh, Todd. Can I ask you something?"

Todd turned, an easy smile on his face, his brows raised. "Sure. What?"

"How do you do that?"

The brows knit. "Do what?"

Okay, maybe he didn't want to have this conversation in the middle of Bavarian Brews. He opened the door and motioned that they should go out on the street. Once outside he wasn't sure how to frame his question.

"What's on your mind, computer man?" Todd prompted him.

"I was watching you with Cecily. You're smooth."

Todd shrugged and took a drink of coffee.

"How do you do it? How do you know what to say?"

"I just say what comes into my head." Todd watched Cecily running across the street toward Sweet Dreams. "She likes being chased. But you know what? She's about ready to let me catch her, and she's going to like getting caught even more." The smile on his face oozed confidence.

Well, Jonathan would have confidence, too, if he looked like Johnny Depp's kid brother. He realized he was frowning. He probably looked like a pitiful loser.

"Woman troubles?" Todd guessed.

"Always."

"Yeah, well, women and trouble go together." He clapped Jonathan on the back. "But you've got to hang in there. Never give up. That's what Winston Churchill said, and he saved England in World War II."

Jonathan nodded and trudged off down the street. Winston Churchill only had to save England. Jonathan wanted to win Lissa Castle. And he didn't look like Todd Black.

He was halfway to the bookstore when he saw Tina Swift coming down the sidewalk from the other direction. Tina was recently divorced and had half the men in town sniffing after her. Hardly surprising, considering how cute she was.

Cute and stuck-up. She'd been in his class, a cheerleader and a member of the top social tier at Icicle Falls High. She'd never paid any attention to Jonathan then or in the twelve years after graduation. It was only once she'd opened a shop that sold imported lace and china three years ago and needed someone to design a website that she'd remembered his existence.

Now she'd spotted him and was smiling as if they were buds, which meant she wanted something. And it sure wasn't a date.

Jonathan pretended not to see and crossed the street.

Undeterred, she called his name and ran after him.

Okay, he gave up. He stopped.

She hardly allowed him time to say a self-conscious hello before asking, "Did you get your reunion invitation?"

"Uh, yeah."

"I hope you put the date on the calendar."

"Well," he began.

She didn't let him finish. "It's going to be even better than the ten-year. We've already heard from a ton of people. Cam Gordon…"

Football fathead and snob. There's someone I want to see.

"Feron Prince…"

The Prince of Darkness. He stuffed me in a locker when we were freshmen.

"Kyle Long. He was a friend of yours, wasn't he?"

"Still is." And Jonathan didn't need to go to the reunion to see him.

"I think Rand is coming."

Which meant Jonathan wouldn't be, for sure.

"Did you know he got married?"

Married? Jonathan smiled. "No." So Rand was out of circulation. Well, well.

"Oh, and we just heard from Lissa Castle, our very own celebrity. She's definitely coming."

Rand was out of circulation and Lissa was coming. Was he imagining it or were the stars aligning? (Whatever that meant.) If he went to the reunion, he'd have a whole weekend of close proximity to Lissa. Maybe he could separate her from her adoring fans long enough to talk with her, impress her, maybe even dance with her. Except he couldn't dance.

"Jonathan?"

Tina was looking at him, eyebrows raised.

He pulled himself back into the present. "What?"

"Like I just said, I was hoping you could help me out with a couple of things. We want a website for the reunion, and I thought maybe you wouldn't mind making one. You do such good work. And you did a wonderful job designing the webpage for the chocolate festival."

But that had been something he *wanted* to do. This, not so much.

"We could put a bunch of pictures from the yearbook up there, along with any current ones we get. Have a place for people to post. You know, that sort of thing."

"You could just do that on Facebook," he said, hoping to dodge this assignment.

"Oh, great idea! Could you do that, too?"

Wait a minute. He hadn't said yes and already she'd doubled his work, and none of it was anything he would get paid for.

But how to say no to a pretty woman? Jonathan didn't have a clue.

"Oh, *please* say yes. I need a tech wizard."

"I guess I could." What the heck. She was going to wear him down, anyway, and they both knew it.

He sighed inwardly. Now he could hear all about how successful his former classmates had been, see pictures of their wives and kids. Yuck.

Meanwhile, here was Tina, gushing away. "Fabulous! Thank you, Jonathan. You are just…"

A sucker.

"…the best."

The best geek. Nothing wrong with being a geek, he reminded himself. It had worked fine for Bill Gates.

"I should get going," Tina said. "I'm late for the committee meeting. But I'm so glad I ran into you."

Yeah, him, too. Before he could say anything, sarcastic or otherwise, she was hurrying off down the sidewalk.

Jonathan continued on toward the bookstore, deep in thought. Lissa would be back for the reunion in August. Now that Rand was married, maybe he stood a chance of at least getting her attention for a few minutes.

Realistically, that was about all he'd get. She'd been way too popular, and practically everyone else would want to hang with her. Still, he and Lissa had known each other for years. Surely she'd want to visit with him, too.

But simply visiting wasn't going to cut it. He had to figure out a way to shake things up, make an impression.

Hmm. Following that line of thought to its logical conclusion... If he wanted to make an impression, he had to come up with a plan.

His earlier conversation with Todd Black returned for a visit. *You've got to hang in there.*

He pulled his smartphone out of his jeans pocket and looked up Winston Churchill's famous quote. *"Never, never, never, never give up."* What chance did he have of winning Lissa's love? About one in a million. If he didn't even try? None.

He squared his shoulders. He was not going to give

up. Somehow he was going to find a way to transform himself from zero to hero, find a way to make her see that her truest childhood friend could also be her truest love.

But how?

He needed a love coach.

Chapter Three

Adam was missing from the next Friday-night poker game. "He decided to stay up in Alaska for the weekend and fish after finishing his sales calls," Jonathan explained to his fellow gamblers.

"Should be good salmon fishing on the Copper River about now," said Vance. "Especially next week. I may have to take a run up there myself."

"Going up to Alaska for a little fishing when the spirit moves you? Business must be great at the bookstore," Kyle observed, his voice tinged with jealousy.

Vance shrugged. "It's okay."

With Vance's lifestyle, it had to be doing more than okay. Vance didn't talk about his business much. For that matter, he didn't talk much about his life at all. Jonathan knew he'd been married and had a daughter, and that was about it. Maybe Vance had a rich uncle who died and left him a fortune. Maybe he was a Microsoft millionaire. Jonathan had no idea. When it came to sharing his personal life, Vance preferred to stick to topics such as his fishing adventures (especially the one that got away), how much he'd won or lost at the casino or his latest wine discovery.

"Okay," Vance said, and started dealing the cards, "let's get down to business. Five-card draw, jacks or better, to open."

As they picked up their cards, Bernardo mused, "I don't know how that boy can go off fishing on the weekend all the time. If I did that, my Anna would not be happy."

"He's already up there, anyway, since that's part of his sales territory," Kyle said, "so he may as well stay. I would."

"You're not married, *amigo*," Bernardo reminded him.

That made Kyle frown. "Thanks for the update."

"If a man wants to keep his woman happy he has to be around," Bernardo continued.

Jonathan supposed Bernardo would know. He'd been married for fifteen years.

"Yeah, they like attention," Vance agreed. "Lots of it. Another reason to stay single."

"If I was with Jillian, I'd give her plenty of attention," Kyle said.

Vance pointed a fat finger at him. "Don't go there."

Kyle frowned again and shoved two cards across the table. "I'll take two."

When Vance gave him two new ones, he was still frowning, but that probably had more to do with thoughts of Jillian than the cards he'd received.

Jonathan kept his thoughts about women in general and one woman in particular to himself. The last thing he wanted was Bernardo's pity or Vance's scorn. Let Kyle take that hit. Jonathan preferred to suffer in silence.

Saturday morning Jonathan attempted to ease his suffering by going with his sister, Juliet, to the library for the Friends of the Library monthly book sale.

A stranger seeing them enter the musty room in the library basement would never have taken them for siblings. Other than their hair color, they didn't look at all alike. Juliet Gerard had big, brown eyes and perfect eyesight, where his gray eyes hid behind glasses. He had a long face, while she'd been blessed with a perfect oval like their mother's. He was skinny and barely five foot eight; she was long-legged and stacked. She'd definitely gotten the looks in the family while he'd gotten the brains. Not that Juliet was stupid, but it quickly became apparent who the family genius was. In the world of kids, that wasn't necessarily a blessing. When they were younger he'd often wished it was the other way around, but then he'd realized how unfair that would have been. Life was easier for a man who wasn't all that attractive than it was for a woman. Theoretically.

Their lives were as different as their looks. Juliet was married and trying to get pregnant, a project that was taking much longer than expected. When she wasn't working at that, she logged in part-time hours at Mountain Escape Books or met with her book club or hosted parties where all her friends had to buy candles or face goop. She was an awful cook, a good dancer and an avid romance reader. And her social calendar was always full.

Jonathan's, on the other hand, had a lot of open space, and he was stuck in nonswinging single limbo. He couldn't dance, but he could fix leaky pipes and install dimmer switches, something both his sis and his brother-in-law appreciated. Unlike Juliet, he read real fiction like action adventure or sci-fi/fantasy, and the monthly fund-raiser book sales gave him an opportunity to try out new authors.

He'd just scored big, finding a first edition of *The Kingdom of Zoon,* when Juliet, prowling the romance section a couple of bookshelves over, let out a squeal.

Hildy Johnson, who owned Johnson's Drugs along with her husband, Nils, was standing next to her and already had several books in her basket, but she eyed Juliet's find with envy. "Oh, Vanessa Valentine. I haven't read that one."

The woman was married and in her fifties. Why was she reading romance novels?

"I'll lend it to you when I'm done," Juliet promised.

Rita Reyes, who'd worked in the bar at Zelda's restaurant, entered the room. She said a quick hi to Jonathan, then moved to join Juliet and Hildy in their treasure hunt. "I hope you haven't taken all the good books."

"We saved you a few," Juliet assured her. "When's Zelda's going to open again?"

"Charley says by June."

"I hope so," Juliet said. "I miss those huckleberry martinis."

"And I miss working there." Rita sighed. "I'll be so glad when we're up and running again."

A fire in December had forced the restaurant to close; it was now in the process of being rebuilt. Zelda's was a popular place in town for both families and singles wanting to mix and match. Jonathan hadn't gone there much.

Rita pointed to the book in Juliet's hand. "I love that one. James Noble is the perfect man."

The perfect man, huh? A character made up by a woman? Oh, brother.

"Look! Here's *Surrender*," Rita said, pulling a paperback off a shelf. "I *love* this book."

A war novel in the romance section? Jonathan edged closer and sneaked a peek. He saw no scene of carnage on the cover, no white flag being raised—only a woman in a low-cut dress and some muscle-bound guy in tights and a shirt he forgot to button doing a back bend over the kind of fancy bed no man would want to sleep in. Looking at the way the guy was holding her made Jonathan's back hurt.

"Oh, my gosh, me, too," agreed Juliet. "There's a hero to die for. I love the scene where he throws himself in front of her and gets stabbed."

"And how often does that happen in real life?" Jonathan scoffed under his breath.

The women stared at him as if he'd uttered blasphemy.

Juliet raised a delicate eyebrow. "Probably as often as a giant bubble floats to earth and gives magical powers to the first fool who touches it."

Rita snickered and Jonathan, properly chastised and feeling like he'd stuck his face in a firepit, moved to a safer corner of the room and perused the home improvement section.

Turning his back on Juliet and her fellow romance junkies didn't shield his ears from their conversation.

"Men," Rita said disgustedly. "Maybe if they read a few romance novels they'd learn something."

"Nils could stand to learn a few things," Hildy said. "Especially in the bedroom," she added in a conspiratorial whisper that carried across the small, now quiet—since everyone was eavesdropping—room.

Balding, scrawny Nils and Brunhilda Hildy in the bedroom together. That was T.M.I. to the max.

"Oh, they all think they're such good lovers." Rita rolled her eyes. Rita was divorced. Obviously, her man hadn't measured up. "If I found a man who could make love like the heroes in those books, I'd take him to bed in a heartbeat."

"If a man really wanted to be a good lover, he should read these books," Hildy continued in her stage whisper.

Rita nodded. "That would guarantee he'd get lucky."

The women finished making their selections. As they went to pay for their books, two gray-haired men and a teenage boy stampeded to the romance section.

Jonathan paid for his book and then left the room with Juliet, who was now wearing a superior smirk.

"Pathetic," Jonathan muttered.

"You shouldn't knock romance novels if you

haven't read them," she said as they walked out of the library and turned toward Bavarian Brews for their ritual post-shopping coffee.

"I guess," he said. "But they all seem so, I don't know, unrealistic." He held up a hand before Juliet could give him another verbal smackdown. "Yes, neither are my sci-fi/fantasy books. But I *know* they're improbable. And at least sci-fi has real science at its roots."

"And my romance novels have real life at their roots," Juliet argued. "They're all about men and women falling in love and working out their problems. People do that every day. And you know what I like best about them? They all have happy endings." Juliet's smile vanished. "Sometimes a woman needs a break from real life and a little encouragement."

His sister was always upbeat. To see her expression suddenly cloudy was disturbing. "Everything okay with you and Neil?" He hated to ask, not because he didn't care, but because female emotions were scary. He'd tried his best to comfort her when their dad died but had felt hopelessly inadequate.

Right now she was looking at him with teary eyes that made him uneasy. He'd rather face the dragon of Zoon than a woman's tears.

"I'm never going to get pregnant," she said.

"You should stop taking those pregnancy tests, Jules." He got that she wanted a baby, but agonizing over the fact that she wasn't pregnant probably wasn't helping.

As if *he* knew what would or wouldn't help. She

should be talking to Mom, not him. How'd they gotten on this conversational track, anyway? Oh, yeah. Romance novels.

"Well, thanks. That was comforting," she snapped.

He slung an arm around her. "Hey, sorry. But seriously, stop stressing. It'll happen." Dr. Jonathan Templar, fertility expert. Oh, brother.

"Maybe it won't," she said in a small voice.

Now he really didn't know what to say. *Don't give up?* Yeah, that'd make her feel better. *You've got someone who loves you?* True but not what she wanted to hear. The only thing she wanted to hear was, "You're pregnant."

He shook his head. "Life sucks sometimes."

Amazingly, that had been the thing to say. She managed a smile and said, "Yeah, you're right. But not all the time." She held up her grocery bag full of paperbacks. "At least I scored big today. I've got a whole bag full of happiness."

A whole bag full of happiness, huh? "I guess."

"These books are full of love and adventure."

"And perfect men," Jonathan added, remembering the conversation in the library.

"A woman's idea of perfect, anyway," Juliet said.

They got their coffee, then sat at one of the café tables outside to enjoy the sunshine and watch their fellow Icicle Falls residents go about their business. They were almost finished when a woman with a baby in a stroller approached. Jonathan opened the door for her and returned to his seat to see his sister's eyes looking ready to spill tears.

"Hey, it'll be okay," he promised, and hoped he was right. "You're only thirty. You've got plenty of time to have a kid." They'd been trying for a year or so. Did it bring the odds down the longer you tried?

She nodded, but no smile this time. "I should get going. See you at my place for dinner tomorrow?"

It was Mother's Day. If he didn't show up, he'd be toast. "Sure." He made a mental note to bring some antacids.

She gave him a hug, then hurried off down the street.

Jonathan drank the last of his coffee and went to throw the cup in a nearby garbage can. He passed a table with a woman sitting alone, nursing a drink and reading a paperback. He glanced down and saw a couple on the cover, this pair dressed in contemporary Western attire. Another romance novel. The woman smiled and turned a page.

What was it about these books that had women so hooked? He reviewed the conversation he'd heard in the library. *There's a hero to die for.... James Noble is the perfect man...perfect man.*

Women wrote those novels and they wrote about perfect men. So if a guy wanted to learn what a woman wanted in a man… Who was that author Juliet and Hildy had been talking about? Vanessa Valentine. Someone with a name like that had to know her stuff when it came to love.

Jonathan tossed his cup, then retraced his steps to the library, hoping the women hadn't cleared every romance novel off the shelves.

Most of the library patrons were gone by the time he slipped back into the musty room on the lower level, either back to their homes to wash cars or mow lawns, or off to go hiking the mountain trails. A few late arrivals browsed the health and finance sections, and one woman was leafing through a cookbook.

Just his luck, the only other section that was occupied was the romance section, where two teenage girls stood, perusing the books. They were cute and skinny, probably cheerleaders. Darn. He'd hoped not to have an audience.

He hovered over by the magazines and CDs, wishing they'd leave. They didn't. In fact, it looked like they were going to camp out over there all day, reading and filling their paper grocery bags, emptying the shelves.

What do you care if they see you looking through a romance? They're only high school kids, he reminded himself. Kids who'd go home and tell their moms about the dork who'd come in looking for love between the covers of a book.

"Oh, my gosh, here's a Vanessa Valentine," said one.

No, don't take that.

She handed it to her friend.

"I haven't read this," the other girl said, and dropped it in her bag.

So much for that book. So much for *all* the books if he didn't make his move soon. He sauntered casually over. A forty-something woman he'd seen around town had joined them now, and he was aware of both her and the girls staring at him like he was some kind of freak as he studied the titles. He could feel himself beginning to sweat. *Just take a book and get out of here.*

He snagged a book about a vampire and another with a cowboy on the cover and was about to leave when, suddenly, he saw it. What was this? Two shelves down in the corner, a few inches past the woman's thighs… Yes! One last Vanessa Valentine.

He bent and made a grab for it just as she leaned over. Oh, no! Boob graze.

"Excuse me," she said in a tone of voice that told him he was done here.

"Uh, sorry," he mumbled, and snatched back his hand.

She took advantage of his consternation and plucked the Vanessa Valentine off the shelf. Then she scooped another half dozen novels into her shopping bag.

That left two and one of the teens got them. The woman was right. He was done here. Face still flaming, he walked to the card table where the library volunteer was taking money.

She was somewhere in her twenties and dressed in black. Her fingernails were black, too. She had piercings all over her face, a collection of earrings running up her ears and wore enough eye makeup to give her a head start on Halloween. Not that Jonathan was an expert on eye makeup, but hers seemed like overkill to him. He preferred a more natural look, like what Lissa wore. Liss, always the gold standard.

But this woman was friendly enough. He'd seen

her volunteering before. He nodded in response to her greeting of "Back for more?"

She took the books to total them and noticed the vampire on the cover of the top one. "Oh, I love this author. Don't you?"

"I don't know. I've never read her."

"You haven't? Well, you're in for a treat. Her vampire is really sexy."

Did she think he was into guy vampires? He opened his mouth to explain that neither guys nor vampires were his thing, but he found it impossible to wedge the words into their conversation.

"He's right up there with Sookie's Eric. Gotta love Eric, don't you?"

Jonathan was aware of the teens tittering behind him. His face began to heat. "Well…"

"I suppose you've read all the *Twilight* books. Are you on Team Edward or Team Jacob?"

"Huh?"

"I say vampires win every time. Werewolves aren't that sexy."

More tittering produced more burning on Jonathan's face. "These aren't for me."

"Sure they're not," came a whisper from behind him.

"They're for my sister."

The volunteer's face fell. "Oh."

Okay. She was embarrassed, he was embarrassed. He held up the vampire. "But I'll have to give this one a try."

"You should," she said, nodding her head and making her earrings jingle. "You'll like it, I promise."

He paid his buck and got out of there. At least he'd managed to get a couple of books. But what he really wanted was a Vanessa Valentine novel. He wandered upstairs to see if he could find any of her works in the fiction section to check out.

Lo and behold, he discovered a copy of one of the books Juliet had found downstairs. He took it off the shelf. *Everlasting Love,* the title read, and beneath the cursive script a beautiful couple posed, dressed in the garb of another century. No bed. This pair was standing in a moonlit garden. From the way they were gazing at each other, they wouldn't be bothering with a bed.

For a moment, the woman's dark hair lightened to a honey-blond and the guy's face lengthened and acquired a pair of glasses. Jonathan blinked.

When he glanced down again, the couple had reclaimed their original looks. Shaking his head at his own foolishness, he turned the book over and read the summary on the back.

Lorinda Chardonnay's life lies in ruins. Her father has gambled away their family's fortune and betrothed her to the Earl of Ryde, shattering her hopes of marrying her childhood love, Sir James Noble. Little does she know that the Earl of Ryde has a terrible secret that will cost Lorinda her life if she learns of it. But James is not about to let her go into danger without someone to watch over her. And if he must ride the King's Highway by night and face his rival's sword to do so, then he will.

Hmm. This sounded kind of interesting. Sword fights, secrets, saving the girl. What the heck. He'd give it a try. He took that one and a couple of other Vanessa Valentine books from the shelf and went to check them out.

Halfway to where Mrs. Bantam, the librarian, stood smiling at him his feet faltered. He'd already gone through enough torture downstairs. He needed cover for his romance novels.

He made a quick detour to the do-it-yourself section and picked up a book on patios, then he went back to— Oh, no. Mrs. Bantam was no longer at the checkout desk and in her place stood Emily Ward.

Emily was fairly new in town. A couple of weeks ago he'd fixed her home computer. She'd supplied him with coffee and then pulled up a chair right next to him so she could watch him work. Customers did that sometimes, but they weren't usually wearing perfume or tops that pouffed out when they leaned forward, showing breasts wrapped in lacy black. She'd gotten him so distracted he'd knocked over his coffee, drenching everything on her desk. She'd been okay about it but he'd felt like a total moron and had been trying to avoid her ever since.

He pushed his glasses up his nose and forced himself to get in line behind an older woman checking out several books, all the while wondering what happened to the good old days when librarians looked like librarians. The only thing even remotely librarian-like about Emily was her glasses, but they were fire-red and were more like some kind of fashion accessory than an aid to sight. She had short, auburn hair with a feather dangling from it and she wore jeans and a clingy top and a ton of bracelets on her wrist. She wasn't as beautiful as Lissa, but she was still pretty enough to make him sweat.

"Hi, Jonathan," she greeted him. "Looks like you've got some reading planned for the weekend."

"Uh, yeah." That was articulate. *Say something else, idiot.* "I bet you've got plans." Wait. Did that sound like he was asking her out? He wasn't trying to start something, not with Emily, anyway.

"Not really," she said, smiling at him.

He nodded. "You getting to know people yet?"

"Slowly."

She took his pile of books and started checking them out to him. Once she'd finished with the book on patios and got to the first romance novel, her eyes widened.

"I'm getting some stuff for my sister," he said. That was his story and he was stickin' to it.

"What a nice brother. I bet you're doing something nice for your mom for Mother's Day, too."

If a box of Sweet Dreams chocolate counted, then yes. He shrugged. "Family dinner."

Now Emily spied his bag of library book-sale treasures. "I see you've been to the sale."

He left the romance novels he'd purchased downstairs in the bag and instead pulled out his earlier acquisition, *The Kingdom of Zoon,* thus proving he was no sissy who read chick books.

She cocked her head and studied it. "That looks interesting."

Interesting. A polite way of saying yuck. People sure were quick to judge a guy's reading material.

Someone behind Jonathan cleared his throat, so Emily got busy and finished the checkout process, and Jonathan scrammed, letting out his breath as he went. Who knew going to the library could be so stressful? He stuck the romance novels in the bag with his other books, then left the library, holding the tome on building patios for all the world to see.

But once he arrived home, the manly book on patios got tossed onto the kitchen counter and Jonathan settled on the front porch swing with Chica to find out what was so special about Sir James Noble.

The rest of the morning slipped away as Jonathan was drawn into nineteenth-century England. It was midafternoon when he poured himself a glass of milk and made a PBJ sandwich. Book in hand, he plunked down at his kitchen table to eat and lost a couple more hours.

Finally Chica, who'd been keeping him company, got tired of sitting around and slipped out her dog door. But Jonathan stayed in the nineteenth century. He remained there through dinner, too, gnawing on a cold chicken leg while the wicked Earl of Ryde entertained spies with everything from roast duck to syllabub. (What the heck was syllabub?) Meanwhile, Sir

James Noble, bound and gagged in a dark dungeon, struggled back to consciousness, his one thought to save the woman he loved.

After much anguish and struggle, Sir James was able to free himself and rescue the fair Lorinda.

"Oh, James, I thought after what happened at the ball, the horrible things he made me say—I was sure you couldn't love me anymore." Lorinda buried her face in her hands and began to cry.

He gently took her hands and kissed each finger. "Don't cry, dearest. He's dead now. He has no power over you. And as for loving you, don't you know? I've never stopped. The sun will turn to ash before I stop loving you."

Now, *that* was a damned good line.

A few more pages saw James and Lorinda happily starting their new life together. Then there was nothing left for the author to write but *The End*.

For Jonathan, however, this was the beginning. He'd found the love coach he'd been looking for. Several, as a matter of fact. Maybe, if he read enough of these novels, took notes, he could figure out how to win Lissa's love.

The thought had barely formed in his mind before he rejected it as hopeless and stupid. Still, what did he have to lose? Surely there was an ember somewhere in Lissa's heart that he could fan into a small flame of love.

Like a detective, Jonathan wandered down memory lane in search of clues.

He saw himself at the age of ten, a scrawny kid with glasses, doing his best to help a little golden-haired girl come down from the boys' tree house, where she'd bravely climbed. Rand, the leader of the pack, had yelled at her for having the nerve to invade their territory, and had left in a huff, taking Lenny Lubecker and Danny Popkee with him. She'd burst into tears, and Jonathan had abandoned guy solidarity in favor of staying behind to comfort her.

Lissa was upset but all Jonathan could think to say was, "Don't cry, Lissa."

"I just wanted to see," she sobbed. "You all come up here and don't play with me. It's mean."

He'd never thought of their behavior as mean. Their "boys only" tree house was a fort, a place where they could go to look down on the world and feel superior to those silly girls.

Except Lissa wasn't silly. She was sweet and she was his friend and now she was upset. "Come on. Let's go to my house and have root beer floats," he suggested.

She sniffed and nodded.

He scrambled out of the tree house and started to climb down the makeshift stairs they'd hammered into the trunk.

She poked her head out, then ducked back in.

"Come on," he called.

"I can't."

He climbed up again and looked inside. He found her huddled in a corner. "Don't you want a float?"

"I'm scared," she said in a small voice.

"There's nothing to be scared of," he assured her.

She shook her head.

"Lissa, you have to come down," he said reasonably.

She shook her head again.

"Come on," he urged. "I'll help you."

"What if we fall?"

"We won't."

But she wasn't convinced, and pressed farther into the corner of the tree house.

"I'll get you down."

"Promise?"

"Promise."

With a little whimper, she slowly scooted forward on her bottom. Once at the edge, though, she moved away again.

"Come on, Liss." He held out a hand. "You can do it."

She bit her lip and studied him for a moment. Then she moved back to the entrance. He went down a couple of steps to give her room. "Okay, now turn around and put your foot out."

That produced another whimper but she turned around. Then she stuck out her foot.

Jonathan breathed an inward sigh of relief.

Until she pulled her foot back. "I can't."

"Yes, you can. You're brave. You climbed up here all by yourself."

"I didn't think about falling then."

"Don't think about it now," he advised. "Here, I'll make sure you find the step."

Once more, she risked sticking out her foot. This time he guided it to the step. "All right! You did it. Come on, next foot."

And so it went, one foot at a time until he got her down to solid ground.

Once there she threw her arms around his neck. "You saved me!"

It made him feel like a superhero. It was also a little embarrassing. What if the guys saw? He pulled away. "No big deal."

"It was to me," she said. And then she did something that forever changed his life. She kissed him on the cheek. "Thank you, Jonathan."

He could feel his whole face burning. The other boys would tease him mercilessly if they got wind of this. Not knowing what to say or do, he ran off toward home and those root beer floats, Lissa right behind him.

His mom had not only made them floats, she'd made popcorn, too, and they'd spent the rest of that Saturday afternoon playing Yahtzee. It had been a perfect day and it had been the beginning of what turned out to be a lifelong, one-sided love affair.

Did Lissa remember that day? She'd never mentioned it again. Although one afternoon when they were walking home from middle school she'd told him he was her best friend.

She'd been talking about Danny Popkee, on whom she had a crush, asking Jonathan for advice on how to get his attention. That had been torture. Jonathan hadn't wanted Lissa to get Danny's attention. She already had a boy's attention. His.

"I dunno," he'd mumbled. "Either he likes you or he doesn't."

"Well, that's no help. What would you do if you wanted someone to like you?"

Walk her home from school, help her with her math and hope I can get up enough nerve to ask her to the eighth-grade dance. He'd shrugged. "Just be nice." That was never hard for Lissa. She was nice to everyone. "Like you always are," he'd added.

"Aw, Jonathan, you're so sweet," she'd said, making him blush. "I don't know what I'd do without you. You're my best friend."

He was her best friend, but she had a crush on Danny. She'd decided to bake Danny some cookies and that was all it took. They went to the eighth-grade dance together.

But she'd made cookies for Jonathan, too—to thank him for all his good advice.

In fact, she'd made cookies for Jonathan a lot, always trying out new recipes. Baking became one of her favorite ways to express her creativity. And to do something nice for her high school pals.

"What do you think of these?" she'd asked, setting a plate of cookies in front of him. He'd come over to her house to help her with algebra, a subject that was threatening to ruin her sophomore year. "They're called kitchen sink cookies."

"Kitchen sink cookies?"

"Yeah, 'cause you put everything but the kitchen sink in them. They have oatmeal and raisins and butterscotch chips and chocolate chips."

Sounded great. He'd taken one off the plate and bitten into it. In spite of all that good stuff they weren't very sweet. This wasn't one of her better efforts, but he didn't want to tell her that.

There she'd sat, looking at him expectantly. "Not bad," he'd managed.

He hadn't mastered his poker face yet and she'd known immediately that something was off. She frowned and chose a cookie from the plate, took a bite. "Eeew."

"Well, they're not your best. But they're okay." He'd valiantly taken another bite.

She'd set hers back on the plate, then took his out of his hand and put it back, too. "You're an awful liar. They're terrible. I refuse to let you eat another bite. I must have forgotten the sugar. How could I do that?"

"Thinking about something else?" he'd suggested. More like *someone* else. Lissa was always falling madly in love—with everyone but him.

He'd watched her take the plate to the garbage can and dump the ruined goodies in. "You know, those weren't totally bad," he'd said.

"Yes, they were." She'd sat down at the kitchen table and smiled at him. "You're a super friend. But you have terrible taste."

Not in women.

He should have said that out loud. Why didn't he? Why hadn't he ever said anything?

Of course, deep down he knew the answer. He'd been afraid of how she'd react. He'd chosen to keep his mouth shut then and during the years that followed in order to avoid the agony of rejection.

Still, all those years of cowardice had produced their own brand of suffering. He was tired of suffering.

He and Lissa had been best friends when they were kids. They could be best friends again, maybe even more than that if he turned himself into the kind of man a woman like Lissa would notice.

He only had a ghost of a chance.

But he believed in ghosts. So tomorrow he'd read about the Viscount Vampire and the Cursed Cowboy. Then he was going to go online (where no one would see what he was buying) and buy a bunch more romance novels. He had a lot of research to do.

Chapter Four

Mother's Day dinner at the Gerard residence with Jonathan's sister in charge was a culinary adventure. To say that the meal didn't measure up to the fancy table setting and fresh flowers would have been an understatement. The roast was done well enough to qualify as jerky and the asparagus was scorched. The cake…well, it wasn't cake, at least not like any Jonathan had tasted—since the last time he ate Juliet's cake. Wasn't cake supposed to be…taller? And, whoa, what was that bitter taste?

Juliet made a face, too. "I shouldn't have added the baking powder at the last minute," she said.

"It does need to be sifted in, sweetie," her mother said gently.

"But I'd forgotten it. And I knew I had to add it."

"But since you did add it, the cake should have risen better," Mom said, playing culinary detective. Even Columbo couldn't solve the mystery of why Juliet's kitchen creations never turned out, so Jonathan didn't know why Mom was trying.

"Then Cecily called about book group and I forgot

the eggs." Juliet sighed. "I hoped the baking powder would be enough."

"The baked potatoes weren't so bad," said her husband, Neil. "Anyway, it's hard to screw those up."

Was that a compliment? Jonathan wasn't sure. That was often the case when he listened to his brother-in-law talking to his sister. "She made the effort and that's what counts." And even if the spuds were a little underdone you hardly noticed after smothering them with sour cream and butter.

"I'm not complaining," Neil said. "My girl's got other talents."

From the way he was looking at Juliet, Jonathan could guess what they were. He held up a hand. "You don't have to tell us." There were some things a guy didn't want to think about his sister doing.

"It was a lovely dinner, dear," said their mother.

"No, it wasn't." Juliet frowned at the frosted yuck on her plate. "I'm sorry, Mom. I wanted this day to be special."

"It is." Mom swept her gaze around the table. "I'm with all of you and that makes it perfect. But if you want to top it off…"

"I'll go get ice cream," Neil offered.

"Oh, I wasn't thinking of anything to eat. I was thinking of—"

"Farkle," Jonathan and Juliet finished with her. Their family had played a lot of games when Jonathan was growing up, and his mother still loved to beat him at Words With Friends. He'd gotten Farkle for her last Christmas and it had become a new favorite.

"I just happen to have it in my purse," Mom said with a grin.

Jonathan wouldn't have been surprised to hear she had the entire population of Luxembourg in there, too. How much stuff women could fit in their purses amazed him.

"Dice," Neil said, rubbing his hands together. "That's a game even I can get into."

Unlike their family, Neil wasn't much of a game player, unless it involved a football and a good dose of aggression. He was a big, well-muscled guy, who used those muscles working in the Sweet Dreams warehouse. Today Jonathan couldn't help thinking (with only a tinge of jealousy) that his brother-in-law could pose for a cover on one of Juliet's books.

Neil's looks—that was what had hooked her in the first place. Jonathan wasn't sure what kept her hooked, although she seemed happy enough with her choice. Other than going dancing at the Red Barn, their favorite honky tonk, they didn't appear to have much in common. Juliet loved to read. About the only thing Neil read was the sports page. When it came to movies, she liked chick flicks and Neil preferred action movies. He was big on eating, she was bad at cooking. Family was everything to her. His family was dysfunctional and he'd moved as far away from them as possible. And he never seemed that excited to see hers.

Although maybe Jonathan was imagining that, because he always felt a little uncomfortable around Neil, rather like a mule standing next to a Thoroughbred racehorse.

Mom had taken the can of dice out of her purse and Jonathan pulled his mind away from thoughts of mules and horses. But later that evening, when he got back home, he found himself revisiting the subject. Some men just seemed to be born babe magnets. Others...

Well, Chica loved him.

She rushed out her dog door to greet him the minute he pulled up back at the house. "Did you miss me, girl?" he asked.

Chica woofed and wagged her tail. *Yes.*

"I bet you're ready for some fetch, huh?" He grabbed her tennis ball from the porch and threw it for her and she raced after it. Dogs were so easy to please. If only it was as easy to please a woman.

After a rousing game of fetch they went inside the house, and that was when Jonathan discovered his loss. Chica had developed a taste for romance and had devoured two of his library book sale paperbacks.

"Aw, Chica," he said in disgust as he surveyed the mess of mangled books and shredded paper on the couch and the living room floor. He picked up what was left of one cover and saw that the Viscount Vampire now bore canine teeth marks all over his face and neck. He'd survived better than the cowboy. All Jonathan could find of him was his Stetson.

He shook the fragment at Chica. "What is this?"

Her tail curled between her legs and her head hung. She turned, slinking off toward the kitchen.

"Yeah, you should be ashamed. Bad dog!" She had a dog door and a huge yard to play in. She didn't need to swipe his books and eat them. "Why did you do that?" he demanded. She didn't make a habit of eating his books. But then, he didn't make a habit of leaving them lying around on the couch. And, he had to admit, these had smelled a little musty. Maybe Chica had mistaken them for something dead.

Well, they were as good as dead now, he thought. He picked up part of a page and read.

"Armande, I have never met a man like you," breathed the contessa.

"And you never will. I will satisfy your every desire. Forever," he whispered as he gently lifted her hair, exposing her lovely white neck.

Desire and a lovely white neck—that was all he was going to see of the contessa and Armande. Jonathan retrieved the waste can from under the kitchen sink and got to work.

Chica watched as he cleaned up the mess.

"Yeah, you did this. Those were research, you know," he informed her.

She whined.

He relented. "Okay, you're forgiven. Come here."

She came, her tail wagging hopefully.

He knelt and pulled her against him and rubbed her head. "I guess those books just looked too good to resist, huh?"

She licked his face.

"Yeah, yeah. I know, you're sorry. I'll find 'em online and download them on to my e-reader. But no more eating my books, okay?"

Chica barked. *Okay.*

Once the mess was cleaned up, he'd spend some time on the island of Crete, with a suave tycoon and a beautiful businesswoman. He'd snitched *The Undercover Tycoon* from Juliet. He'd spotted it lying on top of a pile of books on the stairs and, unable to stop himself, had pinched it and smuggled it out in the pocket of his windbreaker. She'd happily have lent it to him if he asked, but no *way* was he asking to borrow one of Juliet's romance novels. He'd never have heard the end of it, especially from Neil. He'd managed to get it out of the house undetected and he'd get it back in the same way. Nobody would be the wiser.

"No eating this one," he told Chica, showing it to her. "It's not ours."

She yawned and settled down next to him on the couch.

This story had a contemporary setting, and it didn't take long for him to get involved in the plot. Although the hero and heroine were hot for each other, something was standing in the way of their love—the business. Her family used to own it but now she only ran it. And the tycoon wanted to sell it out from under her.

As Jonathan read, he made notes on his iPad, treating the novel as if it were a college textbook, the same as he'd done with the other book he'd read. This particular hero seemed to have an overabundance of testosterone. He was strong and forceful, and while he and the heroine clashed—a lot—she seemed to appreciate that forcefulness. So, women wanted a man who was forceful, a take-charge kind of guy.

Jonathan added that attribute to the list he'd started. Forceful, take-charge. He could be forceful. Maybe.

Adam returned from his Alaskan adventure late Sunday night to make a shocking discovery. His key didn't work in the lock. He wasn't dreaming and he wasn't drunk. This was the right house. His house. But his key didn't work. Even finding the lock had been a pain since his wife hadn't left the porch light on. What the hell?

He rang the doorbell.

No one came.

He rang again.

Still no one.

Chelsea's car was there. What was going on? "Chels," he called. "Chelsea?"

Finally the entry hall light went on and he saw the shadow of a slim body on the other side of the frosted glass panel. She must have fallen asleep.

That in itself was odd. She always waited up for him.

Now she was at the door but it didn't open. And the porch light stayed off, leaving him standing there in the dark.

Her voice drifted out to him, muffled and distant. "Go away, Adam."

What? "Let me in. My key won't work."

"It won't work because I had the locks changed," said the voice.

Maybe he was dreaming, after all. Or she was

joking. "Okay, babe, you've had your laugh. Now open up."

Instead of opening the door, she turned off the entry light and disappeared. "Chels!" He banged on the door. "This isn't funny anymore. Open up."

One neighbor was two wooded lots away and whoever had purchased the house next door hadn't moved in yet. Still, he caught himself checking over his shoulder to see if anyone had heard. He felt like a fool standing there, demanding entrance into his own house. Changing the locks, that wasn't even legal. But what was he going to do, call the cops? He'd wind up sleeping on the couch for the rest of his life.

This was nuts. He took out his cell phone and dialed her.

"What?" she answered.

What, indeed? Who was this snappish woman?

"Do you mind telling me what's going on?" he asked.

An upstairs light went on and a window opened. Their bedroom. For a moment he saw her face, framed by the bedroom light. Chelsea had long, chestnut hair, big hazel eyes and Angelina Jolie lips. The lips weren't smiling.

She held a box wrapped in white paper and tied with a pink ribbon. He recognized that box. And now she was going to... Oh, no. That was breakable. "Don't—" he began.

Too late. She dropped it. The box landed with a crunch. So much for the candy dish the clerk at Mountain Treasures had convinced him to buy.

His wife had lost her mind. "What are you *doing*?"

A moment later, something else came fluttering down, like a poorly designed paper airplane—the card that went with the box.

"All right," he said into the cell phone. "What was that all about?"

"Guess."

"You didn't want to give my mom anything for her birthday?"

Wrong guess. The call ended and the bedroom window slammed shut.

He called her again. "I don't get it."

"Does the number seven mean anything to you?"

Seven, seven. Crap! Their anniversary. Their anniversary was this weekend and he'd forgotten. "Shit," he muttered.

"Yeah, that's what you're in," she said. "It was bad enough you just had to stay up in Alaska and fish, but not to send flowers, not even call…"

"I called." That was feeble. He'd left a message on voice mail telling her what time he'd be in. No mention of their anniversary.

Because he'd forgotten. Forgotten! What was wrong with his brain? A twenty-pound salmon, that was what. He felt sick.

"And then I found the package and thought you'd left it as a surprise." Her voice was wobbly now, a sure sign that she was crying. "And what was it? Your mother's birthday present. And her birthday isn't until next week. And I already bought something because you never remember!"

He wouldn't have remembered this year, either, except he'd been talking to his mom on his cell a few days ago and she'd dropped a hint when he happened to be downtown, walking past a shop. More than a hint. She'd come right out and said, "Your wife is not your personal secretary, Adam, and you should be able to remember your own mother's birthday."

Yeah, and he should've been able to remember his own anniversary, but he hadn't. He'd stuck his mom's present in the closet and forgotten about it. Just like he'd forgotten another important date. "I knew it was coming up," he said. No lie. He'd planned to remember. Lame.

"This is the last straw. I'm tired of you taking me for granted. You do it all the time."

"I do not," he insisted, both to her and himself.

"Oh, yes, you do. And this isn't the first time you've messed up."

All right, so he'd accidentally gotten tickets to a Mariners game on the day of their anniversary the year before last. And she'd never have known he'd screwed up if his brother Greg hadn't called from Seattle asking what time they were meeting at the stadium. He'd done penance and gotten her diamond earrings. A whole carat, for God's sake. He'd even taken her to the game and they'd ended up having a great evening.

And last year he'd remembered. She hadn't needed to remind him the week before. Why did women keep score like that? They kept track of every screw-up and then threw it in your face. In the middle of the night.

"Oh, come on, babe. Cut me some slack. Let's talk about this." She always wanted to talk.

Not tonight. She ended the call and the bedroom light switched off.

Of course he tried to call her once more, but it immediately went to voice mail.

Great. Just great. Where would he go at eleven-thirty at night? He supposed he could go to one of the town's B and Bs, but if he did that, everyone would know his wife had kicked him out.

Since this was only temporary, he saw no point in going that route. Tomorrow he'd take her out to dinner. They'd kiss and make up and everything would be fine.

Meanwhile, though, he couldn't sleep on the porch. He hauled his carry-on back to the car. If that was the way she wanted it, he could sleep there. Except while an SUV would be okay for sleeping, it made for a poor place to shave in the morning.

He started the engine and drove slowly away from his house. His house! He had no idea where he was going. He sure knew where he was, though. In the doghouse.

Jonathan was having an incredible dream. He'd just killed a man in a sword fight, and now the woman he'd rescued—Lissa, in an old-fashioned pink gown—had thrown herself into his arms.

"How can I thank you?" she breathed.

"Well," he said, and lowered his head to kiss her.

"Oh, wait. What's that I hear?" she said, turning her

head just before he could reach her lips. "The church bells."

"That's the bells, all right," he agreed, and tried for her lips again.

"They're summoning you. You must go."

"Who's summoning me?"

He never found out. Between the insistent ringing of his doorbell, coupled with pounding on the door and Chica's barking, he was now hopelessly awake.

He checked the time. Midnight! He swore and threw off the covers, marched out of the bedroom and flicked on the hall light, Chica running ahead of him. Whoever it was, Jonathan was going to kill him.

But then he realized that anyone summoning him at this hour must be in trouble. Juliet! She'd had a fight with Neil?

He picked up his pace. By the time he got to the living room, his visitor was not only ringing the bell and banging on the door, but calling his name, as well. Definitely not Juliet.

Jonathan opened the door and there stood Adam. "I need a place to sleep."

"Huh?"

"Can I crash on your couch?"

"Uh, yeah," Jonathan said, and stepped aside.

In walked Mr. Success, dragging his carry-on luggage behind him. "Chelsea kicked me out."

"'Cause you went salmon-fishing?" That seemed a little extreme.

"No, because I forgot our anniversary."

Jonathan, no expert on women, still knew this was

a cardinal sin. "How'd you manage that?" If he was with Lissa he'd never forget their anniversary. Heck, he'd make *everything* an anniversary—first date, first kiss, first time they slept together. At the rate he was going, that wasn't even happening in his dreams.

Adam paced into the living room and parked his carry-on next to Jonathan's couch. He ran a hand through his hair. "I didn't mean to forget." He fell onto the couch. "She says I take her for granted."

"Do you?"

"No. Well, maybe. Once in a while. I don't know." Like hell he didn't. "Right."

"Okay, so I'm not perfect like those men on the covers of her dumb romance novels."

Jonathan caught sight of his Vanessa Valentine paperback on the kitchen counter and subtly dragged his copy of *PC World* over it.

Adam never noticed. He was too involved in his own drama. "But cut a man some slack, you know?"

Jonathan didn't know.

"She changed the locks."

Whoa. His friend had sailed down the river of no return. "That's harsh."

"That's what I thought," Adam said. "Anyway, I know we'll get it all straightened out tomorrow."

And now who was dreaming?

"Sorry to get you out of bed. You were the first one who came to mind."

Vance lived right down the road from Adam, but Jonathan understood why Adam hadn't gone there.

Vance would have taken great delight in taunting him. Whereas Jonathan…was a soft touch.

"I just need a place for tonight."

Jonathan had a suspicion that his poker pal was going to need a place for longer than one night, but this probably wasn't the time to point that out. Anyway, he was tired and he wanted to get back to bed. Back to Lissa in her pink gown. He pulled a sleeping bag out of the closet and tossed it to Adam.

"Thanks, man," Adam said. "I'll get this sorted out in the morning. Right now, I just need a good night's sleep."

He needed a lot more than sleep. Jonathan didn't tell him that, either. Some things a man had to figure out for himself.

Chapter Five

Jonathan never found Lissa again. Every time he drifted off, he was awakened by the sound of a rumbling train. It didn't take more than the first rude awakening for him to realize that no one had built a train track through his house in the night. No, the horrible noise that dragged him from his dreamland search for Lissa had been Adam's snoring.

He finally gave up on sleep around seven to find Adam still zonked out on his couch, like a giant caterpillar half out of his sleeping bag cocoon, his hair going every which way and his mouth hanging open. There was a sight a guy didn't need to wake up to.

Coffee. He needed coffee.

He had a handy-dandy little coffeemaker that delivered one serving at a time, and he made himself a mug. The aroma of brewing java sure would've awakened Jonathan, but Adam slept on. How could the guy sleep so well when his wife had kicked him out? And didn't he have to be at work? Jonathan's schedule was flexible and depended on what clients he had lined up for the day, but he assumed that on a Monday Adam would have to report in to his office.

Not your problem, he told himself as he filled Chica's dog bowl. *You're not his mother.*

Still, the idea of Adam happily snoozing away after ruining his sleep the night before wasn't appealing. It was quarter after seven now. Time to wake up. Jonathan yanked the sofa pillow out from under Adam's head and whacked him with it.

Adam bolted up. "Wha?"

"Thought you might have to get up."

Adam groaned. "I didn't sleep at all last night."

Right. He'd just been faking. "You snore."

Adam frowned and rubbed his eyes. "What time is it?"

"Quarter after seven."

"I have to get going. Man, I'm shot." He eyed Jonathan's mug. "Is that coffee?"

Jonathan nodded at his coffeemaker. "You can make yourself some."

"Don't mind if I do," Adam said, and unzipped his sleeping bag. "But first things first."

Jonathan watched him wander off down the hall to the bathroom, wearing boxers and a T-shirt. Lucky for Adam he had a suitcase of clothes. It was a cinch he wouldn't be getting into his house for more anytime soon. Poor guy.

From what Adam had said the night before, Jonathan suspected he'd had it coming. Still, he couldn't help feeling sorry for his poker pal. Locked out of your own house. That had to be humiliating.

He heard the toilet flush and suddenly realized that potential humiliation was lying out in plain sight on the toilet tank. Oh, no.

Maybe Adam hadn't seen it....

"What the hell?"

Adam had seen.

Jonathan rushed down the hall and arrived at the bathroom to find Adam holding *The Undercover Tycoon* and staring at it in horror. He looked at Jonathan as if he'd just discovered Jonathan was an ax murderer.

"Give me that." Jonathan strode over and grabbed the book to snatch it away.

Adam wasn't ready to let go. "What the hell is this?"

"Never mind." Jonathan yanked again.

Adam yanked back and Jonathan pulled harder.

"Give me the damned book," Jonathan growled.

Adam let go at the same time Jonathan gave up the struggle. The book did a swan dive, putting the tycoon in the toilet.

They both stood for a moment, watching the paperback floating in the toilet bowl. Who knew what was going through Adam's mind, but Jonathan had only one thought. "My sister's gonna be pissed."

"That's your sister's book?"

"Yes," Jonathan said grumpily, fishing it out. "Well, it was." Maybe he could dry it off, set it out in the sun. Once it was dry she'd never know the difference.

"What are you doing reading your sister's romance novel?"

This wasn't exactly something he wanted to share.

He wished he'd remembered the dumb thing and ditched it while Adam was snoring. "Never mind," he said, and took the soggy tycoon out to the front porch.

Adam was right behind him. "That's a chick book."

"I know," Jonathan said as he laid it out on the porch railing. Chica, who'd come over to see what was going on, sniffed it. "Oh, no, you don't," he said, picking it up again. Maybe if he put it in the dryer.

"So, why are you reading a chick book?"

Jonathan hadn't wanted to tell anyone, but looking at Adam regarding him with disgust was enough to make him reconsider. What the heck. "I'm doing research."

"Research? What, are you going to write one of those?"

This was awkward. "No. I just…" *Don't want to be a loser.* He couldn't bring himself to say that, so instead he clamped his lips shut and went back inside, Adam and Chica following him.

"What? I mean, dude, that's weird."

"No, it's not. I figure I can learn something from these books." If he could keep them from getting destroyed.

Adam gave a disdainful snort. "Like what, how to get the prince to take you to the ball?"

"No. How to figure out what's important to a woman." Jonathan set the tycoon on top of the fridge where Chica couldn't reach him. Then he took his Vanessa Valentine novel out from its hiding place under his magazine. "They're written by women, and the women who read them like what the heroes do.

I'm thinkin' reading some of these is a good way to get a handle on what makes a woman tick and what she wants in a man."

Adam took it from him. "Seriously?"

"Seriously."

Adam turned it over and read the back cover. "Sounds dumb."

Jonathan could feel his cheeks heating. Yeah, what did he know? He was just the dork who'd given Adam a place to sleep after his wife kicked him out.

"So who's the woman you want?"

"Never mind." He went to the kitchen and pulled a box of cereal from the cupboard, keeping his back to Adam, willing the flush of embarrassment from his face.

"No, seriously. Who is she?"

"No one you know." Adam was a relative newcomer to Icicle Falls. He hadn't known Lissa.

"So she doesn't live around here?"

"Not anymore."

"She used to?"

Jonathan got busy pouring milk on his cereal. "Yeah. We went to school together."

Understanding dawned and Adam nodded sagely. "Your high school sweetheart. That's right. You and Kyle have a reunion this summer. I remember you guys talking about it the other night. So, is your old girlfriend coming back for the reunion?"

"We never went out. We were just friends." Jonathan shrugged like it was no big deal.

"And you want to see if you can start something with her."

"Yeah," Jonathan admitted.

Now Adam was looking skeptical. "And reading these books is going to help you?"

"Maybe."

"You're nuts."

Guys like Adam thought they knew it all. He'd probably never had trouble sweeping women off their feet. But it looked like sweeping and keeping were two different things. Old Adam wasn't doing so well himself right now. He was in no position to scoff.

"You got a better idea?" Jonathan demanded. "How much do you know about women?"

Adam threw up his hands. "Nothing, nada, zip. Nobody does. Women are another species."

"I'd say they're a species worth studying," Jonathan said. "Unless you like sleeping on my couch more than you like sleeping in your bed."

Adam scowled and rubbed his chin, then dropped the book on the coffee table. "I've got to get ready for work." He pulled some clothes out of his carry-on and disappeared back into the bathroom.

Denial. The guy was in denial. He was probably hoping to run over to his house later, toss out an "I'm sorry" and watch his wife throw the door wide open. For that to happen Jonathan suspected she'd need to be either brain-dead or under a spell.

"May as well dig out the blow-up bed," he said to Chica. "He's gonna be here for a while."

Adam got cleaned up and was out the door in

twenty minutes, and Jonathan once again had the house to himself. He and Chica ate breakfast and went for a walk. Then it was time to watch *Good Morning, Oregon*.

Today Lissa and her cohost, Scott Lawrence, were interviewing, of all people, Vanessa Valentine, who had a new book out. Vanessa, a brunette who looked to be somewhere in her forties, was the picture of success in a black suit and fancy pearl necklace.

But it was Lissa who held Jonathan's attention. Today she wore a red skirt that showed a modest but alluring amount of leg, and a creamy white blouse that looked as silky and touchable as her hair. As always, she was flashing the sweet smile that must have made viewers feel as if they were her best friend.

And, as always, she was gracious and welcoming. "Vanessa, it's a real treat to have you with us today."

"Thank you," Vanessa said.

"And you have a new book out."

"Yes, I do. *A Fire in Winter* just hit the stands last week."

"So, what can readers expect from this latest Vanessa Valentine novel?" Lissa asked.

"First of all, they can expect a good story. I always try to deliver that to my readers because they deserve it. They pay hard-earned money to be entertained and I want to make sure they get their money's worth."

Now Scott broke in. "And your legion of loyal fans keeps growing. But it's mostly a legion of women, right?"

"My readers are predominantly women, but men read my books, too," Vanessa replied.

"See?" Jonathan said to Chica, who was parked next to him. "I'm not the only guy reading this stuff."

Scott's expression was frankly disbelieving. "So, tell us, Vanessa. Why should men read romance novels?"

Vanessa looked at her host as if he were a fine specimen of stupidity. Then she smiled and said, "I can think of several reasons. For one, romance novels deal with the things that are most important in life— love, relationship, family, working to conquer obstacles. That's worth reading about. Secondly, a man can learn about maintaining a relationship from reading romance fiction. He can also learn how women think. And I hear a lot of you complaining that you have trouble figuring us out," she added with a teasing grin.

Scott laughed reluctantly. "You've got that right. But what about those sex scenes?"

"Yes. What about them?" she quipped. "Men, if you want to know what turns a woman on, you can get a pretty good idea from reading a romance novel."

"Now, if that isn't proof I'm on the right track, I don't know what is," Jonathan said, and Chica agreed with an enthusiastic bark.

"You make a pretty good case," Scott said. "I think I may have to come to your book signing."

"I think so, too," Vanessa said, still smiling.

"Vanessa will be signing her new book, *A Fire in Winter,* tonight at the Lloyd's Center Barnes & Noble at 7:00 p.m.," Lissa said. "So, men, here's your chance to talk to an expert in romance."

"And I guess we'd better start reading romance novels." Scott smiled. "Thanks for being with us today, Vanessa." To the viewers he said, "After this, we have Chi Chi Romero, who's going to show us how to spice things up in the kitchen."

And that was the end of the interview with Vanessa. *Too bad I didn't tape it for Adam,* Jonathan thought. Maybe it would've convinced him he needed to do his homework.

But then again, maybe not. Guys like Adam, who had everything come easy to them, had trouble grasping the concept of homework—that no matter how smart you were, or *thought* you were, you still needed to do it. Jonathan suspected this time was going to be different, though. Once a guy got kicked out of his house, there was no quick route back.

Adam found it hard to concentrate at work. No wonder, with the way his life was going.

He'd called Chelsea when he reached the office, tried to make up for his memory lapse by inviting her to dinner and had been told in no uncertain terms what he could do with his offer. It had all been downhill after that.

As a pharmaceutical rep he spent more time waiting in doctors' offices than he did actually talking to them about the new medicines in his company's catalog. All that waiting gave him way too much time to think, and when he'd finally get a chance to see a doc, he invariably looked like he needed to be taking one of those new antidepressants he was peddling. One doctor even offered to write him a prescription for a competitor's product.

Back at the office he made phone calls and then hung up, wondering what exactly he'd promised, and had to read his emails repeatedly before he understood what he'd read. All he could think about was how mad Chelsea had been. All he could see was the hurt and anger on her face when she'd glared at him from the bedroom window.

The idea of spending another night on Jonathan's couch was anything but appealing. He had to do something. He called Lupine Floral and ordered a huge bouquet to be delivered that day, ASAP.

"What's her favorite flower?" asked the man who answered the phone.

Favorite flower? His mind was a blank. "She likes yellow." She'd painted their whole living room yellow one week when he was gone.

"Well, then, we'll send her a sunshine bouquet— yellow and white daisies and yellow pom-poms and yellow roses in a yellow ceramic pitcher."

Adam didn't care what they came in, as long as they got the job done. "Yeah, that sounds great. Give me the biggest one you've got."

"How would you like the card to read?"

The card. He hadn't thought of that. He didn't want to announce to the whole world that he was in trouble. "How about 'I love you'?"

"That says it all."

He hoped so. He gave the man his credit card information and ended the call. That should do it. Maybe now he could talk about medications without wanting to take a bunch.

He was smiling when he drove down his street after work. Chelsea would have gotten her sunshine bouquet by now and it would have done the trick.

She loved flowers. She worked part-time at Mountain Nursery and she'd planted all kinds of flowers around their house that made it look really nice— roses and a bunch of other things, names she'd rattled off that left him glassy-eyed.

He wasn't into flowers. But he was into his wife and he felt confident his peace offering would prove it.

He lost his smile when he pulled up in front of his place and saw a kitchen trash bag with a yellow flower head sticking out the top. She'd tossed the arrangement? Seriously? And that wasn't the only bag on the porch. Several huge garbage bags sat huddled together, and beside them was his baseball bat, his glove and his fishing gear.

Okay, this was not funny. He got out of the car, marched up to the porch and checked inside one of the trash bags. Clothes. She'd just wadded up his clothes and stuffed them in garbage bags. He was going to have to pay a fortune to get his pants pressed.

He banged on the door. "Chels!"

Of course she didn't answer.

He banged again.

Once more the bedroom window flew open. There she was again, that pretty face, that long, brown hair.

That frown. Sadness overrode his anger. "Come on, baby. What do I have to do?"

"Change."

"I'm trying," he protested. "I sent you flowers."

"That's not changing. That's bribing."

"That's saying I'm sorry," he corrected her.

"Do you see any daisies around here?" she demanded.

He looked around. "Umm."

"I hate daisies. They smell. And if you ever paid attention to anything I said, you'd know that and you wouldn't have sent them to me."

"Sorry."

"Yeah, well, so am I. Go away, Adam," she said, and slammed the window shut.

Now the anger was back, full force. He kicked the bag holding his rejected bouquet off the porch. Then he grabbed a couple of bags of clothes and stormed to his SUV and threw them in.

Another two bags got hurled into the SUV, followed by his baseball stuff and his fishing gear. He got behind the wheel, slamming the door after him. If this was how she wanted to play it, fine.

But by the time he reached his new home, sweet home, the anger had burned off. What was he going to do?

Jonathan was already there and was putting enough hot dogs for two lonely men on the grill when Adam came up the walk, carrying a trash bag of clothes and a fishing rod. He'd known. He didn't say anything, though, and Adam appreciated that. One of the great differences between men and women. Women loved to say *I told you so*. Men didn't say anything.

"Where can I put these?" Adam asked. Only five little words but he almost choked getting them out.

"Upstairs spare bedroom," Jonathan said, and turned a hot dog, "the one with the books. I put a bed in there for you."

Adam walked past Jonathan's bedroom. It was decorated bachelor-style, with only a bed and a couple of blankets, a nightstand with a lamp and a paperback romance— more research, probably—a dresser and a dog bed. He hadn't bothered with curtains at the windows, just a shade.

Pretty different from how Chelsea had fixed up their bedroom—all vibrant reds and gold, lots of pillows on the bed, a hope chest at the end of it. The rest of the house looked equally good, with coordinated furniture, attractive knickknacks here and there, always flowers. He'd taken her decorating for granted, as if houses just sprang up all furnished. Now, comparing it to Jonathan's place, he realized how much she'd done to surround his life with comfort and an atmosphere that said, "Ahhh."

He moved on past another bedroom Jonathan had turned into an office with a desk, chair, bookcase and a bunch of computer equipment and entered the room that would house his clothes and toys. This room, too, was spare. One wall held a giant bookcase. In the corner next to it sat an old overstuffed chair that looked like a family hand-me-down and a floor lamp.

Jonathan had left him a blow-up mattress and an

air pump. Adam started inflating his new bed and watched morosely as it took shape. A night on the couch was one thing. A blow-up bed and his own room was something altogether different. It symbolized what both he and Jonathan knew. He was in deep shit and was going to be stuck here for some time.

He didn't find any hangers in closet so he laid his pants and shirts on the floor. He wondered if Jonathan had any hangers he could borrow. He doubted it. Hangers were one of those things that women remembered to get and men took for granted.

Like they took a lot of things for granted. Adam frowned and went back to his SUV for another load.

Once back in the spare room, he checked out the books on the shelf. He knew Jonathan was a smart guy—anybody who could fix computers was—but it still surprised Adam to see that his pal was such a big reader. Funny how little he knew about the men he played poker with every week, especially their host.

He and Jonathan had met a year and a half ago. Adam had needed some work done on his computer and had hired Jonathan. They'd gotten to talking, and somehow the talk had gotten around to fun guy stuff. Adam had admitted to always wanting to learn how to play poker and Jonathan had mentioned the weekly poker game he was putting together. Next thing Adam knew, he'd found some men to hang with. But that was all they really were.

Except now here he was, rooming with one of them. If someone had told him five years ago that he'd be playing poker with a nerd, he'd have laughed. And if someone had told him he'd be staying with one, he'd have been horrified. Now he was simply grateful.

He read the titles of some of the books on the shelf. *The Dragon of Zoon, Zoon in Ruins, Return to Zoon.* Those all looked dumb. Jonathan also had several volumes of science-fiction anthologies, a ton of novels about wizards, works by Stephen Hawking and some novels by Michael Crichton. Even some money management books. Adam thought of how easily he burned through a paycheck. Yeah, he had a lot of toys to show for his big salary, but he was willing to bet that Jonathan, who probably made a third of what he did, actually had money in savings. The dude was a thinker.

And he was doing research on women. Maybe he had something there.

Adam went back downstairs and found that Jonathan had moved from the barbecue to the kitchen. He had the hot dogs on a plate and a package of buns sat next to them, along with a potato salad from the Safeway deli department. He'd put out ketchup, mustard and hot dog relish and was now busy opening a bottle of beer.

Adam was embarrassingly aware of the fact that he had contributed nothing to this repast but his empty gut. "Hey, man, thanks," he said. "I'll pick up dinner tomorrow."

The thought that tomorrow he wouldn't be going home for dinner took the edge off his appetite.

"Sorry you're still stuck here," Jonathan said, and handed him a bottle of beer.

"I'm in deep shit," Adam admitted. "I sent her

flowers today and you know what she did with them?
She tossed them."

"She's mad," Jonathan said, stating the obvious.

Adam smeared some mustard on a hot dog bun, all
the while tallying how many meals his wife had prepared for him versus the times he'd thanked her for
making them. He took a bite of his hot dog. He loved
hot dogs, but this one didn't taste so good. "She's right.
I do take her for granted."

"I guess that happens," Jonathan said diplomati-
cally.

"I don't know how I'm gonna get her back."

"Research," Jonathan said. Then he went into the
living room, turned on the TV and brought up a sci-
fi thriller.

Adam sat next to him and watched the humans
battling the aliens trying to take over their space out-
post. Battling aliens. If only that was all he had to do.

After the movie, Jonathan went outside to play with
his dog, leaving Adam to do whatever he wanted. Another paperback was sitting on the coffee table. The
couple on the cover looked like they had it all together.
Adam picked up the book and read the back. The heroine had gotten involved with a drug dealer (what a
fool!) and was running for her life. The hero was an
undercover cop out to get both her and the drug dealer.
Wow, they had issues. Why did his wife like reading
this stuff, anyway?

Maybe he needed to find out.

Chapter Six

Jonathan had been thorough in his research and now had what he considered a comprehensive list of important romantic-hero traits.

According to Vanessa Valentine and other female experts, women wanted:

1. A man who's buff and good-looking. (And they give men a hard time for wanting a hottie. Talk about a double standard!)
2. A man who has a smooth tongue.
3. A man who can be forceful and take charge. (Need to stop being a gutless wimp when I'm around Lissa.)
4. A man who knows when to be tender (but it's okay to beat up other guys for her).
5. A man who makes romantic gestures (the bigger the better).
6. A man who will help her when she needs it.
7. A man who will give up everything for her.
8. A man who will fight for what's right (take a stand when it counts).

"Hey, that's pretty good," Adam said as they waited for the rest of the guys to come over for poker night. "You oughta show this to Kyle."

Jonathan shook his head. "It's just stuff I'm seeing in the books. I don't know how to make it work in real life."

"I think you've nailed it," Adam said. He tapped Jonathan's iPad. "All women drool over good-looking guys. That's one we *know* is true. I don't buy the romantic gestures thing, though. It didn't work with Chels."

Flowers were supposed to be a sure winner but they hadn't won Adam any points. "Maybe it wasn't the right gesture," Jonathan suggested.

Adam threw up his hands in frustration. "Nothing is."

Poor Adam. The week hadn't gone well for him. He'd tried everything—texting, phone calls, another visit to the house—but so far his wife had kept the wall of ice firmly in place.

Jonathan wondered if the flowers hadn't worked because the seventh attribute on his list had escaped Adam's notice. But he kept his mouth shut. When a guy was hurting, the last thing he needed was another man poking a stick in the wound. Adam would have to figure out his woman problem for himself, just like everyone else had to do.

Adam was back to studying the list. "That tongue business." He waggled his eyebrows. "I've got that one down."

Jonathan pulled a handful of pretzels from the bag

Adam had bought for the night's refreshments. "Not talking about using it that way. I read somewhere that men fall in love with their eyes but women fall in love with their ears. They want to hear nice things. And be flirted with," he added, thinking of Todd Black. "Sweet talk, flattery, like what the heroes in the books say to their women."

Adam slumped back against the couch cushions. "I can't remember the last time I said anything like that to Chelsea." He rubbed his chin thoughtfully. "I must've said *something.*"

The screen door opened and in walked Kyle Long. "Hope you guys broke your piggy banks, 'cause I'm here to win tonight."

"Yeah, till Vance comes," Adam joked.

Kyle put his six-pack of beer on the counter. "He's just lucky."

Jonathan thought of what Bernardo had said— unlucky in cards, lucky in love. He sucked at poker. Maybe that would stack the odds in his favor with Lissa.

Vance was next in the door with a can of mixed nuts. Right behind him came Bernardo, carrying a platter with vegetables and dip and looking glum.

"Carrots?" Kyle observed, eyebrows raised.

"Anna has me on a diet," Bernardo grumbled.

Kyle made a face. "And she has you bringing them to us why?"

"To make sure I don't cheat," Bernardo said glumly.

"You are whipped," Adam told Bernardo.

"Whipped but sleeping in his own bed," Jonathan muttered. Adam shot him a dirty look so he shut up.

But it was too late. "Who's not sleeping in his own bed?" Kyle asked. Of course there was only one man present who qualified. He stared at Adam in shock. *"You?"*

Adam's face suddenly looked sunburned. "Chelsea threw me out."

Kyle gawked as if he'd just been informed that Santa Claus and the Grinch were one and the same. "You're the king of cool. How could she do that?"

"I forgot our anniversary."

"That's the worst thing a man can do," Bernardo said, helping himself to a handful of pretzels. "That's even worse than dissing her mama."

"Don't women usually, like, remind you?" Kyle asked.

"Well, Chels does. Did," Adam corrected himself.

"It was probably some sort of test," Vance said. "Looks like you flunked. Let's play cards."

"What are you gonna do?" Kyle asked as they moved to Jonathan's kitchen table.

Adam grabbed a beer and took a long draw. "I don't know. I can't sleep in Jonathan's spare room forever, that's for sure."

Jonathan wholeheartedly agreed.

"I need a plan."

"Me, too," Kyle said. "There must be a way to get a chick to see you."

"And to take you back," Adam said. "But hey, I think Jonathan's on to something."

"Jonathan?" Vance said in surprise.

It was embarrassing to have Adam mention him as some kind of expert since everyone knew he wasn't exactly a love machine. Jonathan could count on two fingers the number of girlfriends he'd had in the past ten years. He shook his head and waved away the comment.

"What?" Kyle wanted to know.

"Well, I, uh..." How to confess that he'd been studying romance novels? Surely that had to be the most unmanly thing a guy could do.

"He's been reading chick books," Adam said.

Kyle's brows knit. "Chick books?"

"You know, romances."

The other men looked at Jonathan as if he'd just announced he was getting a sex change.

Now Jonathan's face felt like the top of a lit matchstick. "Research," he mumbled.

"Okay, that's weird," Kyle said.

"Sounds smart to me," Vance said. "Okay, fellas, let's play some seven-card stud." He began to deal. "High-low split."

"I don't get it." Kyle picked up his cards. "Why would you read those?"

"Because he wants to see how women think," Adam explained.

"Hell, nobody has a clue about *that*," Kyle said.

"Our man here does," Adam told him. "He's even made a list of things women want in a man. Right, Jon?"

"Just some observations," Jonathan said.

"I need that list," Kyle told him.

"I want to know what books you're reading," said Bernardo.

"And I want to play cards," Vance said.

That closed the subject until the end of the evening. But once the beer and chips had been consumed and Vance had won the pot, Kyle returned to women and romance novels. "So, how come you want to know what women think all of a sudden?" he asked Jonathan. "Why are you reading this stuff?"

Jonathan needed to say something before Adam blabbed that he was hoping to hook up with some mystery woman at the reunion. Kyle would solve the mystery in a heartbeat. "Thought it might help my love life," he said with a shrug.

"I guess," Kyle said dubiously.

"I never heard of this Vanessa Valentine." Adam picked up a copy of *Surrender* from the coffee table. "But you know, this one's not bad."

Kyle's eyes bugged. "You're reading them, too?"

"Hey, I need to get my wife back."

Kyle frowned suspiciously at the book. "Looks dumb."

"Well, it's not," Adam said, and his tone of voice didn't encourage Kyle to argue.

Kyle held up a hand. "Okay, whatever you say."

Vance chuckled. "See you losers next week," he said, and strolled out the door.

"I'd better get home," Bernardo said.

Jonathan picked up the plate of veggies. "Take your carrots."

"Are you loco? If I take those home, she'll know I didn't eat them. You keep them, *amigo*."

Just what he always wanted, carrot and celery sticks. Bernardo hadn't wanted them, either. He'd eaten half a bag of potato chips but Jonathan didn't remember seeing so much as one carrot go in his mouth.

"*Hasta* Las Vegas," Bernardo said, and followed Vance out the door.

Kyle, however, lingered. "So, you really think there's something to reading those books?"

"Yeah, I do," Jonathan said.

"Dude, show him your list," Adam urged.

Jonathan brought it up on his iPad and passed it to Kyle.

He read, nodding as he went. "You know, this is great stuff. You got all that from reading romance novels?"

Jonathan nodded. "Actually, they're pretty good stories."

"More than pretty good from the way you've been devouring them this week," Adam said.

"So have you," Jonathan retorted.

Kyle picked up the copy of *Surrender*. "Mind if I borrow this?"

"Go ahead. I'm done with it," Jonathan said.

"Thanks." Kyle took the book and made his exit.

"How about sending me a copy of that list so I can keep it on my phone," Adam said.

"Sure." Anything to help a friend…get out of his spare room.

* * *

The rest of Kyle's weekend was busy. His older sister Kimberly and her husband had bought a house, and Saturday it was all hands on deck to help them move. By the end of the day he was perfectly happy that the only date he had was with his computer, where he watched a movie. Sunday was taken up with family dinner. Kerrie's fiancé had joined them and Kyle felt like the Lone Loser with everyone else all coupled up.

Not *everybody* is matched up, he reminded himself as he pulled into his space in his condo building's parking lot. He waved to Cecily Sterling, who owned a condo one floor up and was just parking her car a few spaces down. If a gorgeous woman like her was still single, he didn't have to feel so bad.

"How was your weekend?" she called to him once she was out of her car.

"Great," he called back. "How about you?"

"It always goes too fast."

Not if you were waiting for Monday. He gave her another wave and then hurried to the stairs before she could ask for any details about his great weekend. It looked like she had some groceries so she'd probably take the elevator, and that meant a safe getaway for him.

You could have offered to carry her groceries, he told himself. He would next time. When he'd actually had a great weekend and had something to talk about.

His place wasn't much yet but it was all his. After roommates and renting, he'd finally taken the plunge and purchased it from a retired schoolteacher who'd claimed that Icicle Falls was getting too busy and had relocated. He'd only been in it a couple of months so his living room was furnished with nothing but a leather couch, a spare coffee table his parents had donated and all his computer stuff. He'd hung a couple pieces of digital art he'd done in college on the wall, but it still looked a little bare. The dining table, his newest acquisition, was contemporary with sleek silver chairs. Whenever he looked at it he felt like… Mr. Suave. *I understand, Jillian. It's easy to confuse me with my cousin James. Yes, Bond. But I prefer my martini stirred, not shaken.*

Yeah, right. Some Mr. Suave. More like Mr. Nobody.

Okay, maybe it was time to check out that book he'd brought home from Jonathan's. He got a can of pop from the fridge, flopped onto the couch and turned to the first page.

The family tree of Edward Northfeld, the fifth Earl of Blackthorne, was one that went back for generations, and its roots had been drenched in blood.

Hmm. Not bad. Maybe he could get into this. Another page and Kyle was no longer in his condo in Icicle Falls. He was in nineteenth-century England with Edward, the fifth earl. And he stayed there until almost midnight when he finally closed the book. Man, that was *good*.

He went online and downloaded several more

books by Vanessa Valentine on to his e-reader. Then he downloaded a couple of short stories on to his phone. If anyone asked, of course, he would never admit that he was reading romance novels. He'd say he was doing research. It worked for Jonathan.

He went to bed but took his e-reader with him. What the heck. He'd start one more story. He wasn't sleepy, anyway.

He fell asleep somewhere between London and Gretna Green.

The alarm on his phone jolted him back to the present and he dragged himself out of bed with reluctance. He wished he had a country estate in England instead of a job to commute to in Wenatchee.

Until he remembered that the woman of his dreams was at that job. He showered and dressed and tried to imagine himself as a dashing earl rather than an office peon who entered data into a computer.

Jillian's casual morning greeting didn't do anything to make him glad he was a modern man. As usual, she was saving her best smiles for Ted. What would the earl do?

The answer to that was easy. He'd grab her by the arm and say, "You vixen, do you think I don't know what sort of game you're playing?"

If Kyle did that, he'd get escorted out of the building.

He scowled his way to his cubicle.

"I guess I'd better not wish you a happy Monday," Mindy said as he sat down.

"Oh, go ahead. Make my day."

"That's what you say when you want to shoot someone. I saw that movie on the classics channel."

He smiled. "I promise I won't shoot you."

"Good to know. You look like you didn't get much sleep last night."

"I didn't."

"Busy weekend?"

"Yeah, it was. How about you?"

"I did something really fun."

"A big date?" Had Mindy found someone on that internet dating site, after all? Jeez, everyone had a life but him.

"No," she said.

Then what was she so happy about?

"I played poker."

Poker? Seriously? He wheeled back his chair and stared at her. "You did?"

"Girls can play poker, you know."

Okay, now that was cool. "What did you play?"

She screwed up her face, trying to remember. "Five-card...um."

"Stud," he supplied, and she looked at him blankly. "Draw?"

"That's it. And you'll never guess what we gambled for."

"Pennies."

"No."

"Quarters?"

"Nooo. We gambled for something *way* more valuable than money."

There was something more valuable than money?

Sex. He flashed on an image of Jillian and him playing strip poker.

"And more fun."

There was nothing more fun than sex. "Okay," he said, "I give up. What did you gamble for?"

"Chocolate!" She proferred a little candy dish full of Hershey's Kisses. "I won. Want one?"

"Don't mind if I do," he said, and helped himself. "So, I never figured you for a cardsharp."

"Oh, I'm not. My girlfriends and I are just learning. I have a cheat sheet with all the card values, but even with that I'm pretty pathetic. One hand, I forgot what a full house was and folded."

He chuckled. "You'll learn."

"I will," she agreed. "I want to win more chocolate."

Chocolate, he mused as they got to work. Now there was the way to a woman's heart. Why hadn't he thought of it before?

Chapter Seven

The Icicle Falls reunion page was now live. (Go Grizzlies!) And the Facebook page was up, too. Both were getting a lot of traffic and plenty of comments.

"I'll be there," wrote Feron Prince.

That would be fun, Jonathan thought as he approved the comment on the website. Feron would probably want to demonstrate how he'd stuffed him in that locker back when they were freshmen.

"Me, too," wrote Heidi Schwartz. "I can hardly wait to show off pictures of my baby."

Yes, it would be one big weekend of bragging, Jonathan reflected sourly. By now, those in his class who weren't married with children were sure to show up engaged. What would he have to show for fifteen years?

A house and a business, he reminded himself. He could whip out pictures of his house and show them off. And his dog. *This is my girl, Chica.*

A comment from Lissa came in. "I can hardly wait to see everyone!"

Him, too? He was someone.

Nothing from Rand yet. Maybe, now that he was married, he wasn't coming, after all. No loss there.

The rest of the football team was attending so they could relive their glory days.

Jonathan posted the picture Linc Jorgensen had sent next to the one of Linc from the yearbook. He'd exchanged a football uniform for a suit and was now a Hollywood mover and shaker with a new reality show in production. It looked like his hairline was receding. This observation only made Jonathan feel mildly better.

He scowled as he looked at the other pictures he was about to upload. A couple of guys on the football team had gotten fat but most of them had kept in shape. This was his competition—jocks with six-packs and impressive jobs.

He considered putting up a picture of himself. He could write "business owner" under it.

But the picture itself was problematic.

He'd have to wait until he got in shape.

He hoped Bruisers gym had a fast-track program.

Kyle worked straight through lunch so he could leave work early and get to the Sweet Dreams gift shop before it closed at five. Whoever heard of closing a shop at five? Didn't they know people had to work? Of course, most of the people who popped into the gift shop either worked in town or were tourists, so maybe they didn't need to stay open for commuters like Kyle. At least it was a short commute. He'd get there in plenty of time to choose something for Jillian.

He made it with ten minutes to spare. And found Adam there, paying for a gigantic box of chocolates.

"What are you doing here?" Kyle asked. Well, duh. Same thing he was, trying to buy a woman's affections.

"Chelsea loves chocolate," Adam said. He lowered his voice so Heidi Schwartz, who was ringing up the sale, couldn't hear. "I figure this is like fishing. You've got to use the right bait."

Kyle nodded. "Good point."

Adam studied him. "You buying some, too?"

"Can't hurt," Kyle said.

"What the hell. It's only money," Adam agreed. He scrawled his name on the charge slip. "Good luck," he said, then took his candy and left.

"Hi, Kyle," Heidi greeted him. "What can I get you?"

Kyle looked around at the various displays, suddenly overwhelmed. Should he get fudge? A box of truffles? Dark chocolate? Milk chocolate? "Have you got a box with a bunch of different kinds?"

"Oh, sure," she said. She walked over to one of the displays and picked up a pink box tied with a gold ribbon. "How about this thirty-six-piece ballotin? It has a nice mix—truffles, salted caramels, a couple of our newest flavor combinations."

"Okay, sure."

Heidi rang up the sale. Kyle saw what he'd just spent and swallowed hard. That was more than he'd planned to pay. But you didn't make an impression on a woman by being cheap. And he knew once Jillian got a look at this, he'd definitely make an impression.

"Is this for someone special?" Heidi asked playfully.

Kyle didn't feel like playing. "Just a friend."

"That's some friend," she said, handing over the charge slip for him to sign.

"I'm a friendly guy." He signed and handed it back.

"Are you bringing her to the reunion?"

He pictured himself walking into the Friday-evening cocktail party with Jillian on his arm. He could almost hear the awe in the other men's voices as they said, "Well, will you look at that. Kyle got himself a long-legged hottie. He's short but, man, he's cool." It was a very pretty picture.

"You are!" Heidi was smiling like she'd discovered some big secret.

"We'll see," Kyle said, covering his bases.

But he was smiling, too, as he left. He could hardly wait to put this on Jillian's desk tomorrow. Chocolates, followed by lunch out, followed by dinner out, followed by...oh, yeah.

Bruisers Fitness Center was packed with Icicle Falls residents doing their workouts when Jonathan made his entrance. Over in the corner he saw Blake Preston working out with weights. Next to him was Tilda Morrison with a guy Jonathan didn't know, probably another cop. Joe Coyote was on a cable machine, and one of the local firemen was on a treadmill, listening to his iPod and running nowhere.

Looking around, Jonathan felt the same nervous jitters he'd experienced back in middle school on entering the gym locker room to suit up for P.E. the first time. This was different, though. He wasn't a kid anymore. He was an adult, just another member of the club (as of five minutes ago), coming in to use the equipment.

The woman who'd signed him up for his one-year membership had told him all about their resident trainer, but he'd passed on the offer for the moment. After all, how hard could it be to lift some weights?

He decided to start with the treadmill. He'd never been a treadmill kind of guy, but the thing was computerized, and computers were, after all, his specialty.

He quickly discovered there was a lot more to a treadmill than hopping on and pushing some buttons. Adjusting the speed and the incline, selecting a program, that was easy. Working the program was a different story. He wound up having to lower both the speed and the incline.

He'd been sweating for a simulated mile when his brother-in-law came in. "That thing's kicking your butt," Neil observed.

Jonathan nodded and kept running, sweat dripping down his face.

"What are you doing here?" Neil asked as if Jonathan could huff and puff and carry on a conversation all at the same time.

"Getting in shape," Jonathan panted.

Neil nodded. "You haven't been in before. Did you just join?"

"Yeah."

"I'm about to work out on the weights. If you want I'll spot you."

"Uh, sure." Jonathan wasn't sure at all, but he decided he'd better swallow his pride and get some assistance from somebody who knew something.

Ten minutes later Neil was helping him master the free weights, making comments such as, "Not like that. You want to wipe out your back?"

It didn't take long to establish the fact that Jonathan was a wimp, but surprisingly, Neil was cool about it, actually a lot more encouraging than he'd been when eating Juliet's cooking. "It takes time is all."

Something Jonathan didn't have a lot of. "How long before I'll see any difference?"

Neil shrugged. "I dunno. A couple months, maybe." He studied Jonathan. "You on a schedule?"

This was where it got embarrassing. Jonathan gave a half shrug. "Just thought I should get in shape."

Neil nodded. "Good idea."

He wanted to be more than in shape. He wanted to look like Neil. "I'm thinking maybe I can, uh, bulk up a little."

"I know what you need for that. Follow me."

Jonathan followed him, past rows of men and women sweating on various machines, to the front of the gym. Off to one side of the reception area was a section offering products for sale—sweat bands, water bottles, vitamins and some big plastic jars of…

"Protein powder?" Jonathan read. "This stuff is forty bucks."

"It'll help," Neil said.

What the heck. Jonathan took a jar.

Neil clapped him on the back. "Good luck, bro. See you around."

"Yeah, see you," Jonathan said. He'd be around. A lot.

Adam pulled up in front of his house to find that at last his wife wasn't barricaded inside. She was out in the yard, weeding the flower beds. It would have been a good sign that she didn't up and run into the house at the sight of the SUV except for the frown. Oh, boy. This wasn't going to be easy.

He got out of the car and started toward her, his heart thudding as hard as it had the day he proposed. That was disconcerting. No, terrifying. For the past seven years he'd felt so comfortable around Chelsea, so relaxed. There was no comfort to be had today.

"What do you want?" she greeted him.

"You." He stopped in front of her and held out the box of candy.

She looked at it as if he was holding a piece of crap instead of fifty bucks' worth of chocolate. Then she looked at him as if he was an even bigger piece of crap. "You just don't get it, do you?"

His hand tightened on the candy box. What the hell did she want from him? "No, I guess I don't. Jeez, Chels, I bring you flowers and you toss them, candy and you look at it like I'm giving you dog turds."

She made a disgusted little snort. "In case you forgot, I've been trying to lose ten pounds."

He had forgotten.

"I don't want bribes, Adam. I want sincerity."

"I am sincere!"

"No, you're angry," she said, and went back to pulling weeds. "You've taken me for granted for the past five years of our marriage."

"I have not." But he didn't sound any more convincing to his own ears than he did to hers. They both knew the truth.

"Yes," she said calmly, "you have. You've gone off fishing whenever you felt like it, assuming I wouldn't mind being left alone. You've gotten busy and never let me know you'd be late for dinner. You've even forgotten nights we were supposed to go out."

"Not always," he argued. But she was right; he was a shit. He was king of the shits.

"Not always," she conceded, "but often enough, especially lately. And then to go and forget our anniversary." The way she looked at him made him want to shrivel up and die. "A woman gets tired of always being in second place."

He knelt down beside her. "You're not in second place, Chels. You know that. You're the only woman for me."

"I'm the only woman who would put up with you," she muttered. She sat back on her heels and regarded him, her expression softening.

She was going to take him back, thank God. He held out the candy again.

That had been the wrong thing to do because her

face turned to granite. Oh, yeah. The ten pounds. Uh-oh.

"Back to the bribes." She shifted away from him and stabbed the earth with her trowel. "I don't want to see you, Adam."

"Ever? Come on, Chels, you can't just end things like this."

She kept her back to him. "I don't want to see you until you figure some things out."

He'd figured some things out. "I have. I don't want to be without you."

"Well, I don't want to be with you. Not the way you are."

He felt as if she'd just stabbed him with that trowel. The candy fell from his hand and he stumbled to his feet. The locked door, that had been a punishment. So had the clothes and the flowers on the porch. But *this*. To hear her say she didn't want to be with him.

He forced himself to walk to the car but all the way there he felt like he could barely breathe. A million bees were humming in his ears and he was sure he was going to pass out or have a heart attack. What was happening to him? What was happening to them?

The evening was almost gone and Jonathan was beginning to hope that maybe Adam had convinced Chelsea to take him back when he heard the crunch of car tires on gravel. He glanced up from his online chess game to see Adam walk through the door looking like a man who'd gone a couple of rounds with the grim reaper. His eyes were red-rimmed and his jaw set in determination. He came over and sat on the couch next to Jonathan, enveloping him in a cloud of alcohol fumes. Someone had paid a visit to the Man Cave.

"How much did you have to drink?" Jonathan asked.

"Not enough," Adam growled.

Jonathan frowned in disapproval. "You shouldn't have gotten behind the wheel."

"I didn't. Todd Black gave me a lift."

Great. That meant Jonathan would have to get up early and run Adam over to the tavern to pick up his car. Jonathan shook his head. "You know, I'm beginning to see why Chelsea kicked you out."

Adam's brows dipped into an angry *V.* "What the hell is that supposed to mean?"

"It means you don't think about anybody but yourself. You go and get loaded and somebody has to drive you home. Tomorrow somebody—me!—has to take you to pick up your car. You're a pain in the butt." The words were barely out of his mouth before Jonathan regretted them. Talk about kicking a guy when he was down.

Adam's face crumpled.

Jonathan watched in horror. Oh, no. Now he was going to cry.

Adam bent over, elbows on his knees, and ran his hands through his hair. "Oh, God, I suck."

"Hey, man. I'm sorry."

"No, you're right. I'm a selfish bastard and I deserve what's happening to me. And you, old pal…" He gave Jonathan a slap on the back that almost sent him flying off the couch. "You've been great. I gotta get my life together. You gotta help me, Jon."

"Me!"

"Help me think of something romantic I can do to show Chels I love her. Find me something in one of those chick books."

Jonathan was having enough trouble working out his own romantic plan of attack. "How am I supposed to do that? I don't know what your wife likes."

Adam let out a drunken wail. "I don't, either." And then he did cry.

Jonathan and Chica made a discreet exit. Hopefully, come morning, Adam would have forgotten this humiliation. And remembered his determination to get it right in the romance department.

Chapter Eight

This was it, the moment Kyle would make his big impression on Jillian. He got the box of Sweet Dreams chocolates from the front seat of his car where he'd carefully laid it and made his way into the Safe Hands office building. Wait till she got a load of this.

Jillian was not alone. Lola from accounting and Marie, one of his fellow cubicle workers, were standing at her desk, yakking. Shouldn't they be at their own desks by now?

He slowed his pace, hoping that by the time he reached Jillian they would have drifted off. But there was no drifting. Both women remained where they were—like a couple of boulders. Or guard dogs.

What to do? Should he keep on walking, catch her later? Yes, he decided. He'd give the candy to her later.

He picked up his pace to move past them but Marie, who must have had eyes in the back of her head, suddenly exclaimed, "Sweet Dreams chocolates!"

"Who's the lucky girl?" asked Lola.

Crap. This was awkward.

"Are they for someone here?" Marie asked.

And there was Jillian, smiling up at him. So much for waiting until later. It was now or never. "Well," he began, and set them on her desk.

The women fell on them like starved vultures.

"Oh, are you going to get brownie points for bringing us all chocolates," Lola said before he could finish his sentence, and stuffed a bonbon in her beak.

Not all of you. "Actually," he began, looking at Jillian, "I bought them for—"

"Here comes Mr. Wrangle," Marie said in a low voice.

At the mention of the big boss's name the party was over. The women scattered, Jillian called, "Good morning, Mr. Wrangle," and Kyle, who was five minutes late, left for his cubicle, cursing under his breath as he went. Why hadn't he taken one more minute to tell Jillian the chocolates were for her? What a dope.

"You okay?" Mindy asked as he settled into his cubicle.

"Yeah. Why?"

"You look kind of mad."

Mad? What was there to be mad about? He'd spent a king's ransom on chocolate to impress the woman of his dreams and gotten exactly nothing in return. Not even a thank-you from anyone.

He did get one later when he made a trip to the water cooler. From Mildred Parks, who was old enough to be his grandmother. "Kyle, that was so sweet of you to bring in candy for all the ladies. Thank you."

That was him, Mr. Sweet. "You're welcome."

"But you should save your money," she advised. "Spend it on your girlfriend."

The candy was supposed to be his first step toward making Jillian his girlfriend. He forced a smile and said, "Good advice." How he wished he'd handled the whole situation diffcrently.

As he returned to his desk he caught sight of Jillian, hanging up the phone. Maybe he'd ask her how she liked the candy.

Oh, no. Here came Ted Darrow. Jillian tapped her pencil and gave Ted a little wave. Kyle watched contemptuously as Darrow strolled over and planted a butt cheek on her desk. Was that a new suit he was wearing? And now...aw, shit. She was offering him some of the Sweet Dreams candy. Talk about bad candy karma.

He marched back to his cubicle and plopped onto his seat. This was sick and wrong. Sick. And. Wrong.

The Ted Darrows of the world got everything— height, good looks, cool clothes. Women. Candy other men paid for.

By lunch Kyle had made an important decision. He needed a new suit.

"I thought I'd grab a sandwich down at Filly's," Mindy said.

Kyle didn't have time to go to the in-house café. He had an important mission. "I've gotta run some errands."

"Oh. Sure. No problem. See you later."

He barely heard her. He was already bolting for the door.

He tried not to look as Jillian came out of Ted's office wearing a smile. Office romances—the big boss frowned on them, especially when one of his higher-ups mingled with the little people. That wasn't stopping Darrow from trying to mingle with Jillian. He was going to use her up like toilet paper and then toss her.

But not if Kyle had anything to say about it. Some new clothes, a dinner date, and Jillian would be safe with a man who really appreciated her.

Now she was alone. Maybe he should turn around, go back and explain that he'd gotten that candy for her. He wheeled around to go and talk to her but was thwarted by the appearance of yet another pair of females, purses in hand and ready for lunch. Yakking away, they flanked her on both sides.

Okay, not now. Kyle left the building wearing a frown as well as his unimpressive clothes. Why did women always run in packs? Sheesh.

He was still feeling grumpy when he walked into the Wenatchee Valley Mall. Even trying on a nice suit didn't cheer him up. Yes, the suit fit fine, and he looked pretty darned good, if he did say so himself. But he saw more in the mirror than the suit. He saw a short man. Ted Darrow had a good six inches on him and there wasn't a thing he could do about that. Unless...

He took out his smartphone and did some quick online research. Hey, here was just what he needed, a shoe store that sold "heightening shoes," which promised to add five inches to his stature. And they had overnight shipping. Sold! He purchased a pair of black dress shoes and some loafers. Oh, yeah. Mr. Suave meets Mr. Big.

Betsy did a double take as she drove by the theater. "Oh, my gosh!" she cried, and pulled her car off to the side of the street. She got out of the car and stood on the curb, gaping at the marquee.

Instead of the latest movie title, it read Betsy, I Need You. And there, by the ticket window, stood Gregory, looking hopefully at her.

She tore across the street and threw herself into his waiting arms.

He hugged her as if he'd never let her go. "Baby. I was so wrong. I'll get it right from now on, I promise. Give me one more chance."

"After this, how could I not?" she said, laughing.

He crushed her to him, taking her lips with all the passion he'd stored up on those long, lonely nights apart. When he finally released her, he had tears in his eyes. "I almost lost you, all because of my stupid pride. But never again. I'm a changed man."

"Are you? Really?"

"Oh, yeah," he said. "Count on it." He gestured to the marquee. "This love story is going to have a happy ending."

Adam shut the paperback Jonathan had left for him on the kitchen counter, with a Post-it marking this particular scene. There it was, a perfect example of item number five on Jonathan's list, the romantic gesture.

Also a good way to make a public fool of yourself. But if that was what it took, Adam was willing. Tomorrow morning, he was going to show Chelsea how much she meant to him. He tossed the book on the floor and rolled over on the blow-up bed, trying to get comfortable. Man, he hoped this worked. He couldn't take very many more nights on this thing.

More than that, he couldn't take too many more nights away from Chelsea. He missed her smile, missed being able to tell her about his day, missed having her curled up next to him as they slept. Sleeping alone felt wrong, like half of him had been cut away.

He sure hoped this romantic gesture would do the trick. He wanted his other half back.

He took the next morning off and went to see Emmit Brown, the crusty old man who owned Falls Cinema.

Emmit wasn't as cooperative as the theater owner in that book had been. "I put some love message up for you, then I have to do it for every yahoo in town who's having woman trouble. Pretty soon, nobody knows what's playing, only that Johnny loves Suzie, and pretty soon I don't have anybody coming in to see a movie," he said, and went back to stocking candy.

"You don't, anyway," Adam said. "You get stuff in six weeks after it's hit every other theater in the state."

This turned out not to be the best way to argue his case. Emmit looked at him in disgust and shooed him out of the theater lobby. "Go buy some flowers."

"I tried that," Adam grumbled.

"Then carve your initials in a tree. Hire a sky-writer. I don't care what you do as long as you do it somewhere else."

"Fine. See if you get my business," Adam said. Damn it all, now what was he going to do?

Inspiration hit him when he drove past the Safe-way. *That* could work. Plus he knew the manager. He parked his car and went into the grocery store to see his pal Denzel Wilson. He hoped he didn't strike out again. At some point he had to get back to the office and do some work. How did the men in those romance novels manage to earn a paycheck when sorting out their love lives took so much time?

Fortunately, Denzel was in his office and had a few minutes to spare. Denzel had a wife who was high-maintenance, always expecting him to take her places, making him hang out with her family every Sunday. If anyone would understand Adam's plight, it was Denzel.

Still, Adam had learned from his encounter with old man Brown. After the bro hug, he dangled a carrot. "Been fishing lately?"

Denzel shook his head sadly. "Been too busy."

"Well, whenever you want to borrow my VXP rod…"

Denzel's eyes lit up like the Las Vegas strip at night. "Yeah?"

"Sure. I don't have time to use it right now."

"Sweet. So, what can I do for you?"

"I need a favor. Chels and I are having problems."

"I feel your pain."

"I need to do something nice, get her attention."

"Flowers," said Denzel. "That always works with Letitia."

Adam shrugged. "Tried that. But I did have an idea. You know that sign out in your parking lot where you post what's on sale?"

Now Denzel was looking leery. "Yeah."

"Can you put up a message for me? Just for this afternoon, long enough for Chels to see it."

Denzel rubbed the back of his neck. "I don't know. That's for our store specials."

"Come on, man, I'm not asking for long. I'll pay."

"You don't have to pay." Denzel thought a moment. "Just for this afternoon?"

"That's all. Once she sees it you can take it down."

Denzel scratched his head and thought again. At last he said, "Okay. After all, the store's an important part of the community."

That would be Denzel's story for his regional manager, most likely. Well, it worked for Adam.

"Only for this afternoon, though. That's the best I can do."

"That's all I need. Thanks, man."

"What do you want it to say?"

Oh, that. Too bad Jonathan wasn't here. He'd have been able to think of something. Adam tried calling his cell but it went straight to voice mail. Bernardo would have all kinds of ideas, but he'd be working in his orchard and ignoring his cell. Kyle was clueless and Vance would laugh at him. He was on his own. What to say?

Keep it simple, he decided. "Put 'Chelsea, I love you.'"

Denzel nodded his approval. "Sounds good."

Adam clapped him on the back. "Thanks. I owe you."

"Let me borrow that fly rod this weekend and we're even."

"You got it. Come by Templar's place anytime and pick it up."

"Templar? Jonathan?"

"I'm staying there."

Denzel looked shocked. "You mean she kicked you out?"

Humiliating to have to admit. Adam nodded.

"You weren't kidding when you said you were having problems."

"We'll get it sorted out," Adam said. He sure hoped he was right.

He said goodbye to Denzel and went to the office, where he tried to concentrate on the data about several new medicines he'd be repping soon.

Once late afternoon arrived, he found it almost impossible to keep his eyes focused on his computer screen. His gaze kept straying to his phone. Chelsea would be done at the nursery now. Any minute she'd be driving by the grocery store on her way home. She'd see the sign, know he was serious, call.

Finally his phone started playing Luke Bryan's "Drunk on You," Chelsea's ring tone. He'd selected it a few nights back when indulging in a maudlin moment of self-pity. The memory of better days of her dancing around the house in her T-shirt and shorts, singing along to the country station, had been enough to make it too hot for him to sleep in Jonathan's spare room, no matter how wide he'd opened the window.

Now he grabbed his phone like a lifeline. "Chels."

"Very funny, Adam. Was I supposed to think that was cute?"

No, she was supposed to think it was romantic. What had gone wrong? "I thought you'd like that."

"You thought I'd like being on sale for a dollar ninety-nine a pound? That was mean. And tacky." She ended the call before he could say anything more.

Well, this was a far cry from what had happened in that book he'd read. He left the office and drove back to Icicle Falls to see what had gotten his wife so steamed. It wasn't hard to figure out once he hit Safeway. There, for all the town to see, the big sign outside the store said Chelsea…$1.99 a Pound.

"What the hell?"

He parked his SUV and marched inside the store. The place was packed with shoppers picking up dinner essentials on their way home from work. He found his pal Denzel busy overriding some problem on one of his grocery checker's stands.

Denzel finished up and, catching sight of Adam, smiled at him. "So, how'd it go?"

"How'd it go? I'm in deeper shit than I was before, thanks to whoever put my wife on sale for a buck ninety-nine a pound."

"Huh?"

"Come and see." Adam wheeled around and marched out of the store, positioning himself where they'd get a good look at the very effective job Denzel had done of humiliating Adam's wife.

"Aw, shit," Denzel muttered.

"You can say that again," Adam snarled.

"Man, I'm sorry. I sent one of our baggers out to take down the flank steak loss leader and put your message up. We got busy and I called him in. I thought he was done, since he was just standing out there talking to a girl. That kid's ass is fired."

Another man's life in the toilet all because of a woman. Well, that didn't seem right. "Hey, don't fire him on my account," Adam said.

"I'm not. The kid's a screwup."

Like me, Adam thought miserably as he walked back to his SUV.

He called Chelsea. Of course she didn't pick up. "It wasn't supposed to read like that, Chels," he told her voice mail. "It was supposed to say I Love You. Somebody screwed up."

He ended the call. Somebody screwed up all right. Damn. Why was love so hard?

Juliet was having computer problems. This came as no surprise to Jonathan. Juliet was always having computer problems. This time she'd lost an entire file of recipes. Jonathan wasn't sure if that was a bad thing or a blessing in disguise, but he'd promised to come over and help her after work.

He walked in the front door, with the book he'd drowned in the toilet hiding in his back pocket. He'd baked it in the stove on a low heat and now it was almost as good as new. The pages were a little wavy, but hey, it was a used book. She hadn't looked at it all that carefully at the library. She'd probably think it had come like that.

She started to lead the way into the spare room that served as a study. Her back was turned. It was the perfect moment to return the tycoon to his home. The stack of books was still on the stairs (not unusual since Juliet was a clutterbug). He would subtly drop the book on top of it.

The tycoon didn't have a good landing. The book caught the edge of the pile, making it tip over. Three other books bounced down the stairs. The stairs were carpeted, but Jonathan heard, *boom, boom, boom, boom, BOOM.*

Oh, no. He bent to put them back just as his sister, who could hear better than all the dogs in Icicle Falls put together, turned around.

Think fast. "Uh, they fell."

She looked at him oddly.

He scrambled to put the books back before she could get too close a gander, slipping the purloined book under the others.

But his sister not only had keen hearing, she had the eyesight of an eagle. In two steps she was standing by the stairs. She picked up the traveling tycoon. "My book! I thought I'd lost it." Now she was frowning. She opened the paperback and flipped the pages.

Uh-oh.

"It looks like it got wet."

"Maybe it did at some point," Jonathan said. "It's a used book. Who knows what happened to it? Come on, let's go check out your computer."

"Okay," she said slowly, and followed him down the hall.

The wheels were turning in that busy brain of hers; he could sense it. This was so not good. He sat on the chair in front of her desk and hurried to deflect her attention. "Did you back up your file?"

"I meant to," she said, still leafing through the book. "You know, I would have noticed all this water damage. It looks like someone dropped it in a sink or something."

Or something. "Jules, you've got to back stuff up," Jonathan said, steering the conversation back into safer territory.

"But you can recover it, right?"

"Probably," he admitted. "Still, you should make a habit of backing up anything you don't want to lose."

"I know. And I will from now on," she promised, pulling up a chair next to him. "It's funny about this book," she said as he began his computer detective work. "It was on top of the pile last week, and then I went to read it and it wasn't."

"You should put your books away." Oh, man. Why couldn't she drop the subject already?

"What, or Neil will get into them?" A moment of silence was followed by, "Those were my library sale books."

He shrugged and kept his gaze glued to her computer screen. He could feel sweat beading on his brow.

"You were over here for dinner the day after the book sale."

"Jules, I'm trying to concentrate here."

"And then, just a few days after that, I went to get this off the pile and it was gone," she finished thoughtfully.

He could feel her eyes burning into him.

"Did you take my book?"

He cast about desperately for some plausible answer.

Before he could come up with one, she pointed an accusing finger at him. "You did!"

"No," he lied, searching for his poker face.

"Oh, yes, you did, and after all that talk about how dumb romance novels are."

"I—" He stopped there. How to explain this?

"Why were you reading my book?"

"I just thought I'd check it out. Okay?"

"I'm not buying that."

"I'm trying to get your file here," he said. *And I can't lie and find your lost file at the same time.*

"Jonathan, you may as well tell me. I'm gonna bug you until you do."

"There's nothing to tell." At least not to his sister.

"Well, could you tell me what happened to it?"

He frowned. "I accidentally dropped it."

"In the sink?"

"Uh, in the toilet."

"Eew." She let go of the book and this time the tycoon landed on carpet.

"Don't worry. It doesn't have any germs on it."

"I doubt that," she said, disgusted.

"I'll buy you a new one," he promised. If he'd done that in the first place, he might've gotten away clean with no one the wiser. *Dumb, Jonathan.* How could he be so good at math and computers and so stupid at...life?

She was silent again, but only for a few seconds. "Why would you be interested in romance novels all of a sudden?" she mused.

"I'm not. I just thought I'd give one a try. That's all..." ...*you need to know.*

"You could've asked me. I'd have lent it to you. In fact, if you want to read a good story, let me give you the Vanessa Valentine I got."

"I already checked it out." Crap! Had he really said that? "Jules, I can't concentrate on retrieving your file with you talking."

"Never mind the file. What's going on?"

He frowned at her. "I'm doing some research. Okay?"

"Research on what? Are you going to write a romance novel?"

"No," he said testily.

"Then what?"

"I just... Never mind."

She fell silent. Of course, that didn't mean she'd abandoned the subject. It only meant she was thinking of a new way to wrangle the information out of him.

"Okay, got it," he said.

"Thank you. You're amazing."

"That's me," he agreed. And now he was going to beat it before Juliet began another round of twenty questions. He started to get up.

She grabbed his arm. "Not so fast. Tell me what's going on. I'll find out, anyway."

"There's nothing going on," he insisted. "Come on, Jules, let go of my arm."

"Uh-uh. Tell me."

He glared at her. "Stop being so damned nosy."

"I'm your sister. I'm supposed to be nosy. If you don't 'fess up I'll tell everyone you're reading my romance novels."

She would have, back when they were kids. Now that they were grown-ups, it was nothing more than an empty threat because she'd never deliberately embarrass him. "Go ahead."

She dropped her hand. "You know I won't. I just wish you'd fill me in on what's going on. I tell *you* everything."

"That's because you're a woman. Guys don't talk about stuff."

"Maybe you should. Maybe I could help with… whatever. Did you ever stop to think of that?"

She was going to bug him until she drove him insane. "It's no big deal. I just thought—" Oh, this was so pathetic and awkward. "I thought it would be interesting to see how women think." There. Surely that would be enough information to satisfy her.

"I could have told you that."

"Some things a guy doesn't need to ask his little sister."

"And why this sudden need to know how women think?" She gasped in delight. "You're seeing someone!" She snapped her fingers. "That cute new librarian."

Great. Now they were going to play twenty questions about his love life. "No."

"Then why— Wait a minute. I ran into Tina Swift at Bavarian Brews the other day. You have a high school reunion coming up, don't you?"

"Yeah. So?"

"So does that have anything to do with you snitching my book?"

"Not unless I'm a tycoon."

She was relentless. "Neil told me you joined the gym." She studied him, making him squirm. "Getting buff, reading romance novels…"

He didn't like the knowing look that landed on her face.

"*Now* I get it. This has to do with someone who's coming to the reunion, doesn't it?"

"If you ask me one more question, I'm never working on your computer again."

"I don't need to. I remember who you liked when we were kids." She regarded him, her expression a mixture of pity and exasperation. "Jonathan, please tell me I'm imagining things."

"You're imagining things."

She frowned. "Are you going to stay single all

your life just hoping that one day Lissa Castle will fall madly in love with you?"

That made him sound like such a loser.

Juliet heaved a long-suffering sigh. "She's never wanted to be anything more than friends with you, Jonathan."

"Thanks for the reminder," he muttered.

Juliet laid a hand on his arm. "I'm sorry. I don't want to see you hurt."

"Let me worry about that," he said grumpily.

"I thought you were over her."

He was. For a while. He shrugged.

Juliet fell silent again.

Good. Maybe she'd finally drop the subject.

It stayed dropped for about ten seconds. Then she picked it up again. "So what are you doing to get ready for the reunion?"

He was not discussing this with her.

It didn't seem to matter because she was discussing it with him. "You need new clothes."

He rolled his eyes.

"And a better haircut."

He frowned. "I don't remember asking your advice."

"Big brother, you need it. Let's go shopping next week."

"I can do my own shopping."

"No, you can't. Come on. It'll be fun."

Clothes-shopping was only fun for women.

"So when do you want to go?"

She was going to annoy him until he caved. It was

her modus operandi. "August." By then he'd need a bigger shirt, and he could probably use some help picking one out.

"Oh, you're right," she said as if she knew what he was thinking. "Everything will be on sale by August. Isn't that when the reunion is? Tina's already dieting."

Women were always dieting, whether they needed to lose weight or not.

"Well, when you're ready, you have to take me with you," Juliet said. "If you're going to make an impression, you need someone besides your nerdy friends to help you."

She was probably right. He nodded. Okay, this embarrassing discussion was done. He got up and started to leave.

"What else are you doing to get ready?" she asked, following him down the hallway.

Or not. "Nothing I need help with."

"You have to learn to dance."

"Jules," he protested. Next thing he knew, she'd be offering him a dance lesson.

"I can teach you."

"I am not dancing with my sister," he growled.

"Oh, yes, you are. Stay for dinner. Afterward I'll teach you how to do the nightclub two-step. That's easy, and it's impressive."

Eating his sister's cooking *and* having her teach him how to dance—that would be double torture. "I gotta go. I've got stuff to do."

"Jonathan," she said sternly. "If you want to impress a woman you need to know how to dance. Women love to dance, and most men are too lame to even try. If you can look good on the dance floor, you're already way ahead of your competition."

He shook his head. "I can't believe this."

"What?"

"I can't believe we're having this conversation."

"Well, we don't have to. You can just stumble along on your own trying to figure out what women want… or you can get help."

He *had* help. He had Vanessa Valentine. "I'm okay, but thanks for the offer," he said firmly.

She frowned but gave up pestering him. "Okay, but when you see Lissa Castle dancing with some other man at the reunion, don't come crying to me."

The thought of Lissa Castle dancing with someone else was enough to make a grown man cry. Rather than do that, Jonathan went home and pulled up the latest romance novel he'd downloaded.

This was a contemporary tale about a man returning to his hometown. He'd left a loser and returned a success—a famous race car driver with money to impress the girl he'd never forgotten. Jonathan could almost relate.

Halfway into the book, the hero, who must have known Juliet, got the heroine onto the dance floor.

Joel held out a hand to Leslie. "Dance with me."

She wanted to say no, but the look in his eyes demanded she say yes. "I didn't know you could dance," she said as he led her onto the floor.

He smiled down at her. "There's a lot you don't know about me."

He was right. This was a different man from the one she remembered—strong, forceful. Sexy.

He moved them through an intricate step and suddenly they were dancing heart to heart. His breath ruffled her hair and she felt the heat of desire deep in her belly. "I think it's time we took this relationship to a new level," he murmured.

"Oh?" Now her heart was beating like crazy.

"You want it, I want it. For once, let's not play games."

Jonathan read on as Joel moved Leslie from the dance floor to his bed. Whoa, just one dance led to all that? What if Juliet was right?

He thought back to high school. He'd avoided school dances like the plague. (Maybe it had something to do with way back in middle school, when Lissa had gone to the eighth-grade dance with Danny Popkee—who knew?) He couldn't dance. He didn't have the gene for it.

That night he went to bed and dreamed he was at the Icicle Falls High reunion. All the attendees were dressed to the nines but him. He'd opted for a pair of purple polka dot boxers. While everyone was shaking their booty out on the dance floor, he was pacing along the edge of the crowd, trying to get Lissa's attention. She was out in the middle of the floor with Rand. He was dressed like a matador and Lissa wore a slinky black dress and was twining her legs all around him.

At last they finished and when Jonathan went out on the floor to join them, all the faceless onlookers cheered. "Go, Jon," someone called.

He strutted up to Lissa in his polka dot boxers, showing off pecs that would have put the Incredible Hulk to shame. Like the hero in the romance novel, Jonathan held out a hand to her and said, "Dance with me."

Instead of cooperating like a proper heroine, she cocked an eyebrow. "Do you know how to tango?"

"Well, no," he admitted.

"West Coast swing?"

"Uh, no."

"East Coast?"

"No."

"Any coast?"

He shook his head. "My sister offered to teach me, but I didn't take her up on it."

"You should have," she said. "Now take your polka dots somewhere else. I don't waste my time on men who can't dance."

Suddenly he was no longer in polka dot boxers. He was wearing a clown suit and had a big red nose. Rand reached over and pinched it. "You always *were* a clown. That's why I stopped hanging out with you when we hit middle school. That's why Lissa doesn't want you."

"And you can't even dance," she said. "Your sister offered to teach you but would you let her? Noooo." She gave his red clown nose a pinch, making it honk.

"I can dance," he insisted. Next thing he knew, he

was on the roof of Icicle Falls High, tap-dancing in his clown outfit. And his entire class was standing below, watching him.

"Look at that clown," called Feron Prince. "He thinks he can dance. He should've let his sister give him a lesson."

Jonathan tapped all the harder, shuffling away in his big, red clown shoes. But then he tripped over one of them and off the roof he sailed, heading for the pavement below. "Lissa!"

He woke up with a gasp right before he went splat. "It was only a dream," he told himself.

But maybe his subconscious was trying to tell him something.

If he had any doubts left, the email he got the following morning confirmed what his subconscious had said.

Hi, Jonathan! I guess we're supposed to send pictures to you for the class reunion website. (Why am I not surprised you're in charge of that? You always were a tech genius!) Anyway, here's mine. It was taken at the hot-air balloon festival in Albuquerque. My hair doesn't look so good, but hey, what does that matter when you're having fun? Email back and let me know what you've been up to. It feels like forever since I've seen you.
Lissa

That was encouraging, but the P.S. at the end struck fear into his heart. And you better save me a dance Saturday night!

A dance. With Lissa. Crap! His sister was right. He grabbed his cell phone and called her. "Is that offer of a dance lesson still good?"

Chapter Nine

Adam wasn't giving up. He and Chelsea could work this out. He'd go over to the house after work. No bribes this time, no so-called romantic gestures, just the two of them having a heart-to-heart talk, getting things straight once and for all.

He pulled up in front of the place and found her out in the yard once more, this time watering the roses. She was talking to some man Adam had never seen before. The stranger looked like he was somewhere in his forties and was wearing cargo shorts and a T-shirt. He was short and wiry with a tan, an average face, thinning hair and Ray-Bans propped on his head. Beady eyes. He had beady eyes. Who was this tool and what was he saying to make Chelsea smile?

Adam got out of the SUV and walked over to where they stood, making sure he sent off intimidating vibes with every step.

At the sight of him, Chelsea's smile disappeared. "Adam."

"Hi, Chels." He gave the stranger a tooth-baring smile. "I'm Adam Edwards."

"Dennis McDermott," the man said, and stuck out his hand.

Adam took it and squeezed. Firmly.

His rival grimaced.

"Dennis just moved in next door," Chelsea explained.

"Our new neighbor, huh?" Adam said. "Good to meet you." *Not.* "Where'd you move from?"

"Other side of the mountains, Bellevue."

Adam nodded and wished old Dennis had stayed on the other side of the mountains. "It's a long commute."

Dennis shrugged. "I work from home."

Which meant old Dennis the Menace would be around all the time, popping over for friendly chats with Chelsea.

"Makes life easy," Dennis continued.

It sure made putting the moves on another man's wife easy. "Yeah, I'll bet it does."

"I can pretty much set my own schedule," Dennis added.

Don't even think of scheduling in my wife. "You got a family?"

"Not here. I'm divorced. My kids are in college. I'm pretty much on my own," Dennis said, and smiled at Chelsea.

Yeah, well, you're gonna stay that way, pal. "Chels, I need to talk to you."

Chelsea frowned. "Now is not a good time."

Her putting him down in front of another man made Adam bristle. "This won't take long," he said. "Dennis probably has some unpacking to do, anyway, right?"

"Oh, sure," Dennis said reluctantly. "Nice talking with you, Chelsea. I'll be seeing you."

There was a depressing thought.

"Nice meeting you," Chelsea said, giving the invader a warm smile. As soon as he'd started back across his lawn, though, it disappeared. She glared at Adam and said in a low voice, "That was rude."

"What? Wanting to have a serious conversation with my wife?" He nodded in Dennis's direction. "When did he move in?"

"Just this weekend."

"And he's already putting the moves on you. Did you tell him you were married?"

"No."

He didn't like the way she said that or the look on her face. "Chels."

She didn't stay to listen to what he had to say. Instead, she turned her back on him and started walking to the house.

"Hey," he protested, following her. "I'm trying to have a serious conversation here."

Ignoring him, she bent to turn off the hose. There was a sight that did a man's heart good. It was all he could do not to reach out and pat that nicely rounded little butt. How long was it going to be before they had sex again? It already felt like a million years.

"Chelsea, we need to talk."

She stood up and the look she gave him made him feel like a little kid about to get scolded by his mom. He hated when she looked at him that way. "First you act like a caveman, then you try to bribe me. Now, all of a sudden, you're ready to talk? Adam, you don't really want to fix what's wrong between us. You just want this over so you can move back in."

"Of course I want this over." Who wouldn't?

It had been the wrong thing to say. She scowled at him as if he'd told her she was fat. "I don't want to talk to you until you've done some serious thinking," she said sternly. Then she went into the house—his house!—and slammed the door.

He let out a growl and marched back across the lawn. What was it going to take to get through to her? And how much time did he have before Dennis the Menace moved in on her?

Which he would. The beady-eyed little weasel would have no qualms about fishing in another man's pond.

Adam shot a look to the house next door. The garage door was open and Dennis was standing there, pretending to unpack boxes. He waved at Adam.

Adam gave him a curt salute in return. He used all four fingers, even though the creep only deserved one, the middle one.

He went by Safeway on the way home and picked up a six-pack of beer and some chicken from the deli. Then he drove to Jonathan's to log in another night on the blow-up bed.

He walked into the house expecting Jonathan to be there and was perturbed to see it was just him and Chica, the one-dog welcoming committee. Not that he was in any mood to talk about this latest humiliation, but coming home to an empty house after what had happened made him feel even worse, like a man nobody wanted.

"Where's your master?" he asked.

Chica barked and wagged her tail.

Well, somebody was glad to see him. "Why can't my wife be more like you?"

He went to the kitchen, Chica prancing along beside him. He tossed her one of the dog treats Jonathan kept in the cupboard, then opened a beer and sat in the living room, trying to process what was happening to him.

Two beers and a chicken leg later, he gave up. Women. Who could understand them?

Jonathan had survived dinner at his sister's, thanks to the fact that Neil had barbecued burgers. Now it was time for his first dance lesson.

"We'll start with the nightclub two-step because that's easy," Juliet said.

Easy for her, maybe.

"The man always starts on his left foot. So, you're going to step back on your left foot at an angle, then shift your weight to your right foot and bring your left foot back up. Like this," she said, and demonstrated, counting as she moved. "One and two. Then you do the same thing with the other foot. One and two. See how simple that is?"

Well, it *looked* simple. He tried it. Okay, not so bad.

"Now, here's how you hold her."

Holding his sister, this was weird.

"And don't let your hand drift down to her butt," Juliet cautioned.

No danger of that right now.

"Okay, let's try the step again."

So far so good. Maybe he *could* learn to dance.

Then Juliet added one more step and he was lost. If only there was an algorithm for this.

"Jonathan, you're losing your hold," she scolded. "Here, I'm going to have Neil help us."

"Oh, no," he protested. But she was already calling her husband.

"I need you to show him how to lead," she said once Neil had entered the room.

"Oh, come on, babe," Neil protested. "I'm trying to watch the game."

Jonathan had a flashback to grade school when the kids were picking teams for softball and he was always the last one chosen. *"Oh, come on. Why do we have to take Jonathan?"* He felt his cheeks sizzle and wished he'd just looked on the internet to see how to do this.

"Family comes before baseball," Juliet insisted.

Neil frowned. "I hope you learn fast," he said to Jonathan, upping his stress level further.

"No, I suck at this," Jonathan grumbled.

"We all do when we start," Neil said, making him feel somewhat less embarrassed. "So, the one thing you gotta remember is that you have to be a strong lead if you want a woman to follow. Otherwise, she won't know where to go." He elbowed Jonathan. "It's about the only place left in the world where a man has any control."

Juliet frowned at him. "So not funny."

He ignored her. "Like this." He grabbed Jonathan and demonstrated.

Great. Here he was, dancing with a guy.

"Okay, now try it with Jules."

And...back to dancing with his sister. He was pathetic.

But maybe not hopeless. She gave him an approving smile when they'd finished. "That was much better. A few more lessons and you'll be fabulous. Every woman at the reunion will want to dance with you."

Neil looked surprised. "Is that what this is about? Wait a minute. Now I get it. That's why you joined the gym."

Jonathan's cheeks burned once more. "I needed to get in shape, anyway."

Neil shook his head. "Man, the things we do for women."

Juliet patted his arm. "We appreciate it."

"It's too bad a woman can't appreciate a guy for who he is," Jonathan muttered.

"We do," Juliet said.

"Yeah, right," Jonathan sneered.

She grinned. "Okay, we've been known to drool over a nice set of pecs."

"Seems kind of shallow," Jonathan said.

"Yes, not like you men, who don't care at all what a woman looks like."

"Busted," Neil cracked.

"Seriously," Juliet said, "everyone's attracted to a person who looks nice. That's how you get someone's interest at first, but good looks aren't enough to hold any woman. In the end we don't need a man who's perfect. We just want one with a good heart, someone we can build a life with. That's the most important thing."

If that was the case, Lissa should have fallen for him years ago. "Then why am I learning to dance?" Jonathan demanded irritably.

"Because it's romantic."

Jonathan remembered the latest book he'd read. Obviously, it was.

"And it's a sure way to get a woman to stop and take notice."

He did need to get Lissa's attention, needed her to see him in a new light.

"Trust me on this," Juliet said. "Being a good dancer gives you an advantage."

"She's right," Neil confirmed. "The man who can dance goes home with the girl." He slung a casual arm over Juliet's shoulders. "It worked for me."

Maybe if Jonathan practiced enough, and then had a good stiff drink the night of the reunion, it could work for him, too. He could dream, anyway. "Okay, show me that turn again."

Kyle came to work on Thursday wearing his new clothes, walking tall and feeling like he could pose for the cover of *GQ*. And there, straight ahead of him, sat Jillian at her desk. For once she was alone. No women standing around, yakking at her, no other man flirting with her. Kyle picked up his pace, all the while rehearsing what he'd say to her. *Hey, Jillian, looking good this morning.*

Maybe she'd notice that he was looking good, too. And taller. And maybe he'd ask what she was doing this weekend.

Just as he was almost at her desk the phone rang. He slowed down.

"No, he's not in yet," she said, not even glancing in Kyle's direction. "May I take a message?"

Great. Now she was going to be writing down a message. Would she have time to talk with him? Out of the corner of his eye another obstacle appeared— one of the big bosses. This was not the time to wait for Jillian to get off the phone. Once again, Cupid was not playing for Kyle's team. He went to his cubicle, wearing a frown to accent his new duds.

"Wow, look at you," Mindy greeted him.

At least someone around here was observant.

She scooted her chair a little farther back from her desk to check him out. "You seem taller."

It was the shoes; but he shrugged as if he had no idea what she was talking about.

"I always wanted to be tall," she said.

Him, too. "Being short's not so bad, as long as you're a girl."

"Oh, I don't think being short is so bad when you're a man, either, as long as you're cute."

Was she saying he was cute? He couldn't help smiling.

"And, I have to admit, if I hadn't been short I

wouldn't have been as good a gymnast." She grinned. "I'm death on the uneven parallel bars."

He could imagine her flying through the air, wearing a leotard. It wasn't a bad picture. But it couldn't compare to the mental image of Jillian in a bikini, which he kept on display in the corner of his mind labeled Perfect Woman.

A little more chitchat and they both settled down to work. Well, one of them settled down. Kyle could hear Mindy's keyboard clicking away next to him and knew she was busy inputting data, her mind whirring on behalf of Safe Hands Insurance. He was inputting, too, but halfheartedly. Every few minutes, he kept peeking around his cubicle to see what was going on over at the receptionist's desk.

The first time he looked he saw—big surprise— Ted Darrow, with his butt planted on Jillian's desk, chatting her up. Darrow was such a predator. Why couldn't she see that?

Next time he looked, she was accepting a flower delivery. Some woman was going to get a call to come to the reception desk and collect her prize. But instead of picking up the phone and summoning someone to her desk, Jillian took the envelope from the arrangement and opened it. And smiled. So she was the lucky woman.

He scowled as he watched her unwrap the big, gaudy vase of red and orange flowers. Whoever sent them had probably paid an arm and a leg. It wasn't hard to guess who. Darrow, the desk-sitter.

Well, Kyle had brought her candy. Now might be a

good time to mosey on over and mention that. He left his cubicle and walked casually past the other workers, just a man headed to the water cooler. He stopped and got a quick drink, stealthily looking toward the reception desk. No one there but Jillian. The way was clear. Finally.

He sauntered on over, said a smooth "Hi, Jillian" and planted a butt cheek on the desk in true Darrow fashion. Unfortunately, his landing wasn't as smooth as he'd expected. Even as she squeaked, "Watch out!" he made contact with the flower vase.

He jumped up and turned to catch it, just as she reached for it, resulting in their both missing it. Down the thing went, spilling water and flowers everywhere. That could have been fixed easily enough but to compound his misery, the glass broke. Why didn't they make those vases thicker?

"Gosh, I'm sorry," he said, bending to pick up the flowers.

"It's...okay." That was what her lips said, but the rest of her face added, "Not."

He gathered up the flowers and handed them to her, feeling like a little kid handing over a wilted roadside bouquet.

"Thanks," she said. Again, right words, wrong facial expression.

From some corner of the office Kyle heard a snicker. If only he was a turtle. He could pull inside his shell and hide. There was no hiding here at the reception desk. He beat a hasty retreat to his cubicle, his cheeks burning.

When he got there, he found a chocolate cupcake sitting on his desk.

"I think you need this more than I do," said a soft voice from the cubicle next door.

Mindy had seen. The whole office had seen. He was a loser and here was the booby prize. "Thanks," he managed, and faced his computer screen, wishing he could rewind this morning.

The chocolate cupcake beckoned him. *You'll feel better if you eat me.*

He picked it up and took a bite. Not bad. And he did feel better—as long as he kept his eyes on his screen and didn't look in Jillian's direction. So much for the new clothes.

By the end of the work day, he was ready to get back in the ring and fight again, in spite of the fact that his coworkers had enjoyed several good laughs at his expense.

"You got the flower power, boy," Willie the accountant had teased as they left the office.

Whatever that meant. Kyle had heard the expression somewhere and he thought it had something to do with the sixties but he wasn't sure. Willie would know; he was old enough. Kyle didn't ask for an explanation, though. Instead, he pretended not to hear.

Still, Willie's crack got him thinking. The best way to fix this mess was to send Jillian some flowers, along with an apology—and an invitation to dinner.

He got on the phone to Lupine Floral and placed his order. Heinrich, one of the owners, assured him that Jillian would get her flowers first thing the next morning.

He was smiling when he hung up. Flower power, yeah.

Jonathan finished with his last client by four and went straight to Bruisers to do his workout. For a guy who had rarely lifted anything heavier than a computer, it was a killer. But hey—no pain, no gain. And he was determined to gain muscle and Lissa's attention.

The place smelled like the inside of a gym locker. He could hear the *woosha-woosha* of the treadmills where two women were speed-walking. One of them was about his mom's age. The other was Cecily from Sweet Dreams. She caught sight of him and gave him a friendly wave, and he nodded and hurried to the weights. Did she wonder why he was bothering to come here? He didn't exactly look like the king of buff.

But these things took time. Anyway, he didn't need to be totally ripped. He'd settle for…heck, anything was better than what he had. He looked at the row of weights. Time to move up to something heavier. He chose a set of dumbbells and got to work.

When he was done with those, he made the round of the machines, instruments of torture for an out-of-shape guy. But, he thought as he worked his legs, these sessions were getting a little easier. He had to be making progress. He tried not to look as Garrett Armstrong, one of the local firemen, casually rowed his way to nowhere on the rowing machine. Someday he'd be that fit.

After the gym he went home and showered and had a protein shake. Then he stuck the meat loaf his mom had given him the other day in the oven to reheat while Chica sat nearby, watching hopefully. "Come on now, this is my favorite," he told her. "You don't really think I'm gonna share, do you?"

Of course she didn't think it. She knew it. He was such a soft touch.

No sign of Adam. Maybe he'd finally made up with Chelsea. Jonathan sure hoped so. He didn't mind helping a pal but he wasn't up for having a permanent roommate. Unless it was Lissa.

The mere thought of Lissa reminded him how far he still had to go on the road to self-improvement before he saw her at the reunion. In the not-so-good old days he'd have relaxed before dinner by playing a game of chess online. There was no time for that now. Instead, he had to practice his dance steps.

He probably looked like a fool with his arms around nothing but space, but he'd rather look like a fool now than at the reunion. Anyway, there was no one to see but Chica. *One and two, one and two.* Chica barked encouragement.

And then he heard a new voice. "What the hell are you doing?"

He turned to see Adam walking in the door, bearing a pizza box from Italian Alps.

Okay, he definitely looked like a fool. *Well, so*

what? "I'm learning how to dance," he said and kept moving.

Adam shook his head. "For the reunion, huh? I don't know why you're even bothering. There's no pleasing women. No matter what you do, it's wrong."

"No matter what *you* do, it's wrong," Jonathan corrected him. And he wasn't Adam.

Boy, there was an understatement. Adam had money. And muscle. Jonathan was still a wimpy nerd in jeans and a T-shirt with a picture of Albert Einstein on it. But under that shirt he was slowly building muscle. He'd bulk up and learn to be suave and Lissa wouldn't be able to resist him. He hoped.

That night he had an important book to finish. This one was practically the story of his life. Like Lissa, the heroine had known the hero since childhood. He'd been the cowboy next door, someone she saw as a friend, not a lover. It wasn't until the poor guy nearly got trampled by a bull that she realized how much he meant to her.

"Oh, Justice," Corrine sobbed, taking his hand in hers. "I thought we'd lost you."

"Would it have mattered if you had?" His voice was weak. And bitter.

"Of course," she said, stung.

"You've been so busy with Chase…."

She put her finger to his lips. "Don't say it. I've been a fool."

She knew that now. Chase was charming and handsome.

Like Rand, thought Jonathan.

But he was all flash, like heat lightning, striking hot and hard and then gone. Justice was like the rain, steady and dependable. He was always there for her. He always had been. Why hadn't she seen that before?

Yeah, Jonathan thought. Why?

"I've always loved you," Justice said. "You never gave me a chance."

"I'm giving you one now." She leaned across the hospital bed and gently kissed his lips.

She started to pull away but his arm came around her, surprisingly strong considering everything he'd been through, and his lips claimed hers for another kiss, this one filled with passion long denied.

"I want you, Corrine. I can't let Chase have you. He doesn't deserve you. He never has. You're mine."

There it was again, hero attribute number three on Jonathan's list. Women wanted a man to take charge, to say, "This is how it is. You're mine."

He shut his eyes and tried to envision himself saying that to Lissa. He couldn't, because there was a big difference between him and Lissa and this fictional couple. Deep down, Corrine loved Justice and Justice knew it, thanks to a heated makeout session the author had allowed them earlier in the book. Jonathan had never enjoyed a heated makeout session with Lissa. And they'd only kissed once.

It had been at her Halloween party when they were in middle school. Her parents had turned the kids loose in the basement with chips and pop and candy corn, and they'd decided to play truth or dare.

Tina Swift, dressed as a witch, had dared Lissa to kiss Jonathan. This had been humiliating because Jonathan had known Tina meant the task to be unpleasant.

He'd been the world's scrawniest pirate. With glasses. The girls had giggled and Danny Popkee had threatened to punch Jonathan if he let her. But she was dressed in a princess gown and the prettiest girl at the party. Ever since Jonathan had gotten a gander at Lissa in her first bikini, he'd dreamed of kissing her. He was willing to risk a million punches.

She'd ignored the giggles and the threat, leaned over and got him right on the lips. It had been a heady experience, sending a hormonal current zipping through Jonathan. He was kissing Lissa! It was a dream come true. He savored the moment—until Danny ended it by making good on his threat and punching him.

He left the party with a black eye and heartfelt gratitude to Tina.

Did Lissa remember that kiss? Maybe in a *ha, ha, wasn't that cute* kind of way. He'd been a kid then. He could do better now if given the chance. He just had to find a way to get her to *give* him that chance.

Chapter Ten

On Friday a bouquet even bigger than the one that came the day before arrived for Jillian around eleven. Kyle watched as she took out the card, read it and smiled. That boded well for a dinner date. She put the flowers right up at the front of her desk. Ted Darrow was sure to see them. Ha! *Take that, Darrow.*

Kyle left his cubicle and sauntered over to the desk.

"The flowers are lovely," she greeted him. "You didn't need to do that, though."

"I wanted to," he said. "Sorry about yesterday."

She shrugged. "No big deal."

He was about to nail down the details of the Saturday dinner date he'd suggested on the card when—*oh, no, not now*—Ted Darrow came out of his office. "Jillian, I'm going to need you to compile some reports before lunch." He gave Kyle a distracted smile, then turned his back to him and kept talking.

Kyle got the message. With a frown, he went back to his cubicle. Darrow was a two-legged virus, corrupting Kyle's every attempt to get close to Jillian.

But he couldn't monopolize all her time. Kyle

would get her later. He'd set up dinner plans with her on his way to lunch.

That plan backfired when she walked out with Darrow. Were they going to lunch together?

"Want to grab a sandwich at Filly's?" asked a voice at his elbow.

He turned and there was Mindy, smiling at him. With his new shoes he was a good three inches taller than her. Which meant he'd probably come up to Jillian's chin. But size didn't matter when you were in love. He hoped she realized that.

"Yes? No?"

Oh, yeah. Mindy. "Uh, sure."

Filly's Café was located in the lobby of the office building and offered a few tables and chairs. A couple of paintings of horses hung on the walls in an attempt to make the name work. Mindy ordered a salad and Kyle ordered an egg salad sandwich and a coffee, and they staked out a table.

"How did the flowers go over?" she asked.

Kyle almost choked on his coffee. "Flowers?"

"I work right next to you. Remember?"

"Oh." Jeez, working in this office was like living in a fishbowl.

Mindy stabbed a tomato with her fork and casually examined it. "She's going out with Ted Darrow."

"How do you know that?"

Mindy gave him a pitying look. "Everyone knows."

Everyone but him. Yeah, he'd known Darrow was sniffing around, but... Mindy had to be wrong. Jillian would suck up to him a little, of course. She had to be nice to the bosses. But as far as going out with him, she had better taste than that. "He's a jerk."

"He's also one of the bosses and he drives a Jag."

Kyle set down his sandwich. "So, what are you saying exactly?"

Mindy popped the tomato in her mouth and chewed, leaving him waiting for her sage observation. She swallowed. "I'm saying he's one of the bosses and he drives a Jag."

"And the deck is stacked?"

"Something like that."

"Pretty shallow if that's all that matters to a woman," Kyle muttered, glaring at his sandwich.

"It's not all that matters to every woman. Just some."

"Well, that's dumb. People should look beyond superficial stuff like that."

"Do you practice what you preach?" Mindy asked.

"You bet I do. I'm not shallow."

"Mmm," she said, and took another bite of salad.

After that she changed the subject and they chatted about their plans for the weekend. Kyle had to admit he didn't have any for Saturday yet. But he had high hopes. He kept that to himself, however. Mindy was a skeptic.

Once finished, they still had some time before they needed to return to the office. He could go outside, take a walk down the street, maybe run into Jillian. Maybe she hadn't really gone to lunch with Darrow. Just because they'd left the office together, it didn't mean they *were* together. Right?

He claimed he had to run some errands and Mindy nodded. "Sure. See you back in Dilbert Land."

She left him and he sauntered outside. What now? Was he going to wander up and down Mission Street, peering in windows? That would look dumb. He opted for going to the drugstore. He needed...gum. He could walk partway down Mission and maybe casually run into Jillian that way.

A couple of blocks down the street, he got his Jillian sighting. He was passing a new restaurant that offered casual dining when he spotted her at a small window table with Darrow, two plates of half-finished lunch between them.

He couldn't deny it any longer. Mindy was right; they were together. Kyle suddenly wanted to punch something. What did Jillian see in that jerk, anyway?

Wait a minute. What was this? Was she crying? He slowed down to a stroll and did his best to appear inconspicuous as he peered inside. There she sat, dabbing her eyes with her napkin. Darrow looked as if he wished he were somewhere else. It didn't take a genius to figure out what was going on. Darrow was dumping her. Poor kid.

But she was well rid of him.

Now she shook her head and stood so abruptly her chair almost fell. Off she dashed toward the interior of the restaurant, probably to the women's room.

Darrow frowned. He pulled out his wallet, removed a bill and threw it on the table. Still frowning, he looked out the window and happened to see Kyle looking back. The frown dipped lower. Kyle picked up his pace and kept on walking. Getting the stink eye from his superior was seriously uncool. But knowing the jerk was out of the running was worth a thousand stink eyes.

Kyle got his pack of gum from the drugstore, then walked back to the office. Jillian was at her post again and, for once, she was alone. No one was hovering and the phone wasn't ringing. Her eyes were red.

But now she was about to find out what it was like to be loved by a real man. Kyle stopped at her desk. "You look like you've been crying. Everything okay?"

"Some people are real assholes," she said.

Kyle blinked. His mother and sisters never said stuff like that, and hearing those words come out of Jillian's pretty mouth was a shock. Women weren't supposed to talk like men. They were supposed to be, well, better. But she was hurt. She was allowed. Anyway, it was true.

"Yeah, they are," he agreed. "Anytime you want a shoulder to cry on."

She managed a watery smile. "You're sweet, Kyle. Thanks for caring."

Sweet. It was a good beginning.

The phone rang, and that was the end of their conversation. But they didn't need to say anything more. They had reached an understanding.

And he had proof of it when he returned from his afternoon break to find a slip of paper with a feminine scrawl propped on his computer keyboard. "How about coming over for dinner Saturday night?" it read.

Underneath that was Jillian's address. Very coy. Yeah, he could do that.

He was half tempted to show it to Mindy and crow a little. But he had the distinct impression that she didn't like Jillian and the last thing he wanted was someone raining on his parade. She'd see how wrong she was once Jillian was taking her lunch breaks with him.

He was in a good mood the rest of the afternoon. *I'm king of the world.* Well, if not the world, at least the office. He winked at Jillian when he left at five. She smiled back and gave him a flirty little wave as she talked on the phone. Man, oh, man. Life was good. He wouldn't be at all surprised if he won the pot at poker tonight.

Adam was in a foul mood when the guys showed up for poker.

"You still locked out?" Bernardo asked as they settled around Jonathan's kitchen table.

"Deal the cards," Adam snapped.

Vance nodded. "Still locked out."

"So, uh, the candy didn't work, huh?" Kyle asked.

"No, that went over even worse than the flowers."

"What kind of flowers did you get her?" Bernardo asked.

Adam frowned and picked up his cards. "I dunno. Some arrangement with yellow flowers and daisies. They cost me a bundle. And she tossed them. She doesn't like daisies," he added sourly.

"You should've gotten her favorite flower," said Vance.

Now Adam's frown turned into a scowl. "Hell, who knows that kind of stuff?"

"I do," Bernardo said. "Anna likes tiger lilies."

"I thought all women liked roses," Kyle said.

"That's usually a safe bet," Bernardo agreed. "And a single red rose for no reason on her pillow? A man can score big with that." He shoved a couple of cards across the table to Vance. "I'll take two." To Adam he said, "You know, you're in deep shit, *amigo.* You're gonna have to work hard to dig your way out. You have to court her all over again. Like the knight did in *Wooing Willow.*"

Adam made a face. "Oh, man. Not another romance novel. Those aren't working for me."

"It's because you're not paying attention," Bernardo said.

"I am, too," Adam protested. "I got her flowers and candy, and went over to talk to her. The only thing I haven't done is open a vein."

He was obviously too embarrassed to mention the Safeway sign. Jonathan had seen it and cringed. Something had gone wrong with *that* plan.

"Ah, you're pissed," Bernardo said. "She can tell. She knows you just want everything back the way it was."

"Well, I do. What's wrong with that?"

"Uh, I don't think she liked the way it was," Jonathan said.

"You've got to make her feel special," Bernardo told him. "I'll lend you a copy of that book."

"Is it a Vanessa Valentine one?" Jonathan asked. He should get it.

"It is. Anna has all of them."

"Since when do you read romance novels?" Adam wanted to know.

Bernardo grinned. "Since I saw how friendly my wife got after she read one."

Adam glared at his cards. "Yeah, well, I've been reading, too, and so far it hasn't done me any good."

Bernardo pointed a finger at Adam. "Stop reading with angry eyes. These books are written by women. That means what the men are saying and doing in them is what women want men to say and do. Lose your attitude and maybe you'll learn something."

That made Adam scowl. The others ignored him.

They went around the table twice, throwing out chips, seeing and raising, then Bernardo said, "Call," and everyone showed their cards.

Kyle was the winner. As he raked in his chips, he said, "I gotta tell you, those books are paying off for me." Now he puffed out his chest. "Guess who's got a date with Jillian tomorrow."

Jonathan could feel his eyes getting big. "Yeah? I thought she was hot for Ted Darrow."

"Was. You know they were actually an item? Anyway, the jerk dumped her, and old Kyle is around to help her pick up the pieces. She's invited me over for dinner tomorrow."

"That was fast," Jonathan observed.

Kyle grinned. "I think it was the flowers that did it. But the clothes didn't hurt."

Vance shook his head. "Your deal, Bernardo."

* * *

All it took was another night on the blow-up mattress in Jonathan's spare room to convince Adam he needed to borrow that novel from Bernardo. Saturday morning found him in Bernardo's orchard, walking between rows of trees with Pink Lady apples dangling from them like summer ornaments.

At the sight of him, Bernardo pushed back his straw hat and grinned knowingly. "So, you decided to get smart, eh?"

Adam frowned. Sometimes Bernardo was an irritating know-it-all.

The know-it-all didn't wait for him to acknowledge his inferiority. Instead, he led the way from the orchard to his house, a snug two-story farmhouse, complete with a garden off to the side and rockers on the front porch.

Once inside Adam could smell the remains of breakfast—coffee and a hint of cinnamon. And that reminded him of his wife's cinnamon rolls. From somewhere at the back of the house he could hear Bernardo's wife, Anna, singing.

"You know why she's singing?" Bernardo asked. Then, without waiting for an answer, he said, "Because she has me."

Gag. "Just give me the book, smart guy," Adam said.

"Anna," Bernardo called, and then rattled off a bunch of Spanish Adam couldn't understand. Probably, "The stupid gringo is here."

A moment later, his wife came down the hall.

She was a little slip of a thing with high cheekbones and full lips and midnight-black hair sparkling with strands of gray.

"*Hola,* Adam," she greeted him. "So you want to borrow my favorite Vanessa Valentine book."

"I promise I won't lose it."

She smiled at him and patted his arm. "You read this book, and it will help you learn how to treat your wife well."

How much had Bernardo told her? "I treated her okay." Even as he said it Adam knew he sounded like a fake.

She didn't say anything, just exchanged a knowing look with her husband. Then she ran up the stairs.

Adam stood in the hallway with Bernardo, feeling awkward. He rubbed the back of his neck where the muscles seemed to be constantly knotted. "I wasn't that bad a husband."

Bernardo chuckled. "You weren't that good a husband, either, *amigo.*"

Now his wife was back. She handed Adam a book. The cover showed a couple dressed in the clothes of another era, a time when the only thing a man could drive was a carriage. They were in a garden and he was kneeling at her feet and kissing her hand. Whipped. The man was whipped.

"Chivalry," Bernardo said as if he could read Adam's mind. "These days we take our women for granted. Back then, aah, a woman was a treasure to be won and cherished." His wife was next to him now and he put an arm around her shoulders. "Your wife, she is your best friend, *sí?* It's important to show her that. Right, *querida?*"

She put a hand to his cheek and looked at him like he was Antonio Banderas instead of a short, middle-aged man with a gut.

Bernardo wasn't rich and he sure wasn't handsome, but Adam felt the sting of jealousy. "Thanks for the book," he said, and got out of there.

It was warm and sunny, a perfect day to do some fishing in Icicle Creek. Instead, Adam picked up a sandwich and some bottled tea at Safeway and settled in a secluded spot on the bank. Then he opened the book and began to read.

He found himself shaking his head frequently. Why did the hero even want this woman? Yeah, she was beautiful and she was hot for him, but her family wanted her to marry someone else, and it seemed that every time they were together all she did was argue with him. Rather like Chelsea, he realized.

The man didn't give up, though. Even back then, it seemed flowers were the way to a woman's heart. *You tried that,* Adam told himself.

But how hard had he tried? He'd ordered a floral arrangement but had let another man choose the flowers. The dude in this book had gone on a search for the woman's favorite flower. And when he took it to her, he'd been…humble.

Adam had to admit he hadn't exactly been humble in his approach to Chelsea. He'd been pissed off and demanding. Still, who wouldn't be after getting locked out of his own house?

He shut the book and glared at the cover. Was that what he was going to have to do—get on his knees and beg? Obviously, it was. Was he willing to do that? He thought of how much he missed his wife, missed her smile, missed making love to her. Yeah, he was more than willing.

So, his first mission would be to figure out what kind of flowers she liked. He hiked back to his SUV and cruised past the house. Her car wasn't there, so she'd probably been on the schedule to work at the nursery. The predator next door was mowing his lawn. He nodded at Adam.

Great. All Adam needed was for that tool to see him taking pictures of his own house. He pulled out his cell phone and pretended to take a call. The minute Dennis turned and started mowing in the other direction, Adam snapped a quick picture. Then he drove off. Just a disenfranchised husband, stopping to pay a social call. Humiliating.

His next stop was Lupine Floral. He entered as a middle-aged man was ringing up a sale for Blake Preston, the bank manager. The man behind the counter gave Adam the sort of pleasant greeting one would give a stranger. No surprise, since he *was* a stranger. He and Chelsea had lived here for five years, and other than his desperate phone call a few days ago he'd never once ordered flowers for her. This hadn't bothered him before today.

"Thanks, Heinrich," Preston said. "Sam's going to love these."

"Flowers and a trip to Hawaii." The man—Hein-rich—smiled. "That's some birthday celebration."

"She's some woman." Preston smiled.

Adam found himself wondering when he'd last talked to someone about his wife like that. Man, it had been way too long. He was a skunk. He nodded and said a brief hello to Preston as he left the shop, then walked over to the counter.

"What can I do for you?" Heinrich asked.

He remembered the knight in *Wooing Willow* find-ing one perfect rose to give his lady. "I need a flower." Boy, that sounded cheap.

But it didn't faze the man behind the counter. "What kind?"

Adam brought up the picture on his phone. "What kind are these?" They weren't in bloom yet, but she had a bunch of them. Obviously, she liked them. Hope-fully the florist had some kicking around that looked like flowers instead of big green stalks.

"Ah, stargazer lilies."

"That's what I want," Adam said.

"Good choice. They have a wonderful fragrance."

Adam didn't care about the flower's fragrance. He only hoped that when Chelsea saw his floral offering, it would put her in a forgiving mood.

He didn't stop with the flower. He went to John-son's Drugs and picked up a pad of paper. Writing a note to his wife was going to be harder than any term paper he'd ever written.

It wasn't as if he'd never told her he loved her. He had. He'd told her on their first date. He'd taken her out to dinner and then to an improv comedy club in Seattle and they'd laughed their asses off. He'd known that first night she was the one for him. She hadn't believed him when he said he loved her, accused him of trying to get her to sleep with him on the first date. When he proposed, he'd taken her to Canlis, one of the priciest restaurants in Seattle, and come dessert he'd pulled out a diamond ring and told her again that he loved her. That time she'd believed him.

He needed her to believe him again, needed her to know he meant business, that he was going to do whatever it took to get back together.

Once more, he drove to the water where he could think. After half a tablet of paper and two hours of soul-searching, he was making progress. He read what he'd written so far.

"Chelsea baby, I finally get why you're pissed at me. I've been doing a lot of thinking" (and a lot of reading, but no way was he going to confess that he'd been reading romance novels—she'd never let him live it down) "and the more I think about how I've taken you for granted, the worse I feel. I'm sorry. Not just let-me-come-back sorry, but really sorry."

What to say now? He rubbed his chin. Hell, get down on your knees. For once in your life, act like a knight.

He cracked his heart the rest of the way open and wrote. "You mean everything to me. You really do. I'm asking you to give me a second chance. I know I don't deserve it, but please give it to me, anyway.

I can change. Call me. Tell me you'll see me. I love you. Adam."

Did Chelsea think he could change? He'd soon find out.

He returned to his SUV. Now he'd drive over to the house, leave this note and Chelsea's favorite flower and…what the hell was wrong with this flower? He picked it up from the front seat. It looked as sad and droopy as he felt. Hot car interiors and flowers obviously didn't go together well.

He let out a frustrated sigh. Like it or not, he was going back to Lupine Floral.

The same man was there, chatting with an older woman with red hair. She looked vaguely familiar but he couldn't recall where he'd seen her. Between them on the counter sat a fat arrangement of flowers in white and pale green. "The color is perfect for you," the man said.

Adam wasn't sure whether he was talking about the green sweater the woman was wearing or the flowers.

Either way, the compliment had worked. "Heinrich, you always know what to say to make a woman feel good about herself."

Nobody could accuse Adam of that.

"Well, I'd better get back to the bookstore," she said.

The bookstore. That was where he'd seen her. She owned the place.

He'd gone in once with Chelsea. They'd been running errands and the bookstore had been the last stop. He remembered how he'd whined like a little kid, hurrying her through her selection process. *"Come on, babe. All those books are the same. Just pick one so we can go home and eat lunch."*

How wrong he'd been! None of those books were the same. Well, other than the fact that by the end the hero got a clue. Adam hoped he was getting a clue.

He felt uncomfortably self-conscious as the bookstore woman walked past him. He hoped she didn't remember him.

From behind the counter, Heinrich, his new best friend, smiled politely. "Welcome back."

"Thanks," Adam said. "I need another flower."

Thank God the man didn't ask why.

Instead, he produced another exactly like the last one—well, before it wilted—wrapped a pink ribbon around it and laid it on the counter.

Adam paid and scrammed. Then he drove straight to the house. Chelsea still wasn't back but at least the predator was nowhere in sight. He left his offering on the porch along with the note and prayed this second flower didn't wilt before she got home.

Chapter Eleven

Saturday evening, a little before six, Kyle pulled up in front of a modest house in Wenatchee. It was blue with white shutters and window boxes full of flowers. A front walk had been paved down the middle of a manicured lawn. He could picture himself mowing this lawn. But he couldn't picture Jillian mowing it. Then again, he couldn't picture her making them a cozy dinner, either. She struck him as more of a take-out or take-me-out kind of woman. Well, he'd be happy to take her out. Anytime.

He rapped on the front door, keeping the bouquet of lupine he'd picked hidden behind his back.

The door opened and there she stood, in all her glory. Mindy. His mouth dropped. What was going on here? Was he in a parallel universe?

Not that the Mindy in this universe looked bad. She was wearing jean cutoffs short enough to show lots of thigh and a cropped black T-shirt that accentuated a nice little rack. In fact, she looked good.

But she wasn't Jillian. He frowned. What kind of sick joke was this?

"I see you got my note," she said, opening the door wider.

"*Your* note?" That note had been from Jillian.

Mindy's smile was suddenly uncertain. "Yeah."

"I don't understand."

She cocked an eyebrow. "What's not to understand? You were bummed. I thought dinner would cheer you up."

"Oh. Well, thanks. Except…"

Her eyes narrowed. "Except what?"

"Nothing," he said, and stayed rooted to the porch.

"Are you coming in?"

What was that he smelled? Something tomatoey and garlicky.

"I made lasagna."

His fave.

"And chocolate cake for dessert."

He thought of the cupcake he'd had, and his taste buds told him to be polite and get inside. He did, handing over the flowers.

"Oh! Did you pick these yourself?"

"Yeah." She was smiling at him like he was one of those heroes he'd read about. Damn. Why wasn't she Jillian? What was he doing here? He shouldn't stay. He'd only lead her on.

He walked in farther.

Once inside he didn't know what to do. He stood in the living room, wishing he could leave and inhaling the aroma of lasagna while she took the flowers into her kitchen. He watched as she dug around in a cupboard, then pulled out a vase.

"Sit down," she said.

He sat on the edge of the couch. Yeah, this was one sick cosmic joke. Jillian was free now. He could have been out with her, thought he'd be out with her. But here he was in Mindy's living room while she put flowers that should have gone to Jillian in a vase. None of the books he'd read so far had prepared him for a situation like this. He checked the time on his phone. How long before he could leave? The longer he stayed, the harder it would be. She'd end up thinking they were an item and then everything would get ugly.

He looked up and saw she was watching him. Her smile had vanished.

"Do you need to be somewhere?" she asked.

"Uh…"

Now a frown line appeared on her forehead. "Kyle, if you didn't want to come, what are you doing here?"

"I…" How did he say this without hurting her feelings?

"You?" she prompted.

He had to work beside her every day. This would not go over well, and work was going to be hell on Monday.

But it would only be worse if he allowed the misunderstanding to go any further. "I thought someone else left that note." She looked as if he'd just shot her with a poison dart. Oh, man, he was going to puke.

He never knew a human face could do such a great imitation of a glacier. Right now he'd rather face a glacier. An avalanche. A pack of hungry wolves. Anything.

"Oh, don't tell me."

"Darrow dumped her. I told her anytime she wanted to get together…"

Mindy closed her eyes. Maybe she was envisioning how she'd murder him? "That's what I get for being cute and leaving notes," she said miserably.

"I'm sorry," he said. "But I couldn't sit here and eat your lasagna and let you think…" …what a rat he was. Too late for that.

She shook her head like he was the most pathetic man on the planet.

"Hey, a guy can't help who he's attracted to," Kyle said. It was true. Why did saying it make him sound like such a shit? "Not that you're not attractive," he added, trying to soften the blow.

It was too late for blow-softening. She had tears in her eyes. "You're a fool," she said, then sadly added, "But so am I."

"I should go."

She turned her back and got busy arranging the flowers in the vase. "Yeah, I guess you should. I'm not very hungry anymore."

He didn't have any desire for food, either. What he needed was a good stiff drink.

As he drove away he asked himself if he should have seen this coming. When he played chess he could see five or six moves ahead. But love was a different game altogether, and now he couldn't help wondering if he was ever going to win at it.

* * *

Chelsea didn't call on Saturday evening. No texts, either. This made Adam restless. "Want to go get a beer?" he asked Jonathan.

Jonathan was used to hanging in limbo and had learned how to entertain himself. He was trying to do just that, playing an online game of *Warrior Wizards*. "No, I'm good," he said, concentrating on cornering the dragon on a cliff overlooking a raging sea.

"Maybe my phone's broken," Adam said.

"Maybe she's making you sweat," Jonathan suggested.

"Where's yours?"

"Huh?" Jonathan lost his concentration. He dropped his avatar's force field and the dragon blasted him to cinders. Game Over. He frowned.

"Your phone. I'm gonna call her."

"It's on the counter." Jonathan leaned back against the sofa cushions and watched while Adam tried to make a different phone do what his hadn't been able to—get his wife to talk to him.

Adam frowned, a sure sign he'd been sent to voice mail purgatory. "Hey, babe. Did you get my letter? Call me. Text me. Anything."

He'd never seen Adam so desperate. And here was a new development. "You wrote her a letter? You must've read *Wooing Willow*."

"I took her a flower," Adam said, neither confirming nor denying that he'd succumbed to reading another romance novel. "Stargazer lily. It's got to be one of her faves. They're all over the garden."

How the heck had he known what a stargazer lily was?

Adam plopped down on Jonathan's recliner. "I used to date girls and say I'd call 'em and then forget," he said in a pensive voice.

Jonathan had never done that. But then, he hadn't gone out with as many girls as Adam had. Still, he liked to think he wouldn't have done that, regardless of how many girls he'd dated.

Now Adam was fidgeting. "Want pizza? I'm gonna get us a pizza." With that he was off the recliner and gone, leaving Jonathan in peace.

"What do you want to bet he's going over to the house?" he asked Chica, who was next to him, sprawled on the couch.

Chica yawned, dog language for "I don't care one way or the other."

Jonathan did, though. He didn't want to see his buddy miserable. He especially didn't want to see his buddy miserable here, indefinitely. He hoped Adam would make up with Chelsea and get back in his own place.

Meanwhile, observing him was like being in a college lab class, watching someone else's experiment go wrong and trying to figure out what to avoid so you, too, didn't flunk.

Flunking was still a strong possibility, no matter how much research and observation Jonathan did. Reading romance novels was one thing; applying what was in them was quite another. He still had no idea how he was going to conquer the real-life challenge of winning the love of Lissa Castle. He'd made lists, written down examples of what to say to a woman and what to do for her, but so far he didn't see how he was going to put it all into play.

He decided to do a Venn diagram. As he drew circles for himself and Lissa, he saw that the overlap wasn't as big as he'd thought it would be. What they had in common was a past history, food (she liked to bake, he liked to eat). Games. They'd grown up playing everything from board games to cards. Hmm. What else? Well, dancing. He knew she loved to dance. He...was working on it. What else besides that? Oh, yeah. He grinned and wrote down *movies*.

Their moms and Rand's had often taken the kids to matinees at the Falls Cinema. When they got older, they went on their own, he and Rand and Lissa, sometimes with several other kids. The bigger the group, the quieter Jonathan got.

He thought about the time they'd gone to see *Hook* when they were around twelve. It had just been he and Lissa at first, but somehow Rand got thrown into the mix. Jonathan could still remember the frustration and disappointment he'd felt when Rand met them at the ticket booth.

Of course, Lissa had sat between them. Rand had teased her, trying to put popcorn down the back of her sweatshirt. She'd told him to stop but she'd giggled when she said it, and even Jonathan had known what that meant.

Once the movie started, the goofing around ended

and all of them had gotten caught up in the story. Lissa had cried when Rufio was killed.

"It was just a movie," Rand had said scornfully as they stood in line at Herman's Hamburgers, waiting to order ice cream.

"I don't care," she'd shot back. "It's still sad. Didn't you think so, Jonathan?"

Torn between not wanting to look like a sissy and not wanting to hurt Lissa's feelings, Jonathan had finally said, "At least Tinker Bell didn't croak." For a while that was a running joke when things weren't going well for one of them. *At least Tinker Bell didn't croak.*

Maybe he could find a way to use that line when they were together. Which brought him full circle back to the reunion. How was he going to engineer enough time with Lissa to make her want to spend *more* time with him?

He moved on to creating an activity diagram for the reunion, plotting how he'd greet her. "Find Lissa in bar. Use Dirk Jackson's line from *Smooth Moves*. 'Look at you. I could do it all night.'"

He was still trying to figure out what to do next when Adam came back and dumped another Italian Alps pizza on the kitchen counter. Jonathan didn't ask if he'd struck out. The expression on Adam's face said it all.

"Hey, don't give up," Jonathan said.

Adam's only reply was a growl as he marched off to his room.

Jonathan heaved a sigh. It was beginning to look like his roommate was here to stay.

Love. Sometimes it was more a four-letter word than a feeling.

Chelsea finally called early Sunday afternoon.

"Did you get my letter?" Adam asked.

"Yes, I did."

She sounded more cautious than angry so he had to be making progress. "Will you see me? We could go out to dinner," he said. "I'll take you to Schwangau."

"I can't. I have plans."

Not with Dennis the Menace, please. "With who?"

"With the women from work."

"Oh." Edged out by a bunch of women. That sucked.

"They're coming here. We're having a plant exchange."

Everyone was welcome at his place but him. A week ago that would have really pissed him off. "Monday, then."

"It's Memorial Day. Anyway, Schwangau is closed on Mondays. You know that."

"Okay, Tuesday. Will you go out with me on Tuesday?"

"Are you sure you won't be too busy working...or whatever?" she taunted.

How many times had he forgotten to tell her he had to work late or taken coworkers out for a drink and left her home waiting, always assuming she'd understand? How many times had he gone fishing, either up in Alaska or here at home, figuring she wouldn't care? Obviously, too many.

"You're the most important person in my life," he said. No bull.

"All right."

He'd scored. It was all he could do not to let out a whoop. "I'll make reservations now. Pick you up at seven." He had to go visit his accounts in Seattle that day, but if he knocked off early, there wouldn't be as much traffic on the road. It was only a two-hour drive. He'd get back to Icicle Falls in plenty of time....

Or not. Everything went wrong on Tuesday. It took longer than he'd expected to make his rounds and instead of being done early he got on the road half an hour later than he'd planned. But okay, he could still get there by seven.

On I-90 he had a flat tire. By the time he'd finished changing it, he was sweaty and cranky. Why did stuff like this only happen when you had to be someplace?

He'd barely gotten on the road again when an accident turned the freeway into a parking lot. And now it was six-thirty and he was stuck in traffic. The last thing he wanted to do was call his wife and tell her he was running late. What could he say? How could he spin this? *Somebody stole my car. And mugged me. I'm at the police station.... I'm in the emergency room, I was hit by a truck....* Or the truth. *You're not going to believe this but I'm stuck in traffic.*

Neither option sounded good. Still, he had to say something. He decided to go with the truth.

She didn't bother with hello when she picked up. Instead, she went straight to, "Where are you, Adam?"

"I'm stuck in traffic."

"You're still in Seattle?"

"No, I'm on I-90."

"You're in Seattle."

"Look, I got done later than I thought I would." But only half an hour. If it hadn't been for the flat and this traffic snarl he'd have made it home in plenty of time.

"Gee, what a surprise. And then I bet you just had to take someone out for a drink."

"No. Then I had a flat tire."

"Right," she said, her voice dripping scorn.

"I did. And now I'm stuck in traffic."

"Oh, please. How dumb do you think I am? You may as well just admit you forgot. You haven't changed at all and I still come in second after…everything." Before he could insist that wasn't true, she ended the call.

"I have, too, changed!" He called her back. Of course she didn't answer. She probably had steam coming out of her ears. He should have knocked off at three, not tried to go back to Virginia Mason and catch Dr. Rogers. That had cost him an hour. And now, here he was, crawling along at the pace of a dying slug.

"Leave me a message," her recorded voice instructed him.

"I'm not lying. I'm stuck in traffic," he growled, and gave the car horn an aggressive honk to prove it. Which prompted the guy in front of him to stick his hand out the window and give Adam the finger.

"Dude, you're not telling me anything I don't know," he grumbled.

Six forty-five. He should have been driving over to pick up Chelsea right about now. Tonight they'd have had a romantic dinner, he'd have promised to do better, presented her with the emerald necklace he'd bought her for their anniversary. Then they'd have gone home and made love.

No lovemaking tonight. No dinner, no chance to see his wife's face light up at the sight of her belated but stellar present. He was back at square one. He swore and pounded the dashboard with his fist.

This was not fair and he didn't have a clue what he was going to do about it.

But sitting here on the freeway, he sure had lots of time to think of something.

Chapter Twelve

Adam was on his way to visit his accounts in Idaho when Chelsea called him. "I checked on the internet. There was an accident on I-90 last night."

Vindicated! "Did you really think I was lying to you?"

"I thought you were looking for an excuse."

After everything he'd been doing to try to get her talk to him? Either his wife thought he was the biggest idiot on the planet or he'd worn her trust down so close to the bone there was none left. Neither possibility made him feel good.

"If you want to go out, we can," she said.

At last, an open door. If only it had opened when he was still in town. "I'm on my way to Boise," he said.

"When you get back then. Friday?"

"Friday is poker night."

"What?"

Had he just said that out loud? "Nothing. Friday is perfect. I'll make reservations at Schwangau for seven."

"You sure you'll be back in time?"

"Absolutely. I'm coming home Thursday."

"Okay," she said dubiously.

"I'll be there," he assured her.

It was three in the afternoon on Thursday and Adam was zipping down the freeway when his trusty company car decided it no longer wanted to be trustworthy. He limped off the freeway to the nearest auto repair shop.

"Well, good news," said the head mechanic after keeping Adam waiting an hour. "It's only a fan belt."

Adam breathed a sigh of relief. "Great." It shouldn't take long to put in a fan belt. He could probably be on the road in an hour.

"We don't have that particular belt in stock so we'll have to order it."

What was with his life lately? Had some gremlin put a kick-me sign on his butt? "How long will *that* take?"

"I'll order it now. We'll have it first thing tomorrow."

If they got going first thing in the morning and were done by nine he'd still be okay. He'd drive like a madman and make it back to Icicle Falls by six-thirty, with a half hour to spare. "How long will it take to fix?"

The mechanic shrugged. "An hour or so. Part should be here by ten. We'll have you on the road by eleven."

Eleven? "That's too late. I've got to get home to Washington. My wife—"

The mechanic, a middle-aged family man type, pointed a finger at him and completed his sentence before he could. "Is having a baby. Right? Due any day?"

"Well, no."

The guy looked disappointed. "So she's...sick?"

"Uh, no. But we've got an important dinner."

"Oh, your anniversary."

That sounded better than a let-me-come-back-home dinner so Adam said, "Yeah. And it's really important I be there."

The mechanic was now the picture of a man ready to bust his hump to help another man stay out of trouble with his wife. "I hear you."

"So can you get me on the road any sooner?"

The mechanic shook his head sadly. "Afraid not. You'd better change your plans to Saturday."

Okay, they could go out Saturday. After all, it wasn't his fault that the car had crapped out.

"Meanwhile, we can give you a loaner," said the mechanic. "There's a nice Best Western just down the road."

Adam got his loaner car, checked into a motel room and then made the dreaded call to his wife.

"Why are you calling?" she asked suspiciously.

"Because I..." *She's not gonna believe you.* Lie! "I couldn't get a reservation for Friday."

"Really?" she said, a world of scorn in her voice. "I wonder if you're having trouble getting a reservation because Friday is poker night."

"What? No! No, that's not it."

"You can always get a reservation for a Friday when you call a couple of days ahead."

"Well, I couldn't this time," Adam insisted.

"Adam, you're lying. I can tell."

"I'm not lying," he lied.

She ended the call, leaving him talking to the dial tone.

He was going to have to tell her the truth, fantastical as it sounded. He called her again.

"What?" she snapped.

"You're right, I was lying. But I was lying because if I tell you the truth you'll think I made it up."

"Try me."

"I'm stuck in Idaho. My car died and I need a new fan belt. They can't get the part until tomorrow and God knows when they'll get the car fixed."

"You could've told me that in the first place," she said. "I'd have believed you."

Just like she had when he was stuck in traffic.

"I always know when you're inventing stuff."

No, she didn't. In the past he'd told some fibs and sweet-talked his way out of trouble more than once. He decided to not to argue the point.

"I'll make it up to you on Saturday," he said. "Seven o'clock."

"Okay." But her tone of voice added, "And you'd better not screw up."

"Where's Adam?" asked Kyle as the men settled around Jonathan's table with their cards and their snacks.

"On his way home from Idaho," Jonathan said. "His car crapped out."

"First his wife, now his car. He's sure having bad luck lately," Kyle said.

"When it comes to women, there is no such thing as bad luck, my friend," Bernardo informed him. "You either put in the work and are rewarded or you don't and you lose."

"Not buying that theory," Vance said as he dealt the cards. "Sometimes bad luck comes in like Godzilla and stomps everything to shit."

What had happened, Jonathan wondered, to make him such a cynic? He suspected Vance had a story to tell but he didn't ask. Unlike his sister, he didn't believe in butting into somebody else's business. If Vance wanted them to know about his love life, he'd say something.

"I agree with Vance," Kyle said as he anted up. "Here I thought I was going to Jillian's, and it turns out that dinner invite was from...another woman." He frowned. "Sometimes a man hasn't done anything wrong but he still loses."

"You don't think chasing after the wrong woman is doing something wrong?" Bernardo countered.

Kyle frowned. "What are you saying?"

"He's saying maybe you're fishing in the wrong stream," Vance explained.

"You know," Bernardo said, "before I met my Anna, there was this girl. Whoo, man, she was *muy caliente*. I was so sure I was in love with her."

"Yeah? What happened?" Kyle asked, throwing in a poker chip.

Bernardo shrugged. "She liked my best friend more."

I feel your pain, Jonathan thought.

"Why didn't you get in there and fight and take her away?" Kyle asked.

"That is a fight you think I would have won?" Bernardo sounded incredulous. "No, when a woman is determined on a man, that is the man she gets."

"Well, that stinks," Kyle said, and scowled at the cards in his hand.

"Oh, at the time, *si,* it does. But things have a way of working out. You let go of that one and someone even better comes along. A year later I met my Anna and she was perfect for me."

"And what about the other woman?" Kyle asked, throwing in a blue chip. "What happened to her?"

"She married my friend. They had six girls. Oh, that house, every day there is drama. And my poor old friend, he is always in trouble. No, I am happy with the woman I got and I'm glad things didn't work out the way I wanted. It would have been me being nagged and yelled at because I wasn't making enough money. So, you see, when it comes to women, there is no such thing as bad luck," Bernardo concluded.

Jonathan and Kyle chuckled. Vance, however, didn't even crack a smile. Instead, he threw in two blue chips. "I'll raise that by four bits."

What *had* happened to Vance to make him so bitter? Whatever it was, Jonathan hoped it wasn't contagious.

"Well, I'm gonna create my own good luck," Kyle said. Then he frowned. "There must be some way I can get Jillian's attention."

"Read *Wooing Willow* when Adam's done with it," Bernardo suggested.

"I don't have time to wait for Adam to be done with it."

"Then buy the damn book," Vance said. Everyone folded and the pot was his. "You all are such a bunch of cheapskates," he muttered as he raked in the chips.

"I'm not," Jonathan protested. "I've spent a fortune on books."

"Good man," Vance approved. "You're helping some hard-working writer pay her bills."

Jonathan had never thought about whoever wrote those books needing to earn a living. He'd been more concerned with learning something. Now he was glad he'd laid down some hard-earned money for the latest novels he'd been consuming.

"Hey, I've been buying books, too," Kyle said. He shook his head. "I don't know how the men in those stories think up all those cool things to say."

"That's easy," Jonathan said. "They're written by women, who put the words in their mouths."

"How do you learn that stuff?" Kyle asked. "I mean, I'm reading it but I haven't got a clue about applying it. How do you know what to say to get a woman to fall for you? There oughta be an app."

Jonathan grabbed his smartphone. "Let's ask Ida."

"Who's Ida?" Bernardo asked.

"Not a who, a what," Jonathan told him. "It stands for Instant Data Acquired. It's an app, a quick reference. You ask Ida a question, she finds the answer."

Bernardo whistled in admiration. "No kidding," he said.

"You can ask it anything from 'Who was the fourteenth president of the United States?' to 'Where can I hide a body?'" Jonathan continued.

"You'll have better luck asking it where to hide a body," Vance said.

Jonathan brought up the app, held the phone to his face and asked, "What do women want to hear?"

"May as well use a Ouija board," Vance continued.

"I'm sorry, I can't help you with that," said a female voice, making Bernardo laugh.

"That's because it's impossible," Kyle grumbled.

"Stick with the books," Bernardo advised as Kyle dealt the cards for the next hand. "And then practice what you read," he added, dredging a potato chip through the onion dip. His platter of veggies sat on Jonathan's counter, completely ignored.

"That's great advice, except I don't have anyone to practice on," Jonathan complained.

"Adam's still here. Practice on him," Bernardo said.

"I don't think so," Jonathan said in disgust. He was already dancing with his sister. That was as far as he was willing to go.

"Look," said Vance, "pick out some good lines the heroes say in those books and then memorize them."

Jonathan thought of the line he'd written down. Okay, he was on the right track.

"A lot of those are one-size-fits-all," Vance went on. "You can use 'em anywhere."

Jonathan remembered a line he'd read earlier. *You're my very breath. My every heartbeat whispers your name.* That pretty well summed up the way he felt about Lissa. He'd tried to move on, get a life. After all, he wanted a family, wanted someone he could spend the rest of his life with. The problem was, there was no one else like Lissa.

It had been hard to see her dating other guys over the years, but he'd known he wasn't good enough for her. Maybe, if he was lucky, by the time he was done getting buff and becoming a real-life hero, he would be. He sure hoped so.

"Hey, are you in or out?"

Vance's irritated voice brought Jonathan back to the game. So far he'd lost ten bucks. He figured he'd lose more before the evening was over. It wasn't easy to outbluff Vance.

They were halfway through the night when Adam finally rolled in. "Want us to deal you in?" Kyle asked.

"The way my luck's been running?"

"Deal him in," Vance said with a grin.

Adam grabbed a beer and pulled up a chair. "So, what's happening?"

"Vance is skinning us," Kyle said.

"What else is new?"

"Nothing new with you, I guess. You're still here," Vance said.

"Did you read that book?" Bernardo asked.

"Yeah, I did. And Chelsea and I are going out to-morrow."

This was encouraging news. For both Adam and Jonathan. "That's cool," Jonathan said.

Adam nodded. "I just hope she takes me back."

So did Jonathan.

Saturday night Adam showered, shaved and doused himself with cologne, then went to pick up Chelsea. It felt weird to be walking up his own front walk as a suitor instead of a husband. He felt stupid ringing the doorbell rather than just walking in. He reminded himself that he had to *earn* the right to walk back in.

The door opened and there stood his wife, looking tantalizingly beautiful in a blue sundress and heels. Her hair, which she often wore pinned up when she was at work or out in the yard gardening, was down. The way he liked it. He wanted to reach out and touch it, but he didn't. That was another right he was going to have to earn back.

"You look good, Chels," he said.

"Thank you," she said primly. No smile.

It was going to be a long, uphill battle. He stood aside and let her pass, then watched the sway of her hips as she walked to the car. His wife had the cutest butt in the world.

"Hi, Dennis," she called.

The predator next door was sitting on his front porch, reading a book. Probably for cover so he could watch Chelsea, too. Adam frowned as he opened the car door for her. "I don't like that guy," he muttered.

"He's perfectly nice," she said.

Yeah, he was being perfectly nice for a reason. The same reason Adam was on his best behavior. He walked around and got behind the wheel. "You know, he can't be all that perfect. He's divorced."

"His wife left him," Chelsea said.

"Well, that proves it. There must've been a reason."

The words were barely out of his mouth when Adam realized he'd said the wrong thing. Next to him, Chelsea raised an eyebrow. "I know you had good reason to kick me out," he said.

"I did." She said it defensively, almost as if she was trying to convince both him and herself that she'd done the right thing.

Well, maybe she had. Maybe he'd needed a major wake-up call. "Thanks for going out with me tonight. I want to make this work."

"So do I," she said softly. "I've got an important reason."

He got that. "We always said we'd never be like our parents, never split up."

She bit her lip and nodded. "I know."

At the restaurant the maître d' led them to a quiet corner table covered with a snowy linen cloth and gleaming silver and crystal. A little candle added a romantic glow and the flowers in the vase were fresh. Schwangau was the fanciest restaurant in town, and it was the place to go if you wanted to impress a woman. Tonight Adam needed to do some serious impressing.

Their waiter appeared and asked if they'd like to start with drinks.

"Yes," Adam, said and proceeded to order Chelsea's favorite—champagne.

"No champagne for me," she said.

Nothing to celebrate. This didn't bode well. "Okay," Adam said. "What would you like?"

"Lemonade."

"I'll take a Pilsner," he told the waiter, who nodded and left. Now it was just the two of them and suddenly Adam didn't know what to say. He tried to remember something, anything, from one of those books he'd read and drew a blank. So, instead, he pulled her present out of his pocket and slid it across the table. "Happy anniversary. I promise I'll be on time next year." *Please, God, let there be a next year.*

She smiled. It was the first one he'd seen since she kicked him out of the house. There was hope!

He held his breath as she picked up the package and unwrapped it, opened the jewel case and gave a little gasp. It reminded him of when they made love. How he wanted to hear that little gasp again.

"It's beautiful," she said. She took out the emerald necklace and held it up.

"I wanted to give you something special, to make up for..." Here he faltered.

Now the waiter was back with their drinks. Adam grabbed his and took a big gulp. After seven years of marriage he was back at square one, nervous and tongue-tied with a beautiful woman he wanted to impress.

She held the necklace out to him. "Help me put it on?"

He took it and came around to her side of the table. He pulled aside her hair, exposing her neck, and flashed on the image of doing the very same thing when they were in bed together, then kissing her neck. He wanted to do that now, but he clasped on the necklace and returned to his chair.

"Adam, did you mean all those things you said in that letter?" she asked.

"Of course I did." He'd poured his heart into that letter. How could she even ask?

She lowered her head and studied the menu.

"I know I wasn't perfect, but was I really that bad a husband?"

She looked over the menu at him. "Sometimes, yes."

"But not all the time."

"Not all the time," she conceded. "Not at first."

Now the pesky waiter was back again, needing to know what they wanted to eat. A restaurant was not the place to be when you were trying to have a serious talk with your wife.

They placed their orders, the waiter left and Adam said, "Okay, finish what you were saying." He wasn't sure he wanted to hear, but it was the only way they were going to settle this and get back to normal. The *new* normal, he reminded himself. The old normal hadn't worked so well.

"Remember when we were first dating?" she asked.

What did that have to do with anything? He nodded.

"You called all the time. You drove across the mountains in a snowstorm to see me at Christmas."

"Because I wanted you." He still did.

"And then you got me. But after a couple of years…" She shrugged.

"What?"

"You started taking me for granted. Like that fish in the rec room."

"What?"

"The fish you caught in Mexico."

"The marlin." He'd had that baby mounted.

"I was like that marlin. You got me, and then you didn't need to work anymore. I might as well have been hanging on the wall along with the fish." In case he hadn't gotten the symbolism, she added, "You've been taking me for granted, practically ignoring me. I want to be with someone who wants me all the time, not just some of the time, like when he's after sex or needs something picked up from the cleaners."

Ow. "Come on, Chels, I can't have been *that* bad."

"Yeah, you could."

"What do you want—I shouldn't work?"

Now she was beginning to look perturbed. "Of course not. You know that's not what I'm saying."

All right, yeah. Deep down he did.

"You do a lot of things that don't include me."

"So do you. You've got your book group…."

"That's only once a month. You, on the other hand, have softball, fishing, poker."

Was she going to make him give up poker night? Fishing? Well, okay, if that was what it took. At this point he'd give up anything. Hell, he'd cut off a leg. "Chels," he began.

She raised a hand to silence him. "I'm not saying you have to give all that up. I get that you want to be with your friends and do your guy things. But what about doing something with me once in a while? How about doing more things with other couples?"

Okay, he could do that. "Sure. Have your friend Juliet and her husband over. I like Neil."

"We don't have to be together 24/7, but we could be a little more like when we were first married," she added.

They used to do things all the time—going to dinner, to the movies, playing gin rummy on a rainy Sunday afternoon.

"You could take me fishing."

"Fishing?"

"Yeah. Fishing. Why do you always have to go with men?"

"You wouldn't like it." She'd be bored. She'd want to talk, and you didn't talk when you were fishing.

Now she looked like she was going to cry.

"Okay, we can go fishing. We can find all kinds of stuff to do."

She'd complained before that they didn't spend enough time together. Whenever she did, he'd take her to a movie or out to dinner and then everything would be fine.

Until he relapsed. Somehow, he never noticed when

he was slipping back into his bad habits. Not that he'd thought of his behavior as bad habits. Not that he'd really thought at all.

Now, taking a critical look at his life, he realized that when it came to his marriage, there was hardly anything he hadn't taken for granted. He'd assumed Chelsea would care for the house and cook the meals on top of working, and that all he'd have to do was bring in the big bucks, mow the lawn and wash the car once in a while. She even paid the bills. She'd taken on that chore when they were first married and he'd happily let her. He hadn't wanted to be bothered. He'd never thanked her for everything she did. Heck, he'd hardly noticed. And while she kept their household running smoothly, he played poker with the boys, fished and convinced clients to prescribe his company's medications. And all the while, his marriage kept getting sicker.

"Adam, I love you."

Relief washed over him. They were going to be okay.

"But I can't go on like this. I won't."

He felt his heart stop. "I'll change, I promise."

"You need to, because I'm pregnant."

"What?"

Great. Here was the damned waiter with their first course.

Adam felt like he was going to explode waiting for the man to go through the ritual of peppering their salads. Once he'd left, Adam asked the question that had been burning its way through his mind. "How can you be pregnant?"

Not the right words to say. Her eyes flashed. "How do you think?"

"I mean, but…" They'd been told they couldn't have kids. The doctor had said…

"It's a *miracle,* Adam, that's what it is. And look at you. Instead of being thrilled to hear this, you're acting like I just told you the world was coming to an end." She threw down her napkin and stood.

"Where are you going?"

"Home."

"Come on, Chels, don't do that. We haven't even eaten yet."

"I'm not hungry anymore. You and your selfishness, you took away my appetite."

With that, she ran from the restaurant.

How was she going to get home? He didn't want her walking, not when she was pregnant. He threw down some bills and tore off after her.

She was already halfway down the street when he caught up with her. "Chels, come back and get in the car. I'll take you home."

"I don't want to get in the car. I don't want to be with you. Not after the way you just acted." And to prove it, she kept walking.

"Cut me some slack. I was surprised, that's all."

"I can see it in your face—you're not happy."

"Of course I'm happy," he insisted, walking along beside her. At least he would be once he'd adjusted to the idea. First he had to get past the panic. All this time, he'd thought they wouldn't—couldn't—have kids. He hadn't worried about the future or put much of anything in savings. Suddenly, they were about to have another mouth to feed, a college education to pay for, maybe a wedding. It was overwhelming. And, unlike him, Chelsea'd had time to get used to the idea. "How far along are you?"

"Two months."

"You've known for two months?"

"No. I found out when you were in Alaska." She stopped right there in the middle of the sidewalk so she could put all her energy into glaring at him. "I was going to tell you on our anniversary."

And he hadn't come home. He'd not only forgotten their anniversary, he'd denied her the chance to share an important milestone in their lives. And now, his panicked surprise had been the final nail in his coffin.

"You are the most selfish man I know," she said, and started walking again.

"Chels, come on. Let me drive you back to the house. You shouldn't be walking all the way home. It's not good for the baby." Well, maybe it was. What did he know?

"The baby will be fine, and so will I. And we'll both be better off without you."

Would they end up with Dennis the Menace? No, not that. "Let's talk about this."

"I'm done talking and I'm done with you. And if you don't quit following me, I'm going to call the police and have you arrested."

Her words stopped him in his tracks. At dinner

she'd told him she still loved him. She couldn't mean what she'd just said. He started moving again. "You can't do this, Chels. It's not fair. You have to give me a chance."

"I just did and you blew it."

"Well, give me another." He caught her arm, forcing her to stop.

She scowled at him.

"Let me take you home."

"You're not staying."

He nodded. "I know."

The ride home was a silent one. Chelsea was still steaming and he didn't know what to say.

Back at the house she was out the car door before he could even come around and open it for her. He watched as she ran up the walk. There went the most important person in his life. How little he'd done to show her that she was. Why had he thought his marriage could run on autopilot? Hadn't he learned anything from his folks?

As a kid he'd felt both confusion and frustration over the disintegration of their marriage. He'd hated it when they fought, hated seeing his mom in tears. Now his wife was in tears. Oh, boy.

He drove slowly away. If there was a romance novel that told a man how to deal with this kind of mess, he sure needed it. He had to find his way to a happy ending—and soon.

Chapter Thirteen

The more people who posted on the website Jonathan had set up for the reunion, the more panicked he became. It was June. The reunion was ten weeks away. He had ten weeks left in which to get buff. He was going to have to double his efforts. Work less, work out more.

At least the dance lessons were going well, he thought as he used one of the instruments of torture at the gym. Lately he'd been meeting Neil after five a couple of days a week. Neil wasn't done with his shift at the Sweet Dreams warehouse and this wasn't one of their regular days, but Jonathan figured he knew what he was doing now. He didn't need babysitting. He increased the weights on the machine and got to it.

Did women have any idea how hard guys worked to get their attention? Almost everything a man did centered on winning a woman's approval. The jocks showed off their moves on the football field or the basketball court, while the brains tried to impress with their smarts. Brain or brawn, all guys spent a fortune on dinners out, concert tickets or jewelry, whatever it took to get the women of their dreams. They did things they would never even consider in their saner moments, like joining a gym.

Oh, man, this was a killer. Maybe he shouldn't have increased the weights so much. Push through, that was what Neil had said last time they were here. Okay, pushing through, pushing, pushing. Ow! What the heck? He stopped and rubbed his upper arm. Something had just gotten pushed too far. That couldn't be good. He decided he'd had enough for the day.

Anyway, he had to go home and get cleaned up. He was due for another dance lesson at his sister's that night. She'd offered dinner, as well, but he'd made an excuse to avoid that. She was trying to master the art of chili and he wasn't sure he'd survive it. He wasn't sure he'd survive the lesson, either. Tonight was East Coast swing, which Juliet had promised would make him look like a rock star on the dance floor. She and Neil had given him a demonstration after he'd passed nightclub two-step with flying colors and she'd declared him ready for something new. It looked like fun, except with all those spins and twists and flips, it also looked incredibly hard. But, hey, being a rock star wasn't all fun and games.

He played some Frisbee with Chica, ate a tuna sandwich and then showered and put on some cutoff jeans, along with his favorite T-shirt which said Real Men Play Chess.

Chica knew she was being abandoned and she wasn't happy about it. "Don't worry," Jonathan told her. "Adam will be home pretty soon."

Not that Adam was very good company these days. His date with Chelsea had been a disaster and, once more, she was refusing to take his calls, which made him sullen and antisocial. Actually, Jonathan didn't mind the fact that Adam had taken to hanging out in his makeshift bedroom, watching movies on his computer. It beat having him camped like a thundercloud on the living room couch, making snide remarks as Jonathan practiced his dance steps.

This sour-lemon version of Adam was someone Jonathan hadn't seen before. Normally the guy was fun to be with. He'd changed since Chelsea had kicked him out. Well, women did that to you. One minute you were happily boogying down the road of life. Then you met a girl, fell in love and you got detoured to Shit City where the sky was always gray.

Jonathan had visited there often enough, every time Lissa acquired a new boyfriend. Now he wanted to check out the real estate in someplace new. He hoped the dance lessons, among other things, would take him there.

A horrible smell greeted him as he walked into Juliet's house, along with the shriek of a smoke detector. He remembered a joke Neil had made once: "Dinner's ready when the smoke detector goes off." Juliet hadn't been pleased, and Jonathan had told him that wasn't funny. Instead of apologizing, he'd gotten defensive. "Why don't *you* eat dinner here every day for a couple of years and see how you like it?" Of course, Juliet had started to cry. Neil had apologized, and they'd kissed and made up. At the time Jonathan had thought he was a shit. But smelling this burned…whatever, Jonathan had to admit he'd probably get a little tired of bad cooking, too. He wondered if Juliet ever got tired of trying. And if she ever got tired of Neil.

This called to mind something she'd said when he showed up for his first dance lesson. *In the end we don't need a man who's perfect.* Good thing, because Neil wasn't perfect.

Jonathan knew he had no room to talk; he wasn't perfect, either. Had Lissa reached a point in life where her opinion was the same as Juliet's when it came to men? If she'd stopped looking for Mr. Perfect, maybe he had a chance.

He went out to the kitchen and found Neil and Juliet in a cloud of smoke. The kitchen door was open and she was trying to fan it outside while Neil waved a broom in the general direction of the smoke detector. "Babe, I know you like to read," he shouted over the noise, "but how about not doing it when there's something on the stove?"

"I'm sorry," she shouted back. "It really was going to be good chili."

"I know," he shouted, then swore and fanned the broom harder.

At last the smoke detector, having done its job, settled back into vigilant silence.

"Uh, hi, guys," Jonathan said.

"I hope you weren't invited for dinner," Neil muttered.

Jonathan was glad he'd been wise enough to wiggle out of it. Her husband couldn't do that.

Juliet looked sadly into the pan. "This is ruined."

"You think?" Neil said grumpily.

At that she burst into tears.

He was at her side in a shot, hugging her. "It's okay, babe. I felt like pizza tonight, anyway. How about I go over to Italian Alps and pick up a large mushroom and onion?"

She nodded and he left. "I suck at cooking," she said miserably.

There was an understatement. "Maybe you need lessons."

She frowned.

"Seriously, Jules. Maybe cooking is for you like dancing is for me. You just need some instruction. I bet if you took a class, you'd be great."

Well, maybe. He remembered a few sessions in the kitchen with their mom. The time Juliet started a fire on the stovetop was about the last time Mom insisted she learn how to cook.

She considered this. "Maybe that's not a bad idea. I think Neil's getting tired of my cooking."

Eating Juliet's cooking for four years—Neil wasn't a shit. He was a saint.

Jonathan watched as she tried to scrape the mess out of the pot. She'd have better luck finding the end of a black hole. She finally gave up and dumped the pot in the garbage. Now he knew what to get her for Christmas. Pots and pans and some cooking lessons. There was a present Neil would appreciate, too.

She looked like she was going to cry again, so

to distract her, Jonathan said, "Hey, what about that dance lesson?"

She wandered out of the kitchen, looking like a mourner leaving a gravesite.

But once she started talking about dance steps, the sad face vanished. "This is such a fun dance. Women love it."

Yeah, but did every woman know how to do it? "What if she doesn't know the steps?"

"It doesn't matter as long as you're a strong lead. Anyway, women pick up dance steps pretty quickly."

By the time Neil had returned with the pizza, they'd mastered the basic step and were moving on to a variation. "Lookin' good," he said.

But not feelin' good. Thanks to his workout at the gym, his arm was killing him. No pain, no gain, he reminded himself. Still, he was glad to take a break and join them.

After the pizza was consumed, Juliet was ready to teach Jonathan a new move. This proved to be more than his wounded muscle could take. He swore under his breath and dropped his arm.

"Are you okay?"

"Uh, yeah." He rubbed the screaming muscle.

"Did you work out today?" Neil asked.

Jonathan nodded. "I think I pulled something."

Neil disappeared into the kitchen, then came back a moment later with a bag of frozen peas and a tea towel. He wrapped the peas in the towel and pressed them to Jonathan's arm. "Ice, Advil and rest. And lay off the workouts for a couple of days."

Lay off? Just when he needed to be working harder. Like Juliet's cooking, this sucked.

Ever since returning to work after his mistaken-identity weekend, Kyle's cubicle had felt more like a refrigerator than a work space because of the frosty atmosphere between him and his cubicle buddy.

Make that *former* cubicle buddy. Mindy was a walking ice sculpture. Her polite good-mornings were enough to give him frostbite and there was no banter anymore. He was in outer Siberia and suddenly he hated his job. He'd never realized how much more fun she'd made it.

"She gave up on Ted," he heard Karen Carmichael saying to Sarah Schillman as he approached the water cooler. "Now she's on to someone new. She'd be perfect for a reality show. You could call it Gold Diggers of the Northwest."

Ow.

Sarah giggled, but on seeing Kyle, she said a quick "Hi, Kyle" to alert her friend to shut up.

Karen turned and saw him, and her face flushed tomato red. "Oh, hi, Kyle."

"Hi," he said with a disapproving frown. The women left but the comments lingered. Kyle got his cup of water and returned to outer Siberia, where Mindy was typing away in frozen silence.

He hadn't meant to hurt her. If he'd known the dinner invitation was from her, he would've turned her down right away. But instead she had to leave that cutesy little note. Why had she done that? Why hadn't she just asked him if he wanted to come over for dinner? Maybe asking in writing had seemed safer than doing it face-to-face.

He could identify with that. Many a time he'd sweated bullets over how to ask a girl out. It looked like connecting with the opposite sex wasn't any easier for women than it was for men.

Although Jillian had no problem. Was she really on to someone new? And if so, who?

By the end of the day, Kyle knew exactly who. Si Klcin, the company's top salesman, stopped by her desk and she lit up like Christmas in Icicle Falls' town square. Si said something, and she smiled and tossed her hair. She sure had recovered from her broken heart in a hurry.

Si was probably twenty years older than Jillian. His hair was thinning, he was getting a gut and he didn't drive a Jag. He drove a Mercedes convertible. And he had a condo in Vegas. The ugly truth walked up to Kyle and smacked him in the face. *She* is *a gold digger.*

And he was a fool. Like countless other men, he'd been taken in by a pretty face. He'd overlaid the real Jillian with a fantasy Jillian who was sweet and adorable and clever. Well, she was clever, he'd give her that—clever at finding men who had what she wanted and making them want her.

But they didn't stick with her. Darrow hadn't.

A conversation he'd once had with Mindy came back to him.

"Sometimes I think I'd rather be pretty than smart."

He hadn't known quite what to say. Mindy wasn't bad-looking. "Why's that?" he'd asked.

"Because men care more about pretty girls than they do smart ones."

Well, she was right in a way. Nobody wanted to date a dog. Still, "I dunno. There's got to be more to a woman than her looks. Otherwise, a man would get bored."

Now Kyle wondered why Darrow had dumped Jillian. It sure wasn't because the woman was unattractive. Something had turned him off. Was it because he'd looked behind the facade and saw there wasn't enough to hold his interest?

Kyle didn't want a facade, either. He wanted someone he could connect with. Now he realized it wasn't Jillian.

Following that hypothesis to its logical conclusion—if not Jillian then who? A vision of Mindy in shorts and a clingy top sneaked into the back of his mind. Too late. That Mindy was gone. She'd been replaced by the ice queen sitting next to him.

The atmosphere was far from festive when the guys sat down to play poker. Kyle was suffering from the pain of disillusionment and had concluded he was never going to find Ms. Right, let alone get laid anytime in the next century. Bernardo was grumpy because Anna was mad at him for cheating on his diet.

And Jonathan was frustrated, plagued by visions of buffness denied. On top of that setback, he'd gone to the eye doc and learned that yes, indeed, he still wasn't a candidate for Lasik surgery. He'd tried contacts and had no success, so that meant he was stuck with his glasses. Unbuff and bespectacled. How was he going to get Lissa's attention at this rate?

But everyone's problems paled compared to what Adam was going through. Chelsea still wanted nothing to do with him. "And we're gonna have a kid."

Jonathan felt a stab of envy. A kid. He wished he had a wife and was expecting a kid. Then he remembered the mess Adam was in.

"Congratulations," Bernardo said. "Now the fun really begins."

"So do the bills," added Vance.

"Is it a girl or a boy?" Kyle asked.

"How the hell should I know?" Adam growled. "I'm lucky I even know she's pregnant. I thought I was in trouble before, but now… Oh, man, I'm in deep shit."

"Since you're having a kid, I'd think she'd be more open to taking you back," Jonathan said. But what did he know?

"She would have. We were this close. Until I blew it. Damn. But it came at me out of nowhere."

"What did you do?" Bernardo asked.

Adam gave them the lowdown on his meeting with his wife. "Now she's back to not talking to me," he finished. "I should have said…something."

"You did," Vance pointed out. "You said the wrong thing."

"What the hell am I going to do?"

No one answered him. Probably, Jonathan figured, because no one had any idea what he should do.

"You know," Adam said, "it's funny how when you first meet a woman, all you see is a pretty face and a great body you want to get your hands on. Then you go out with her and things change. You can't get enough of seeing her, being with her. Before you know it, she's your best friend, your whole life. She gets to be like breathing, something you don't have to think about. You assume she'll always be there. You forget how much you need her, how much…"

Oh, no, Jonathan thought, *he's gonna cry.*

The crisis was averted when Adam turned a sob into a cough and cleared his throat. "I don't want to lose her."

"You ought to tell her what you just told us," Bernardo advised.

"Why don't you do something to show her you're glad about the kid?" Vance suggested. "That's a big thing to her."

"Hey, it's a big thing to me, too," Adam said. "But it's scary."

"Women never want to know you're scared," Vance told him. "It doesn't give 'em any confidence in you."

Adam frowned. "It shouldn't be this hard, dealing with women."

Vance's smile was cynical. "Yeah? Who said?"

The game continued halfheartedly. Until Bernardo ran out of money. Then, with a sly grin, he took the copy of *Wooing Willow* Adam had returned to him and laid it on the table.

"Hey, you were gonna lend that to me next," Kyle protested.

"Well, *amigo,* now maybe you can win it and keep it."

"That's mine," Kyle said. "Call."

Adam folded. "I'm done with it."

Vance showed his cards. He had a pair of kings.

Jonathan had garbage. He shoved in his cards, face-down.

"Ha!" Kyle crowed. "Three of a kind. Come to Papa."

The game resumed. Fortunes shifted, short-term loans were made. Pretty soon Jonathan was low on money. "Okay. I'm out of cash." He grabbed a couple more romance novels from his coffee table. "These should be worth a few chips."

A discussion ensued regarding how many chips a library sale paperback was worth.

"At least twenty blues," Jonathan argued. He held up Vanessa Valentine's *The Swan and the Leopard.*

"Oh, yeah, put that in," Bernardo said. "Anna hasn't read it yet."

"And what makes you think you're gonna win it?" Adam taunted.

"I'm feeling lucky now that Vance has lent me five bucks," Bernardo said.

The game continued and two more of Jonathan's books found their way to the poker table. "I'll see your Vanessa Valentine and raise you a Harlequin Super-Romance."

Vance let out a whistle. "High rollers. Fold."

Bernardo and Jonathan followed suit, and then it was down to Kyle and Adam.

Kyle scowled. "Fold. You were bluffing, weren't you?" he demanded as Adam raked in his winnings.

Adam just grinned.

Bernardo chuckled. "You scored big, *amigo*. Hope you read those and learn something."

"Man, I need to," Adam said. "I've got to get Chelsea back. I've got to make things right, got to show her I'm cool with the baby."

"Try doing what the hero in *A Delivery for the Doctor* did," Jonathan said. If anyone overheard this conversation, they'd think he and his friends were nuts.

"What did he do?" Adam asked.

"He went out and bought a bunch of stuff for the kid," Jonathan said. "Put a different gift on the woman's doorstep every day for a week."

"And then what happened?" Adam asked.

"The last day he stood on the doorstep with a big stuffed bear. She took him back."

"As easy as that, huh?" Adam mused.

Vance frowned. "Don't be a dip. When it comes to women, nothing is easy."

"But it's worth trying," Bernardo said.

Adam nodded vigorously. "At this point I'll try anything."

"Well, that takes care of you. Wish I could wrap up my love life like that," Kyle said sourly. "I was wrong about Jillian and I think I blew it with Mindy."

Bernardo looked confused. "Who's Mindy?"

"She works next to me. She's a lot of fun, and she doesn't care what kind of car a man drives." Kyle shook his head. "I keep asking myself, what would Vanessa Valentine do?"

"Yeah, well, we'd all like to know that," Adam said.

It occurred to Jonathan that Vanessa Valentine, queen of romance, would probably have the solution to all their problems. Was she anywhere in Washington? Did she ever make house calls? "I saw her on TV. I wonder where she lives."

"Are we gonna play cards or what?" Vance growled, and Kyle started dealing.

At the end of the evening Adam was the big winner. He held up a copy of *A Delivery for the Doctor*. "I'm reading this one first."

Bernardo took a handful of chocolate chip cookies out of the package on the counter. "Looks short enough. You should be able to handle it," he said with a grin. "*Hasta* Las Vegas, *amigos*."

The party broke up, Adam opened his book and Jonathan decided to check out Vanessa Valentine's website. He got his iPad and did a search. Of course, big-name writer that she was, her name came up all over the place. He didn't bother reading the articles and interviews but went straight to her website.

It wasn't what Jonathan had expected. Instead of a girlie home page, all pink and plastered with lacy hearts, Vanessa had opted for a simple, cream-colored page with her name written across it in a black scrawl. There was only one heart on the page, and it was her logo—a small, red heart with two interlocking *V*s inside it, which occupied the upper right-hand corner. Under her name he read, "Home of the bestselling romance writer." Various tabs took visitors to pages where they could read book excerpts, enter contests or check her appearance schedule.

He went to her bio. There she was, in her black suit and pearls, posing with arms crossed in front of a bookcase stuffed with Vanessa Valentine novels. He started reading. The woman had written a ton of books, been on every bestseller list known to man and even had one of her books made into a movie. And, whoa, what was this? She lived in Seattle!

He scooted over to the page that listed her appearances. She was all over the country, hitting every major city from New York to L.A. But hey, she was making an appearance in Seattle at Emerald City Books.

Emerald City Books? That was Vance's bookstore. Vanessa Valentine was coming to his bookstore and he hadn't said anything. What was with that? Who knew? But there was one thing Jonathan did know. He was going to Seattle to meet Vanessa Valentine.

Chapter Fourteen

Jonathan arrived at Emerald City Books on a balmy Tuesday evening. There hadn't been an inch of space on the street for blocks, and he could see why as he looked in the store window. He'd be lucky to find a seat.

A tall, middle-aged man in jeans and a polo shirt was walking a small Boston terrier back and forth on the sidewalk in front of the store. The dog saw Jonathan and went into a barking frenzy.

"No, Bubba," the man commanded.

Jonathan could tell Bubba was all bark and no bite. He knelt to pet the dog.

Sure enough, Bubba was happy to make instant friends with anyone who wanted to pet him and started jumping on Jonathan, licking his hands.

"Are you here for the signing?" Jonathan asked the man.

The guy looked at him as if he were insane. "My wife is."

And he and Bubba were keeping their distance. Jonathan understood. He'd been like that himself. Until he became enlightened.

He gave the dog a final pat, then entered the bookstore. Once inside he found himself in a steamy fog of perfume thick enough to give a guy an asthma attack. The Vanessa Valentine book party wasn't scheduled to start for another twenty minutes, but the store was packed with women of all ages and hotter than an oven in spite of an open door and two fans working overtime. And the noise level—between that, the perfume and the sight of women everywhere, he was teetering on the brink of sensory overload. Everyone was talking, laughing, eating chocolate and grabbing books.

The women came in all ages—good-looking babes decked out in tight jeans and clingy, sleeveless tops and not-so-good-looking babes, hiding extra pounds under baggy tops (he recognized that strategy—baggy tops worked to hide a lack of body, too). Then there were the cougars with fancy jewelry and tantalizing makeup, and older women, many with gray hair and spreading waistlines. It seemed half the women in Seattle were there, each one clutching the new Vanessa Valentine hardback. Many also carried other books, a mix of hard- and paperback, for her to sign, and Jonathan wished he'd brought his other Vanessa Valentine novels from home.

Watching the disappearing inventory, he decided to get over to the checkout counter before the store ran out. In addition to snagging a copy for himself, he wanted to get one for Bernardo's wife and for Juliet, who would kill him if he didn't bring her a book.

Heck, she was probably going to kill him when she found out he'd gone to this without her. But he was on a mission, and it wasn't the kind of mission where a guy brought his sister.

He swam through the sea of estrogen to the counter, where a pretty, brown-haired woman around his age was ringing up sales, along with the only other man in the place—Vance. It was Vance, wasn't it?

This version of Vance didn't look like him, though. He'd shaved, and he'd exchanged his slob uniform for slacks and a shirt and sport coat. Here in the store, with his game face on, he not only looked like a different man, he acted like one, too. He was smiling and genial, flirtatious even. It was as if his body had been taken over by an alien life force. Who was this Vance? Jonathan could feel his jaw dropping.

The alien Vance caught sight of him and mirrored Jonathan's expression. Then he frowned. "Jonathan. What the hell are you doing here?"

Jonathan frowned back. "I saw on Vanessa's website that she was doing a signing here. You coulda told us, you know."

"I didn't think you'd want to come. These things are a zoo. Anyway, I was going to bring you all signed copies."

"You were?" Now, that was darn nice of him.

Vance took four books off a rapidly shrinking stack. "Here. On the house."

"Thanks. Uh, can I have one more? For my sister. I'll pay."

Vance shoved another book at Jonathan. "What the

hell. Just take it. That stack is all presigned so now you can leave this circus."

Jonathan didn't want to leave the circus. "I'll stay. Juliet will want Vanessa to write something personal to her."

For some reason this didn't seem to make Vance all that happy, but he shrugged and said, "Suit yourself. But don't expect her to have time to talk to you."

That was exactly what Jonathan was hoping for.

"She's on a tight schedule and she doesn't want to be here all night. She can't stay and yak."

Jonathan supposed that was how it went with celebrities. What he wanted to ask was something no one in his right mind would ask someone like her. But he was going to do it, anyway.

Books in hand, he searched for a place to sit. The crowd had already taken up most of the folding chairs arranged in rows on one side of the store. If very many more people showed up, there wouldn't be enough to seat everyone.

As he scanned the rows of seats he got another surprise. There, over in a far front corner, was Pat from Mountain Escape Books, along with Cecily's mother, Muriel, and Dot Morrison. Oh, boy, this was awkward. Would they wonder what he was doing here? Of course they would. Enlightening as romance novels were, he was still embarrassed to 'fess up that he read them, especially in front of Dot, who was bound to have some dirty crack ready to embarrass him.

Maybe they wouldn't spot him in the crowd. He

positioned himself toward the back, next to a middle-aged woman who gave him a friendly once-over.

"It looks like you're a big fan," she observed.

He was suddenly conscious of a petite brunette settling in on his other side. Her curiosity was palpable and the room got even hotter. "Uh, these aren't for me," he explained.

"For the women in your life, right?" the woman asked, and he nodded.

"That's so sweet," said the brunette. "Is one of those for your girlfriend?"

Was she coming on to him? When was the last time *that* had happened? The answer was easy. Never. He couldn't help smiling. "No."

She cocked her head. "Got a girlfriend?"

"Not yet. But I hope I will soon." Had he just said that to a perfect stranger?

"Oh." She looked disappointed. "You're seeing someone."

He'd been "seeing someone" all his life. She'd just never seen him back. "Sort of."

"I should have known that a man who reads romance had to be taken," the brunette said.

Here was another benefit of reading romance, Jonathan realized. Obviously, carrying around a romance novel was almost as good as having a dog when it came to attracting women. Who knew?

As anticipation grew, so did the buzz of female voices. Women began checking the door for a first glimpse of Vanessa. Up near the front, Pat turned around in her seat, probably also looking for her.

Jonathan hunched down and dropped his gaze, willing himself to blend in with the crowd. It would have taken a grand wizard to accomplish that. He stuck out like a rhino at a tea party.

When he finally ventured to lift his head, it was to see Pat staring at him in astonishment. Now that they'd seen each other, though, she smiled and waved at him. He raised a hand in return and she leaned over and said something to Dot and Muriel. It wasn't hard to guess what, since they both turned, smiling and waving. Dot's smile was downright puckish.

He waved back, his own smile strained. Great. Just what he needed. Using a romance novel as a ploy to attract a woman was one thing; having all of Icicle Falls learn that he read them was another altogether. Maybe if he offered Dot free computer maintenance for life he could buy her silence.

"You've got a fan club," the middle-aged woman said.

Was that what you called it?

Now Vanessa Valentine was in the building, and a burble of excitement followed her as she worked her way through the crowd up to the front, where a podium stood ready for her and, nearby, a signing table decorated with a vase of red roses. Tonight she was wearing a flowery summer dress, her dark hair falling onto her shoulders. She was a pretty woman, and if Lissa hadn't owned Jonathan's heart, lock, stock and barrel, he'd have been smitten, in spite of the fact that Vanessa probably had ten years on him. He hoped his brain wouldn't freeze when it was his turn to talk to her.

Vance joined her at the front and held up his hand for silence. The women quickly obliged.

"Thanks, everyone, for coming out to meet Vanessa." He turned to her. "It's always a treat to have you at the store."

"I'm always happy to come see my friends at Emerald City Books," she said.

She'd been at the store before. She knew him. How come Vance never mentioned that when they were all talking about her books on poker night?

"And we have another popular writer here tonight. Muriel Sterling is with us. We carry several of her books," Vance continued, "and, if you want to buy one, I'm sure she'll be glad to sign it. Muriel, it's good to have you here."

Muriel murmured her thanks and added, "I'm a big Vanessa Valentine fan."

"Who isn't?" one of the women in the crowd called out, and several fans giggled.

"Before Vanessa reads from her new book, we're going to start by giving you all a chance to ask her some questions," Vance said.

A dozen hands shot up, and he pointed to a pimply-faced teenage girl in the front row. Jonathan had seen her earlier and felt sorry for her. In addition to the zit issue, she was overweight. It wasn't hard to imagine what life at school was like for her. Books were a world she could escape to, where she could enjoy vicarious pleasure as she watched the heroine work out her problems and come out on top. He hoped the girl would come out on top in her own life.

"Where do you get your ideas?" the girl asked.

"You know, they can come from anywhere. One place I love to find inspiration is in art museums. Paintings, especially traditional paintings, tell a story. Sometimes I'll see a woman in a painting and it's as if she's saying, 'Tell my story, Vanessa.'"

Pretty impressive, thought Jonathan.

"How did you get started?" the girl asked in a small voice.

"By writing all the time. If you work hard, you can make your dreams come true."

The girl beamed at Vanessa, and with her smile her whole face lit up. There was a pretty girl in there. Jonathan hoped she'd find someone who could really see her.

Another woman asked, "How long does it take you to write a book?"

"That depends," Vanessa said. "Each book is different."

The answer seemed a little vague to Jonathan, but the crowd was satisfied.

"How do you write?" another woman asked. "At a computer?"

"Oh, not at first. I have a lovely garden, and in the summer I like to sit outside on my patio with a glass of lemonade and write on a tablet. In winter, I sit in my sunroom with a vanilla candle burning and Adele playing in the background."

"What do you drink then?" someone called.

"Tea. Lady Grey."

Jonathan wasn't sure what tea had to do with writing, but the women all nodded like members of an exclusive club who knew exactly what she was talking about.

Vance ended the chitchat. "I know you all want to hear Vanessa read, and we have to save time for her to sign your books. So, Vanessa, are you ready?"

"Of course." She slipped behind the podium, opened her book and began to read.

The women—and Jonathan—listened, spellbound. Who'd have thought tea and candles could inspire all that?

"'Jean Pierre picked up his sword. The old wound hadn't healed, but he couldn't wait for that. If he did, it would be too late to save Lily Auguste. Her life was infinitely more precious than his. His only regret was that now he would most likely die without ever having kissed her. He would die before he had ever really lived.'" Vanessa stopped there and shut the book.

There was a moment of awed silence, and then the room exploded in applause. And no one was clapping harder than Jonathan. Man, that was good stuff.

Vance was back in control. "All right, ladies, if you'll form a line to my left, Vanessa will sign now."

Again, Jonathan marveled at how different Vance was in this environment. Every bit of snark had been buried under a veneer of charm.

The women surged forward but Jonathan stayed at the back of the bookstore, happy to let her other fans go ahead of him. He didn't need eavesdroppers.

Vance joined him. "You still here?"

"Yep." He held up the books. "I'm gonna get all

these personalized. By the way, why didn't you tell us you knew her?" Jonathan added accusingly.

"What, you want a date?"

"I want to meet her. I'm thinking she might have some good advice."

Vance looked heavenward and shook his head. "She writes fiction. Remember? It's all made up. She's not Dear Abby."

"Well, I still want to meet her."

"Suit yourself," Vance said again, and left him to go ring up sales.

The line moved slowly. Everyone wanted to meet Vanessa.

Pat, Muriel and Dot, who had been near the front of the line, were now leaving the party. They stopped next to where Jonathan stood.

"Jonathan, I didn't know you read Vanessa Valentine novels," Pat greeted him.

"He's reading them for the hot sex," Dot teased. "God knows that's why I read them."

As usual, Dot had succeeded in making him blush. "I'm getting a book for my sister. And…the others are for her friends," he announced on a burst of inspiration.

"That's sweet of you," Pat said. "Juliet was really disappointed to miss out."

His sister had known about this? Sheesh. *She* could have told him.

"It's too bad she got sick at the last minute," Muriel remarked.

"I guess she didn't need me to get a book for her, then," Dot said.

"If we'd known you were coming you could have ridden over with us," Muriel told Jonathan.

"Jonathan wouldn't want to be trapped in a car listening to three women talk about romance novels," Dot said. "Anyway, you'd have been stuck here. We're spending the night in town, staying at the Sorrento and then doing the Pike Place Market tomorrow."

The middle-aged woman he'd been sitting next to had been eavesdropping shamelessly and now joined the conversation. "Oh, I love the market. I always come home with one of those beautiful flower bouquets."

And so the conversation continued, with two more women joining in. Jonathan felt a little like he was in the middle of a cluster of rapidly multiplying cells, talking cells that made it hard to concentrate on what he wanted to say to Vanessa.

Dot and company finally left and Jonathan breathed a little easier. They'd stood talking for so long, he'd begun to worry that maybe they'd wind up accompanying him right to where Vanessa sat and listening in on their conversation.

Speaking of listening in… He turned to the middle-aged woman behind him. "Why don't you go ahead of me."

"Oh, no. I don't mind waiting my turn."

He could see her now, jumping into the conversation. *You want help with your love life? How interest-*

ing! "No, it's okay," he said, motioning her forward. Far away. Then he moved to the very end of the line.

It was an hour before everyone else had finished talking to Vanessa and Jonathan finally got his turn. She was wearing a wedding ring and a fat diamond. Jonathan tried to tell himself that because she was married, she was less intimidating. It didn't work.

"That's quite a pile of books," she said. "Are you doing your Christmas shopping?"

"No." *Impressive, Jonathan.* He pushed his glasses up his nose. "One's for my sister." He set the book on the table. "Can you sign it to Juliet?"

"Sure."

She personalized it and he put another book in front of her. "And for Anna."

She signed that one and looked up expectantly.

He laid down two more. "And for Adam and Kyle. They're my friends."

She smiled. "Your friends have good taste in books."

"We all play poker. With Vance," he added, nodding to where Vance stood at the register, along with the younger woman, bagging a book for one of the last customers.

"So you're one of Vance's buddies."

Jonathan nodded again. "We all read your books. We're, um…" Oh, boy. This was going to sound so stupid. "We're…" He scratched the back of his head. "They make good textbooks."

"Textbooks," she repeated, and held out her hand for the last copy.

Jonathan passed it over. "Can you sign this one to me?"

"And you are…?"

"Oh, uh, Jonathan." *The village idiot.* His face burned.

"So, Jonathan, tell me more about how my novels make good textbooks."

"Well, they're all about, uh, love. And getting it right. And my friends and I—we need to get it right."

"I see." She was serious now, and the teasing light was gone from her eyes.

Jonathan cleared his throat. "I need an expert."

"I'm not exactly an expert."

"When it comes to a guy being a hero, you are. Your men always know what to say and do."

Now she looked uncomfortable.

"Not at first, maybe," he hurried on. "But they figure things out. I need help figuring things out. So does my pal Kyle. Bernardo, well, he's got it together, but he'd love to meet you, anyway. And Adam, he's really in a mess. His wife is so mad at him she kicked him out. But they're gonna have their first kid. He's got to get his act together."

"Sounds like it," she agreed.

Good. She saw the need. Now he had to put it all on the line and ask. "I read on your website that you live here in Seattle, and I was hoping maybe you'd be willing to come to Icicle Falls and meet the guys, let them pick your brain. It's a great town. We'd pay for your lodging. And feed you."

"What the hell are you doing?" demanded a gruff voice at his elbow.

Jonathan turned to see Vance scowling at him. The burn on his face got hotter. "I'm just seeing if Vanessa would like to meet the guys."

"Jon, she's a busy woman. She has other appearances. Deadlines."

Of course she did. He'd been stupid to think a big-name author would have time to come all the way to Icicle Falls and act as a personal love coach to him and his friends.

"When?"

Jonathan blinked. "What?"

"When?" Vanessa repeated.

"Vanessa, you don't have time for this," Vance told her.

"Maybe I do. For your friends," she added, sounding more like his mother than his guest author. "Anyway, Pat from Mountain Escape Books was asking me earlier if I'd like to come up and do a book signing. That would be fun. So, when were you thinking?" She looked expectantly at Jonathan.

"Uh, Friday night?"

She nodded. "Absolutely. It so happens that I'm free this weekend. You can show me around town on Friday and I can meet your friends. Then I'll sign books at the store on Saturday." She turned to Vance. "I think it's high time some of your friends met Vanessa Valentine, Vance. Don't you?"

Vance didn't look at all happy to share. "Just remember what I told you," he cautioned Jonathan. "She's not Dear Abby."

No. She was even better.

He called Kyle as he walked to his car. "I just scored big-time."

"Yeah?" Kyle sounded surprised. "With who?"

"Vanessa Valentine."

"What!"

"I just met Vanessa Valentine."

"And she slept with you?" Kyle asked, incredulous.

"No, you dork. I didn't score *that* way. I asked her to come and meet with us on Friday and…she's coming."

"Seriously?"

"Yep."

"Oh, man, that rocks."

"We're gonna have to put her up somewhere, though. Can you chip in?"

"Where?" Kyle asked suspiciously.

"I'm thinking Icicle Creek Lodge."

"That's kind of pricey."

"She's a big-name author. I've got to put her someplace nice. And the lodge is the nicest place in town."

"Yeah, I guess you're right. Count me in," Kyle said.

"Me, too," Bernardo agreed when Jonathan called him. "I'm going to have her sign every book of hers we own. Anna will be thrilled."

"You're shittin' me," Adam said when Jonathan got home and shared his big news.

"Nope. She's coming." Jonathan pulled a beer from

the fridge and plopped down on the couch. "This is gonna be *great*."

The only one who didn't think it was going to be great was Vance. "You guys are a bunch of clucks," he said when Jonathan called to see if wanted to throw in some bucks toward her lodging and entertainment.

Maybe, but they were an excited bunch of clucks. The rest of the week, when he wasn't busy with customers, Jonathan spent his free time cleaning. Adam pitched in, too, ordering flowers from Lupine Floral and, on Friday, picking up fancy cream puffs from Gingerbread Haus. Bernardo and Kyle contributed champagne and chocolate and a scented candle because, according to Kyle, Jonathan's place smelled like dog.

Vanessa arrived in town around noon on Friday and, squired by Vance, met Jonathan for lunch at Schwangau. He was having lunch with Vanessa Valentine. He could hardly believe it.

"You know, this is one of my favorite restaurants," she confessed as they were seated in at a corner table.

"You've been here before?" Jonathan asked, surprised.

"A couple of times, when I've come up to see my brother."

"You have a brother who lives here?" Who the heck was her brother?

"Oh, yes. He doesn't invite me here very often, which is too bad since I love the shops."

"He probably realizes how busy you are," Vance said.

"Family is important, though. You know that, Vance."

"Of course," he said, and looked distinctly uncomfortable.

"I bet you didn't know Vance has a daughter," Vanessa said to Jonathan.

"Yeah, I heard." Jonathan didn't normally get nosy but he couldn't help asking, "Does she live anywhere around here?"

"Over in Seattle. She's a good kid," Vance said.

"Yes, she is. And Vance is a good father."

Jonathan noticed the way Vanessa smiled at Vance when she said that. There was some emotion packed into that smile. Did Vance have something going with this woman? Maybe they were just friends. Close friends.

"That's enough about me," Vance said firmly. "Why don't you tell Jonathan about the new book you're working on."

"Well, I don't know too much about it yet. I'm still getting to know my characters."

"I guess it takes a while," Jonathan said.

"It can. It's not easy being a writer." She flashed Vance a smile. "People don't always understand you." Now she sobered. "And a lot of writers have a tendency to bury themselves in their work and hide from life."

Vanessa didn't strike Jonathan as the type of person to hide from life and he said so.

"You'd be surprised," she said.

Vance picked up his menu. "So, what looks good? I think I'll have the sauerbraten."

The rest of lunch was taken up with conversation, mostly Vanessa talking about the different cities she'd visited on her book tours and how glad she was to have some time at home with her husband and her cats.

But then it got personal. She wanted to know how Jonathan had discovered her and what, specifically, he'd learned from reading her books.

"I've made a list," he confessed, "but I'm not sure how to follow it."

Vance sighed loudly. "This stuff between men and women, you can't learn it from a book. You've got to get out there and live it."

"And keep living it," Vanessa said, looking pointedly at Vance.

He shook his head. "I'm too old for that."

"You're never too old for love," she insisted. "And it's never too late to learn," she said to Jonathan. "But I don't know if I'm the one to teach you."

She wasn't going to back out, was she? "No, you are. You're the closest thing to an expert we've got."

She leaned back in her seat and studied him. "You poor, deluded man."

"So, who's for dessert?" Vance asked.

After lunch, they visited Pat at Mountain Escape Books. Then Vanessa wanted to shop. "I'd love to go in that cute little shop with all the nutcrackers in the window," she said. "Oh, and the one with the imported lace."

Jonathan wasn't interested in nutcrackers or imported lace. And he wasn't wild about running into Tina, which they were bound to do since the lace shop was hers, but he valiantly said, "Sure."

"I can take her if you need to work," Vance offered, clearly anxious to be rid of Jonathan.

Now Jonathan knew what was going on. Vanessa was Vance's Lissa. She considered him a good friend; he wanted it to be more. But it couldn't be. Vanessa was married.

And she obviously needed someone along to make sure Vance behaved himself. "I don't have anything planned," Jonathan said.

Vance shrugged. "Fine."

So the three of them went to the cute little shop with all the nutcrackers, where Vanessa bought several. "I always like to shop ahead for Christmas," she explained.

Then they went to the lace shop, where Tina fawned all over Vanessa and looked frankly shocked to see that she was with Jonathan. "Jonathan, you never told me you knew Vanessa Valentine."

As if he and Tina were good buds and he'd simply forgotten to mention it. He didn't even try to respond to that.

He didn't need to. Vanessa linked her arm through his. "Jonathan and I are friends. Aren't we, Jonathan?"

They were? "Uh, yeah."

Once outside the shop she said, "Don't tell me, let me guess. That woman thinks she's better than you."

Jonathan blinked. "Well. Yeah."

Vanessa wagged a finger at him. "Don't ever let women like that intimidate you."

His first advice from Vanessa Valentine. He wasn't sure he could follow it, but he appreciated it.

"I could have told him that," Vance muttered.

"But I bet you didn't," she retorted.

Vance just kept walking.

Vanessa dragged them from shop to shop for two more hours. They looked at everything from Christmas ornaments to funny hats. They visited Gingerbread Haus and Jonathan bought her one of Cass Wilkes's popular gingerbread boys. Then it was off for more shopping. Jonathan's feet were beginning to hurt. How did women have the stamina for all that shopping?

By five o'clock shops were starting to close. "I'll take you over to the lodge," Vance said to Vanessa.

Did he want time alone with her? What was going on with these two? "Would you like to go out to dinner?" Jonathan asked. No matter what was going on, he was determined to be a good host.

"Actually, Vance and I need to discuss a few things," Vanessa said, and suddenly Vance seemed uncomfortable.

"Uh, okay," Jonathan said.

What the heck did they need to discuss? Whatever it might be, it was none of his business.

"I'll bring her by at seven," Vance promised.

Jonathan had secretly hoped for a chance to talk to her about his situation with Lissa at some point during the day, but shopping had been all-consuming.

So it looked like he'd have to wait until later, like the rest of the gang. He hoped she'd have time to solve all their problems.

By quarter to seven, four men, showered, shaved and dressed in their best clothes, waited in Jonathan's living room for their heroine to arrive.

Bernardo had brought a stack of books for Vanessa to sign for his wife. "Anna's pissed she didn't get to come," he said.

"This isn't a party. This is serious business," Adam said. "We need help."

"Not all of us," Bernardo informed him.

Vance's car pulled up outside.

"She's here," Jonathan announced, his heart banging like a jackhammer. He pushed his glasses up his nose and started for the door.

"I don't see her," Kyle said, looking out the window. "All I see is Vance."

"What happened to her?" Adam turned to Jonathan in panic. "You were just with her today."

"Maybe she's...I don't know." Where *was* she? Jonathan opened the front door and in walked Vance. All by himself.

"Where's Vanessa?" Jonathan demanded.

"Right here," Vance said. "You're lookin' at her."

"Real funny," Adam snapped. "Now, where is she?"

"Like I said, you're lookin' at her. I'm Vanessa Valentine."

Bernardo guffawed. "Right."

"Yeah, you look just like her," Kyle added.

Vance walked over to the counter. "Flowers. You

shouldn't have." He picked up the box of chocolates. "For me? You fellas went all out."

Jonathan snatched them away. "Those aren't for you."

"If they're for Vanessa, they're for me." Vance snatched them back. "I tried to talk you fools out of this, but you wouldn't listen to me." He settled in Jonathan's recliner, opened the box and helped himself to a truffle.

"You *can't* be her," Kyle protested.

"Of course I can. Ever hear of a pen name? Otherwise known as a pseudonym."

Jonathan felt as though he'd entered a parallel universe. "But the woman at the book signing, the woman we were with all day—"

"Is my younger sister, Valerie," Vance said, and popped another chocolate in his mouth. "She handles all my publicity and acts as my front woman when I need to make appearances." He frowned. "She gave me hell for not telling you guys and threatened to tell you herself if I didn't 'fess up."

The shock reverberated around the room as the men realized their idol had feet of clay. Big, hairy feet.

Kyle made a face. "You wrote those sex scenes I read? Oh, man. I'm gonna puke."

"I can't believe it," Jonathan said, and sank onto the couch. Except that did explain the fond look she'd given Vance earlier at lunch. No wonder she knew so much about him! "I thought maybe you two had a thing going."

"You thought I was getting it on with a married

woman?" Vance snorted in disgust. "I've got standards, you know."

"Some standards." Adam pointed a finger at Vance. "All this time, you let us make fools of ourselves, let us think there was actually something to those stupid books."

Vance lifted his shoulders. "There is."

Jonathan wanted to walk right over and punch Vance in that smug face of his. Instead, he asked, "How'd you ever get started writing chick books, anyway?"

Vance's whole face shut down. "None of your business."

"Yeah, it is," Adam said. "You made fools of all of us."

"Nope. You made fools of yourselves."

"My wife loves your books," Bernardo said. "I'd really like to know how you got started."

Vance stared out the window. Finally he said, "My first wife—"

"First wife?" There was more than one?

Vance ignored Jonathan's outburst. "—she was hell in high heels. The woman was psycho." He shook his head. "After we got divorced, I vowed never again. But then I met Lydia. She was the sweetest woman— always happy, always laughing. And she loved romance novels. She started writing one, had her pen name all picked out."

"Vanessa Valentine," Jonathan guessed.

"She never got a chance to finish it."

"Shit," Adam said in a low voice. "She died?"

Vance nodded. "Breast cancer. Twelve years ago. I finished the book for her. Learned about the business, found an agent. Got it published." He gave a mirthless chuckle. "Even dedicated it to her—'For Lyddie. You finally got your happy ending.'"

"But you didn't stop with that one book," Jonathan said.

Vance was looking at the woodland scene outside Jonathan's dining room window and seeing something none of the other men could. "No, I didn't. I kept going. I decided the best way I could keep her memory alive was to make her a household name." He shrugged. "Anyway, I got so I liked doing this. Every time I wrote, it felt like she was sitting right there with me. Still does."

"Ah, now *there* is a story you should write, *amigo,*" Bernardo said.

"That's cool and all, but damn, I thought you owned a bookstore." Kyle's tone of voice plainly said he felt cheated.

"I do. I bought it so my kid would have a job." He shook his head again. "She was a lit major. Not much you can do with that. She runs the store."

"Was that the woman ringing up sales at the book signing?" Jonathan asked.

"Yeah, that's her. Emily."

He never would have figured it out. Other than having similar coloring, she didn't look anything like Vance. Which was a good thing for her. "But those books... They sound like something a woman would write," Jonathan said. "How do you do that?"

Vance shrugged. "I ask myself what my wife would do. If I go too far off base my sister pulls me back. She reads everything before I turn it in to my editor. Like I said, you can thank her for getting me here. She thought it was only fair to tell you guys the truth. By the way, we canceled the reservation at the lodge. You're all getting a refund."

"Yeah, well, it would've been nice if you'd told us a few books back," Adam growled. "I spent a fortune."

"Hey, you got a good read out of the deal," Vance shot back.

"We weren't buying them for a good read," Jonathan said. Although he *had* enjoyed the books.

"Yeah, I know. You all want to learn how to fix your woman problems."

"That's a bust," Adam grumbled.

"Oh, quit your whining. There's still good information in those books. My sister makes sure of that. And those other books you've been reading, those were written by women," Vance added.

"How do you know?" Adam asked.

"I go to the writers' conferences with my sister."

"What, in drag?" Adam demanded.

"No, as her business manager. I've met most of the authors."

Jonathan frowned. "I was hoping for some one-on-one coaching."

"Me, too," Adam said grumpily.

Vance shook his head. "You don't need it. Think of Dorothy."

Dorothy? Jonathan didn't remember a Dorothy in

any of the Vanessa Valentine novels. "Which one of your books is she in?"

"None. Didn't you clowns ever watch *The Wizard of Oz?*"

"When I was a kid," Jonathan said. Where were they going with this?

Vance frowned at their obtuseness. "Come on. The wizard at the end told her she'd always had what she needed to get home. With the number of books you've read, you guys have all the information you need to get your women. You just have to use it."

Adam stared at him. "That's it? That's all the help we're gonna get from the great Vanessa Valentine?"

"It's all the advice you need. Oh, and try to think like a woman. Now, let's eat."

Try to think like a woman. No problem.

Jonathan went to the fridge and pulled out the cream puffs. They were on a fancy plate he'd borrowed from his mother. He set them on the counter. "Here...Vanessa," he said bitterly.

Vance joined him and slapped him on the back. "Thanks."

Jonathan frowned. "I really wanted to get some expert advice, not *Wizard of Oz* crap."

Vance expelled a long-suffering sigh. "Okay, what do you want to know?"

Jonathan shook his head. Maybe Vance and Vanessa were the same in real life but they sure weren't in his mind. "Forget it."

"You've been reading those books, taking notes

like crazy. I don't know who you're after, but whoever she is, you just need to apply what you've learned."

Yeah, and click his ruby shoes together and chant, "There's no place like home."

"Pay attention and tell her what she wants to hear— give her what she wants." Vance poked him in the shoulder. "Don't give up, kid. You're on the right track."

"How do you know? You're a guy," Jonathan retorted in frustration.

"I'm not writing this stuff in a vacuum and I've been around the block a few times. I know this much—you act like a hero, you'll get the girl. Love always wins in the end."

Vance helped himself to a cream puff. "Just remember to find yourself a woman with a big heart, one who looks beyond the cover-model pecs, and you'll be okay."

And with that bit of helpful advice, Vanessa Valentine, aka Vance Fish, took his cream puff and walked over to Jonathan's kitchen table. "Come on, let's play cards."

Jonathan would play cards, but he was done gambling for Vanessa Valentine novels.

He didn't buy a book at the signing at Mountain Escape Books the following day, either. He didn't even go.

"I can't believe it," his sister said when he showed up for his next dance lesson. "Vanessa Valentine is a *man*?"

Jonathan nodded glumly. "And I thought maybe I'd learn something about women from those books. Everything the heroes did was bogus."

"No, it wasn't," Juliet said. "Everything they did was right. Romantic and noble."

"But they're written by a guy," Jonathan protested.

"Well, I don't care if they're written by a space alien. They're wonderful books. And those heroes are the kind of men women dream about." She smiled at Jonathan. "A good man is a good man, no matter who's telling his story. And not every book you read was written by Vance. Anyway, believe me, if more men would read romance novels, there'd be more happy marriages."

Uh-oh. Wasn't Juliet happy?

As if reading his mind, she shook her head at him. "Don't worry. I'm perfectly happy with Neil. I know sometimes he says dumb things and sometimes I do dumb things, but we always make up. He'd do anything for me, and in the end that's what counts." She grinned. "Still, if he'd read a few romance novels, he'd sure get some brownie points." She sighed. "Why can't more men be like romance-novel heroes?"

Probably because trying to become one was practically a full-time job. Still, if a guy did the job well, maybe it paid off, Jonathan told himself. After his disappointment over Vanessa Valentine, he'd been ready to pack in this whole romance-hero scheme, but now, listening to his sister, he changed his mind. No matter who was writing this stuff, they knew something he didn't. Which wasn't saying a lot.

During their dance lesson, Juliet raved over the progress he was making, and by the time he'd finished, he'd come to two important conclusions. One, although he didn't have the dancing gene he could overcome his handicap with hard work. And two, if Vance could write a romance so could he, and he was going to write a real-life one. With Lissa.

Chapter Fifteen

On Saturday Adam entered a new shop in downtown Icicle Falls. Crossing the threshold of Oh, Baby was like setting foot on foreign soil—in a place where there were no men. Women in varying stages of pregnancy browsed among doll-clothes-size dresses and tiny football and basketball jerseys. Tables were piled with blankets and sets of what looked like blue and pink long underwear. He saw bonnets, miniature sundresses and shoes that were small enough to fit in the palm of his hand. Babies were so little. How did you handle one without breaking it?

A surge of terror rose in him and swirled into the excitement already present. This was really happening. Was he ready to be a dad? He hadn't even mastered being a husband.

But he was working on that. People could change. He'd be a better husband and he'd be a great dad, too, one who really deserved that Father's Day tie.

It seemed appropriate that he was starting his campaign to prove himself a worthy husband and father on Father's Day weekend. Tomorrow, just like in the book he'd read, he'd lay a gift on Chelsea's front porch with a note attached. The next day, another would appear with another note and so on until the following Saturday. Then he'd show up and ask her to Zelda's grand opening night. He'd already made reservations for eight o'clock. Lucky for him he'd called when he had. Charley, who owned the restaurant, told him he'd gotten the last available table.

He hoped this plan worked. If it didn't he was out of ideas and out of luck.

Where to start? What to get? Everyone in here was staring at him. It was like they were gang members and he'd wandered onto their turf. He looked around and fought the desire to run.

A short brunette who seemed to be in her mid-thirties greeted him. She was the only one, besides him, who didn't have a bulging belly, which meant she was probably the owner. "Hi. Is there anything I can help you with?"

"I'm having a baby," he said. Several women smiled and one snickered, making him feel even stupider and more exposed. He might as well have been walking around in his underwear. He cleared his throat. "I want to buy some baby stuff."

"Well, you've come to the right place," the woman said. "Do you know what you're having?"

"A baby." More snickers. "I mean, I don't know if we're having a boy or a girl. We just found out."

"Well, you can probably use almost anything, then," the woman said.

"I need seven presents," Adam said. "I want to give my wife one a day."

"Oh, that's so sweet," said a woman who was standing nearby, checking out blankets. She looked like she had a watermelon under her dress.

Oddly enough, she looked kind of sexy. Adam imagined Chelsea with a big belly, a belly growing their baby. He smiled.

"Maybe a mix of necessary basics and fun things?" the shop owner suggested. She picked up something with a bunch of snaps. "How about a Onesie? If you go with a neutral color like green or yellow, you'll be fine whether it's a boy or a girl."

The watermelon woman stepped over, holding a light green blanket that made him think of ice cream. "This would be nice," she suggested.

"Thanks," he said. The panic began to subside.

Now another woman was at his side. "Here's something cute."

It was a sort of pajama thing—orange with tiger stripes.

"Oh, and you'll need these," another woman said, handing him a package of bibs.

Before he knew it, he had an armload of baby things. "I think you met your quota," the shop owner teased.

All except the last present, which had to make a statement. And there it was, sitting on a shelf, beckoning him—a big, blue stuffed elephant. *An elephant never forgets.* And he wasn't going to forget the lessons he was learning the hard way. "I'll take that elephant, too," he said, pointing to it. "And can you wrap all of these up?"

"Of course," said the owner. "How about a variety? Some in gift boxes, some in bags?"

"Sure." He didn't care how she did it. It all just needed to look nice.

"Your wife's a lucky lady," said the watermelon woman, smiling at him.

"No, I'm a lucky man," he corrected her. He was lucky to have found Chelsea. Now, with a little more luck, maybe he could keep her.

Father's Day was still hard for Jonathan. This Father's Day was especially hard. He kept thinking how proud his dad would have been to see some muscle actually forming on his scrawny son. He could have talked with Dad about Lissa, asked him for advice on how to proceed. Instead, he was going out with his family to Der Spaniard in memory of Dad.

"Your father loved to eat here," Mom said.

This was hardly a newsflash but sharing it obviously made her feel good, so Jonathan nodded.

"I wish he was still here," Juliet said, "because this is a very special Father's Day."

She was smiling like a woman who'd won a free shopping spree. Happy sister, comment about this being a special Father's Day—it could mean only one thing. Jonathan didn't steal her thunder by guessing her news.

Sure enough. She and Neil exchanged sappy grins, then she announced, "We're pregnant."

"Oh, darling, that's wonderful!" her mother cried, and hugged her.

"Congrats, man," Jonathan said, shaking Neil's hand.

"Thanks." Neil was looking like he'd won the Nobel Prize for science.

Jonathan couldn't blame him. They'd been trying for two years.

Mom dabbed at her eyes with her napkin. "Our first grandchild. Your father would have been over the moon."

"I'll be an uncle." Jonathan smiled. "Uncle Jon. I'll teach him how to play chess."

"No nerd stuff," Neil said firmly, making Jonathan frown.

"What if he's a she?" asked his wife.

"Girls can play sports," Neil said.

"They can be smart and play chess, too," Juliet pointed out.

"And they can learn to cook," her mother said. Then, as if realizing she might have stepped in it, she took a quick drink of her lemonade.

"Actually, I'm learning to cook," Juliet said.

When? This was news to Jonathan.

"I signed up for a class Olivia's offering at the inn. It's called Comfort Cooking and we're going to make old classics with new twists."

"I can hardly wait to see how you twist those," Neil said.

Neil needed to read some romance novels.

"Or you can just take over the cooking," Juliet told

him. "Because," she added, "next time you insult my cooking, that's what's going to happen. I'm tired of it."

Her lower lip was trembling and her eyes were filling with tears. This was awkward. Jonathan got busy on his enchiladas and Mom took a sudden interest in something outside the restaurant window.

"Hey, babe. I'm sorry," Neil said, and covered her hand with his.

"I know I should have been a better cook," she continued. "And now that we're starting a family, I'm going to learn. I want to set a good example for my daughter. Or son. And I want you to set a good example, too, so no more insults. My daddy never insulted my mom."

"Okay, got it," Neil said, and he suddenly got busy with his enchiladas.

"Have you thought about names?" Mom asked, moving them away from the awkward moment.

Juliet smiled. "We still haven't agreed on a girl's name, but for a boy, we're thinking Jonathan."

Jonathan nearly dropped his glass. "What?"

Juliet beamed at him. "In honor of a good brother and a good man."

Naming their son after a nerd? What did Neil think about this? "Are you okay with it?" he asked Neil.

"Yeah." Neil pointed his fork at Jonathan. "But you still don't get to teach him chess."

"Unless he wants to learn," Juliet corrected.

The possibility of having a namesake had him so choked up he could barely say thanks but he managed.

"And don't worry," Juliet said to Mom. "He'll have Daddy's name, too."

"Jonathan Frederick. It has a nice ring to it," Mom said.

Jonathan figured the kid would rather be called Jon than Fred. Thank God his parents hadn't named him Fred, Jr. He'd had enough to cope with in high school as it was.

"Well," Mom said, raising her glass, "here's to our new family member."

"To the new member," Jonathan echoed, and they all clinked glasses.

For the rest of the meal, talk centered on the baby, and that was fine with Jonathan. His sister had waited a long time for this and he was happy for her.

A nasty little gremlin hopped onto his shoulder and whispered in his ear, "This may be the closest you ever come to getting a kid. You're a nerd and a loser."

You act like a hero, you'll get the girl. Vance's words came back to him and he used them like a sword, taking out the gremlin with one swift move. Damn it all, he *was* going to get the girl.

Of course, Chelsea wasn't home when Adam pulled up. But Dennis the Menace was out, mowing his lawn. Was that all the man ever did?

He waved at Adam and turned off the mower. "She's not home."

He didn't need old Dennis to tell him what he already knew. It was Father's Day and she'd be in Seattle with her family. They'd always spent Father's Day weekend over there. Right now he was sure she was at the Windjammer with her father and her two sisters and their families, enjoying a crab Louie. And telling everyone what a rat he was.

But he was done with rathood. He was a new man. Hopefully, these presents would prove it.

Here was Dennis again, intruding on his thoughts. "She's in Seattle, visiting her family."

A nasty little jab. "I know," Adam said through clenched teeth. "Father's Day," he added, getting in a jab of his own. "How come you're not with your kids?"

"Saw them yesterday," Dennis said.

Instead of returning to his own lawn and his own business, he stood there, smiling a rival's smile, eyeing the package in Adam's hand. Had Chelsea mentioned to him that she was pregnant?

Now he nodded at it. "Chelsea's birthday?"

"No," Adam said. It was none of this slimy little predator's business what the gift was for. Adam marched up to the porch and left his offering there. Then he marched back down the walk.

"I'll see she gets that," Dennis called.

Like he was her personal assistant? Or her boyfriend? It was all Adam could do not to walk over there and punch that superior expression off his face. "She'll find it," he said curtly.

Dennis shrugged and started his mower back up.

Adam imagined him running over his foot and smiled.

But his smile didn't last long. It was hard to smile standing on the edge of a ruined marriage.

It's not ruined, he told himself. At least it wasn't yet. He could still make things right. By next Father's Day he wanted to be a family, not a divorce statistic.

Father's Day. When he was little, it had been a day for backyard barbecues and a chance to play with his cousins. After his dad split, it had turned into a rare opportunity to hang out with his old man. Dad would take him and his older brother, Greg, to see the Mariners play or out to Wild Waves water park. Those times were fun but they couldn't make up for his dad not being around much the rest of the year. Staying at Dad's apartment every other weekend was a novelty that quickly wore off. The weekend was always over too soon. And then when Dad got a new wife who came with sons of her own... Adam frowned. He didn't want his kid to have to compete with some stepbrother or -sister.

He drove back to Jonathan's, his home away from home, where he settled on the porch with the dog for company and put in a call to his dad. Maybe he'd have some sage advice. After all, he'd screwed up two marriages. He had to have learned *something* from that.

The old man answered on the second ring.

"Hey, Pops, I'm calling to wish you a happy Father's Day," Adam said. "How's it going?"

"Oh, all right."

"You doing anything today?"

"Nah. Greg's got things going on with his wife's family."

And the old man hadn't been included. That wasn't

surprising, considering the fact that his brother and father had grown apart.

"And Joe and Mark both had plans."

The words came out sharp and bitter. But what did the old man expect? He wasn't with their mom anymore. Stepsons didn't owe loyalty to a man who'd divorced their mother.

"So how's it going over there?" his dad asked.

Now was Adam's chance to confess that he was in trouble and needed help.

But before he could say anything, the old man was on to a new question, steering them into shallow conversational waters. "You still like small-town life?"

"Oh, yeah, this is a great place. Good fishing."

His father had always promised to take him fishing but had never gotten around to it. Too busy. He'd promised to take Mom to Hawaii, too. That had never materialized, either. Dad had managed a trip to Reno with his tennis team, though.

"Well," Dad said, "one of these days I'm going to have to come up there and check out your place, see if the fishing is as good as you say."

"Sounds like a plan."

Even as Adam said it, he knew that would never happen. His dad was semiretired now and he had the time, but he'd never make the effort. Just like he'd never made the effort to work at his marriages. And now he was alone on Father's Day.

Adam was going under for the third time but he realized his father was no lifesaver. He was his own personal shipwreck and he'd be no use to his son.

Adam said goodbye and ended the call. Now he was more depressed. Had he just been looking at his future?

He stopped by the house the next morning on his way to work and saw that yesterday's present was no longer on the porch. Good. She'd gotten it. Or Dennis had filched it. Adam wouldn't put it past him.

Adam decided to think positive. Of course Chels had found the present. Had she read the note he'd included? It had been short and to the point. "I'm happy about the baby. I wanted you to know that."

Today's offering was the blanket. The accompanying note read: "This blanket made me think of you. It's soft and pretty. I can see the baby wrapped up in it. Wish I could wrap my arms around you like a blanket." Had that been too mushy? Probably not. From what he'd read in those books, a man couldn't get too mushy.

He wanted more than anything to ring the doorbell and wait for her to open the door so he could give her the blanket in person, but something told him this wasn't the time. He needed to simply leave her every present, like Santa Claus. Then, maybe, by Saturday she'd be ready to see him.

If she was, he had to make sure he played it right. Deep down he knew this was his last chance. If he blew it there wouldn't be another. No three-strike rule in this game. He'd be out in two.

But he wasn't going to strike out. Chels still loved him and he loved her. What was it Vance had said to Jonathan on Friday night? Oh, yeah. *Love always wins in the end.* He hoped Vance knew what he was talking about.

Mindy not speaking to Kyle had been bad enough. Mindy speaking to other men, that was torture.

And she wasn't just speaking. She was flirting. She flirted with Willie the accountant, which was kind of sick if you asked Kyle, considering how old Willie was. She flirted with Harold, one of the claims analysts. And when Kyle followed her down to Filly's, he found her parked at a table flirting with Dave, the kid from the mail room.

She glanced up and saw Kyle, and instead of the warm look she used to give him, her expression hardened. Then she returned her attention to Dave and flashed the kid a hundred-watt smile.

Fine. If that was how she wanted it, fine. Kyle ordered a sandwich to take back to the office. He sat down at his desk and ground his sandwich to smithereens with his teeth.

He knew when Mindy had returned to the office. He could hear her laughing as she came in. What had Dave said that was so funny?

Other people were returning from lunch, too, smiling and happy. Everyone was smiling and happy but him.

"I guess you had a good time at lunch," he said sourly as she sat down at her desk.

"Actually, I did."

It was the first time she'd talked to him since that

disastrous Saturday, but it didn't improve his mood. "Did Dave ask you out?"

"You know, I don't think that's any of your business."

That shut him up. But it didn't stop him from seething. He didn't want Mindy flirting with other guys. He wanted her flirting with him. What was he going to do?

He had no idea, but he'd better get one soon. Mindy was moving on at the speed of light, and pretty soon she'd be completely out of reach.

Once home from work, he picked up his reading device and sank onto the couch, prepared to spend a few hours in the nineteenth century with a hero who was just about as dumb as he was. Oh, man, and now Alan Tremaine had really blown it. Kyle went to the next page and read on.

Opal hurried to take refuge in her favorite spot, the little stone bench at the heart of the garden maze. How symbolic that she should come here, after all she'd been through. What a fool she'd been. But no more. She could live without Alan Tremaine. She could find another man and be perfectly happy.

"Don't do it," Kyle groaned. "Give him another chance."

She arrived at the quiet spot to see a single rose lying on the bench. She hurried to pick it up.

"I can't pass by a blooming rosebush without thinking of you, Opal," said a soft voice at her back.

She turned and saw Alan standing there. A flush of embarrassment heated her cheeks as she remembered that humiliating scene the night before. "It's cruel of you to mock me," she said, and moved to rush past him.

He blocked her way. "I'm not mocking you, truly. I'm hoping with this rose we can grow something new. I've been blind a long time, but you've opened my eyes to what true love is."

She looked at him in disbelief. "And what, pray, is it?"

"It's shared laughter and challenges faced together. It's standing beside a man even when he's acted the fool. It's so much more than I thought it was when I pursued a woman with a head as empty as your father's pockets."

At the mention of her family's straitened circumstances, Opal bowed her head in shame.

A gentle hand raised her chin. "I don't need a fat dowry. What I need is you. What I need is a second chance, if you'll give it to me."

How could she not? "Oh, Alan," she cried, throwing her arms around him.

"Ah, my girl," he said, and kissed her. "We were always meant to be together. I can't believe now that I didn't see it."

She dimpled up at him. "Nor can I. But I'm glad you've found your sight at last."

"Me, too," Kyle said.

Opal and Alan went on to enjoy a lavish wedding and a wedding night that sent Kyle to a cold shower.

In this latest Vanessa Valentine (make that Vance Fish) novel, it was almost as if Vance had taken Kyle's situation with Mindy and given it an historical setting. Like him, Alan Tremaine had been a shortsighted idiot who couldn't see that the right woman for him was standing under his very nose. And like Kyle, Alan Tremaine had blown it big-time. But he'd redeemed himself with a chick-friendly peace offering and a humble request for a second chance.

Of course, he'd been able to redeem himself because Opal Carew, the heroine, had loved him since they were kids and was willing to give him that chance. Mindy had known Kyle for a year and even he wasn't so naive as to think she was in love with him. She was interested, that was all. And the disastrous nondate at her place had done a lot to kill her interest. He wasn't sure any kind of romantic gesture could resurrect it.

But it was worth a try. He'd tried hard enough to get a woman who only cared about the size of a man's bank account. Mindy had appreciated him for who he was, didn't care if he was short or tall, rich or poor. She'd simply liked him. Wasn't she worth at least as much effort as he'd put into chasing Jillian?

Absolutely. And if it was too late, well, that was no more than he deserved.

The next day he hurried into Safeway before going to work and picked up a bag of Hershey's Kisses.

Mindy was already at her desk when he got to the office, typing away on her keyboard, too busy to say hi.

Kyle pretended they were still pals and said, "Good morning."

The only response he got was the tap-tap of her keyboard.

He opened the bag of chocolates. "You still playing poker?" he asked, and tossed a Hershey's Kiss over the cubicle wall. He heard it land on her desk.

The tapping stopped a moment, then resumed.

"I'm betting I can get you to laugh before the day is over," he said, and tossed a second chocolate.

The tapping picked up speed.

He tossed a third one. "I'll see that chocolate kiss and raise you another."

The tapping stopped and he smiled.

Until she scooted her chair back, leaned over and grabbed the bag. "Some of us are trying to work," she snapped, then disappeared behind the cubicle wall.

So much for that idea.

A moment later a chocolate kiss sailed onto his desk. All right. "Are we friends again?" he asked.

Another chocolate came over to visit. "I'll think about it."

Thinking was good. Thinking let him hope he had a winning hand. Now it was time to bet all his chips.

On his way home from work he went to Gingerbread Haus and ordered a gingerbread girl and a gingerbread boy. Cass Wilkes was on duty and at his
request she happily wrote his name on the boy and
Mindy's on the girl.

"That is really sweet," she said. "And clever."

"You think my friend will like it?" *You think she'll
want to be more than a friend?*

Cass handed over the box with the cookies. "Of
course she will. What's not to like about a man doing
something so thoughtful?"

He'd paved the way with chocolate. He sure hoped
this gingerbread couple wouldn't encounter any road-
blocks.

The following morning he got to the office ten minutes early and set the gingerbread couple on Mindy's
desk. Then he sat down at his computer and started
going through the motions of work. He pretended not
to notice when she walked past him and tried to ignore
the sudden increase in his heart rate. She set down her
purse. He felt sweat beading on his forehead.

"What's this?"

He peered around the cubicle wall and saw she'd
opened the box. "That's you and me going to the grand
reopening of Zelda's restaurant in Icicle Falls. I hope."

She stared straight ahead at her computer. "What,
Jillian wasn't available?"

"I don't know and I don't care." What had Alex
Tremaine said to Opal Carew? Kyle couldn't remem-
ber a single word. Crap. He was on his own. "Look,
I was dumb. I don't want someone like Jillian. I want

someone who's got heart, someone I can laugh with."
This was coming out all wrong. He tried again. "I
had a chance for dinner with a really cool woman
and I blew it, plain and simple. I'd like to try again if
you'd let me."

She still wouldn't look at him, but she was nibbling
her lip, a sure sign she was considering his offer.

He gave her one last nudge toward yes. "Hey, at
least I'm a step up from those internet losers you
dated. I've got a job. And I'm not writing a book on
mushrooms."

That made her smile. "Yes, but can you compete
with Willie?"

"It'll be hard, but I'll try."

"I could do worse, couldn't I?"

"Hell, yeah." He suddenly remembered her pre-
requisite about a man being a churchgoer. "I mean,
heck. Heck, yeah. What do you say? I think I'm done
being stupid about women. Give me another chance."

"All right."

He pumped the air. "Yes!"

"People are trying to work here, you know," said
Eleanor Gumm, several desks over.

Kyle shut up and got busy, grinning as he worked.
It was going to be a great day.

Chapter Sixteen

On Friday Adam had to visit his customers in Seattle, so he got up extra-early and was at Chelsea's door before dawn, this time setting out the tiger-striped jammies. The accompanying note read "I have something to ask you tomorrow and a promise to make. Will you open the door when I come by?" He knew she wouldn't be working. He'd actually called the nursery and found out. He'd show up right after breakfast, before she got busy in the yard. He hoped to heaven the presents had been enough to convince her he'd changed.

The work day seemed unending, and he lost twenty bucks and three romance novels to Kyle at poker that evening. "I can't concentrate," he said. "Tomorrow is do or die. Either Chels takes me back or I'm in Jonathan's spare room forever."

Jonathan had the world's worst poker face and it was impossible for him to hide the utter panic this announcement inspired.

"Don't worry," Adam assured him. "I was just kidding. If things don't work out with us, I'm moving to

Seattle. I don't want to hang around here and watch her hook up with some other man."

"I don't blame you," Bernardo said. "That would be tough."

"It'll work out," Vance predicted.

Adam frowned at him. "How do *you* know...Vanessa?"

The jibe didn't faze him. "Because she's going to have a kid. She wants security."

"If that's all she wants, why didn't she take me back sooner?" Adam demanded.

Vance shook his head as if sorely tried by having to deal with such a slow learner. "She wants to make sure she's got you trained before the baby arrives, dolt."

"Trained?"

"Yeah, trained."

"What, you think she's been manipulating me?" Vance shrugged.

"She's been jerking my chain."

"Maybe it needed jerking," Vance said.

Adam considered his behavior over the past couple of years. "Yeah, maybe it did."

The next morning at ten he and the stuffed elephant parked in front of his house to find Chelsea already outside, weeding the flower beds. She wore cutoffs and a yellow T-shirt and her hair was pulled up in a ponytail. And there, walking up and down the lawn—his lawn!—pushing a lawnmower—his lawnmower!—was Dennis the Menace.

He grabbed the elephant and stomped over to Dennis, falling in step with him. "What are you doing mowing..." he shouted over the roar of the lawn-mower.

"What?" Dennis shouted back.

"Why are you mowing..." Dennis turned off the mower, leaving Adam to finish his sentence loudly enough for all of Icicle Falls to hear. "My lawn?"

"Just helping out," Dennis said. "You haven't been around and your grass was getting high. I offered."

"Well, you don't need to offer. I can mow my own lawn," Adam said, attempting to wrest the mower out of Dennis's greedy paws.

Now Chelsea had joined them. "Adam," she began.

Adam thumped his chest. "I can mow the lawn."

"Not if you're not here," Dennis said, giving the mower a yank in an attempt to regain control.

"I'm here now." Adam yanked back.

"Adam, come away," Chelsea coaxed. "What have you got there?"

"A big, dumb animal?" guessed Dennis. "How symbolic."

"I'll symbolic you," Adam said, and whacked him with the elephant, tipping his glasses sideways.

"Hey, not cool," Dennis growled.

"I'll say. Over here trying to steal my wife. My grass." Adam took a swing.

The little weasel ducked and before Adam knew what hit him, or rather who, Dennis landed a lucky punch. Adam and the elephant went down.

It was broad daylight but Adam saw stars. His jaw was broken, he was sure. Some other man was all over his lawn and would be all over his wife next and here he lay like a beached whale. He groaned and shook his head.

"You shouldn't mess with me. I was a lightweight champion in college," Dennis said.

"That was a mean thing to do," Chelsea snapped, and Adam couldn't tell whether she was saying it to him or to Dennis.

"You shouldn't mess with my wife," Adam said. Ow, that hurt. He clutched his jaw.

"Oh, your poor jaw." Chelsea was kneeling next to him now, concern plainly written on her face.

It had been a long time since he'd seen even a hint of kindness on that pretty face. Adam decided he could do a little manipulating, too. "I think my jaw's broken."

"Someone should break your head," Dennis informed him. "To just up and leave a sweet woman like this?"

Up and leave? Adam looked at Chelsea in confusion. "I—"

"Come on in the house," she said, helping him up. "Let's get some ice on your jaw."

He let her help him up, him and the elephant.

"Leave the lawn," Chelsea told Dennis. "Adam can finish it."

Yeah. So there.

"If you need anything, call," Dennis said to Chelsea, giving Adam a look that promised a smashed nose to follow his broken jaw.

Once in the kitchen she sat him down at the table. It felt like years since he'd sat here. He soaked it all in—the pretty oak cabinets, the vase of flowers on the table, the smell of bacon left over from her breakfast. But the best sight of all was Chelsea herself.

He watched as she loaded ice in a plastic bag and then wrapped it in a kitchen towel. "What did Dennis mean about me leaving you?"

"He saw you were gone and jumped to conclusions."

"And you never said anything different?" She'd let him look like a jerk. Granted, he'd been a jerk—long before Dennis arrived on the scene—but not *that* big a jerk.

"I never said anything, period. He just assumed you'd left."

Adam chewed on that for a moment. "I guess it's easy to assume things about people. Like they'll always be there, no matter how much you take them for granted."

She looked at him, surprised as a math teacher with an obtuse student who'd finally grasped a simple equation.

She came over to where he sat and pressed the ice on his chin.

He winced and pulled away.

"Don't be such a baby," she chided.

Baby. The word brought him back to what he'd wanted to say when he first arrived. He held up the stuffed elephant. "This is for the baby."

"It's sweet," she said softly. "You've been sweet," she added, and the tone of her voice encouraged him to hope that if he played his cards right, he'd be back home tonight.

"I'm gonna be like that elephant, Chels. I've learned my lesson. I won't forget."

She sat down opposite him, tears in her eyes. "Do you mean that? Really?"

"What else can I do to prove it?"

"Be different from now on. Make time for me. Make time for your family."

He was done being a selfish bastard. "I can change," he told his wife and himself.

"You have to. We've got a baby on the way. It's time to man-up."

"I will," he promised.

She smiled. How he'd missed that smile! Then she leaned across the table and kissed him. It was as smooth and satisfying as fine bourbon. When she pulled away, the look in her eyes promised more.

"Will you go out with me tonight?" he asked. "Zelda's is reopening. I got reservations."

She nodded.

He wanted to jump up and down, shout his success from the rooftop, go pummel Dennis McDermott into the ground. Instead, he played it cool. "Good," he said. "And now, I'm gonna mow the lawn."

Kyle and Mindy were enjoying salmon baked in puff pastry almost as much as they were enjoying each other's company when Adam and his wife came into Zelda's to swell the crowd by two. It seemed most of the residents of Icicle Falls had showed up to celebrate the reopening of the popular restaurant. The bar where they'd waited for their table had been packed, and here in the dining room not a table was free except for one down by the fireplace, their obvious destination.

Charley, the owner, was beaming as she led them to their table. She had every right. She'd worked her butt off turning the restaurant into someplace special, and after the fire she'd worked even harder. The restaurant was better than ever with a slick new rustic decor and a bigger bar, complete with a nice-size dance floor. Jake O'Brien, hometown boy, and his band Ricochet were going to be performing there later. Jake's first CD was out and he was busy playing the county fair circuit, but since his wife and Charley were friends he was squeezing in this appearance as a favor. Yet another reason the place was packed to the rafters. Adam had made his reservation fairly late; he must have pulled some strings to get in. Well, good for him.

He had his arm around his wife's waist and he was smiling like he owned the world. With his wife back, Kyle supposed he did. He stopped to give Kyle a handshake. "How's it goin'?"

"Great," Kyle said, and made introductions.

"We'll have to get together some time," Chelsea said before they continued on to their table.

Getting together with other couples, being a couple. Kyle sure liked the sound of that.

"Is that one of your poker buddies?" Mindy asked.

Kyle nodded, although with everything they'd been going through lately, he was more like a comrade-in-arms.

"He's nice. So's his wife. It would be fun to do something with them."

That seemed positive. Kyle took a casual drink of his beer. "So, are you saying you'd like to do more things together?"

She smiled at him. "What do you think?"

He grinned. "I think I'm glad I asked you out."

"Me, too," she said.

And later, when he took her home, she asked, "You want to come in for a drink. Or something?"

A drink sounded good. "Or something" sounded even better. "Yeah," he said, "I do."

He followed her inside and looked around the tidy little house, taking in details he'd missed the first time he was here. Being stupid. Paintings of flowers decorated the walls. She had a bowl of fruit sitting on her kitchen table. It was all homey and welcoming and he could already envision the two of them stretched out on that couch on a winter's night, in front of the fireplace. A big orange cat regarded him warily from its perch on a rocking chair, then bolted for safety to another part of the house.

"You've got a cat," he said, stating the obvious.

"That's Snookums. She's kind of shy." Mindy continued on to the kitchen. "What would you like to drink?"

He joined her. She opened the fridge and bent over to inspect its contents. It was a lovely sight to behold.

"I've got Pepsi, lemonade, some white wine."

"Huh?" Oh, yeah, he was supposed to be focusing

on the contents of the fridge, not the woman in front of it. "Pepsi's fine."

She got out two cans and took glasses from the cupboard. She probably couldn't reach the top shelf without a stepladder. Smiling, he remembered what his mom used to tell him every time he complained about his lack of height. *Good things come in small packages.* Mom had been right.

Mindy put ice in their glasses, poured in the pop and brought them over to where he leaned against the counter. As she smiled at him, it dawned on Kyle that, at last, he was writing his own romance.

There she stood, her eyes inviting him to kiss her. Her lips parted in anticipation. He took the glasses out of her hands and set them on the counter, saying, "Later." Then he reached out and drew her to him.

She came willingly, a smile on her full lips.

Savoring the moment, he threaded a hand through her dark, silky hair. She was beautiful, a perfect little package.

She closed her eyes and tipped up her face, ready for his kiss.

The minute his lips touched hers, he knew his search was over and he'd found the woman of his dreams.

Oh, yeah. This was better than anything Vance could write, Kyle thought, and deepened the kiss.

It was long and juicy, and when they'd finished, she asked, "Are you sorry you're not out with Jillian?"

"Jillian who?" he said, and kissed her again.

Jonathan and Chica had gone hiking on Lost Bride Trail. Legend had it that when you were about to get hitched, you caught a glimpse of the ghost of Joshua Cane's bride, who mysteriously disappeared back when Icicle Falls was nothing more than a mining town. Jonathan hadn't seen a thing.

He'd returned from his hike in a grumpy mood and heated a pizza. He should've been in a better mood since he'd finally lost his roommate. Adam had collected all his stuff that afternoon and was now over at Zelda's celebrating the grand opening with his wife.

Kyle was there, too, on a date with his pal Mindy. Bernardo and Anna were out with her family. Even Vance had plans. His editor was in Seattle for a conference and they were having dinner. Juliet and Neil were going dancing at the Red Barn. It seemed like everyone was doing something tonight except him.

"We're doing something. We're having fun right here, aren't we?" he said to Chica as he pulled out the pizza. Pizza and the sci-fi channel. Life was good.

If you considered that a life. Halfway through *Aliens versus Aliens* he decided he'd had enough. He was going out. He donned a clean T-shirt that said Nerd Is a Four-Letter Word, then left Chica in charge and headed out the door to join the gang celebrating Zelda's grand opening.

The parking lot was full and there was a crowd inside the door waiting to be seated. There was barely room for them with all the floral arrangements and balloons saying Congratulations. No surprise that this was such a big deal. Both the restaurant and its owner, Charley, were popular.

But it was more than that. The people of Icicle Falls loved real-life Rocky Balboa stories. They supported one another, and when one of their own fought her way back from failure to success, everyone celebrated. The town itself had once been on the verge of extinction and came back strong, turning itself into a German-style alpine village. Failure happened and that was okay. Letting it beat you was not.

Jonathan passed up the restaurant, which was obviously catering to couples and families, and entered the bar, just another swinging single out for a good time.

Except once in the bar, he became acutely aware of the fact that although he was single, he was far from swinging. The bar was a mob scene. No one under the age of forty had stayed home, and the air was thick with perfume and aftershave. Jake O'Brien's latest hit, "Baby, You're Back," was playing in the background, a warm-up for his band's appearance later in the evening. There were lots of singles, but they'd been here long enough to form couples and groups.

Jonathan saw Tina Swift at a corner table, yukking it up with Priscilla Castro, who worked at the town hall, and a couple of guys from the bank. She saw him and waved, but didn't beckon him over to join them.

Of course she wouldn't. He wasn't part of their circle. If this was a historical romance they would've been nobility or gentry. He, on the other hand, would have been a stable boy. He worked for them, kept their equipment running, but he wasn't one of them.

Billy Williams, the popular cowboy who worked on a nearby guest ranch, was the center of a group of giggling women, being his usual hammy self. He was the court jester. Everyone loved the jester. Nobody noticed the stable boy. But then, you weren't supposed to notice him, even if he'd acquired some muscle.

Jonathan didn't last more than a few minutes. The crowd was too intimidating, too happy, too…connected. He didn't belong. He got out of there.

Now he felt more morose than he had at home. Might as well go back to Chica and some cold pizza, he told himself. That was depressing.

Almost of its own will, his car turned toward the edge of town. In a few minutes he was pulling into a potholed parking lot in front of a tavern where he saw several trucks and a couple of muddy Jeeps. Its outside wall sported a painting of a Neanderthal dressed in a pair of lederhosen and bearing a club. The Man Cave.

The place was darker and seedier than Zelda's. It wasn't as packed, probably because it was all guys, busy with the important business of shooting pool and drinking. A country song was playing, accompanied by the clack of pool balls.

No one here was any more welcoming than they'd been at Zelda's, but he didn't feel so out of place. Was that because everyone here was a stable boy, too? He went to the bar and sat down.

The bartender was a beefy guy who looked a little

like the Neanderthal on the outside wall. "What can I get you?"

"I'll take a Bud," Jonathan said.

The bartender nodded and a moment later Jonathan had a beer to keep him company. He was halfway through it when a voice at his side said, "Hey there, computer man. What brings you to our man cave?"

He turned to see Todd Black at his elbow, dressed casually in jeans and a plain gray T-shirt. Plain gray, no catchy nerd talk on it anywhere. Jonathan felt like a dork. He crossed his arms over his shirt in an effort to hide the clever saying. "Uh, hi, Todd."

"You out slumming?" Todd asked, surveying his kingdom.

"Just thought I'd get a drink."

"You're not over getting one at Zelda's?"

Jonathan shrugged. "I checked it out. It's a little too crowded for my taste."

Todd nodded as if he completely understood, which, of course, he didn't. He couldn't. Cool guys like Todd never did. "Yeah, it's a zoo."

"You were there?" Jonathan asked in surprise. When? Had Todd seen him there, lost in the crowd, a geek in a foreign land?

"I was there earlier. Stopped by to say congrats to Charley."

Probably somewhere in all those floral arrangements was one from Todd. The guy sure knew how to please women.

Todd clapped him on the back. "Enjoy yourself, my man. Make yourself at home, shoot some pool."

With the other guys who were here without women. Maybe some of them were here to get away from their women. But as Jonathan looked around, he saw that most of the left-hand fingers had no gold glinting on them. Saturday night, and these guys were here, shooting pool. No one had a date, no one was over at Zelda's, picking up girls. Saturday was loser night at the Man Cave. And here he was with the rest of them.

Not for long, he promised himself. Not for long.

Chapter Seventeen

With the exception of Bernardo, who complained that his wife was starving him to death, all of Jonathan's poker guests were in a festive mood. Vance had just signed a big book contract, and Cupid had come through for both Adam and Kyle.

"I took Chels out to dinner before I came here." Adam grinned. "It's like when we were first dating. We can't get enough of each other. I gotta say, that last book I read did the trick. Thanks for making me do my research," he said to Jonathan.

"Hey, what about me? I wrote 'em," Vance said.

"Not the one that helped me, so don't go getting a fat head," Adam said genially.

"Well, his books helped me," Kyle insisted. "So did the others. In fact, I learned something different from one book I read. Plus it was fun. Who knew chick books were so cool?"

"I did," Vance said with a grin.

"I'm taking Mindy to the street dance," Kyle announced.

Icicle Falls celebrated the Fourth of July in a big

way. On the Fourth, residents enjoyed picnics, a parade and a street fair and, at night, fireworks over the Wenatchee River. But the big kickoff was the street dance the evening before. Vendors sold everything from burgers and corn on the cob to shaved ice. All of Center Street closed down. There was always a climbing wall and bounce house and space for chalk drawing on one end and, down by the bandstand, dancing. This year, two different bands would be playing, one offering fifties and sixties classics, the other covering the eighties clear through to the latest hits. Anyone who was anyone would be there. Jonathan was not looking forward to it.

"Are you going?" Kyle asked him.

"I might, for a while." A very short while.

"It's a great place to make your dancing debut," Juliet had said. "And it'll give you confidence and help you get used to dancing in public."

"I'm not ready," he'd protested. He needed another six weeks, needed every day and night until the reunion. Then he'd have the whole package—new dance steps, new clothes and more new muscle.

But Juliet had insisted he climb out of his shell and attend.

"Should be fun," Kyle said.

Yeah, for him, now that he had a woman. For Jonathan it was going to be torture.

Juliet made sure they all arrived early. The band wasn't due to go on for another hour but already the street was packed—couples visiting with one another and eating ice cream, clumps of teens meeting up and kids darting in and out of the crowd. At the end of the street, the bounce house and climbing wall were doing a brisk business. The aroma of grilling onions and sausages danced on the air.

"I haven't been to this in years," Mom said as she, Jonathan, Neil and Juliet sat at a picnic table in the food court consuming hamburgers from Herman's. "I'd forgotten how much fun it is."

If you were coupled up. If you were single, not so much, Jonathan thought as he watched a couple en route to the bandstand stop for a kiss. What was he doing here? Oh, yeah. Making his dancing debut. His palms suddenly felt sweaty and he wiped them on his jeans. *You'll do okay,* he told himself. Who was he kidding?

Kyle joined them, happy to show off Mindy. She was cute, even shorter than Kyle, with a tight little body wrapped in jeans and a tank top. She seemed nice and she looked at Kyle as if he was ten feet tall. *He'd* done okay.

Next Adam and Chelsea stopped by, bearing plates of burgers.

The way Chelsea's eyes lit up when she looked at Adam made Jonathan think of sparklers. There was a happy woman. All it had taken for Adam to win her back was mastering the art of the romantic gesture.

Not for the first time, Jonathan was still racking his brain, trying to think of some romantic gesture he could make to impress Lissa. Well, he had a few weeks left.

The sounds of a guitar warming up drifted over to where they all sat and Juliet nudged him. "Hey, it's almost time to dance."

Whoopee.

"Are you going to save me a dance?" his mother teased.

"You can have the first one," he said.

"Oh, I'll take the second one," Mom said. "We'll let your teacher have the first. I can hardly wait to see you both in action."

"They're not bad," Neil said.

Coming from Neil, that was high praise indeed.

Another ten minutes and the band had started playing "Dancing in the Street." Juliet grinned at Jonathan. "That's our cue. Okay, everybody, let's get footloose."

"All right!" Mindy hopped up, Kyle immediately behind her.

Jonathan rubbed his hands on his pant legs and pushed his glasses up his nose. He told himself to stand up. His legs didn't get the message and his hind end stayed firmly rooted on the picnic-table bench.

"Come on," Juliet urged, yanking at his arm. "You have to do this sometime."

Sometime could be another time. Someplace less public.

Juliet gave another insistent tug and he reluctantly rose to his feet, feeling like he was about to take a plunge into the icy river. *You've done that and lived,* he reminded himself. And once he was in the water, he was always fine. Once he survived the first dance he'd be good.

The band had switched to something faster now, drawing a crowd…of listeners. Only two other couples were actually dancing.

Juliet dragged him through the listening throng to where the four exhibitionists were going at it. "This is perfect for swing dancing."

He pulled back. "Let's wait until there are more people." He'd stick out like a clown at a funeral. Clowns. He remembered his dream and his feet went from cold to frozen. "I can't do this."

Juliet got right up in his face. "Do you want Lissa Castle or don't you?"

"That has nothing to do with this."

"Yes, it does. If you can't dance here, you'll never be able to dance at the reunion. Now, come on." She gave his arm another fierce yank that about pulled it out of its socket. Who would've guessed his little sister was so strong?

He stumbled after her and, next thing he knew, there they stood for all the world to see.

"You can do this," she said. "Now, *go*."

It took superhuman strength to start that first move but once he had, muscle memory took over, his feet doing the steps, his arms confidently shifting Juliet back and forth. He was a passenger in his own body, watching in amazement as he went through the routine she'd taught him. The crowd made room and someone hooted encouragement.

"Flip me," Juliet commanded.

"But…you're pregnant," he protested.

"Barely, and the baby's well-cushioned in there. Come on, Jonathan."

Why not? urged his newfound confidence. The song was almost over. They might as well go out with a bang. He obliged and, dance queen that she was, Juliet landed perfectly. The end.

The crowd went wild, invigorating him with their cheers and applause, and the lead singer up on the bandstand said, "That was some show, folks."

Kyle slapped him on the back and Adam, who was at the front of the crowd with Chelsea, gave him a thumbs-up.

Success! He felt like he'd completed the Boston marathon. His heart was pumping like crazy and he was on such an endorphin high he was sure he'd never come down.

Neil had joined them now. "No more of that sailing through the air stuff, Jules," he said to his wife. "You're gonna make the baby sick."

"I knew we shouldn't have done that," Jonathan muttered.

"Oh, don't be silly," she said to both of them.

"No, I mean it," Neil said. "We don't want anything to happen."

That sobered her. "Okay," she promised. "No more flips."

Neil looked relieved. "Good job, bro," he said to Jonathan.

"I *knew* you could do it. You'll be the hit of the reunion," Juliet added, and kissed him on the cheek.

He was certainly the hit of the street dance. After

a showy nightclub two-step with his mom, he wasn't lacking for women who wanted to dance with him.

Dot was next to claim a dance, surprising him with how well she followed. "I was something in my time," she informed him.

"You're something now," he said, earning him a smile and the offer of a free breakfast at Breakfast Haus.

Just as the band was starting another fast number, Daphne Robard came up to him. "Jonathan, hi. Remember me?"

Daphne had been in his graduating class and would be attending the reunion. A star of all the high school musicals, she'd always had a larger-than-life personality. And she'd been popular. Other than a hello when they passed in the hall, she'd never paid too much attention to Jonathan, partly because she'd been busy dating the entire football team. She'd finally made her selection and married Jimmy Miller, one of the fullbacks, then moved to California. She'd only recently returned to Icicle Falls. Rumor had it she'd gone through a messy divorce and come away with a bundle of money and that she was looking to invest in a shop in town. She'd gained more than money since Jonathan had last seen her. Daphne had lost a husband and found an extra sixty pounds.

"Sure," Jonathan said. "How are ya?"

"Free as a bird. Dance with me." He hadn't said yes, but she was already towing him toward an empty spot in the growing crowd of dancers. "I haven't danced in years. That SOB I married was a couch potato." Before

Jonathan could even get the beat to lead them into the first step, she started boogying, happily leading herself. "It feels so good to be free! How've you been?" she shouted over the music.

"Fine." He could feel people's gazes on him again. Daphne always drew a crowd. His hands began to sweat.

"Spin me, Jonathan," she commanded, and then spun herself. "Wheee!"

Yeah, wheee. When would this dance end?

"Flip me like you did that other girl."

Oh, no. That would be a disaster. Even with the muscle he'd gained, Daphne would be too much woman for him.

Before he could protest, she'd hurled herself into the air. None of the lessons his sister had given him had prepared him for a situation like this. Acting out of instinct and sheer terror, he tried to get an arm under Daphne, in the hopes of making sure she landed well. But she knocked him off balance. Before he knew it, he was staggering backward with his arms full of Daphne, bouncing off people like a ball in a pinball machine. They'd taken out two couples and half the skin on his arm by the time they finished their bumpy landing with Daphne on top of him.

With a grunt she struggled to a sitting position and glared at him. "I thought you knew how to dance."

"Uh."

That was as far as he got. Daphne pushed herself off him and stormed away, leaving him lying like an upended turtle in the middle of the laughing crowd with a sore butt, a bleeding arm and his whole face on fire.

A hand reached down and pulled him up. Adam. "What were you thinking, dude?"

"She asked me! What could I do?"

"Just say no."

Then Juliet was by his side. "Are you okay?"

"Yeah," he said, and started walking. The walk quickly turned into a limp. Great. Now he'd be too sore to work out at the gym.

"Where are you going?"

"Home."

"You can't just leave! You were doing great."

"I've had enough for one night." Jonathan had never enjoyed being the center of attention and this… If he didn't dream about clowns tonight, it would be a miracle. "Can you take Mom home?"

"Yes." She was frowning, clearly not happy with him.

Well, that made two of them. He nodded and limped off, wiping the blood from his shirt as he went. He should have worn something different tonight. Maybe a T-shirt with Loser printed on it.

Jonathan kept a low profile the rest of the Fourth. He joined his family for a picnic by the river but avoided the parade and the rest of the hooplah downtown. The last thing he needed was to run into anyone who'd been a witness to his abysmal debut at the street dance.

"That wasn't your fault," Juliet insisted, guessing the reason he was going to hide out.

"Anything goes wrong, it's always the guy's fault."

"You catch on fast," Neil said, and Juliet frowned at him. "Hey, you're the one who says the man's in charge on the dance floor."

"You're not helping," she told him.

He shrugged. "Don't worry about it, Jon. Arnold Schwarzenegger couldn't have flipped her. And before that, you had 'em lining up. They were all hot to dance with you."

"If you'd have stuck around you could have danced with a bunch more," Juliet put in.

He hadn't wanted to dance with a bunch more women and he didn't care about anyone but Lissa being hot to dance with him. And now, after what had happened, he wasn't so sure he wanted to keep dancing as part of his plan to win her.

Juliet gave up on turning him into a party animal. "Okay, you're off the hook. Go home and lick your wounds. But I expect you at the house on Wednesday for your dance lesson, same as always."

"Uh."

She pointed a finger at him. "No excuses. When you fall, you have to get right back on the horse."

So the next week he was back on the horse, learning how to salsa.

"Not bad," Juliet approved. "But you've got to move your hips more."

"I can't. It makes me feel like a girl."

"Trust me. You won't look like a girl when you do it."

Who said he was going to do it? Ever?

"Next week we'll try some country two-step and then I'll take you to the Red Barn."

"Oh, no." Jonathan shook his head. "No way."

"You have to get out and dance in public again," Juliet said.

This salsa lesson had given him second thoughts. Man wasn't meant to do stuff like that in front of other people. He didn't think he wanted to get back on the horse, after all. "I probably won't dance at the reunion." That would be safer, both for him and all the other dancers.

"You're a good dancer. You'd be crazy not to."

He'd be even crazier to risk a public fiasco like the one he'd experienced at the street dance. "Look, Jules, I appreciate all the lessons, but I'm gonna stop. I don't think I was meant to be a dancer."

Her eyes narrowed. "You're going to *quit?*"

Why did she make avoiding public humiliation sound so wimpy?

"One more lesson," she pleaded. "Then, if you still want to quit, we will."

"Okay, one more," he said. He actually did enjoy dancing in the safety of his sister's living room. If only he could ask Lissa to come to his house and dance.

Was Juliet right? Was he a quitter? That wasn't heroic.

But then, dropping women at dances wasn't heroic,

either. The very thought of another public humiliation was terrifying.

His sister didn't seem to get that, because he showed up for what was to be his final lesson to find several women waiting for him in her living room. What was this?

"I imported some new dance partners for you," Juliet told him. "My book club."

Jonathan's hands went clammy. *Think fast!* "Uh, I can't stay. I just came by to say I have to…" What? "Run some errands," he improvised.

"You can do them later," his sister said. "Anyway, all the shops are closed now. There's no place to run." She grabbed his arm in a vicelike grip and hauled him into the living room.

"Hi, Jonathan," said Chelsea, Adam's wife. "This is going to be fun."

Not for him…

"I'm sorry I didn't get to dance with you at the street fair," said Cass Wilkes, owner of Gingerbread Haus. "I really wanted a chance to learn that slow dance you did with your mom."

"And I wanted another swing dance," put in Dot.

"I want to learn to swing dance, too," Cecily Sterling said.

Oh, Lord. Dancing with Cecily Sterling. He wouldn't remember a single step. Charley Albach was just as intimidating.

He didn't care if Juliet was related to him. He was going to kill her.

"Okay," she said, "who wants to go first?"

"I'll break the ice," Dot said. "Come on, kid, let's show 'em what we're made of."

Juliet had her playlist all cued up and she started with a fast vintage rock number, "Betty's Lou Got a New Pair of Shoes."

Jonathan pushed his glasses up his nose and then wiped his sweaty hands on his jeans. The beat was pounding like a jungle drum but he couldn't seem to hear it. Where was the beat?

"You can do it, kid," Dot said.

He swallowed hard, nodded and wiped his hands on his jeans again. Then he rubbed an imaginary itch on his forehead.

"Okay, wait here," Dot said, and stepped away.

He released his breath and watched as she pulled the other women into a chick huddle. The huddle broke up and they all turned their backs. What the heck?

Now Dot was back. "Okay, kid. Nobody's watching. It's just you and me. Let's get some dancing in before this song ends."

She put a hand on his shoulder and held out her other hand for him to take so they could start in a closed position. As he took her hand, she smiled encouragingly at him, nodding her head to the beat.

Oh, there it was. He started them dancing. Then, much to his surprise, he was dancing like a pro on *Dancing with the Stars*. Every move Juliet taught him came as naturally as breathing. Dot was smiling and suddenly the other women were clapping and cheering. Out of the corner of his eye, he saw that they'd all turned around again and were watching him, but now it didn't matter because he'd found his groove.

Until Dot said, "Flip me, kid."

Flip her? Here? Now? Daphne's face superimposed itself on Dot's. He could see them flying across the room, landing on the coffee table and breaking it.

"I don't weigh much," said Daphne-Dot. "You can do it."

"Oh," he said weakly.

"Get back on the horse," Juliet barked.

"Go for it!" Chelsea shouted.

"Come on," Dot urged, "prove you've got what it takes."

He didn't have what it took. Everyone knew that, including him.

Juliet was at his elbow now. "Do it," she growled.

"I won't take you down, I promise," Dot said.

Dot was no spring chicken. What if she broke something?

"Hey, I don't get that many thrills at my age. Do an old lady a favor."

Oh, what the heck. Jonathan braced himself and flipped her.

A pair of scrawny legs sailed past his vision and then Dot was safely back on her feet. Everyone in the room was cheering and clapping again. He'd done it! He'd gotten back on the horse and stayed on.

After that, the night was one big Jonathan fest, with the women taking turns, begging for one more dance whenever he said he was tired. Juliet put on the AC, but he was still sweating by the time they finally let him sit down and drink a Coke.

"I had a great evening," Stacy Thomas said as they tore into the gingerbread treats Cass had brought.

"I wish Adam would learn to dance," Chelsea said wistfully, and Jonathan made a mental note to tell Adam he'd better sign up for dance lessons.

"You ever want to take a free cruise, kid, you could hire on as a dancer," Dot told him. "They're always looking for handsome studs to dance with all the single women."

He was a handsome stud? Dot was either losing it in her old age or she needed glasses.

"You," Cecily said as the party broke up, "are the best-kept secret in Icicle Falls."

He had to smile at her remark. "Thanks," he said.

Juliet shut the door on her guests and turned to gloat. "I *told* you that you could do it. You were like Derek Hough 2.0. You could go on *Dancing with the Stars* right now and win that mirror ball trophy."

He should still be pissed at her. It was hard, though, when he was feeling like the dancing king. Still. "That was a dirty trick."

"This was the only way to get your confidence back," she said. She took the last gingerbread boy from the plate sitting on her coffee table. "You are so ready for the reunion." Then she studied him critically. "Well, for dancing, anyway. Now we need to upgrade your look."

His appearance, the next frontier.

"You've buffed up, big bro. With some new glasses and a J.Crew style, you're going to be seriously hot."

He made a face. "Yeah, right."

"I'm not lying to you," she said. "Trust me. Before we're done with you, you'll be able to have any woman you want." She winked. "Even one whose initials are L.C."

He left his sister's house wearing a big grin.

Chapter Eighteen

On the first Saturday in August, Jonathan found himself up early and driving over the pass with Juliet riding shotgun. Why they had to go all the way to Seattle for clothes was beyond him, and he said as much as they cruised into the parking garage next to Macy's.

"Because Seattle has a bigger selection," Juliet explained. "And until someone decides to open up a men's clothing store in Icicle Falls, that's where we're going."

"I could just order something online," he grumbled.

"Yes, well, I've seen the kind of clothes you order online. You can't be trusted not to buy some outfit that makes you look like a walking ad for geekhood. Not that it's a bad thing to be a geek," she added quickly.

"Thanks."

"But you don't want to dress like one when you're trying to impress a woman. For that you need stud duds."

"Stud duds, huh?"

"Yes. Clothes that make you look sexy, not geeky.

That's where I come in. I want you to try on everything and I want to see it."

What was this *everything* stuff? Wasn't he just buying a shirt and pants? "Uh, define *everything*."

"Clothes for every event at the reunion and beyond, brother dear. We are going to deck you out like a Christmas tree."

What had he gotten himself into?

"It's about time you let me help you get a sense of style. And that's all I'm going to say about that."

Thank God, Jonathan thought. She'd been after him for years, always trying to get him to change his image, giving him sweaters for Christmas that he never wore, shirts for his birthday that stayed in his closet. One year she'd even given him boxers. Sheesh.

Still, he realized now that she'd been right. He was wardrobe-challenged. But he didn't need it rubbed in his face. Anyway, if he'd worn any of that stuff he'd have felt like a dork playing dress-up.

Which he was probably going to feel like today.

Juliet had insisted they leave early, claiming they had a full day's work ahead of them. At the time, he hadn't seen how buying a couple of shirts and a pair of pants could take so long, but now he was beginning to get an idea.

"This is going to be fun," Juliet said.

Fun. Yeah, about as much fun as hitting your finger with a hammer.

"Once we get you in some decent clothes, you are going to feel like a different man," Juliet predicted.

He could go for that. He *wanted* to be different. Better. A hunk. Well, okay, that was stretching it. Better. He'd be happy with better.

It wasn't hard to find a salesclerk eager to assist them. In fact, the guy's enthusiasm over dressing Jonathan made him slightly uncomfortable.

"He needs an entire new wardrobe," Juliet told him.

"I can see that." Ellis, a slim twenty-something guy with a slick metrosexual style, studied Jonathan from head to toe, shaking his head over Jonathan's black T-shirt sporting the symbol for pi set inside a steaming pie plate. (Caption beneath: Bring on the Pi.) "But I see potential," he said with an encouraging smile.

"So, casual clothes to start with," Juliet decided. "He needs some low-rise jeans and a slim fit shirt."

"Plaid," Ellis said. "And blue," he added. "Great with your coloring," he said to Jonathan, finally including him in the discussion. "Pant size? I'm thinking maybe a thirty-two, thirty-two."

Jonathan nodded.

"And shirt?"

"Medium," Jonathan supplied. "Fifteen and a half neck."

Ellis took in Jonathan's chest. "I'm thinking we might want to try a large."

From a medium to a large. Yes! All that sweating at the gym had paid off.

Within minutes Ellis and Juliet had assembled two armloads of clothes. Did they really expect him to try on all of that?

Evidently they did.

The first ensemble was jeans and the blue shirt.

He wasn't used to his pants riding that low. But once he'd pulled off his T-shirt and seen his reflection in the mirror, he realized they did a pretty good job of showing off his emerging six-pack. "Whoa." He didn't look half-bad.

"Let's see," Juliet called from outside the dressing room.

He pulled on the shirt and buttoned it up, then came out, buttoning the cuff.

"No, no," she said, slapping away his hand. Instead, she rolled the sleeve halfway up his forearm and undid the top button on the shirt. Then she stepped back to admire her handiwork. "Oh, yeah. My brother the hunk."

Ellis was on hand with a black-and-gray striped rugby hoodie. "And put this on."

Jonathan obliged and Juliet sighed. So did Ellis.

"If you weren't my brother, I'd have a serious crush on you."

"I already do," Ellis said, making Jonathan's cheeks sizzle. "Okay, now back to the dressing room. Oh, I feel just like Clinton on *What Not to Wear*."

Another ensemble, another glance in the mirror, and Jonathan was doing something he hadn't done in front of a mirror in, well, ever. He smiled.

Yeah, he still wore glasses, but they were losing their dork power. Maybe he *could* turn himself into somebody cool.

He modeled another outfit for his sister, who clapped in delight.

"An absolute transformation," Ellis said dreamily.

"We need movie theme music." Juliet began searching on her phone.

As Jonathan stepped back into his dressing room to try on a tan polo shirt, Jo Dee Messina's "Sharp-Dressed Man" blasted in after him. He turned in the mirror and admired his new and improved self, and it nodded in approval. Yes, he was becoming a sharp-dressed man.

Forty minutes later, he'd spent more on clothes than he had in the past two years combined, and Ellis was giving him his card, offering to help him with any needs he should have in the future. And Juliet was just getting warmed up.

"Shoes and socks next," she said, steering him toward the shoe department.

"I'm not made of money, you know," he protested.

"Don't give me that. You've got money in savings, you miser. It's time you invested some of it in yourself."

The investment didn't end at the shoe department. They went to a men's suit store and got him a suit, to another department store's optical department for new glasses frames and then to a fancy hair salon that catered to both men and women.

"I made an appointment for both of us," she said blithely. "After this you can buy me something to eat." And with that she left him in the capable hands of a hairdresser named Desiree, who gave him a pricey haircut and sold him an equally pricey jar of pomade. But worth every cent, he decided, checking out the new and improved him.

When they met in the reception area an hour later, Juliet beamed like Henry Higgins looking at Eliza Doolittle. "Wow! You are now officially a lady-killer."

"Yeah, right." Okay, that was taking it too far.

But as they set off down the street toward Wild Ginger, he caught a twenty-something woman checking him out. Him. Really? He glanced over his shoulder to see if there was someone behind him. Nope.

"Yes, she was looking at you," said Juliet, who could read minds. "You are going to be the surprise hit of the reunion."

Probably not compared to the likes of Rand or Cam Gordon or Feron Prince. But that was okay. He wasn't out to wow every woman from the class of 1998. Only one.

Were the new clothes enough? Lissa had always tended to get sidetracked by guys with a flashy facade. Sadly, she'd often had trouble seeing behind the facade.

"I can't believe he cheated on me," Lissa lamented the Thanksgiving weekend of their sophomore year in college.

She and Jonathan were both home for the weekend, and their families had gotten together on Friday night to share leftovers. The turkey sandwiches had been consumed. Lissa's older sister had been trying to settle her two-year-old so the families could play Trivial Pursuit. Lissa and Jonathan had drifted out onto the porch to compare notes on college and had wound up discussing her love life.

"Seriously, Liss? I knew when you brought him home last year that he was a player. He was flirting with my sister. You didn't see that?"

Her eyes widened, then her lower lip trembled. "No. Oh, Jonathan, why do I pick losers all the time?"

Because you don't pick me. As always, he thought it but didn't say it. He was too afraid that if he did, he'd see by the expression in her face that she believed he was a loser, too. Not the rotten, cheating kind of loser, of course. Just a subpar guy with no commanding presence. He simply wasn't sexy. Even his college major wasn't sexy. Who wanted to date a guy whose major was computer science?

A girl who was majoring in math, of course. Caroline Schnook wasn't as beautiful as Lissa (who was?), but she liked to play chess and she liked to read. They had plenty in common. He could be happy with her. That was what he told himself. But the happiness hadn't seemed so happy anymore after he'd seen Lissa.

"At least you've found someone nice."

He'd shrugged. "She's okay."

"Okay? You're settling for someone who's only okay?"

"There aren't enough Lissas to go around." It was the closest he'd ever come to telling her how he felt. Just saying those words had made his heart pound.

"Oh, Jonathan, you're so sweet. But you shouldn't be with a girl you're not crazy in love with."

"I think we're going to break up." He'd thought he could be happy with Caroline, but after talking to Lissa he'd known that, as she put it, he'd only be settling. And while that might have been okay for him (since he was reaching for the stars with Lissa, anyway), it wasn't fair to Caroline. Every woman deserved to have a man deeply, madly, breathlessly in love with her. Who wanted to be settled for?

"Gosh, Jonathan," Lissa said, "what's with us? How do we keep winding up with the wrong people?"

Because we're meant to be together. Just say it! he told himself.

As he opened his mouth to take the big gamble and put his heart on the line, the front door opened and her dad poked his head out. "Hey, you two, come on. We're about to start playing."

Lissa went back inside, leaving Jonathan to follow. The moment had passed.

What would have happened if he'd said, "Just a minute, Mr. Castle. I have something really important to say to your daughter." It would have blown up in his face, that was what would have happened. He'd looked nothing like the guys she dated. He'd looked like a geek.

But he didn't look like one now. He wasn't the same guy he'd been back then, either, and he was going to prove it to her.

The new and improved Jonathan hosted the next poker night.

Adam stared at him in surprise. "Whoa, what happened to you, dude?"

Jonathan shrugged as if it was no big deal that he'd

just spent a small fortune on clothes and glasses and a haircut. "Got some new clothes."

"Got some new everything. Crazy good improvement," Adam said, nodding.

"You don't even look like you," added Kyle, who'd come in with him.

A good thing, since the last person Jonathan wanted to look like was himself, at least his old self.

"So, does this mean you're going to the reunion, after all?" Kyle asked.

Jonathan pretended he hadn't given it much thought. "Maybe."

Kyle, too, nodded his approval. "Now that you're Mr. Hot it would be dumb not to."

Mr. Hot. Kyle was as full of it as Juliet.

"You really are a cutie," she'd informed him when he dropped her off at home after their shopping expedition.

"Whatever," he'd said.

"I'm serious. Yeah, you were geeky when we were kids, but you were never ugly. And now that you've hunked up *and* you're showing off the merchandise, you're going to have no problem getting any woman's attention."

Family loyalty, he'd thought. And the guys were just being good friends.

Except Vance never worried about boosting a man's ego and even he gave the new and improved Jonathan a thumbs-up. "I may have to put you in a book."

"Put *me* in a book," Bernardo said, thumping his chest.

"As what?" Vance scoffed.

"As a Latino lover."

The guys all chuckled and got down to the business of playing cards and that was the end of any talk about Jonathan's makeover.

But other people were still talking. "Look at you," Elena greeted him when he entered the Sweet Dreams office to run some diagnostics on one of their computers. *"¿Qué pasó?"*

The attention was both embarrassing and gratifying. "I just got some new clothes."

"You look great," Cecily said.

Dot, too, was impressed when he went to her place to assist with a computer emergency. "My, my, wait till our local girls get a gander at you in those new clothes."

It did seem like the local girls were taking a gander. Jenni, the barista at Bavarian Brews, gave him a once-over and cooed, "I like your new glasses."

"Uh, thanks," he said. *Well, that was smooth.* He might have been a new man on the outside, but inside he was still his same geeky self. He was going to have to work on upping his suave factor. He thought of item number two on his list of hero attributes—a smooth tongue. Yeah, he had a ways to go in the sweet-talker department.

That evening, after a hike with Chica, he pulled out his list and studied it again. He was making progress, he reminded himself. He was now at least semi-buff and as good-looking as he was going to get. And he could check off dancing. But he definitely needed some work in the smooth-tongue department. How did a guy learn to be a smooth talker?

He decided to throw out the question at the next poker night. "What kind of stuff can you say to get women to like you?" he asked.

Kyle, who was now an item with Mindy, was suddenly an expert on women. "You have to be sure and tell them they look nice."

"And never tell a woman she looks fat," Bernardo added. "Even if she says she has to go on a diet." He frowned. "Every time a woman goes on a diet, you end up on one, too."

Adam, who was seated next to him, slapped Bernardo's gut. "You need to be on a diet, dude."

"Hey, don't do that to a man!" Bernardo rubbed his middle. "That's how Houdini died. Anyway, I *am* on a diet. Remember?" he said as he helped himself to another one of the cookies Adam had brought.

"Yeah, I can tell," Adam said, looking in disgust at Bernardo's pudgy gut. "Doesn't your wife ever wonder why you're not losing any weight?"

"I *am* losing weight," said Bernardo. "I'm doing it slow."

"So, you just go up to someone and say, 'You look nice'?" Jonathan asked, bringing them back to the subject at hand. Pretty boring. He liked the lines he'd read in his novels better.

"Dress it up a little," Vance said. "Be creative. And concentrate on one thing, like her eyes." He demonstrated, lowering his voice. "I could get lost in those eyes of yours."

"Why, thank you," Bernardo said in a high falsetto and batted his lashes, making Adam and Kyle snicker.

Jonathan shook his head. "I'd feel like an idiot saying stuff like that."

Vance shrugged. "Women like it."

If women liked it, then men should say it. Jonathan stood in front of his bathroom mirror later that night and practiced. "I like your hair…." No, wait. That was dull. "Your hair, it looks like, um…" He thought of Lissa. "Spun gold. Like honey pouring down." Okay, that was good. It was true, too. He tried a second line. "Has anyone ever told you that you have enchanting eyes?" Oh, that was another good one. He smiled in the mirror and tried out his favorite line, culled from one of his novels. "Look at you. I could do it all night." Oh, yeah. That was a killer.

The next time he was at Bavarian Brews he tried a bit of flattery on Jenni, just to see if it would work. "Seeing you, I almost forgot what I came in for." He'd thought that one up all on his own and it was an excellent line, if he did say so himself.

Her cheeks turned pink and she smiled as if he'd given her chocolate. "Aw, Jonathan, that's sweet."

"I like your hair," he added.

"Really? I just got it cut," she said.

He hadn't noticed that. He made a mental note to be more observant. "Uh, yeah."

Now Jennie was looking at him speculatively, as if he might be good date material. He didn't want to lead her on; that wouldn't be right. He placed his order and moved away. Obviously flattery was powerful magic and should be used sparingly.

"Pretty smooth, computer man," said a low voice behind him.

Todd Black, the king of smooth. A whoosh of embarrassment carried away Jonathan's suave. He turned. "Uh, hi, Todd."

"I like the new look, man. Who are you out to impress?" He nodded in Jenni's direction. "Should I take a guess?"

"No, no. I was only…" *Practicing.* "Being nice."

"A word of caution," Todd said quietly. "Don't be too nice. Women take it the wrong way and then you're in deep shit."

So he'd just realized. He decided he'd better go back to practicing his lines in the mirror.

Kyle walked out of Ted Darrow's office feeling like he was ten feet tall, Ted's words ringing in his ears. "You've really been going the extra mile lately, Kyle. We've got a new position opening up in claims. I want you to apply for it."

That had been damned nice of Darrow. Maybe jealousy had led Kyle to misjudge him. Maybe Darrow wasn't such a bad guy, after all. Just as he was seeing his supervisor in a new light, Ted Darrow was obviously seeing him differently, too.

Well, he was seeing himself in a new way. These days he walked taller (even without the heightening shoes, which sat abandoned in his closet). He looked the bosses in the eye and smiled, volunteered for projects, even suggested ways the company could improve, like going to a paperless filing system. He supposed it all boiled down to confidence, and he knew who he had to thank for that. He could hardly wait to tell her.

"Hi, Kyle," Jillian said as he passed her desk. "Good news?"

Her voice had been pure silk and she was giving him the kind of flirtatious smile she used to give Darrow. Now, that was interesting. "Maybe," he said, and kept walking.

"Okay, spill," Mindy said as he tried to settle back down at his computer. "What was that all about?"

"I'll tell you at lunch," he promised.

"You'd better," she said with a smile.

Funny things, smiles. They could be fueled by any number of motives. Sometimes they meant a woman was happy. Other times, as in Jillian's case, they meant she was after something. Or someone. Someone who could give her something.

He sent up a little prayer. *Thanks, God, for not letting me have the woman I wanted.*

"Why am I not surprised?" Mindy said when he shared his news with her at lunch.

"I don't know. Why?"

She leaned over and kissed him. "Because you deserve it. You're great and they're lucky to have you."

"And I'm lucky to have you," he said. "How about coming to my class reunion with me? I want to show you off."

"Yeah? Even though I'm not tall and blonde?"

"Blondes are overrated. I prefer short girls," Kyle said, earning himself a kiss. "So, you wanna go?"

"Of course. Otherwise, some other woman might steal you."

No chance of that but Kyle decided he wasn't going to disillusion her.

"Mindy's going with me to the reunion," Kyle announced at poker night.

"There's a shock," Jonathan said, trying not to be jealous. How he wished that, like Kyle, his love life was all sewed up.

"You've gotta go, Jon," Kyle said. "I mean, the new clothes, the new muscle. That's what you've been doing it for, isn't it?"

Jonathan shrugged. He was glad he'd kept his mouth shut about Lissa, glad he hadn't committed to attending the damned reunion. He'd paid his money but that didn't mean he had to go. A guy could change his mind—and that was exactly what he'd done. After what he'd learned earlier that day about Rand, he was glad.

"And what's the point of reading all those romance novels if you aren't gonna put some of that into play?" Kyle continued.

"Reunions," Vance said. "They're such a bunch of B.S. People never go because they want to see their old pals. They go because they want to show off or prove something."

Or get someone, Jonathan thought.

"So I guess you never went to any of yours," Adam said.

"Oh, yeah. I went to my ten-year. Met my old girl-friend there. Married her six months later." Vance shook his head. "I never should have gone."

And if that wasn't confirmation that Jonathan had made the right decision, he didn't know what was. So much for the new clothes and glasses. So much for sweating at the gym. Damn Rand Burwell, anyway.

"I guess he's divorced now," Tina had said when she gave Jonathan the revised list—with Rand's name at the top—to put up on the webpage. Good old Rand was free as a bird and coming to the reunion.

Jonathan had been in a foul mood ever since. "Are we gonna play cards or what?"

The other guys looked at him in surprise. "Sure," Adam said. "Ante up, dudes."

That was the end of the conversation for the night, but Kyle lingered after everyone else had left. "Okay, what's up with you?"

"Nothing," Jonathan snapped.

"Wait a minute. You just updated the reunion web-page, didn't you?"

"So?"

"So what happened to piss you off? Who's com-ing?" Jonathan could tell by his friend's expression that he'd answered his own question. Sure enough. "Oh. Rand."

"Yeah, Rand."

Kyle frowned. "Well, so what? This isn't high school and you're not the same person you were back then. Heck, you're not the same person you were three months ago. Are you gonna let Rand intimidate you?"

As a matter of fact, yes.

"I'll bet he's got a gut on him now. Probably losing his hair, too," Kyle threw in for extra measure.

"Not according to the picture he sent."

"Oh. Well, what do you care? Rand's not competition for you anymore." Kyle's face clouded. "Wait a minute. There wasn't someone you were hoping to hook up with, was there?"

"No." He could feel his cheeks heating. Where was his poker face when he needed it?

Kyle pointed an accusing finger at him. "Lissa."

Jonathan tried to cover up his embarrassment with bluster. "There's nobody I want to see. All those people are a bunch of fatheads."

"Except Lissa. You always had the hots for her. Damn it all, Jon, I thought you'd kicked that habit."

"I did," Jonathan muttered.

"Yeah, I can tell. Come on, buddy, don't do this to yourself. You're in la-la land, just like I was with Jillian."

Well, he liked it in la-la land. He busied himself putting away the cards and poker chips.

"Okay, so you've still got it bad for Lissa. I think you're nuts, but okay," Kyle said. "Then what are you doing running away like a nerd chicken because Rand's coming? I heard he's married. He'll probably have the wife in tow."

Jonathan shook his head. "He's divorced. He'll be

out looking for someone to hook up with." And they both knew what that meant.

"I still think you should go," Kyle said.

That was the last thing he wanted to do—go to the reunion and watch Rand and Lissa hook up again.

"If you don't, you're just giving her to him on a silver platter," Kyle said. "But hey, it's your life," he added, and left.

Yes, it was. And if he wanted to give up and be alone and miserable, he could.

He put the beer bottles in the recycle bin, then went to bed. He had a half-finished Vanessa Valentine paperback lying on his nightstand. He ignored it, turned out the light and rolled over. Screw Vanessa Valentine. Screw Rand. Screw the reunion. Screw everyone and everything. And with those pleasant thoughts, he drifted off to sleep.

Where he dreamed once more that he was at the Icicle Falls High reunion. This time they were all at the dining hall at the Icicle Creek Lodge and he was a waiter, serving everyone. A waiter dressed in a clown suit. Bearing a silver platter under a big silver dome, he came to where Rand sat yukking it up with Feron Prince and Cam Gordon. He bent over Rand and lifted the lid to reveal a miniature Lissa, laid out like a roast pig with an apple in her mouth.

"All right," Rand said, rubbing his hands together. "Just what I've been wanting. Thanks, Jonathan."

He took the apple out of Lissa's mouth and she looked beseechingly at Jonathan and cried in a tiny voice, "Help, Jonathan! Save me!"

He awoke with a start, sat up and blinked. What the heck was that?

Last call for the reunion, that was what.

Okay, he was going.

Chapter Nineteen

Class of 1998 Reunion Schedule of Events
(Welcome, Grizzlies!)

Friday, 5:00–7:00 p.m.
Cocktail party at Icicle Creek Lodge,
followed by dinner

Saturday, 9:00 a.m.
Grizzly Girls breakfast at Breakfast Haus
followed by shopping

Saturday, 9:00 a.m.
Grizzly golf tournament at the
Mountain Meadows Golf Course

Saturday, 12:00–4:00 p.m.
Grizzly grub picnic at Riverwalk Park

Saturday 8:00 p.m.–midnight
Dance at Festival Hall

Sunday, 10:00 a.m.–12:00 p.m.
Farewell brunch at Icicle Creek Lodge

The third weekend in August had finally arrived. This was it. Jonathan was scrubbed and shaved and dressed to kill in new shoes (dark loafers, no socks), jeans with a hip shirt, tie and a white linen blazer. He nudged his glasses in place, even though they already were perfectly settled on his nose, and examined himself in the mirror. His chest had broadened and he was now sporting a six-pack under his shirt. Or the beginnings of one, anyway. Maybe he could survive this.

Of course he could survive this. He had a new look and a smooth tongue.

And a red rose he'd picked from his mother's garden to give Lissa. He'd considered a number of memorable romantic gestures he could make. His first thought had been to hang a banner over the door of the Icicle Creek Lodge proclaiming Welcome, Lissa. Except he'd decided Tina would probably take it down, not wanting to single out anyone in particular (unless it was herself). Anyway, he'd tried the anonymous gesture before, back in high school, and that had backfired. If he was going to do something romantic, he needed to make sure he got the credit for it. He'd also thought of having the band play a special song just for her. *This goes out to Lissa from Jonathan.* That had seemed like a good idea when it first struck, but the more he'd mulled it over, the less he'd liked it. It made him think of people sitting at home at night, listening to the radio. *Play Misty for Me.* He'd seen that old movie on the classics channel, and he didn't want to do anything that might come across as psycho. Hiring a limo and picking her up to take her to the first event? What if she'd made plans to go with a girlfriend? Or Rand. (*There* was a depressing thought.) In the end he'd settled on the rose. It was tasteful and classy. Like the new him.

Chica, who'd been watching him, followed him out the front door, whining.

"Sorry," he told her. "This is a human party. You can't come."

He gave her head a good rub and in return she gave his hand a little nip that might or might not have been playful.

"You stay here and guard the house. Okay?"

She lay down on the porch with a groan.

"I'll be back," he said. Hopefully, not until late.

Rose in hand, he climbed into his Volkswagen Beetle and made the short drive to the Icicle Creek Lodge. Tina and her decorating crew had gone all out. Across the front door hung a banner that said Welcome Home, Class of 1998. Once inside the lodge, he saw flowers and balloons everywhere in their school colors of red and gold. A few people were chatting in the lobby— he recognized Bobby Burns, basketball star, and his pal John Corallo, as well as April Anderson, who'd been president of the Grizzly Girls.

He ducked past them and followed the noise to the dining hall, which was packed with tables covered with linen tablecloths and fancy settings, and people standing about, already enjoying drinks and reminiscing. His heart rate began to pick up. He forced himself to walk into his past.

Feron Prince seemed to be six inches taller than

the last time Kyle had seen him and had bulked up even more. No beer belly there. At his side stood a woman who looked like Beyonce's kid cousin. The huge rock on her finger said they belonged together. Next to him, Cam Gordon stood with a drink in his hand. Cam hadn't weathered the past fifteen years as well as Feron. His hair was thinning and he was starting to grow a gut. But the clothes he wore said he'd also been growing his bank account. Two other former jocks joined them. Jonathan could feel the waves of testosterone coming at him. He turned his gaze in a different direction.

In another part of the room, several women were gathered around Daphne Robard, laughing hysterically. Another group of women nearby included Heidi Schwartz, who was showing off a picture on her phone, probably of her kid. He wished he had something, anything, to show off.

He started to pass another group of chatting women. One of them looked appreciatively at him and waved him over. It was Tessa Newton. She'd been a cheerleader.

"Hi, there," she greeted him. "Are you here with someone?"

"Uh, no." *Oh, boy. Great way to be suave.* He tried again. "Just here by myself, looking for pretty ladies." That sounded dumb.

Dumb or not, Tessa ate it up. She grinned at him, revealing a dimple. "I'm Tessa." She held out a hand for him to shake.

Of course she didn't recognize him. He was

tempted to be a smart mouth. *I'm Jason Bourne.* Instead, he opted for politeness and took her hand. "You probably don't remember me. I'm Jonathan Templar."

"J-Jonathan?" she stammered.

He smiled at that. It looked like clothes did, indeed, make the man.

She blinked, obviously trying to line up what she was seeing with the image she had stored in her memory bank.

"Nice seeing you, Tessa." *Not really.* He moved on.

"Jonathan, hi."

He turned to see a guy in slacks and a button-down shirt waving at him. He'd lost the specs but he was still as skinny as ever. Darrell Hornsby, one of his old chess club buddies. Jonathan smiled, happy to see a friendly face. And who was that standing next to the friendly face? He gasped at the curvy brunette in the clingy black dress. She resembled a movie star. Or a high-class hooker. What was *she* doing with Darrell?

Jonathan moved over to where they stood and said hello.

"You look good," Darrell said, taking in Jonathan's new clothes. "What happened?"

"Darrell!" the woman chided in soft tones.

"Oh, sorry. I mean, well, gosh, you look good."

"Thanks." All his hard work had been worth it. Now, if only Lissa would notice. Where was she?

"Meet Bridget," Darrell said.

"Hi, Bridget."

"Nice to meet you," she said, looking him over and smiling. "Darrell's told me a lot about you."

What was there to tell? "Uh, really?" *Smooth.* Jonathan got in touch with his inner Todd Black. "Well, I can see why he didn't tell me anything about you. I wouldn't want to share, either, if you were mine." Not that he'd seen Darrell or talked to him in the past five years but it sounded nice.

It sounded nice to Bridget, too. She beamed at him. Oh, yeah. He had his suave on. He could do this.

"You're never going to guess where Bridget and I met," Darrell said.

He wasn't even going to try.

"Online. There's this site for people who are too busy with their careers to date."

Jonathan remembered that Darrell had a software company. He was clearly doing okay.

"It specializes in—" Here Darrell faltered.

Fortune Hunters? "Matching beautiful women with successful men?" Jonathan supplied.

"That's it," Darrell said, grinning.

Jonathan didn't know a lot about women's jewelry but he did know expensive when he saw it, and the necklace Bridget was wearing couldn't be cheap. Kudos to Darrell, he decided. The guy had done well. He'd bribed a beautiful woman to be with him and he'd probably impress everyone at the reunion.

"Well, they did a terrific job," Jonathan said, trying not to stare at Bridget's boobs. "Hey, I need to, uh—" He pointed in the general direction of the crowd.

"Okay," Darrell said. "We'll catch up with you later."

Jonathan nodded and started to move away.

Now here came Kyle and Mindy. "Man, what a crowd, huh?" Kyle said.

Don't remind me, Jonathan thought. There were a few people he was looking forward to talking to—some of the chess gang, a couple of old buddies from band, but for the most part he was in hostile territory.

"Hi, Jonathan," Mindy said. "It's nice to see you again."

"Thanks," Jonathan said, trying to surreptitiously scan the crowd.

"Want us to save you a couple of seats at dinner?" Kyle offered.

A couple of seats, that was thinking positive. *Yeah, think positive.* "Sure," Jonathan said, and returned to his hunt for Lissa.

She had to be here somewhere. He craned his neck, trying to see past the dressed-to-impress herd. The crowd shifted, and he caught sight of the bar set up in one corner of the dining hall. There, a little off to the right with a martini glass in her hand, talking to Laurie Poznick, stood Lissa.

He didn't want to go over and talk to Lissa with another woman standing there, but she'd probably have someone standing next to her for the whole cocktail party. There would be no perfect time to make his first move. Now he saw—oh, no!—Rand in all his muscled glory approaching from another corner of the room, zeroing in on Lissa like a stealth bomber. No beer gut there, no hair loss. Rand looked as good as he had in high school. No, better—more filled out, more mature. He was a man in his prime.

Jonathan's grip on his rose tightened. A thorn pricked him and he swore under his breath. Once Rand reached Lissa, he'd never leave her side. She'd end up going in to dinner with him, and Jonathan wouldn't stand a chance.

He shouldered his way through the crowd, practicing his line as he went. *Look at you. I could do it all night. Look at you. I could do it all night. Look at you.*

Yes, look at her. She was so beautiful, wearing a blue sundress, her hair hanging in golden waves down past her neck.

Look at you. I could do it all night.

Now he was practically in front of her. She was even *more* beautiful close up. He took in those pretty lips, all pink and glossy, and his mouth went dry.

Laurie saw him first and smiled. Then Lissa turned her head. Now what was it he was going to say? *Looking.* Something about looking.

"Uh, Lissa," he said, and held out the flower.

"Oh, Jonathan, how sweet! I was hoping you'd be here. Wow. You could be on the cover of a magazine."

"I could look at you doing it all night," he blurted. Wait a minute. That had come out all wrong.

Lissa's eyebrows drew together and Laurie frowned at him as if he was a perv.

"I mean, I could look at you all night," Jonathan amended. His face was a raging inferno. He turned to the bar and grabbed a water bottle. Stress (or all those workouts) had apparently given him superhuman strength and he about throttled the bottle taking the cap off. Water gushed out like a miniature Old Faithful, spilling down his shirt and onto his pants.

Laurie giggled and even Lissa was smiling.

Jonathan managed a nervous grin. "Uh, cheap plastic."

"I guess," Laurie said.

He had to get out of here before he did anything else dumb. "I'd better, uh…" *Go shoot myself and be done with it.*

He backed up, encountered a body and spun around, spilling the rest of the contents of his water bottle on Daphne, who'd been heading full steam for the bar.

"What the hell?"

"Oh, uh, sorry, Daphne," he said, and put out a hand to wipe off the rivulets. Only…they were running down her breasts. Not a good idea. He yanked his hand away.

She scowled at him. "You ought to wear a sign that says Hazardous," she snapped.

"Sorry," he mumbled, and beat it, retreating to the farthest side of the dining room, willing his hands to stop sweating and his heart to calm down. How many people had seen that?

Now Rand was with Lissa and Laurie. He said something and Lissa smiled. Was it an I'm-majorly-glad-to-see-you smile or simply a polite one? Had she thought of Rand these past few years?

There he stood, well-groomed and well-dressed. Expensively dressed, with a fancy signet ring on his right hand so all the world could see he had money.

Money wasn't everything.

And no ring on his left hand, so all the world could see he was on the prowl.

Now he leaned over and whispered in Lissa's ear and her cheeks turned pink. What had he said? Probably that he could look at her all night. Rand would, naturally, get the line correct.

Jonathan became aware of a presence looming next to him. Feron Prince.

Oh, no. Fresh torture.

"Glad to see you here, Jon," Feron said.

Jonathan couldn't imagine why. "Uh, same here," he managed, even though it was a total lie.

"I missed the ten-year."

What a shame.

"There's something I've been wanting to say to you."

Jonathan looked at him suspiciously. "What?"

"I'm sorry I was such a damned bully in high school. I acted like a real shit stuffing you in that locker and I've felt bad about it for years."

Jonathan blinked. Feron Prince was apologizing to *him?* "It's okay."

"It's not. It never was. But thanks for saying that." He held out a hand and Jonathan shook it. Obviously nerds weren't the only ones who could change....

Jonathan's thoughts were interrupted by the squeal of a microphone. Tina had one and was now tapping it. "Is this on?"

Well, duh.

She tapped it again. "Welcome, everyone, to our

fifteen-year reunion. I'm glad so many of you could make it."

It would have been nice if a certain one of them hadn't. Darn it all, why couldn't Rand have stayed married and stayed home?

"I think they're about ready to start serving, so let's all find our seats."

Rand put a hand on Lissa's back and began to steer her toward a table.

Never, never, never, never give up. Go sit on the other side of her, Jonathan commanded himself.

Keeping an eye on Rand and Lissa, he began to move toward their table. He'd almost reached them when he realized that Laurie was taking the other seat next to her. What would Winston Churchill do?

He had no idea, but he knew what *he* was going to do. He passed the table Kyle had chosen, motioning to his destination. Kyle nodded and gave him a thumbs-up as he weaved his way past chatting classmates toward her table to claim a seat opposite them.

The table was set for eight and already occupied by six. There sat Lissa, Rand and Laurie. And with them, Cam, Tina and Doug Immeressen, another superjock who'd enjoyed intimidating scrawny geeks. Jonathan would rather have swum in shark-infested waters.

Who was he kidding? These *were* shark-infested waters. With a gulp, he pulled out a seat and sat down, nodding at the others.

"Well, here he is," Rand said genially, "the king of the chessboard."

Not everyone had changed.

"That's me," Jonathan said, pretending it wasn't an insult.

Rand studied him for a moment. "You lost the geek look."

Jonathan shrugged. Maybe. He still had all his favorite button-down shirts in his closet and his nerdy T-shirts in a drawer at home. You could take the boy out of the geek clothes, but you couldn't take the geek out of the boy. But for the weekend, that side of him was going to stay firmly hidden.

Unlike Rand, Doug and Cam didn't comment on Jonathan's appearance. They didn't even bother to say hello, just kept talking with Tina. She was cute and single again, so that was hardly surprising. But they wouldn't have said anything anyway.

"I think he looks fantastic," Lissa said.

"Thanks." Jonathan felt that was encouraging. So was the fact that she had her rose. She laid it carefully in front of her plate.

Okay, maybe he was going to survive this. Maybe he was going to do more than survive. Maybe he could find a way to be suave and entertaining. "Congrats on how well your career's going. I've been watching you every day," he told Lissa.

"What, through binoculars?" Rand chortled at his own humor.

"On TV. You're great."

"Lissa's always been great," Rand said. He lowered his voice and Jonathan strained to hear. "I was a fool to let you go."

Rand was a fool. Period.

Lissa blushed and took a sip of her martini.

The chair next to Jonathan was pulled out and down plunked—oh, no, Daphne. "Don't spill anything on me," she cautioned.

"Wouldn't dream of it," Jonathan assured her.

But he did. In his haste to pass the poppyseed dressing to Lissa when the salad had been served, he managed to let the little pitcher slide off its tray. It tumbled right onto Daphne's plate and rained salad dressing into her lap.

She scooted back with a yelp.

Jonathan could feel his cheeks burning. "Sorry, Daphne," he said. This couldn't be happening. Now truly panicked, he grabbed for his napkin and in the process, tipped over his water glass. Water slid across the table toward Tina, who was on his other side, amid ruthless chuckles from Rand.

Jonathan was vaguely aware of someone asking, "Who invited this clown to our table?" He thought it was Cam but it could as easily have been Rand or Doug. He didn't know. Everything was one ugly blur. He was living his nightmare.

Daphne was standing up now, holding out the skirt of her black dress. "I have to go change. This dress is ruined."

"I'll pay for a new one," Jonathan offered.

"You bet," she snapped, and made her exit.

"You always were a klutz," Rand reminisced.

Grown men don't cry. Jonathan wished he could run away, to another city, another state, another country. India, maybe.

"It was an ugly dress, anyway," Lissa said in an obvious effort to make him feel better.

That was Lissa, kind to everyone and everything— lost puppies, little kids, clowns. Jonathan managed a nod.

The evening crawled tortuously on. Daphne came back to the dining hall but found a seat at another table. "Well, you got rid of *her*," Rand cracked.

It was about the only other thing he said to Jonathan. Hard to believe they'd been childhood friends. Rand had turned into a selfish braggart. Everyone at the table heard about his film agency in Hollywood and his house in "the hills." Lissa heard about how his wife had never understood him, how next time he was going to pick a woman with heart. "A woman with blond hair and pretty blue eyes," he added, and gave a lock of her hair a playful tug.

Jonathan gave his breaded chicken a vicious slice with his knife, sending it skittering off his plate. He didn't check to see who saw that one. Instead, he kept his head down as he stabbed it with his fork and returned it to his plate. He didn't touch it again. His appetite was gone, as were his chances of impressing Lissa.

He sneaked a look at the table where Kyle was sitting with Mindy and Darrell and Bridget and two of his old friends from the band. They were all chatting, smiling, enjoying themselves. He should have sat there, with people who liked him.

Dessert was served, a chocolate mousse topped with fresh raspberries that the women all raved over.

As far as Jonathan was concerned, the best part of dessert was that it signaled the end of dinner.

"Time for fun," Tina said, and left her seat.

Fun? Oh, no. What did that mean?

She picked up her microphone and asked, "Is everyone having a good time?"

No.

Hoots and claps asserted that everyone else present was, indeed, enjoying the party.

"Well, now we're going to see how good your memories are. Melody is passing out some pop quizzes. Don't anyone turn your papers over until I say."

"Oh, man, just like in Ms. Crow's history class," complained Cam.

Cam had never been good at history. Actually, Cam had never been good at anything scholastic. His specialty had been football and getting laid.

Jonathan wished he hadn't been so good with the books himself. Look where that had gotten him. Melody gave him a sheet of paper and he dutifully turned it facedown.

Not Rand and Doug. They were already comparing answers. Bunch of cheaters.

"Okay, now, turn over your papers," Tina said merrily.

The questions were properly goofy. *Which teacher was nicknamed the Smurf? Who was famous for her bad hair days? (Hint: her initials are L.P.)* Lissa saw that one and gave Laurie a playful elbow. *Who got caught smoking pot in the boys' bathroom?* Jonathan had no idea. He'd never smoked the stuff. *Who did we lose the football championship to? Who cared? Where was the best place to go when you wanted to be alone after a hot date?* Ha! He knew that one. Even he had done a little smooching parked at the entrance to the Lost Bride Trail. *Who starred in our 1998 production of* The Music Man? Daphne, of course.

Jonathan's hand suddenly went clammy and what little of the chicken he'd consumed started doing the chicken dance in his stomach. *What superbrain got "trapped" in his locker when he was a freshman?*

Seriously? He'd been Tina's reunion tech slave and this was the thanks he got? He crumpled his napkin into a tight ball. Okay, enough. He'd had enough, enough of this so-called game and enough of these people. Almost all of them were stuck in high school with their stupid snobbish pecking order. He didn't need to stay for this.

He shoved out his chair and stood.

"What's the matter, Templar?" Cam called after him.

Jonathan didn't bother to answer, merely said goodbye with his middle finger.

He was halfway across the lobby by the time Kyle caught up with him. "Hey, where are you going?"

"Home. I don't need to sit around and take this shit."

Kyle frowned. "Don't leave, man. If you do, they win."

"Easy for you to say," Jonathan growled. "You didn't make it into the pop quiz."

"Come on. Come back in and sit with us. You *can't* let them win."

Yes, he could. He shook off his friend's hand and started walking.

"You leave, and you'll really look like a loser," Kyle called after him.

That stopped him in his tracks.

"Anyway, you're not that guy anymore. Are you?"

Hell, no. Jonathan turned around and marched back to the dining room.

Chapter Twenty

He arrived just in time to hear his fellow classmates' chuckles. Of course. They were laughing at him. He clenched his sweaty palms and made his way back to his table.

"We were just talking about you," Rand greeted him.

Maybe so, but as it turned out the giggling at the moment was over another question, one he hadn't read on to see. *Who fell into the garbage can while trying to fish out her retainer?* Someone had done that? Why didn't he remember?

"I can laugh about it now," Tina was saying, "but at the time it wasn't all that funny."

"We got a great view of your ass, though," Cam called, and she shook her head at him.

"All those embarrassing things that happened to us in high school," she said. "Didn't they seem like the end of the world back then?"

Yeah, they did.

"But they didn't really matter half as much as we thought."

Well, he didn't know about *that*.

"'Cause look at what a super bunch of people we've turned into," Tina was saying, sweeping the room with her cheerleader smile. "I hope you're all having as much fun as I am catching up with everyone. We're going to need to get out of here pretty soon, but I know you'll all keep the party going at Zelda's or the Man Cave."

Jonathan shot a look across the table. Sure enough, Rand was whispering something in Lissa's ear. She gave him a considering smile, then nodded. It would probably be Zelda's for them and that meant there'd be no chance for him to get any one-on-one time with her tonight.

"But before we go, I want to thank my reunion committee for all their hard work. Laura and Heidi, stand up."

Laura and Heidi stood, and everyone gave them a hearty round of applause.

"And a big thank-you to Jonathan Templar, my favorite nerd, for doing our webpage for us and getting everything up on Facebook."

Applause was a little less hearty now, except for Kyle's table where there was much cheering. Jonathan felt the flush from his neck clear to the roots of his hair.

"Okay, everyone, now just a quick reminder about our schedule of events for tomorrow. All you Grizzly Girls don't forget our breakfast at Breakfast Haus and our shopping spree. Let's support our hometown economy!"

Go, Grizzly Girls, Jonathan thought sourly. Lissa would be part of that, so there was no point in asking her out for breakfast.

"For you golfers, we have the golf tournament, and then, in the afternoon the picnic, where we can get a chance to see how everyone's families have grown."

He already knew how that would go. Lissa would be surrounded by girlfriends; she'd be busy holding their babies, playing with their children. For a moment he could picture them together as a couple, her holding a baby girl with blond curls, him chasing a dark-haired little boy around.

"And I hope you brought your dancing shoes so you can show off your moves at the dance," Tina finished. "That's it for tonight. See you all tomorrow!"

"See you at the picnic?" Jonathan asked Lissa.

"I won't be at the picnic, but I'll be at the dance so don't forget to save me one," she said before Rand whisked her off.

Jonathan stood, his hands clenched into fists. Why was he even trying? Damn Rand Burwell, anyway. His heart twisted as he watched Lissa smile up at Rand. New clothes, new muscle, slick words—what did it matter?

Suddenly, Lissa did one small thing that gave him hope. She sniffed her rose and smiled at him over her shoulder. Just one smile, but it was enough to unclench his fists, to send him home whistling. To assure him that his story wasn't over yet.

* * *

"You gotta go to the picnic," Kyle said when he called Jonathan the next morning.

Jonathan preferred to save his energy, both physical and mental, for the dance. "It's only gonna be families."

"I'm going. So's Darrell. And remember Simon Jacobs?"

"Yeah." Simon had been another member of the chess club. "I didn't see him last night." Not that he'd been looking. The only person he'd been looking for had been Lissa.

"He didn't get here until late last night. But he's coming to the picnic. He's got a wife and kid now."

Simon Jacobs had been even skinnier and geekier than Jonathan. And he'd had a major zit issue. And yet even he was married. Jonathan was now officially the last man from the chess club—heck, on the planet— who didn't have anyone.

"He's gonna want to see you," Kyle said.

"Yeah, I'd like to see him, too. He'll be at the dance, right?"

"When I talked to him he wasn't sure. His wife's pregnant and about to pop."

"Oh. Well." Jonathan still didn't want to go to the picnic. "Tell him I said hi."

"Tell him yourself. Come on, don't wimp out on me here. We need some chess club solidarity."

"You and Simon can stand solid."

"Don't be such a wuss," Kyle said in disgust.

"I'm not a wuss," Jonathan protested.

"Oh, yeah, you are. You need to go to this stuff, Jon. People want to see you."

He'd noticed how much people wanted to see him the night before.

"Come on, just for a while," Kyle wheedled.

Jonathan sighed. "Okay, okay." He'd go, but only long enough to say hi to Simon.

He arrived a little after noon at the Riverwalk Park with his bucket of chicken from the Safeway deli to find the picnic area packed with young families. Juan Fernandez, the senior class president, was manning the barbecue, and the aroma of sizzling burgers was heavy on the air. Women were setting out food on one of the tables, while their guys stood in groups, drinking pop and talking. Kids swarmed the nearby play area and chased one another, darting among the adults. Everyone here had someone. He was going to look like a fool wandering around with only his bucket of chicken for company.

You're here now, he told himself, *make the best of it.*

But who to make the best of it with? That was the question. The crowd looked like it was all cheerleaders and jocks and class officers. All the shy souls had stayed home. Which was what Jonathan should have done.

Oh, but wait. There, staking out a table at the edge of the crowd, was Kyle. And with him? It had to be Simon and his wife. Except the guy didn't look like the Simon Jonathan remembered. Simon had missed their ten-year reunion so Jonathan hadn't seen him in fifteen years. A guy's appearance could change a lot in fifteen years.

He thought of how different *he* looked now. Heck, a guy's appearance could change a lot in a few months.

He deposited his contribution to the feast on the buffet table, then started working his way to where his friends were waiting.

Nearby, one rambunctious little boy in shorts and a red T-shirt came running out of nowhere and managed to collide with Jonathan. He ricocheted off Jonathan's legs and landed on his backside, a shocked expression on his face.

"You're a pretty fast runner," Jonathan told him, setting him back on his feet. "What's your name?"

"Mikey," the child said. "I'm six."

Now Tina had joined them. "Mikey, say you're sorry for running into Jonathan."

So this was Tina's kid. Now that she was here, Jonathan saw the likeness. He was a good-looking kid. He'd probably grow up to become a member of the in crowd.

"Sorry," Mikey muttered.

"That's okay," Jonathan said.

Mikey didn't hear him. He was already off and running again.

Tina watched him go, smiling fondly. "That boy has no off switch."

But Tina did, especially when it came to fraternizing with the unimportant people. "Janelle," she called, and hurried off to visit with a fellow cheerleader who was holding a toddler on her hip.

Jonathan continued on his course, steering past laughing groups of mothers and their kids, and finally landed at the table with Kyle and Simon and his family.

"Hey, you made it," Kyle said. "This was the last table we could find," he added.

On the fringe, just like in high school. But so what? They'd all be on the fringe together and that was better than being alone.

"Jon!" Simon greeted him. "Great to see you."

"You, too," Jonathan said, taking in his old pal's new and improved appearance. The zits were gone and so were the specs. "What happened to your glasses?"

"Lasik surgery."

Lucky Simon. He'd shed a major geek accessory. Jonathan had to beat back the green-eyed monster threatening to sour this moment of reconnecting with an old pal. *So what if you're still wearing glasses? Glasses are cool these days.*

Except he didn't feel cool. He had a new body, new clothes, yeah, and even new glasses, but he was still uncool. He'd proved that at the dinner the night before.

"This is my wife, Beth," Simon said, putting his arm around a plain-faced, very pregnant woman. "And this—" he hoisted a toddler from the picnic table bench "—is Bobby."

"Named after Bobby Fischer?" Jonathan surmised.

"Why not? It'll give him good chess karma."

A burst of laughter from one of the other picnic tables drew their attention. Doug Immeressen had just succeeded in slipping an ice cube down Tina's shirt.

Yup, stuck forever in high school, Jonathan thought,

not for the first time. He studied the group. There they were, the superstars of Icicle Falls High. Were any of them superstars now? Yeah, Tina owned a shop in town, and he'd heard Doug was managing a car dealership in Yakima. He had no idea what Cam Gordon or Feron Prince were doing but he hadn't seen Cam on TV playing in the Super Bowl. So what made them any better than a guy who owned his own computer repair company?

"Okay, everyone, food's ready," Tina announced. "Bring your plates and get your Grizzly grub."

Jonathan noticed that old Doug was first in line. Doug had been a fullback, first string, and he'd probably dated half the girls in the school. He'd been known for both his monster size and the appetite that matched it. Now filling his plate took higher priority than flirting with Tina or paying attention to her little boy.

Did Jonathan want to be like the Doug Immeressens of the world? No, thanks. The guy might have been something back in high school, but today, like Jonathan, he was a guy alone floating in a sea of families. Old Doug was nothing to be jealous of.

"So, how's it been going?" Simon asked. He checked out Jonathan's hip jeans and shirt and the casual flip-flops. "Kyle says you've got your own company. And you built your own house," Simon continued. "Looks like life's agreeing with you." His voice was channeling the green-eyed monster's bro.

Jonathan nodded. *Weird,* he thought. What did *he* have to be jealous about?

"Your business must be doing well."

"It's okay," Jonathan said with a shrug. He was making a living but he wasn't exactly getting rich.

"There's more to life than money," his dad used to say. "Find yourself a good woman and you'll be the richest man in the world."

He'd found the woman, but so far he was still locked outside Fort Knox.

"Let's get some food before it's all gone," Kyle suggested, grabbing a paper plate.

The food line was long, and once the first string had gone through, the pickings were slim, but Jonathan scored some pasta salad and the last burger on the barbecue.

"Jonathan, you're just in time," Juan told him.

Juan, too, had moved in the top circles in high school, but he'd always been an okay guy, happy to be friends with everyone. Even now, Jonathan was impressed that Juan remembered his name. Of course, Juan was running for representative for the fourth congressional district. As a politician, it was his business to remember names.

"Great to see you," he added, and even though he was a politician, Jonathan suspected he meant it.

"As usual, the jocks got all the good stuff," Kyle grumbled.

"You're the one who wanted to come," Jonathan reminded him as they walked back to their table.

One of Jonathan's band buddies showed up with his wife and their twin boys and Jonathan's party squeezed together, making room for them at the table. Visiting with another old pal, Jonathan decided it had been worth his time to come to the picnic. He kept the kids laughing by making funny faces and demonstrated his talent for hanging a spoon on his nose. Very uncool but the kids loved it.

Once they'd finished eating, the twins ran off to play. Jonathan noticed that his pal kept a watchful eye on them.

Which was more than he could say for some of the other parents. Many of them were too busy yukking it up and remembering the good old days to pay attention to what their offspring were up to. Like Tina, who was in a giggling huddle with the other cheerlcaders.

Meanwhile, Mikey ran in ever-widening circles, chasing the bigger kids. He'd probably grow up to be a distance runner. Tina was right; little Mikey didn't have an off switch.

But Simon's two-year-old did. "I think we need to get back to your mom's for a nap," his wife said.

"You guys coming to the dance tonight?" Kyle asked.

"That depends on whether or not I get *my* nap," Beth said.

Simon gave her bulging belly a pat. "She's sleeping for two."

And Simon was proud of it. A wife, a son and another kid on the way. Once again the green-eyed monster had to be slain.

"I guess there's no point in hanging out here much longer," Kyle said, watching them go. "I wish I'd brought Mindy."

And Jonathan wished Lissa had been there. He

hoped she was doing something with her mom and wasn't out somewhere with Rand, who was also M.I.A. He scanned the crowd. There was no one here he wanted to hang with. No baby pictures he needed to comment on.

As his gaze roamed the herd of picnickers, he realized someone was missing from the picture. Little Mikey. Where was the kid? Not with his mom, who was busy flirting with Doug.

Jonathan suddenly got a sick feeling in his gut as he looked toward the river and caught sight of a small figure in shorts and a red T-shirt through the foliage at the river's edge.

"Shit!" He took off running.

"What?" Kyle called after him, but he didn't reply.

He was vaguely aware of Tina's voice, casually calling, "Mikey."

This particular stretch of the Wenatchee River was no lazy river. Its current would be too much for a small boy with a yen to go swimming.

Now Tina was calling her son, her voice laced with panic. "Mikey? Mikey!"

Jonathan kept on running. He got to the riverbank in time to find the boy in the process of removing his second shoe.

"Hey, Mikey," Jonathan said, keeping his voice relaxed. "Whatcha doin'?"

"I want to swim in the river," Mikey said, and pulled off his sock.

"That sounds like fun, but let's go check with your mom first. I'll give you a horseback ride."

Mikey shook his head and stood, clearly more interested in a swim.

Jonathan moved to position himself between the boy and the river. "You ever ride a bucking bronco?"

"What's that?"

"It's a big old horse like the cowboys ride in the rodeo. It's a real fun ride." Jonathan squatted down in front of him. "Hop on. I'll show you."

The river was abandoned in favor of the bucking bronco and Mikey climbed onto Jonathan's back, arms clasping his neck. Jonathan breathed a sigh of relief. A chorus of people calling for Mikey drifted to where they stood by the water. By the time anyone had thought to look here, it would have been too late.

He scooped up Mikey's shoes and socks and straightened. "Okay, are you ready?"

"Yep."

Jonathan managed a tolerable neigh and did a couple of jumps, bouncing the little boy and making him laugh. "Now we're gonna ride on over to your mom. Hang on." He started loping, throwing in a jump or two and producing more laughs.

They'd only gone a few feet when Doug thundered through the huckleberry bushes, catching Jonathan in midjump. "What the hell?"

"He was about to try to swim in the river," Jonathan said.

"Holy shit. Come here, kid," Doug snapped, and pulled Mikey off Jonathan's back. Then he plucked the shoes out of Jonathan's hand. "Jeez, kid, don't you know any better than to go near the river?"

Doug's sharp tone was enough to make Mikey cry, but Doug didn't waste time comforting him. Instead, he strode off, forgetting—or maybe not bothering—to say anything to Jonathan.

"All in a day's work," Jonathan muttered, following behind. Doug would come back a hero. Doug would probably get laid tonight. "You're welcome. Glad to help."

Now Kyle came running up to Jonathan. He'd passed Doug on the way, but Doug hadn't said anything to him.

"Did you just do what I think you did?" Kyle asked, falling in step with Jonathan.

"Yep. Another future jock saved."

"To grow up and torture some helpless nerd in high school," Kyle added. "Look at that," he said as they approached the picnic area.

Jonathan could see. He didn't need it pointed out to him that Tina was now hugging her son and looking gratefully at Doug as if he were a hero straight out of a Vanessa Valentine novel.

Kyle clapped Jonathan on the back. "We know who the real hero is."

"Yeah, the Invisible Man."

"You won't be invisible on the dance floor tonight."

Damn straight he wouldn't. He had some moves to show off.

Jonathan could hear the music from two blocks down as he walked over to Festival Hall from where he'd parked. The dance was in full swing. He entered as the DJ started spinning "Raise the Roof" to see a mob of dancers partying under a ceiling hung with balloons and red and gold crepe paper streamers.

There were Simon and his wife, dancing at the edge of the crowd. She looked like she'd swallowed one of those balloons. Simon was grinning down at her. Watching her smile up at him, Jonathan realized she wasn't so plain, after all. Beth was actually pretty cute.

Maybe love did that to people. If so, it was the world's best beauty treatment.

Jonathan forced himself farther into the room, although he found it difficult to move into the fray when he was so obviously alone. He knew other people were alone, too—but they were confident they wouldn't leave alone. He wished he had that confidence. He wished he was a stronger, take-charge kind of guy. How did a man get the confidence it took to swagger into a room? Maybe he should have read fewer romance novels and watched more action movies.

Cut it out, he told himself. *Grow a pair.*

His tough self-talk only served to make his heart race. What would a romance hero do?

He wouldn't give up; that much Jonathan knew for sure. Any hero worth his salt had to fight for the woman he wanted. Heroes didn't give up.

He saw Kyle and Mindy off to one side of the dancing crowd, shaking it. Kyle looked like a man who'd won the World Poker Tournament. Who could blame him? He'd found a woman who thought he was fabulous.

Jonathan wanted that happy ending, too. *Now's the*

*night to make it happen. You can do it. Stand tall,
look cool.*

He scanned the room for a glimpse of Lissa but
didn't see her. He started walking along the edge of
the crowd. That reminded him of his nightmare and
made him sweat. Crap. The evening had barely begun
and already his confidence was sinking into the toilet.
He worked his way to the bar and grabbed a bottled
water. *Remember, these people are nothing special.*

The song ended and the DJ went into another fast
number. Jonathan tried to look nonchalant, as if standing by himself was something he'd *chosen* to do.

"Hi, Jonathan," a quiet voice said at his side. "Remember me?"

He turned and saw a short, slender woman with
a heart-shaped face and short, dark hair. Amanda
Adams. She'd been in band with him. "Sure," he said.
"How are you?"

"Good." Amanda had never been much of a talker.

Jonathan had never been much of a talker, either,
and his clever one-liners would only take him so far.
He conjured up a nervous smile.

She gave him an equally nervous one in return.

"Uh, would you like to dance?"

She looked at him gratefully. "Okay."

This wasn't how he'd envisioned making his dancing debut. But Lissa was nowhere to be seen and
Amanda clearly wasn't having any more fun standing on the sidelines than he was, so what the heck.
He'd envisioned holding out his hand to Lissa, just
like the hero had in the book he'd read. Instead, here

he was taking Amanda's hand, which was a little on the clammy side.

He could identify. He smiled at her. "This'll be fun," he promised.

Once he had them on the floor, he went into his steps and her eyes lit up. She was tentative and clumsy-footed, but since she didn't weigh much he was able to strong-arm her into most of the moves. He was vaguely aware of a few people watching, so he got bolder. He swung her out and then drew her back and spun them in a showy circle. The song was about to end, so he pulled out a couple more fancy steps. And then he got really bold and flipped her. Success!

This was greeted by applause from the people nearest them as the song ended.

"Wow," Amanda said. "Jonathan, you're an incredible dancer."

"How come you couldn't do that with me?" demanded Daphne, who was coming off the dance floor at the same time.

"I just...I don't know," he finished lamely.

"Well, if you're lucky, I'll give you a second chance," she threatened.

"Uh, thanks," he muttered, and got away from her as fast as he could.

He didn't get far though. Another one of the girls from band had him by the arm. "Jonathan, how about a dance?"

"Sure," he said.

"Can you spin me like you did Amanda?"

"Oh, yeah," he said with newfound confidence.

After that dance, two more girls were waiting.

And so it went for the next hour, Jonathan spinning girls right and left like so many plates. He finally pleaded thirst and went in search of a drink.

There at the bar, as if she'd been waiting for him, stood Lissa in a black dress that hugged her every curve. Looking at her took his breath away, and the fact that Rand was standing beside her was irrelevant. "You're pretty popular tonight," she said.

"I guess," he murmured.

"That's a switch," Rand sneered.

Jonathan ignored him, choosing to concentrate on something more important—smiling at Lissa.

"I didn't know you could dance like that," she said.

"I have a lot of hidden talents," Jonathan told her, and asked the bartender for a beer.

"So, did you save me a dance?"

"Anytime you want it."

"After this one, maybe," Rand said, and began to escort her away.

Jonathan remembered the list he'd made. A hero was forceful, took charge. This, he concluded, was the time to show a little strength.

He blocked their way. "How about now?" he said, and took Lissa's hand and drew her toward the throng of dancers.

"Oh, well, sure," she said, following him, meek as a lamb.

The DJ had just started a slow song, U2's "Sweetest Thing." It had a funky beat but he thought he could make it work for a nightclub two-step. If he didn't have a heart attack first. The old ticker was suddenly thumping like crazy.

This was it, the moment he'd been waiting for since middle school. He was finally getting to dance with Lissa. A true romance hero would start this dance off with an impressive one-liner. All Jonathan could think of was, "You look lovely tonight."

"Thanks," she murmured, then added, "I'm not sure I can keep up with you."

"I bet you can," he said with a smile. "I'm betting you know the nightclub two-step."

"That I can do."

And she did it beautifully. She matched him step for step, keeping up with every clever move he threw at her. It was as if they'd been dancing together for years.

They had, in his dreams.

The song was half-over; he needed to make the most of it. He drew her against him so they were chest to chest, heart to heart. Close up her face was perfect, her skin like cream. Look how long her lashes were. She smelled like a flower garden in bloom. Best of all, she felt like he'd always imagined she would— soft, womanly, a perfect fit for him, as if they'd been made to go together.

He folded her hand in his. "You know, this is the first time I've ever gotten to dance with you." And he was going to remember it all his life.

She smiled, showing off the dimples in her cheeks. "You make it sound like that's something special."

"It is."

"Aw, Jonathan, you're so sweet."

He didn't want to be sweet. He wanted to be sexy. He wanted to be someone she wanted, not just her old childhood pal or her favorite math tutor or computer nerd.

He was about to say that when the music ended, and there was Rand, sweeping her off. "Come on, Liss, you've already wasted one slow dance. Don't cheat me out of any more."

She made a face at him and shook her head, but she let him take her away. How could she not? Rand was like a steamroller, twice as forceful as Jonathan.

Frowning, he went back for his beer. He found Kyle at the bar, getting drinks.

"You were lookin' good out there," Kyle said. "Until you let that ape take your girl."

"She's not my girl," Jonathan said grumpily. He picked up the beer and chugged it down.

"Yeah, and she won't be at the rate you're going." Kyle gave him a friendly nudge. "Come on, man. You're the dancing king here tonight. Lissa'd be glad to go another round with you. Heck, every woman on the floor has her eye on you. Even Mindy wants to know if you'll dance with her." They both spotted Daphne coming toward them, a determined look on her face. "If you're not gonna dance with Lissa, you'd better go hide before Daphne traps you."

"Tell her I went to the john. She can't get me in there."

"I wouldn't put it past her."

Damn it all, he didn't want to hide out in the john

all night. Instead, he'd melt into the crowd. He'd done that all his life.

He moved to another side of the hall, but Daphne followed him like a heat-seeking missile. After dodging her for two songs, he resorted to making his escape to the men's room and shut himself in a stall so he could think. He had to figure out how to stay a free agent so he could get Lissa away from Rand. That jerk didn't deserve her. Never had.

And you do?

Okay, truth be told, he didn't, either. She could do much better than him. But she could do a ton better than Rand.

But maybe she *wanted* to be with Rand. Maybe she wanted to rekindle the old flame. If she did, who was Jonathan to tell her she couldn't? He leaned his head against the stall door, a defeated man. Why the hell hadn't Rand stayed married and in California? Jonathan swore and gave the stall door a whack.

The sound of voices alerted him that he now had company in the men's room. One he was pretty sure he recognized as Cam Gordon. The other—Rand. Jonathan's hands curled into fists.

"I've never seen anybody who can move as fast as you," Cam said. "You planning on sleeping with Lissa tonight?"

There was a depressing image.

"Why not? She wants it."

Cam snorted. "For old times' sake?"

"Something like that."

"Well, I'm not one to ruin anybody's good time, but

don't you think it's kind of shitty?" Cam said. "Considering you're still married."

"Separated," Rand corrected.

"Yeah, sure. I heard you say this morning that you two were getting back together."

"I might have said that. But she's not here, so what the hell."

That shit! Jonathan burst out of his stall just as Rand was zipping up. "You bastard," he growled, and went right for his neck.

"What?" Rand whirled around.

Jonathan almost succeeded in getting his hands on his rival's neck, but Rand had had a lot more experience being a bully than Jonathan had being a hero. It was a short scuffle. Jonathan took a punch to the jaw and went down. He was still trying to cope with the spinning room and the stars twinkling in front of his eyes when Rand said, "Help me get his pants off."

Next thing he knew he was missing his britches and was receiving a friendly kick in the gut for good measure.

"You just stay here, Twinkle Toes, and mind your own business," Rand growled. And on that bit of advice, he and Cam and Jonathan's pants left the men's room.

Chapter Twenty-One

Jonathan lay on the floor of the men's room, trying to cope with the agony in both his body and his heart. The throbbing in his jaw and the pain in his stomach were fighting for attention and making it hard to concentrate on even sitting up. He managed to get to a kneeling position but was sure he'd pass out right there on the floor.

The heroes in the novels he'd read all seemed to survive the most brutal of attacks, stagger up and race off to save the heroine. Or at least help her save herself. And right now Lissa needed help. She needed to know that Rand was about to use her.

There would be no racing off here, though. He could barely breathe. Why didn't any of those novels tell you how to cope when you'd been beaten up? He sat there, hunched over the pain, trying to take in air. *Get up. Go find Lissa. You can do this.* His body didn't seem to agree.

After what felt like hours, he made it to his feet and got to the sink, where he splashed cold water on his face. After that he couldn't do much more than lean there, concentrating on the all-important task of breathing.

The bathroom door opened and Jonathan became aware of a new pain, the pain of embarrassment. He was now officially in his nightmare, at his fifteen-year high school reunion in his boxers. What had he ever done to deserve this kind of humiliation?

"What the— Jonathan?"

He turned his aching head to see Darrell Hornsby staring at him.

"I was mugged." Pain shot across his jaw and he put a hand to his face. He looked in the mirror. The bruise was already showing.

"You're kidding. Here?"

Mugged in Icicle Falls. Boy, there was a good story for the police blotter. *Local man beaten at high school reunion. Assailants take victim's pants.* He didn't want to be a victim and he wanted his pants back!

"They took your pants," Darrell said, just in case Jonathan hadn't noticed.

Which had his cell phone and his wallet. God knew what they'd done with them. He had to get to Lissa. How was he going to do it without his pants? He needed pants.

He needed his posse. "Get Kyle."

Darrell nodded and rushed off.

A few minutes later, he was back with Kyle. "My God, I can't believe it!" Kyle rushed up to him.

"Who did this? Rand?"

Jonathan nodded. "And Cam."

"Are you okay?"

It was hard to talk around his throbbing jaw. "I need...pants."

"You need a doctor!"

Jonathan shook his head. "No time for that. Find my pants. They've got to be in a garbage can somewhere."

"Too obvious," Darrell said. "You could look all night and never find them."

"Hang on. Didn't Adam say he was taking Chelsea to dinner at Schwangau?" Kyle pulled his cell phone from his pocket. "He can grab some pants from your place and be here in ten minutes. And I'll get some ice for that jaw. We'll have you fixed in no time," he promised.

"I don't have ten minutes! Ow, that hurts." Jonathan put a hand to his throbbing jaw.

"Okay, I'll look around here and see if I can find where they ditched your pants, but meanwhile I'm calling for backup. And then those guys'll pay."

Kyle came up to their shoulders. The last thing Jonathan needed was his friend getting the crap beaten out of him. "Not your fight," he said. "Just find me some pants."

Kyle nodded and strode from the room, punching numbers on his phone as he went. "Go outside and keep watch," he instructed Darrell. "We don't want anybody seeing our boy like this."

Darrell scooted out after Kyle, valiantly ignoring the need that had brought him to the men's room in the first place.

Adam and Chelsea were snuggled together in a quiet corner booth at Schwangau when his cell phone started vibrating in his pocket. He'd promised Chelsea he'd turn it off, but had decided that switching to vibrate was a good compromise. Now, with her cuddled next to him, he realized that some things a man shouldn't compromise on and ignored the vibrating phone.

He'd learned his lesson. He smiled at her and raised his wineglass in toast. "Here's to the prettiest mom in Icicle Falls."

"I'm not a mom yet," she said, but she smiled and clinked his wineglass with her water glass.

"Okay, the prettiest mom-to-be." He laid a hand on her leg. It was so good to be able to do that, to be here with her, back where he belonged.

The phone in his pocket vibrated again. Damn. Who was it and why the hell were they bugging him on a Saturday night?

The waiter came and they placed their orders.

"I love this restaurant," she said happily after he'd left.

"And I love you," Adam said. He leaned over and kissed her.

"You really have changed," she said.

His pocket vibrated again.

She made a tiny frown. "What's that I hear?"

"Gas," Adam improvised. "I've got gas."

"For a minute I thought your phone was vibrating."

"I said I'd turn it off."

Fortunately, she didn't ask, "And did you?"

The thing vibrated again. Okay, whoever it was,

Adam was going to kill him. "I'm gonna hit the john. I'll be right back," he said, and gave her another kiss.

Once in the bathroom, he pulled out his phone and saw that all the calls had been from Kyle. He was at his high school reunion with Mindy. Why the hell was he calling Adam, to give him a blow-by-blow report?

Adam called him back. "I'm right in the middle of a romantic dinner. What do you want?"

"Pants," Kyle said. "Somebody beat the crap out of Jonathan and took his pants and he needs another pair."

"What?"

"Pick up a pair of his and bring 'em over to Festival Hall. He's in the men's room."

Kyle hung up before Adam could ask why the hell Kyle couldn't go fetch pants for Jonathan himself.

Great. Here was his wife waiting for him at their table and his pal waiting at Festival Hall for pants. Chels was right; he should have turned off his cell.

But he owed Jonathan big-time and he couldn't leave the man stuck shivering in the bathroom in his tighty whities. He'd given Jon back the key to his place. How did Kyle think he was going to get in, climb through a window? Go through Chica's dog door? His own house was closer. He and Jon were about the same height. He could bring a pair of his.

Could he be back before Chels figured out that he'd taken off? If he drove fast… Yes, he could do it. He'd race to his place, then over to Festival Hall, throw some pants at Jonathan and be back in time for…if not the salad, at least the entree.

He slipped out of the bathroom, then down the fashionably dark hall and out the door. He was in his Corvette in less than a minute and rocketing down the street. He could do this.

He was halfway to his house when the siren and flashing red light stopped him.

"This should help," Kyle said, handing over a bar towel full of ice.

Jonathan winced as the contact caused fresh pain.

Kyle gave him a bottle of water and a couple of aspirin. "Take these."

"Where'd you get them?" Who knew about this?

"Mindy."

He'd told her?

As if reading his mind, Kyle said, "Don't worry. She doesn't know what's going on. Nobody does. I couldn't find your pants, but Adam's gone to get you a pair. And Darrell's outside watching the door. If anybody comes in, we'll hustle you into a stall."

"Where's Lissa?"

Kyle made a face. "This is not the time to worry about Lissa."

"Yes. It is. Rand's still married. He's looking for a one-night stand and he's going to seduce her. I heard him telling Cam."

"That asshole."

"She needs to be warned." But the clock was ticking. For all he knew, Rand could already be spiriting her away. He didn't have time to wait for a new pair of pants. "You've got to find her."

Kyle nodded and left.

Jonathan slumped against the sink. He'd imagined so many scenarios for tonight, all of them with Lissa ending up in his arms. Now she was going to end up in the arms of a creep who only wanted to use her to feed his ego. And here he was, stuck in the men's room in his underwear. Some hero.

"Do you know how fast you were going?" Tilda, the cop, asked Adam.

"Yes," he admitted. "I had an emergency."

"License and registration, please. A fire?"

Oh, boy. Now, he'd stepped in it. If he said he was on a mission to get pants for his friend, she'd want to know why. If he told her that Jonathan had been mugged, she'd want to go to the scene of the crime. Everyone would see Tilda going into the men's room. Everyone would find out that Jonathan had gotten beaten up and had his pants stolen. That was no way to help a friend. But what to say now?

Nothing, that was what. "You know, I guess it wasn't that big an emergency," he said. "I'll take the ticket."

"Good choice," she said, and took her own sweet time walking back to her patrol car to write it up.

So much for getting Jonathan's pants to him in a hurry. And so much for getting back to his wife quickly. Adam ground his teeth.

Kyle returned to the bathroom. "She's gone."

Rand had already gotten her away. Under different

circumstances Jonathan would have admitted defeat
and let Rand make off with the woman of his dreams.
If that was what she wanted, that was what she wanted.
This wasn't some historical novel where he needed to
save a woman's virtue. These days women didn't want
their virtue saved.

But they also didn't want to be used. Jonathan felt
even sicker than he'd felt after Rand had kicked him.
Rand was a modern-day villain who didn't care about
anyone but himself. He was going to seduce Lissa and
she'd wind up getting hurt. She didn't deserve that.
And Rand didn't deserve her. Where was Adam with
his pants?

"Drive carefully," Tilda admonished, giving Adam
his present from the Icicle Falls police department.

His phone vibrated in his pants. He pulled it out.
This time the call wasn't from Kyle. It was from Chelsea. She was either looking for him or testing to see
that he'd turned it off. He put the phone back in his
pocket and drove away. Slowly...

Tilda followed him for three blocks to make sure
he remained a model citizen. He should never have
bought a red car. Cops hated red.

Finally she took off. He drove like an old geezer for
another block, just to be certain the coast was clear,
then floored it. Even with the pedal to the metal he felt
like he was swimming through syrup. He screeched
to a halt in front of his house, left the motor running
and dashed up the front walk.

"Everything okay?" Dennis the Menace called.

They'd mended fences, so to speak, but Dennis was still a pest.

"Fine," Adam called back. He unlocked his front door, took the stairs to the bedroom two at a time and raced down the hall. He careened into the bedroom, yanked open the closet door and hauled out a pair of slacks. And a belt. Jon had buffed up, but Adam still had a few inches on him. Then it was back down the hall, the pants flapping behind him like a flag. Out the door, down the walk, ignoring his gaping neighbor, and into the car. Now off down the road.

He slowed down when he hit the town limits. Another ticket would only delay him further.

After what felt like forever, he was at Festival Hall. He wadded up the pants and strode inside, going straight to the men's room.

A skinny guy with a scrawny neck was standing outside the door. Now he leaned his head in and said something.

"'Scuse me," Adam said, and pushed past him. He got in just as a stall door closed. There was Kyle, standing nonchalantly at the sink, washing his hands.

He turned and, at the sight of Adam, frowned. "What took you so long?"

"Tilda got me for speeding. Where's Jon?"

The stall door opened and out stepped Jonathan, wearing a pair of black silk boxers. "Nice shorts," Adam observed, giving him the slacks and belt.

Jonathan snatched them and climbed into them. They hung only a little loosely on him but he cinched them up with the belt . "Sorry about the ticket. I'll pay it. Can I borrow your car?"

"What? How am I supposed to get back to the restaurant? And what am I supposed to tell Chelsea when it's time to leave and we don't have a car?"

"I'll return it as soon as I get my spare set of keys," Jonathan promised.

"But—"

"Give me your keys," Jonathan snarled.

This new, angry Jonathan startled Adam into reflexively handing over his keys.

"Thanks," Jonathan said, and bolted out of the bathroom.

"Bring the car to Schwangau," Adam called after him, and hoped he heard. He turned to Kyle and demanded, "What the hell is going on?"

"Jon has to go save Lissa," Kyle said.

"With my car."

"Don't worry. He'll get it back to you."

"Well, I hope he gets it back to me before we're done with dinner. Otherwise, I'm gonna have a hard time explaining to Chelsea. I wasn't even supposed to have my cell phone on."

Kyle slugged him in the shoulder. "You're a good man to have around in a crisis. Come on, I'll drive you to the restaurant."

Adam frowned. "Chels thinks I'm in the bathroom."

"Well, then, you're clear."

"I've been in the bathroom for…" He took out his cell and checked the time. "Twenty minutes."

"You had the runs."

"I had the runs," he told her when he finally returned to the table to find her scowling at him. "Sorry." The salad had been delivered. So had their main course. He sat down in front of his steak, ready to dig in.

"Are you feeling okay now?" She laid a hand on his arm. "Maybe you shouldn't eat anything heavy."

"No, I'm fine now," he insisted. But he wouldn't be so fine if Jonathan didn't bring back his car.

Chapter Twenty-Two

Jonathan had pants and he had a car, everything a hero needed to save a damsel in distress. Now all he had to do was track down Rand and Lissa. Icicle Falls had some great B and Bs and guesthouses. They could be anywhere.

He started his search at the Icicle Creek Lodge. "I missed meeting up with a friend of mine," he told Olivia, the owner, who was minding the desk. "He's in town for our class reunion and I think he's staying here."

"What's his name?"

"Rand Burwell." *The Skunk.*

Olivia shook her head. "That doesn't ring a bell." She checked her computer. "Sorry, Jonathan. There's no one here by that name."

"Hmm, I must have been confused," Jonathan said. "Thanks." Strike one.

Aware of the ticking clock, he ran back to Adam's car, got in and floored it. That was a mistake. Out of nowhere an Icicle Falls patrol car appeared, lights flashing. Great. Just great.

He pulled over to the curb and watched as Tilda Morrison got out of the car. She was tall and buff and intimidating. Jonathan *so* didn't have time to be intimidated.

"Jonathan," she greeted him. "What's the hurry?"

"I'm sorry, Tilda. I know I was speeding, but I've got an emergency here."

"There seems to be a lot of that going around tonight. And in this car," she added, frowning. "Is your house on fire?"

Cute. "No."

"Are you having a heart attack?"

He was definitely having heart trouble, but it wasn't the kind he could explain in one minute. "No."

"Then I'd say you don't have an emergency. License and registration please."

He found Adam's registration on the visor and handed it over. "I can't give you my license."

She frowned.

"I lost it. It's in my pants." He shouldn't have said that. He was rattled and it was affecting his ability to think clearly.

"And where are your pants?"

"Uh, they're gone."

She peered in the window, still frowning. "So what's that you're wearing, a skirt?"

"These aren't… Never mind. Can you just give me my ticket?"

She crossed her arms. "No. Not until you tell me what the heck is going on in this town."

So he told her and then she gave him his ticket.

She also gave him a lift. "What that creep is doing isn't illegal but it's damned rotten. Get in the squad car."

They made it to Gerhardt's Gasthaus in record time, where Jonathan struck out again.

"That means they're staying at the Bavarian Inn," Tilda deduced.

Stood to reason. Like Icicle Falls Lodge, it was expensive and the rooms all had balconies with a great mountain view. Perfect for seduction. Tilda chauffeured Jonathan to the Bavarian Inn. At top speed.

"I'm trying to find my friend," he told the girl at the desk. He'd seen her at Bavarian Brews a couple of times, but he didn't know her. It would have been easier if he did. "Could you tell me what room Rand Burwell is staying in?"

"Gosh, we can't give out that information," she said.

"This is kind of an emergency," Jonathan pushed.

"Well, I'd be happy to call his room for you."

And alert him that Jonathan was there? No way. "Uh, no, that's okay." Now what to do? He tried a new tack. "I wanted to surprise him. Can you make an exception just this once?"

Her brows knit. "I thought you said it was an emergency."

"It's, uh…" If he'd played chess like this, he'd have been laughed out of the chess club. "His wife just had a baby." That was a good emergency. Except if his wife was having a baby, he'd probably have been with her. Or someone would have called him on his cell. "He lost his cell phone."

The woman behind the reception counter wasn't buying it. In fact, she wasn't even buying Jonathan's being there. "I'm sorry, sir. I can't help you," she said, her friendly expression hardening into something not so friendly. "Is there anything else?"

Jonathan got the message behind the question. *If not, scram.* "Uh, no." Except. He ran a hand through his hair. "I really have to find him. Is he here?"

"I'll ring his room for you," she said, sticking to the party line.

He shook his head. Just then, the phone rang and she picked it up and turned her back on him. He was done here. What to do now?

Calm down. Think like Rand. What would Rand do?

It was still early in the evening. Rand had always had charm in spades. Would he bring Lissa back to his room and start boinking her right away? No. He'd order champagne, sit with her on the balcony, sweet-talk her.

Jonathan left the lobby and went to the back of the building where all the balconies were located. Several people were out on them, enjoying the warm evening and the last pink of the summer sunset. Sure enough, on a balcony down at the end of the building sat Rand and Lissa at a little table. As Jonathan drew closer, he saw that Rand had, indeed, ordered champagne. They looked like the ideal couple—Rand big as a boulder and dark-haired, Lissa lithe and pretty in her dress, a light summer breeze ruffling her golden hair.

Jonathan marched along the walkway toward them.

Rand saw him first, his pleasant smile melting into a glare of suppressed anger. His words drifted down to Jonathan. "It's getting cold out here, Liss. Let's go inside."

"Don't!" Jonathan called, and picked up his pace.

Lissa looked at him, a smile on her lips. "Jonathan?"

Now he was directly beneath them. "He's trying to seduce you." *Well, duh.*

Lissa's smile lost some of its glow. Hardly surprising since he'd just announced this to all the other hotel guests.

"You guys were a couple once and you can do whatever you want, but you need to know he's married."

Now there was no smile whatsoever. Lissa turned to Rand. "Is that true? You told me you were divorced."

"He's not. He's separated."

"Same thing," Rand said, and called down to Jonathan, "Get lost." He put a hand on Lissa's back. "He's jealous, Liss. He always has been. I wouldn't lie to you about something so important," he said, steering her back toward the door.

"He sure would if it meant he could get what he wanted. And yeah, I'm jealous, and it bugs me that a rotten liar like Rand could lure a nice woman like you back to his room. But *I'm* not lying." They were inside now, the sliding door to the balcony sliding shut. "He told Cam Gordon just this morning that he was getting back with his wife," Jonathan hollered. "He wants a good roll in the hay before he does. He's out to use you."

A murmur of voices had served as backdrop during this exchange, and more people had come out on their balconies to eavesdrop. But now someone new had arrived at the party, a big burly guy wearing a polo shirt that proclaimed him a Bavarian Inn employee.

"I'm sorry, sir," he said, "but you need to leave."

"In a minute," Jonathan said.

"No. Now."

The man took his arm and Jonathan tried to yank free. But the man's hand was a vise and the vise merely tightened. He started to lead Jonathan away.

"He's a cheat and a liar, Liss. You need to know that," Jonathan yelled at the top of his lungs. "Ask him who really taped all those hearts on your locker on Valentine's Day," he added. As if that mattered. As if she could even hear him anymore.

That was about all he had time for because Mr. Friendly was leading him off at a brisk trot. "He's using her," Jonathan explained.

"It's a free country," the man said. "And you're bothering our guests."

Jonathan doubted that. He had an awful suspicion that they'd all been enjoying the show.

But the show was over. There was nothing left to do but to give up and leave. He'd tried.

And failed. Lissa and Rand were now firmly shut away in their love nest. At this very moment, he was probably convincing her that Jonathan was a jealous, lying nerd.

It was a silent ride as Tilda drove him home to get

his spare car keys. Then she took him back to where they'd left Adam's car.

"Want me to follow you and give you a lift back to your car?" she offered.

He shook his head. "No, but thanks. And thanks for all your help."

She didn't offer him any sappy advice or embarrassing sympathy. She just nodded and drove off.

He returned Adam's car, parking it in front of Schwangau. He left the keys with the maître d', instructing him to give them to Adam and to ask if he'd dropped them. Then he trudged back to his own car and drove home.

Chica was glad to see him, jumping up in excitement, running alongside him as he made his way to the house. Inside he donned a ratty pair of sweats and his Einstein T-shirt. Full circle, back to what he was when he'd started this dumb journey, back to what he'd always be.

He was done. Done with love, done with hope, done with Lissa. He was especially done with those stupid romance novels. He found his e-reader and removed every last deceitful tale of happily-ever-after. Next he crumpled his list and tossed it in the trash. He'd done everything on that damned list. Tried the smooth talk and the romantic gesture. He'd buffed up, toughened up and danced his feet off. He'd done what was right, and in the process made a fool of himself trying to save her from hurt and humiliation. It had all been a waste of time.

He gathered paperbacks from every corner of the

house, putting them in a grocery sack. In went the ty-coons, the viscounts and the earls. *A bag full of happiness,* his sister had said when they went to the library book sale. Jules was deluded.

No corner of the house escaped. He took books from the bathroom, under his bed, the coffee table, adding them to his bag. In went the barons and the cowboys. In went the playboys. In went the vampires and spies. And in went every blasted Vanessa Valentine book, even the first-edition signed hardback he'd paid a fortune for on eBay. He should have burned every last one of those the minute he learned Vanessa Valentine was Vance. What a sucker.

Well, he was done being a sucker. He took his bag of books to the fire pit behind the house, Chica trotting beside him. With a growl he tore up a sheik's sorry tale and dumped it in among the ash and charred bits of wood. He gave a Vanessa Valentine historical a savage rip, taking full advantage of the muscles he'd built up working out at the gym. That, too, went on the pile. He threw in two more books, then squirted them with starter fluid and dropped a match on them. They burst into flame with a satisfying whoosh.

"Good symbolism," he told Chica.

She thumped her tail as if she understood.

Another book went on the funeral pyre. Dead. All his dreams were dead. Women were fickle and there was no such thing as a happy ending.

The fire was going strong now. The flames dancing against the dark night were almost hypnotic.

He slumped into one of his camp chairs and stared at them.

Chica's sudden bark pulled him out of his trance and he looked over to see Lissa walking toward him. He'd hypnotized himself into thinking she was really here. He turned back to the fire, hoping the illusion would go away and leave him in peace.

She didn't. Instead, she gave Chica's face a rub and settled on a nearby chair.

Okay, he was dreaming. He blinked and shook his head, but when he opened his eyes she was still there. "Why aren't you with Rand?" he asked her.

"Why should I be?" she countered, still petting the dog. "He's a rat."

"He's always been a rat."

"Well, I never realized it." She leaned back against the chair. "At least, I never admitted it to myself. I mean, if I had, what would that have made me?"

A hero wouldn't say what Jonathan was thinking. Well, he wasn't a hero. He was done with that stuff. He looked at her. Hard. "Stupid, Liss. That's what it would make you."

She bit her lip and nodded.

"Double stupid, because you let him fool you in high school and you let him fool you again now."

"I've never been very smart when it comes to men, I guess," she said.

This was no news flash. He said nothing. Instead, he grabbed a Vanessa Valentine paperback and tossed it on the fire.

"What are you doing?" she asked.

"What does it look like?" He sounded like the king of grumps but he didn't care.

She plucked a book out of the bag. "You're burning romance novels." She said it as if he was committing sacrilege.

"They're a crock."

"Whose are they?"

"Mine."

"You've been reading romance novels?"

The shocked expression on her face irritated him. "Guys can read romance novels."

"Oh, well. Yes, of course they can."

Now she was trying to placate him. Well, he didn't want to be placated. "Liss, why are you here?" *Why aren't you back at the reunion, being Miss Popularity, picking up a new guy?*

"I wanted to thank you. For keeping me from making a very big mistake."

He shed some of his prickly attitude. "You're welcome." He picked up his hardcover signed first edition.

She laid a hand on his arm. "Oh, don't. I love that book."

"You've read it?"

"I've read all her books."

He handed it over. "Well, then, here. You can have it. It's signed."

"Really?" She opened the book to check for herself and smiled. "Lucky you," she teased.

"Yeah, lucky me," he grumbled. "I spent a fortune on these dumb books and all for nothing."

"Jonathan, why are you here by yourself, burning these books? Why aren't *you* at the reunion?"

"Because the one person I wanted to see left early with Rand. And I'm burning the books because they're useless." He took a paperback, ripped it in two and dropped it onto the fire.

"Oh, not another Vanessa Valentine," she groaned.

"She's not even a woman, you know. Vanessa Valentine is a guy."

"She is not! I've met her."

"Yeah, she is. I play poker with her. Him."

"Really?" Lissa turned over the book he'd given her and looked at the picture on the dust jacket. "Then who's this?"

"That's his sister. She's his front. And those books are as bogus as he is."

"Then why were you reading them?"

It was the last straw. Lissa had been clueless ever since he'd known her. She needed to get a clue. "Because I thought they'd give me some idea about how to get your attention," he snapped.

"What?"

"Damn it all, Lissa, I've been in love with you since we were kids. I thought that if I turned myself into some superstud, some romance hero, in time for the reunion, maybe for once, you'd see me. Really see me." He wanted to cry, wanted to punch something, take his chair and throw it through a window. Instead, he stood and dumped the rest of the books in the bag onto the fire, sending sparks flying in all directions. "These are all crap. They end up with the guy getting the woman he's in love with. Well, the guy *doesn't* always get the woman of his dreams because the woman of his dreams doesn't always see what's right under her nose, even when he tutors her in math, even when he tapes hearts to her locker. Even when he takes dance lessons for two friggin' months—all so he can impress her when she comes back for the reunion."

Had all of that just come out of his mouth? Now he'd really made a fool of himself. He fell back into his chair and glared at the fire.

"Oh, Jonathan," she said softly.

Now she felt sorry for him. That was the greatest humiliation of all. "Go back to the reunion, Lissa. There are lots of people who want to see you."

"But there's only one person I want to see right now, and that's my old friend Jonathan."

"I don't want to be your damned friend."

She knelt in front of him and laid a hand on his arm. He snatched his arm away.

"You really are a good dancer."

"Damn straight I am."

"How about another dance?"

"I don't want to." He sounded childish and he knew it. Heroes didn't act like that.

"Please."

He was being a total shit, which she didn't deserve. It wasn't her fault she'd never seen him as anything more than a friend. It wasn't her fault he was a fool.

He sighed. "Liss, I'm sorry. Forget I said any of this, okay? Go back to the dance. I know they're still going strong."

She shook her head. "I don't want to go back to the dance. I want to hang out with you."

Yeah, he really believed that, just like he still believed in Santa.

"Remember the time all our families had that big bonfire down by the river?"

He remembered everything they ever did together. He nodded.

"What were we in, sixth grade?"

He nodded again.

"Rand kept setting his marshmallows on fire. He never wanted to let them turn golden brown. He said he didn't like to wait."

Rand had always looked for the easy way—whether it was toasting marshmallows, taking credit for high school acts of gallantry, or getting a little on the side when his wife was back in California. Jonathan frowned.

"You toasted one for me."

He couldn't help smiling at the memory. "The perfect marshmallow."

"We took a picture. I still have that picture in one of my old photo albums."

Her dad had taken it. They'd been sitting side by side in front of the campfire with him displaying the marshmallow, her giggling.

"You were always doing nice things for me."

"You were easy to do nice things for."

"So, now do something nice and dance with me. Please?"

She was just humoring him. But okay, so what if

she was? He'd never have her, not the way he wanted, but here by the firelight he'd hold her in his arms one last time. If he couldn't keep the girl, he'd take the memory. He stood and moved away from the fire and held out his hand.

She took it and let Jonathan draw her to him.

"There's no music," he said.

"We don't need no stinkin' music," she joked.

He showed off a couple of his swing steps. She followed haltingly, laughing. Then he moved them into something slower.

She mirrored his steps and soon they were moving perfectly together. He turned her and pulled her against him, wrapping his arms around her and swaying gently, treasuring the thrill of feeling her body so achingly close. He laid his head against hers. Her hair was so soft.

"Thank you for the hearts on my locker," she whispered.

Credit where credit was due. And it had only taken sixteen years. He smiled. "You're welcome."

"You really are a wonderful dancer."

"I could be wonderful at a lot of things…if only you'd give me a chance."

"Maybe I'm giving you a chance right now."

Maybe she was. Maybe he'd never get another. He spun her into a turn, this time bringing them face-to-face. Once more he drew her close until they were touching. There in the dying firelight it was hard to read what was in her eyes. Was that a hint of desire he saw or was he imagining it?

There was only one way to find out. Channeling every romance hero he'd studied, he lowered his lips to hers and kissed her. It was tender and packed with a lifetime of love, a kiss worthy of a Vanessa Valentine novel, the kiss of a lifetime. And he'd remember all his life that right now, for just this moment, she was his. It was with great reluctance that he ended the kiss.

She pulled away enough to look up at him. And now there was no mistaking what he saw in her eyes. But he couldn't believe it. "Jonathan, have you really been here, right under my nose, the whole time?"

He felt like his chest was filled with fireworks, all going off at once. He smiled at her. "I've always been here for you, Liss, and I always will be."

"Oh, Jonathan." She took his face in her hands and kissed him again. And this kiss was even better than the one before.

He was barely aware of the sound of car tires crunching on his gravel drive, of a car door shutting, of Chica barking and someone calling his name.

"Hey, Jon!" Kyle ran around the corner of the house, carrying Jonathan's pants. "We found your—" At the sight of Jonathan and Lissa in each other's arms, his mouth dropped. Thinking fast, he whipped the pants behind his back. "I was just dropping something off." He started walking backward, nearly stumbling in the process. "I'll leave it on the front porch. Good to see you, Lissa." Then he grinned. "Good to see you with Jon." After that he faded into the darkness.

Lissa looked questioningly at Jonathan. "What was that all about?"

"Nothing important," he said.

The fire was down to a flicker now. Lissa shivered and rubbed her arms.

"Let's go in the house," Jonathan suggested.

She smiled at him and nodded. Hand in hand, with Chica tagging along as chaperone, they went inside and settled on Jonathan's couch, where they talked for hours. The talking led to kissing, and as the sun finally came up, Jonathan learned one final lesson— what a woman wants most is a man who will always be there for her.

What He Always Wanted

June, ten months after the reunion

Jonathan stood at the front of the Icicle Falls Community Church, wearing a white tux and a pink rosebud boutonniere, waiting for the most beautiful woman in the world to walk down the aisle to him. Kyle and Adam stood next to him, and Chica, who'd been the ring bearer, was sitting at his feet. Off to the side sat his mother, Neil and Juliet, who had baby Jonathan on her lap, along with his grandmother, who'd flown in from Arizona for the event. All three women were already dabbing at their eyes.

Tina Swift had come down the aisle, followed by Laurie Poznick. After Laurie, it was time for the bride.

And here she was, escorted by her proud papa. Jonathan had just about burst his buttons when Lissa told him what her father's reaction had been on hearing they were engaged. "Thank God you finally got it right, Liss."

Her father wasn't the only one who was grateful. The sight of her all dressed in frothy white, walking down the aisle, carrying a bright bouquet of spring flowers, took Jonathan's breath away. He'd dreamed about this for so long, but even his wildest dreams couldn't come close to matching reality. This woman, who was as lovely on the inside as she was on the outside, was going to be his wife.

He would remember every moment of this day for the rest of his life, every word of their vows—even though speaking them in front of all these people made him as nervous as the thought of their dance at the wedding reception.

But it wasn't hard to say "I do." And it wasn't hard to ignore the hoots and cheers and applause of friends and family when it came time to kiss the bride. He was so caught up in the moment that everyone and everything faded to a background blur.

"I love you, Lissa," he whispered after they'd kissed. "I always have and I always will." He couldn't help adding the immortal words of romance hero Sir James Noble. "The sun will turn to ash before I stop loving you."

"Oh, Jonathan," she said, "I love you, too, and I think I always have." Then she kissed him again to more applause and laughter.

The reception was to be held at the Icicle Creek Lodge. Jonathan had finally thought of the perfect romantic gesture, and they left the church in a horse-drawn carriage.

The reception line formed in the lobby, giving people a chance to greet the bride and groom, and then move to the dining hall for appetizers and drinks.

"I knew some girl would find you and take you away," Dot teased. "Unless...are you two going to live here?"

Jonathan shook his head. "We're moving to Portland. Lissa's got her TV show there."

Lissa beamed. "He's giving up his life here for me."

That had been hard. Jonathan was very attached to his house, and he liked living in Icicle Falls. But giving up everything for the woman he loved, that was the number-one thing a hero did, and he was happy to be Lissa's hero.

"But we'll be back on long weekends and holidays," Lissa said. "We don't want that gorgeous house Jonathan built to go to waste," she added, smiling at him.

"Well, *amigo,* you are a married man," Bernardo said, shaking Jonathan's hand. "Now the adventure really begins."

Jonathan was more than ready for it.

Dinner, courtesy of Zelda's, was fit for a king— salmon in puff pastry, Caesar salad and grilled vegetables. All the guests received special party favors—signed Vanessa Valentine paperbacks (Vance's wedding gift to Jonathan). While the guests ate, they were treated to a slide show on a big screen. Pictures flashed by of Lissa on Lost Bride Trail, then at the falls, where she claimed she'd seen the ghost of the lost bride, an omen that meant a wedding was around the corner. Then there were shots of Lissa's bridal shower, along with ones of Jonathan's bachelor party in Vegas. (Vance had flown the poker guys down for the weekend.) There were lots of sentimental sighs when the picture of Jonathan, Lissa and Chica sitting on his front porch showed up. The last one in the loop made his friends clap the loudest. It showed Jonathan and Lissa poring over a Vanessa Valentine novel.

The big hit of the evening was the wedding cake, which had been done by Gingerbread Haus—a giant romance novel, open for all to read. On one page it read, "Jonathan and Lissa found each other and lived happily ever after." The following page proclaimed, "The Beginning."

"We *are* going to live happily ever after," Lissa said as they cut the cake. "How can we do anything else since I've married my hero?" And that made Jonathan's heart swell.

There was much ado about throwing the garter. Amid loud encouragement, Jonathan removed it from Lissa's leg. Later that night he was going to kiss every inch of that beautiful leg, and all the rest of her. He took off the garter and shot it out—and his old pal Darrell Hornsby caught it. Darrell was with a new babe now, another internet matchup named Angelica. He grinned at her and she grinned right back. Go, Darrell.

Plenty of giggling women gathered to catch the bouquet, but to everyone's surprise the throw went wild, and it landed in the reluctant hands of Vance Fish. Jonathan couldn't help laughing.

Adam grinned at Vance. "Well…Vanessa. You know what that means. You better go stock up at Victoria's Secret, 'cause it looks like there's love in your future."

"Cute," Vance said with a scowl.

Next it was time for dancing, bride and groom first. All those people watching… *Who cares?* Jonathan thought as Lissa stepped into his arms. They did a waltz worthy of *Dancing with the Stars,* and Jonathan ended it by scooping her up and spinning in circles with her, raising a burble of female sighs from around the room.

"She's so lucky," he heard one of her friends say as other couples began to join them on the floor.

Now *there* was something he'd never figured he'd hear anyone say. But he knew who the lucky one was. He'd finally gotten the girl of his dreams. Vance had been right; love did win in the end.

"It's true," Lissa said, smiling up at him. "I got the most wonderful man in the world."

"Well, at least in Icicle Falls," he joked.

She made a face at him. "I'm serious. Jonathan, thank you for never giving up on me. For never giving up on us."

"Well," Adam said later as Jonathan and his posse stood watching Lissa and her girlfriends doing a line dance together, "you did it. You got her." He shifted his baby daughter in his arms and kissed her.

"Thanks to you, we all got our women," Kyle added. He and Mindy would be getting married in August.

"You'd have figured it out without me," Jonathan said.

"Not if you hadn't started us reading those books." Kyle smiled at Mindy, who was showing off her engagement ring to Dot Morrison. "I gotta say, though, even with all the books I read, sometimes I *still* don't know what she wants."

The music had ended and now Lissa came toward Jonathan, smiling at him as if he was Prince Charming.

"I think maybe that requires a lifetime of research," he said. He grinned. And what a wonderful life he was going to have doing just that.

* * * * *

Acknowledgments

I had so much fun writing this novel. And I have some important men to thank. Huge thanks to Clay Moyle for answering all my poker questions. And for playing poker with me! Someday I am going to master that card game. Thanks to Rob Rabe for sartorial advice and for helping me with my questions about life at a big insurance company. And to my pal Eric Schneider for telling me about his life as a medical rep. Thank you and lots of kisses to my darling husband, Gerhardt, who is an excellent copy editor. (And a pretty darned good husband, too!)

And now for the girls. Ruth Ross, I owe you a huge debt of gratitude for reading this story when it was nothing more than a mess in progress and for giving me so many good ideas. As always, thanks to the brain trust: Susan Wiggs, Lois Dyer, Anjali Banerjee, Kate Breslin and Elsa Watson. You guys are great! Huge thanks to my fabulous editor, Paula Eykelhof, for your invaluable insight and guidance, and to all the great people at MIRA who continue to make me feel so welcome and such a part of the Harlequin family. And last but surely not least, thanks to my wonderful agent and friend, Paige Wheeler. You're the best.

New York Times Bestselling Author

SHERRYL WOODS

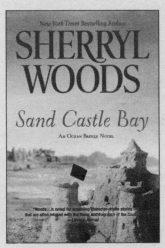

In a trade-off she's lived to regret, Emily Castle left home years ago to become an interior designer. The youngest of three sisters, Emily desperately wanted to prove herself. Success, though, came at the cost of leaving behind the man she loved.

For Boone Dorsett, losing Emily left his heart shattered, but another woman was waiting in the wings. Now a widower with a young son, Boone has a second chance with Emily when a storm brings her home. But with his former in-laws threatening a custody suit, the stakes of loving her are higher than ever.

Will fate once again separate them—or is the time finally right for these two star-crossed lovers?

Available wherever books are sold.

Be sure to connect with us at:
Harlequin.com/Newsletters
Facebook.com/HarlequinBooks
Twitter.com/HarlequinBooks

MSW1436

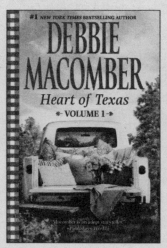

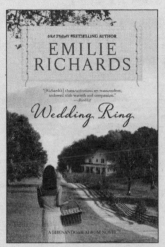

REQUEST YOUR FREE BOOKS!

2 FREE NOVELS
FROM THE ROMANCE COLLECTION
PLUS 2 FREE GIFTS!